MB

PERSEPHONE

JULIAN STOCKWIN

PERSEPHONE

HODDER &
STOUGHTON

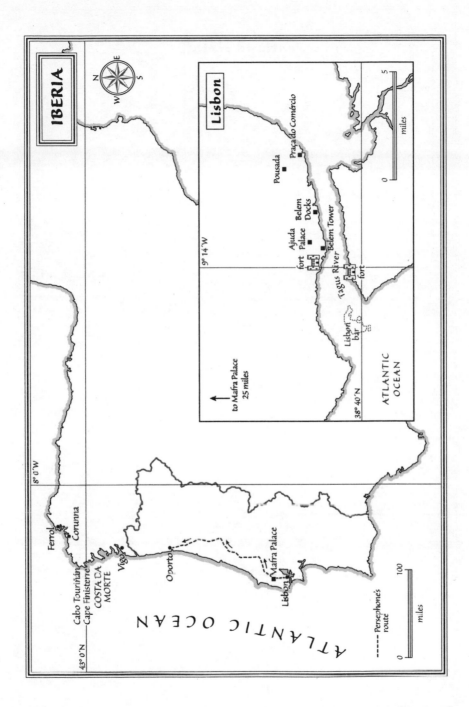

IBERIA

Lisbon

Praça do Comércio

Pousada

Belem
Docks

Ajuda
Palace

Belem Tower

fort

Tagus River

fort

9° 14'W

Lisbon
bar

to Mafra Palace
25 miles

ATLANTIC
OCEAN

38° 40'N

miles

0   5

Ferrol

Coruña

Cabo Touriñán

Cape Finisterre

COSTA DA
MORTE

Vigo

Oporto

Mafra Palace

Lisbon

ATLANTIC OCEAN

8° 0'W

43° 0'N

- - - - Persephone's
         route

miles

0   100

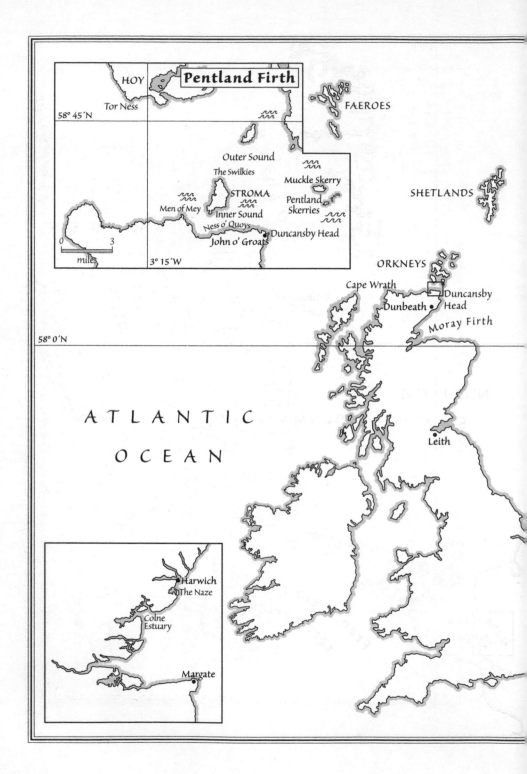

Pentland Firth

HOY

Tor Ness

58° 45′N

FAEROES

Outer Sound

The Swilkies

Muckle Skerry

STROMA

Men of Mey

Pentland Skerries

Inner Sound

Ness o' Quoys

Duncansby Head

John o' Groats

0   3

miles

3° 15′W

SHETLANDS

ORKNEYS

Cape Wrath

Duncansby Head

Dunbeath

Moray Firth

58° 0′N

Leith

ATLANTIC

OCEAN

Harwich

The Naze

Colne Estuary

Margate

NORWAY

SWEDEN

•Oslo

Kristiansand

Skaggerak

The Skaw

Gothenburg

Hirshals

Kattegat

JUTLAND

DENMARK

Esbjerg

NORTH

SEA

North Sea
Squadren

French conquered

territories

Harwich

Margate

4° 0′E

N

W E

S

0   200

miles

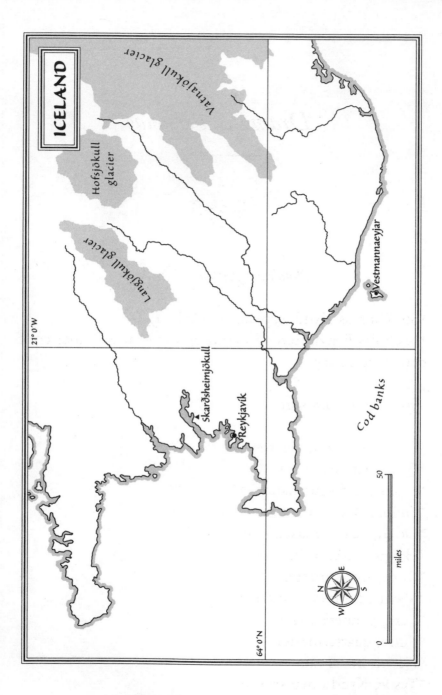

ICELAND

Vatnajökull glacier

Hofsjökull glacier

Langjökull glacier

Skarðsheinjökull

Reykjavik

Vestmannaeyjar

Cod banks

21°0'W

64° 0'N

50

0

miles

N
W E
S

Dramatis Personae

(*indicates fictitious character)

*Sir Thomas Kydd, captain of HMS *Tyger*
*Nicholas Renzi, Earl of Farndon, friend and former confidential secretary

Tyger, ship's company

*Bowden, second lieutenant
*Bray, first lieutenant
*Brice, third lieutenant
*Dillon, Kydd's confidential secretary
*Doud, quartermaster's mate
*Halgren, coxswain
*Joyce, ship's master
*Maynard, master's mate
*Stirk, gunner's mate
*Pinto, quartermaster
*Herne, boatswain
*Tysoe, Kydd's manservant

Ot

An
*B
*B
Ca
Ca
*C
Do
Do
Do
Du
Ed
*F
*G
Ha
*Je
Jør
Jun
*La
*L
*L
Lou
Mc
Mc
*P
Pel
Per
*Sa
She
Sm
Ste

Chapter 1

In the captain's cabin of HMS *Tyger*, Charles Dillon delicately plucked off his opponent's stones and placed them with the others in the centre of the backgammon board. He paused for a moment, then bore off one of his own for the second time in a row, murmuring apologetically, 'I'm persuaded my distinguished commander may be distracted.'

'Oh, forgive me, dear chap,' Captain Sir Thomas Kydd replied distantly to his confidential secretary, staring out through the stern-windows at the crowded Yarmouth Roads where the rest of the ships that had seized the Danish fleet lay at anchor.

Newly returned from their Baltic deployment with Gambier's expedition from the North Sea Squadron, *Tyger* gently heaved at the swell from the east, and with her company on liberty ashore, the ship was quiet.

While Copenhagen had suffered under a cruel bombardment, the Danish gunboats throwing themselves heroically at the great British fleet and Wellesley decisively beating their army in the field, *Tyger* had been engaged in the most important job of all – sealing off the scene from any prospect of outside intervention. Now, victualled and watered, she waited for new orders.

'Shall we remain with the squadron do you think?' Dillon enquired, as Kydd's manservant Tysoe brought in sherry and biscuits.

'Probably not,' Kydd murmured. 'Matters are now resolved – *pro tem* – in these waters.'

With the exception of Portugal and Sweden, the entire seaboard of Europe from end to end was now in Bonaparte's hands but the ruthless action of the British had not only saved the crucial Baltic trade but had robbed the tyrant of the Danish fleet to use against England.

An uneasy calm lay upon the world while Napoleon Bonaparte contemplated his next move.

'I'm sanguine His Lordship will be grateful to lay his head down in peace at his estate,' Dillon offered.

'Still more his countess,' Kydd added.

Lord Farndon, Kydd's closest friend, and his wife, who also happened to be Kydd's sister – had been rescued from the inferno of Copenhagen and carried to England in *Tyger* but he'd seen them leave with a pang of envy. There was no question in his mind that he, commander of the tautest frigate in His Majesty's Navy, was blessed, but the intimacy of their happiness had stirred something in him that left him restless.

It was ludicrous, of course, for as one of the golden frigate captains of the age he had but to step ashore and graciously accept the adulation, lauded as a god of the sea. Yet . . .

A breathless midshipman appeared at the door, whipping off his round hat. 'Sir, respects from Mr Maynard an' the flagship's mail boat is approaching.'

'Thank you,' Kydd acknowledged. 'Carry on, please,' he added, as the lad stood irresolute. The youngster blinked, then scurried off.

There had been no need to inform the captain but Kydd knew the reason for it. Any one of the twice-daily deliveries of mail distributed by the fleet post office could bear their orders from the Board of Admiralty, and every man aboard had an interest in what they contained – it could see them halfway across the globe, to the frigid monotony of the Nova Scotia station, the deadly paradise of the Caribbean or cruising athwart lucrative trade routes.

Kydd heard the muffled cry of the hail to the boat, then sensed the bumping of the vessel alongside.

The officer of the watch himself brought down the much-awaited communication.

As soon as he took it Kydd knew by its thin, single-folded appearance, with no enclosures, that this was no stirring call to a far station. Although signed for, they were not sealed secret orders and almost certainly implied a workaday and unexciting assignment.

'Shall I?' Dillon rose to afford Kydd privacy. Maynard remained wordlessly at the door, waiting.

'No, I shall attend to this later. We'll finish the game.'

At their crestfallen looks Kydd relented and, with a grin, slit the letter open and read quickly. 'Ah.'

'Sir?' The two voices spoke in unison.

'Portsmouth for orders.'

It was odd that there was no mention of a flag – the Downs Squadron, Channel Fleet or other. It smacked of a temporary shift of some sort.

'We're under sailing orders. I'll have the Blue Peter aloft if you please, Mr Maynard.'

Chapter 2

It was a hard beat into the teeth of an early winter westerly. They raised St Helens on a grey morning and, taking his pick of the empty Spithead anchorage, Kydd had his barge quickly in the water manned by a boat's crew in yellow and black striped jerseys, *Tyger*'s colours.

Vice-admiral Montagu had served as far back as the American war, and as an admiral under Howe in the early days of the French wars when Kydd had been a common seaman. He rose to greet Kydd in old-fashioned dress coat and silver stick. 'So Boney's in confusion after Copenhagen,' he remarked amiably.

'At cruel cost to the Danes,' Kydd replied.

'Yes, well, that's all over. You're under my command now. Refreshment?'

This was unusual, not to say puzzling. Rather than an interim holding, it appeared to be a formal placement under this admiral's flag. A port admiral had few men-o'-war of his own and they only for immediate defence of the port, and while these included a pair of frigates, why the famed *Tyger*?

4

'Thank you, sir. Er, in the article of activity against the enemy, what might we expect here as it were?'

'Sir Thomas, your zeal is a caution to us all. I see that you've not yet smoked why you're here.'

'No, sir.'

'Then let me be open with you. Unless the Downs Squadron finds itself in a moil there are no actions anticipated in these waters.'

'But—'

'Your appointing is at the gracious behest of their lordships to afford you and your stout ship some belated respite from the rigours of your recent hard-fought encounters. I do advise that you take satisfaction and joy from this notice of their approbation, old chap. Oh, and you have my leave to sleep out of your ship, of course.'

Kydd saw through it. The Tory government was no doubt under pressure following the contentious Copenhagen expedition and found it convenient to flourish a public hero. It would blow over in time and then he'd be back at sea where he belonged. 'I'm flattered at such attentions, sir. Perhaps I shall go up to London for a mending of the spirit.' The sooner he did his duty in the way they wanted, the sooner he'd be back aboard.

'Do so, old fellow, with my blessing. Oh – your ship is stored and watered still?'

'Sir.'

'Good. For there's a little matter that needs attending to before you go to your rest. Bonaparte is much discomfited by our actions in Denmark and is now rattling his sabre, threatening he'll march on Portugal. We've sent a squadron of some force to lie off Lisbon to show everyone which way the wind blows – it's doubtful this will take more than a week or two and then you'll be back. My contribution to the cause, as it were.'

This implied a special squadron, one created for a particular service and under direct Admiralty control rather than a station detachment and therefore, its object completed, his early return was assured.

'Sail at once, sir?'

'If you would. Just to put in an appearance, is all.'

Chapter 3

❦

The five-hundred-foot heights of the Cabo da Roca firmed
out of the morning mist: the extreme westernmost point
of the continent and an unmissable sea-mark of centuries
past for the port of Lisbon some few miles further on. And
beyond – a British squadron of nine sail-of-the-line under
easy canvas squarely across the mouth of the Tagus. The
120-gun *Hibernia* was an unmistakable bulk in the centre and
she flew her colours at the mizzen top-gallant masthead
signifying a rear-admiral. After acknowledging *Tyger*'s salute
the flagship hung out the squadron signal to heave to.

Kydd stepped aboard through *Hibernia*'s ornamented side
port. A slightly built, sensitive-featured and fastidiously
dressed admiral waited to greet him.

Kydd recognised the gifted and bafflingly contrary Sir
Sidney Smith immediately. He'd first encountered him
commanding at the epic struggle at Acre, which had seen
Smith pitted face to face against Napoleon Bonaparte himself
in a land battle, the first and last English commander to do

so. He had prevailed and Bonaparte, abandoning his army, had fled to France.

They'd met again at the inglorious action a year ago before Constantinople when his genius for irritating his superiors had nearly cost him his flag.

'A warm action in the Baltic I've heard,' he said distantly, offering his hand with practised hauteur. Kydd was aware that his own knighthood was impeccably English while Smith had not yet been so honoured, instead affecting an earlier Swedish award.

'As would keep you tolerably entertained in my place, sir,' Kydd replied evenly.

'Yes. Well, I won't pretend that your presence is anything but gratifying but there's much you need to know before I can let you loose. Come – we haven't much time.'

The admiral's quarters were palatial and characteristically in Oriental style with hangings, framed sayings in Arab script and a rich carpet in place of the stern chequerboard deck and polished mahogany of the usual flag-officer cabin.

Settled in a Persian chair, Kydd waited. There was a stately sway as *Hibernia* took up again on her slow sweep across the Tagus.

'What is your conceiving of why we're here, pray?' Smith asked.

'Sir. To make motions off the port of Lisbon that shall cause Bonaparte to reflect on his position.'

'Wrong in general, wrong in the particulars,' Smith said crisply. 'Like all Gambier's crew you think that Copenhagen has put a stopper on the man's ambitions. I've certain knowledge that he's made pact with Spain to bring about an end to Portugal as the only nation left in Europe defying him.

He's brought an army from France and means to invade, dividing the spoils with the Spanish.'

'As I said—'

'And you were wrong. Here we have your Copenhagen over again. A neutral country with a mad ruler caught between two greater powers – and which possesses a battle fleet that is the greatest prize of all to both. Do we demand of this demented queen she hands over her fleet into our protection before Boney can lay hands on it, or do we set ashore our siege engines for a bombardment and seize it? The country wouldn't stand for it, of course.'

'You're – *we*'re to see they don't sail.'

'Bravo! Our task is to keep watch until Regent Dom João shows his hand. Failing we receive a satisfactory pledge of surety, it will be our melancholy and desperate duty to destroy the fleet where it lies.'

The Tagus was notorious for its sandbanks and currents – this would be no closing under a press of sail in line-of-battle: it could only be fire-ships and boats sent in against ships-of-the-line.

'A desperate measure indeed, sir.' Kydd was appalled by the prospect.

'It shouldn't be long,' Smith went on, with a bored expression. 'General Junot is at Bayonne and has probably marched by now. Dom João must choose his fate very soon.'

Chapter 4

Tyger took her place in the line and prepared as best she could. This would be no fleet action, and until the fire-ships and mortar sloops arrived, there was no clear plan to neutralise the Portuguese fleet.

A day later word came that Junot was poised at the border with an army of twenty-five thousand men, cavalry and infantry with three Spanish divisions as well marching to join.

Would Bonaparte violate the neutrality of a sovereign nation? Later the same day the answer came: the invasion had begun. Junot was striking direct for Lisbon, taking the shorter but more difficult direct route along the valley of the Tagus. Goaded by an impatient emperor, French soldiery could be expected at the gates in days rather than weeks.

From the deck of *Tyger* Kydd watched scores, then hundreds of vessels make for the open sea as the news spread. This was very different from Copenhagen – there was no sea girdling Lisbon that the navy could take for its own to deny the enemy passage; it was only a matter of time before Lisbon would see Bonaparte's legions.

Hibernia signalled, 'Heave to and all captains.'

Sidney Smith was a cunning and resourceful commander, who had wreaked great destruction on the trapped French fleet in Toulon early in the war. What was he planning for this much more dangerous and urgent mission?

Three charts lay face down before the admiral, who waited with a slight smile as the nine captains filed in and sat around the big table.

'Gentlemen. In the matter of the Portuguee navy I have—'

A lieutenant appeared at the door. 'Sir – the ambassador is alongside.'

'Be damned to it. Send him in.'

In respect the captains rose as a fine-drawn, red-headed young dandy entered in sheer pearl silk jacket and elegant cravat.

'Lord Strangford. I'm sensible of the honour of your visit, but at this moment am in conclave with my captains to consider how to deny Bonaparte the Portuguese fleet.'

'Then it's as well they hear what I have to inform you.' The voice was high-pitched and peevish.

'My lord, please go on,' Smith said heavily.

'Then it is this. The Regent Dom João has this day made statement that he intends to accede to the "continental cause" by which is meant that he moves Portugal to Bonaparte's side. I have demanded my passport and am here to seek asylum in your good ship.'

'Dear God. Is it war, then?'

'Not yet. He responds to the tyrant's demands, which are to cleave to his continental system of economic warfare against Great Britain. He believes by declaring this he might yet stem the emperor's wrath and retain his throne.'

'You have remonstrated with the man.'

'I have – his response is to send orders to arrest on sight all British citizens and seize their goods.'

There was a rustle of dismay about the table.

'I can land above a thousand armed seamen and marines should you believe it necessary for security,' Smith said curtly.

'I can't think that a good idea, Admiral. The city is in a ferment and the *partido francés*, the French interest, would make much of it. No, there is another way.'

'Do tell, sir.'

'On my instigation a secret convention has been agreed in London, which provides for British support for any move by the Portuguese to transfer their monarchy and seat of government to the Brazils, thereby putting out of reach the legitimate head of state, whatever puppet Bonaparte finds to inhabit the Mafra Palace.'

'Then?'

'His Highness does not see fit to avail himself of this convention, believing the French want merely to deny Lisbon and its trade to the English, which is what he undertakes to do at once.'

'My lord, you have just tied my hands in the matter tighter than those of a topman aloft in a blow. If I proceed against their fleet it will be in the character of an assassin, for I must act before Junot arrives and puts Dom João's words to the blush. The fool must be made to see the folly of grovelling to Boney before it is too late.'

'Quite. Yet the man must be accounted obtuse and of little understanding of the world. You will understand that for autocracy and benightedness this kingdom is hard to beat. He will not hear me and I fear the end must not be long delayed.'

Smith bit his lip. 'You may have a cabin aboard this ship. Your followers must berth on the mess-decks – we're not an Indiaman. Now, you tell me the British are hunted down and—'

'I didn't say that. Dom João has to satisfy the French spies he's doing something, and to this end he's rounding up stragglers and confiscating the odd cargo in a half-hearted sort of way. Do recollect Portugal is our oldest ally.'

'So gratified to hear this.'

Strangford pursed his lips. 'Admiral, I shall be recommending to the government that—'

'Recommend away, my lord. I shall be steering a more direct course.'

Kydd hid a smile. This was more the Sidney Smith he knew.

'Which is, might I ask?' Strangford wanted to know.

'As of this hour there is a close blockade clamped on the port of Lisbon.'

'And what, pray, do you conceive this might achieve?'

Smith's contempt was barely concealed. 'By this your sainted Dom João may see for himself at the first hand the consequences of his siding with the tyrant. An instant ceasing of trade – no Customs revenue, taxes. No imports, exports – need I go on?'

'This is an illegal act!'

'If it were formally declared, yes. But it will not be. We are protecting our national interests in accordance with our own orders-in-council issued to counter the French Milan decree. Namely, that we may stop and search whatsoever ships we will for contraband, which they will discover is to be a monstrously long-protracted delay.'

'It will—'

'It will demonstrate to the meanest wits that siding with the French now or in the future will have catastrophic consequences that we are quite able to enforce.'

'Very well,' Strangford reluctantly conceded. 'But what of the British residents and citizens trapped ashore? Should you not make provision for them to flee before the French arrive?'

'If I open the floodgates every species of Portuguee riff-raff will clamour for passage.' Smith reflected for a moment and went on, 'So I'll flag a transport or two for their extricating should these prove to be *bona fide* subjects of His Majesty.'

'How will you know this?'

'Ah. I shall set up a rendezvous ashore that shall make examination of those desiring passage, manned by one of my commanders.'

Smith looked about the table before fixing on Kydd with a genial smile. 'I believe Sir Thomas Kydd would best be suited to calm their fears.'

Kydd gave a tight nod. The admiral's reason for his selection was unanswerable: a frigate would have little role in any operations leading up to the neutralising of the Portuguese fleet other than keeping watch on the seaward approaches, a task quite within the powers of his first lieutenant. Was this merely a ploy to put a popular hero in his place? It had happened before with Smith, he recollected, in those fevered last days in Egypt.

His orders were brief to the point of rudeness: the establishing of a rendezvous for the purpose of substantiating the claims of British citizens to passage out in a government-chartered transport. How he did this was entirely up to him, always provided he was able to furnish a thrice-daily report of the number and boarding details of successful applicants for planning purposes.

There was no question that he had the authority needed to deal with any complications – but it was hardly a job for a warrior.

Chapter 5

Leaving the evocative Drake-era Belém Tower to larboard, *Tyger*'s boat sailed the remaining five miles or so to the old town of Lisbon, left in ruins after an earthquake in 1755, but now a great trading city again. Kydd had no strong interest in the sights and history but Dillon, seated next to him, looked out eagerly. The coxswain, the big Swede Halgren, was as imperturbable as usual, while the boat's crew knew better than to rejoice in their release from ship's routine.

One, however, sat trying to hide a smile as his gaze almost caressed the shoreline. Fernando da Mesouta Pinto, quartermaster aboard *Tyger,* had been with Kydd in his first ship. Then a young sailor, now a grizzled mariner, he was stepping ashore in his birthplace for the first time in many years. He had a bundle stowed under a thwart, which Kydd was careful to ignore. Inseparable friend of gunner's mate Stirk, he'd been included as guide and translator.

It was surprising how much shipping was still crowding the channels – and across the opposite side were the dense-packed lines of Portuguese battleships in their anchorage.

Kydd noted with surprise they had no sail bent on the yards and therefore were not about to put to sea for some time.

He'd given some thought to the situation after conferring with Strangford before he left. There could be no question of taking an armed marine escort with him as this was not a lawful act in a neutral country. However, he was assured that a Portuguese colonel named by the ambassador would in his own interest provide any protection needed.

For the screening process Kydd had nothing to go on other than instinct. Besides those with documentary evidence he would have to accept as well any who could show they were native Englishmen only by accent and manner – but what of the multitudes of nameless souls of vague allegiance who swarmed in every sea-port and would swear to a British connection? With the French closing in, was it right to turn any away for lack of proof?

All he could do was play it as seemed best at the time.

Under direction from Pinto they arrived to the left of a vast hollow square plaza – the Praça do Comércio, with its large bronze equestrian statue.

Kydd sent Dillon with Pinto to let the authorities know of their arrival while they lay off to a kedge anchor.

An hour later the pair returned with several officials and two army officers, and Kydd stepped ashore.

The city was in a ferment of noise, cries and gathering crowds. All about them people pushed and jostled but Kydd had prudently chosen to be out of uniform and they were largely ignored. For the sake of amity between their countries it was agreed that a rendezvous of the kind proposed would be tolerated and a waterfront office provided.

Kydd knew why he was being favoured: if events took a more serious cast he would be conveniently close for high officials to demand to be taken off. But this would be a problem for Smith to deal with.

The office was large, a hurriedly emptied Customs inspection hall with a handily placed inner office suitable for interviews.

Dillon and Pinto were sent off again to find the colonel to provide guards and Kydd set about preparing the rendezvous. Ledger books were ruled off to take the details of the fortunate. Included would be their names and present addresses. He would compile from them his reports to Sidney Smith.

As it was unknown how many days they would be required, Kydd took steps to self-sufficiency in a proper seaman-like manner. He sent for the men's hammocks and ones for himself and Dillon – the hall would be a very adequate mess-deck. And ship's rations could be brought back with the regular boat delivering reports.

Printed placards announcing their presence went up overnight and produced an immediate crowd at first light, an ill-tempered, noisy, seething press of humanity held back only by the bayonets of the five-man guard.

'Hands, turn to!' Kydd roared.

He took his place at the desk in the office with Dillon by his side, a ship's clerk at the ledgers. 'Pinto, go out with Halgren and pick the first dozen who look the ticket. Send 'em in here to wait.' He braced for the flood.

Chapter 6

The traveller was tired and aching after the donkey trip from the interior, and waiting for her, instead of a hot bath and indulgences, was a terse note. In view of the dreadful news of the French advance, her tour party had unanimously voted to quit the country by the swiftest means possible; they trusted she would follow as soon as she'd returned from her travels.

Their flight was understandable but it left her abandoned. All because she'd conceived a desire to go up-country while the others dallied in the capital – to Évora, three days inland, where she'd been promised a fine Roman temple and a cathedral dating from the 1200s. It had met all expectations and she'd lingered in the sense of the exotic, the romance of the foreign.

But now Lisbon was in a frenzy of despair and panic. The spectre of Napoleon Bonaparte had risen and the result was terror and civil breakdown.

Curiously, out on the Tagus, ships showed no signs of putting to sea. One of the staff at the *pousada* told her bitterly that they were prevented from leaving by a British fleet, which she might see for herself, out there far to seaward, ceaselessly patrolling off the port.

She wondered what quirk of international relations had brought this about. Were they at war?

Then, barely concealing his rancour, the man added that posters had gone up overnight promising passage out, but only for the English.

She tidied herself and set out hurriedly for the waterfront to search for the promised rendezvous.

Ahead, near the big square, she saw a Union flag above something that looked like a Customs hall. It was besieged by a restless crowd, wailing and shrilly demanding. A detachment of soldiers barred the entrance. Drawing near, she saw that there was no way she could get through. Then she spotted two men in the entrance between the soldiers, one arguing with the crowd and the other standing impassive behind. Both were unmistakably seamen.

'That man ahoy!' she called loudly, her patrician authority cutting through the din. 'Yes, you, sir!' she added, seeing the larger man's face turn in surprise to her.

Hesitating, he shouldered his way through to her. 'Ma'am?' he said, taking off his black japanned hat.

'I desire you take me to the officer in charge of this rendezvous.'

Pausing for only a moment, he said, 'Yes, ma'am. This way, if y' please.' He turned and bullied his way through the crush; she kept close behind him.

The hall was nearly as full, in lines waiting their turn. They glared at her as she was hustled through to the front, then to an inner office with grimy windows.

She saw several figures sitting inside and another standing in a respectful manner.

'I'll tell him ye're here, m' lady.'

The standing figure turned and came out. It was a woman of years and she was weeping brokenly.

Taking his cue, the sailor leaned inside. 'A lady t' see ye, Captain.'

'Tell her she waits in the queue like the others, damn it,' came back an irritable bark, a voice that was tired but somehow familiar.

She pushed past and entered the room. Faces looked up from their writing in surprise – and there in the centre was a man in plain, well-cut clothes. The firmly incised lines in his handsome face gave it an edge of hardness and strength born of experience.

In a wash of feeling she recognised him immediately. Thomas Kydd, late commander of a brig-sloop . . . and the man who, those years ago, had spurned her for a country maid. And if the newspapers were to be believed, he was now a famous frigate captain and knight of the realm.

'Sir, shall I ask her to leave?' Dillon offered hesitantly.

Kydd's expression was unreadable. 'No, the lady is known to me,' he said, in a low voice.

Then, as if recollecting himself, he rose to his feet. 'A pleasure to see you again, Miss Lockwood.' He made to take her hand but she did not offer it and he fell back on a stiff bow. 'Is there anything I can do for you?'

The voice was husky, and maturity had given it a potent masculine resonance that in any other circumstance would have been unsettling. But it brought back unwanted memories, poignant and bitter. She fought a rising tide of feeling, annoyed at being taken off balance by him of all men. 'I would have thought it self-evident why I'm here, Sir Thomas,' she replied coldly. 'A passage back to England would satisfy.'

Kydd resumed his seat. 'We will require your details,' he stated formally.

Dillon came in: 'Full name, madam.'

'Belay that,' Kydd muttered. 'I'll give you a steer later.'

It pierced her, the bluff navalese remembered from those far-off days.

Dillon continued, from his sheet, 'Then what is the number of your party?'

'Myself alone.' It came out almost rudely and she instantly regretted it.

Kydd looked up abruptly. 'No servants? That is to say, you have no maidservant – or husband?'

'For reasons that need not concern you, I repeat I am not accompanied, Sir Thomas.' She was back in control. It had been the shock of seeing him while unprepared.

'Your address in Lisbon?' Dillon asked politely. 'Which is to say, where you'll wish to be advised when the transport is due to sail.'

She gave the details of the *pousada*. 'Am I then to understand there is no difficulty with a berth?' she asked neutrally.

'How's the numbers in *Álvares Pereira*, Dillon?' Kydd snapped.

'All berths taken. Passage in the hold only remains.'

'Can't we . . .?'

'No, sir.'

'Very well. Miss Lockwood, there is no passenger berth available. Do you have objection to sleeping in the hold?'

'Do know that I'm never a martyr to seasickness. Provided it allows me a safe return to England I care not, sir.'

Kydd looked as if he was about to say something but evidently thought better of it.

'Sir, those Portuguee transports are no place for a gentle-woman,' Dillon reproved.

'What are you saying?' Kydd snapped.

'Why, surely the least we should do is offer her a berth in *Tyger*, sir.'

Kydd stiffened. 'There's no room in the frigate.'

'Perhaps your great cabin would answer, sir.'

Persephone Lockwood intervened tartly: 'I will not inconvenience the captain, Mr Dillon. Your Portuguee will suffice.' The last thing she wanted was to be in close quarters with a defensive and graceless Kydd.

'Sir.'

'What is it now?'

'It may appear offensive to Admiral Montagu and others should we refuse passage to a lady in peril. After all, Lord Nelson himself did—'

'I know what Lord Nelson did,' Kydd muttered.

'Really, there is no need for this fuss. I shall go home in the transport.'

'And, sir, she need not board until we're released from station to return,' Dillon persisted.

'Very well,' Kydd said heavily. 'She shall have my great cabin. Do you have much baggage, Miss Lockwood?'

'Not as who should say,' she retorted.

'Then kindly stay within hail of this address. When I have sailing orders I shall send word and expect you to be ready to depart immediately. Do you understand me?'

'Perfectly, Sir Thomas,' she answered icily. 'Good day to you.'

The big sailor escorted her back through the crowd and she was on her own again.

Chapter 7

As Persephone Lockwood walked up the hill to the *pousada*, she was flooded with memories of the awkward but transparently decent and modest sailor of humble origin, awed by his entry into even the provincial society of Devon. His uncomplicated strength of character, so different from that of others, had reached out to her, while his direct manner and resourceful handling of her ambitious mother had warmed her to him, not to mention the sheer physicality of his presence.

There had not been an engagement but an understanding was quickly forming when, shockingly, he had called on her to withdraw his affections. It had been a bitter blow that had upset her more than she had been willing to admit, and in the desolate months that had followed she had tried to make sense of Kydd's choice of a rustic maid.

Hers had been a privileged upbringing. Well educated and connected, society was hers by right. Kydd, on the other hand, was from another place, gauche and ill-at-ease in polite company. That had not troubled her but must have intimidated him. His chance encounter with a simple country girl must have held its attractions.

In the end she had accepted what had happened and her mother had busied herself conjuring young men of birth and varying levels of desirability. Persephone was only in her twenties and her beauty had attracted numerous admirers. She had turned them all down. No doubt a man to whom she could give her heart would eventually enter her life, but until he did she would never let any man affect her so.

To recover her spirits and to escape the pressure of her mother, she'd travelled to Scotland on the pretext of a painting expedition. Taken by the appeal of Romanticism, she'd sought out the sublime in nature that had inspired the new wave of artists, and found it in the wild glens of the wind-torn craggy Highlands, the monstrous seething seas, which ceaselessly battered noble headlands, and secret moss-encrusted rivulets where stillness lay all around.

Her soul had responded with an emotional release that had found expression in sketchbook after sketchbook until, replete, she'd returned home. And in her little attic studio she had worked on the result: a grand and almost fearful view of Glencoe from the northern peaks, dark, potent with bloody history and only in the upper right a single shaft of sunlight hinting at another existence beyond the Grampians.

After several months she had laid down her brush. Her parents' reception of the painting was not what she had hoped. Her mother had scornfully dismissed it as unworthy of a well-brought-up young lady, while her father's eyes had widened and he'd shaken his head wordlessly. She could not bring herself to turn her back on her art for there was so much of her in it. On the other hand the world did not admit maidenly artists, certainly not in the genre of High

Romanticism, so she could never hope to see it hung in public.

On a whim she had shown it to an art dealer, who had asked her, with gratifying words of astonishment and awe, about the artist, whom he didn't recognise from the simple 'PL' signature. She replied primly that it was a dear friend, a Mr Polonius Loxley, whose reclusive nature did not permit him to take the public eye. After the barest minimum of discussion he had named a price that had staggered her, contingent on the provision that he would be granted first refusal on any further Loxleys.

While England trembled, then triumphed at Trafalgar, she was in Ireland painting *Hibernian Idyll*, which was even more rapturously received. Pembrokeshire inspired *Sleeping Dragon* and, in due course, she found herself of independent means, able to indulge her fancy as she chose.

Lately she had gone abroad with a private tour group to widen her horizons. With limited opportunity for continental travel, she'd enjoyed Sweden, with its Scandinavian and Viking mysteries, and then had gone on to Portugal, the last of Europe not to fall under the tyrant's sway. Piquant with a history of empire that was longer by far than Britain's, and with all the colour she could desire, it had been a wonderful interlude until Bonaparte had seen fit to send in his legions – and Thomas Kydd to intrude into her life.

Well, he was a figure of the past and would remain there. The irony was, of course, that he was tied to his simple country girl, who would now be a sad hindrance as he moved in the circles to which his fame had elevated him.

She almost felt sorry for him.

Chapter 8

The flood of petitioners gradually subsided and, but for latecomers, Kydd's rendezvous had done its work. It was time to return to his ship. His detailed reports were in: numbers had been such that two transports would be sufficient. Now it was a matter of final arrangements. The French were somewhere in the remote interior at an unknown distance but there would be warning from fleeing countryfolk before they finally appeared to menace the city, plenty of time for all the successful claimants to get aboard.

He slumped into a chair in his cabin in a foul mood. It would probably be weeks rather than days before he could turn *Tyger*'s bows homeward, and now this unwelcome intrusion, this reminder of an interlude from the past he would have preferred to leave there.

It all came back. His infatuation with a woman so very different from any of his acquaintance. The giddy realisation that he'd taken the eye of a full admiral's daughter. Then before it had come to fruition – if ever it could have – along had come the sweet, other-worldly, innocent Rosalynd whose love had promised a union of unsophisticated simplicity. He had made his choice, but in a cruel quirk of Fate the very sea that was his life had taken her, as ruthlessly as a rival in love.

He had turned his face from Persephone but he could hold to his heart that he'd had the courage to go and confess it to her in person. She had taken it calmly and, no doubt, had gone on to higher things for, as he had just been made so uncomfortably aware, she had blossomed into an arresting beauty who must have attracted quantities of admirers.

It was obvious from her manner that she was as perturbed as he at their latest meeting, perhaps still resenting him for the humiliation of his rejection. It would be an awkward few days' sail back but he would make sure she boarded *Tyger* at the last possible minute.

She was unaccompanied, and he could not guess why she had no chaperone. Did this mean she was not married? Almost certainly it did not: society ladies sometimes travelled to get away from an odious husband and if she'd ended up with some crusty colonel then this was understandable, as was the possibility that he had been posted abroad. With her accomplishments she would have been bored by wealthy idleness.

He almost felt sorry for her.

Chapter 9

Dark-panelled and gloomy, sparsely furnished with a minimum of ornamentation, it was not a chamber to be expected within the magnificent Mafra Palace. But here the fate of Portugal was being decided.

Regent Dom João had summoned a council of state in the dispatch room. His heavy, dark-jowled face was set in a mask of anxiety and he did not look up as his ministers entered one by one and took their places. Nothing less than the survival – or extinction – of his nation was on the agenda. An absolute ruler, only he could command the course that would preserve his country from the all-consuming war that had thrown Portugal between the two titanic powers locked in mortal striving for mastery of the world.

With his mother, the queen, insane, and court intrigues sapping the vitality of the archaic state, it had been a near impossible task to rule not only Portugal but its old empire, which stretched west to the Americas, south to Africa and even as far as China. The ramshackle, decaying system that had been in place for centuries was now facing terminal decline.

A solitary creature, he had the misfortune to be married to the shrewish and quick-tempered Spaniard Doña Carlota Joaquina, whom he had banished to another palace. Here in Mafra, at least, he could comfort himself with the bells and chants of religious rituals performed by its hundreds of monks and friars and maintain the antiquated court ceremonials hallowed by the centuries.

Dom Rodrigo coughed politely. He was the first of the ministers to speak. 'Sire, there are those who contend that our hour is upon us, that we must choose or be damned. The English say that a sword is either sheathed or it is drawn – there can be no more equivocation. It is without question that our interests and those of the empire are all to seaward where their battle fleets reign supreme. It were folly to ignore their request.'

'That I defy the emperor of the French?'

'No, sire. They desire only that our own fleet is withdrawn from his grasp before it is too late. That we sail it to Madeira or even to the protection of their own fleet at Cádiz. I counsel that—'

Antonio de Araújo E Azevedo, Conte da Barca and foreign minister, glared. 'All that is required by Napoleon Bonaparte is that we adhere strictly to his Continental System. No more, no less. That it requires we turn our back on old friends is regrettable but the alternative is worse, as his soldiers close on us. We must humble ourselves and bend to his wishes in all respects. Now, sire!'

'Conte, I have already sent my emissary to allow we are moving to meet his demands. But these have increased beyond measure. I am now required to withdraw my ambassadors and close every port in the empire to the English. Then I should join my naval forces to his and declare war on Great Britain. Only this will placate him.'

'We should do it!' snarled Azevedo. 'Anything less will—'

'We do, and we lose our empire to the English fleet! Without our colonies' revenue we become the paupers of Europe. Is this what you want?'

'Fool! There is neutral shipping ready and willing to shift our cargoes or did this escape you, Rodrigo?'

In reply, the minister for marine commerce slapped his palms to the table and retorted, 'It has clearly escaped you, Azevedo, what happened so lately in Copenhagen. The hard lesson there is that, should we not comply with their insistence, it shall be without a doubt visited upon us – a bombardment of Lisbon and seizure of our navy!'

A silence descended. Rodrigo shifted in his chair, then spoke softly: 'What is not in contention is that our sovereign lord faces an insurmountable dilemma. Events are forcing themselves on us and one of only two choices is left. Either meekly to surrender to Bonaparte in all particulars, which will cost us our empire and probably the crown, or align with the British to stand and fight with them.'

'A third is possible,' observed First Secretary Joaquim Louriçal quietly. 'Príncipe Dom João removes to Brazil out of reach of both, there to rule.'

'I cannot abandon my people to flee in their sight. I will not do it.'

Louriçal shrugged.

'All are pressing me to take sides with one or the other. This will be attended with dolorous consequences whatever is my course.'

'Then—'

'I have chosen.'

'Sire?'

Dom João spoke firmly: 'It is my fervent hope and prayer

31

that in the very near future the offer of the Russians to mediate in this great war will be taken up by Great Britain to the infinite relief of all Europe. The British are hard pressed and, with the entire continent arrayed against them, there is little doubt but they must see where their best interests lie.'

'So?'

'I have given this much thought and have decided on a number of steps to this end. I shall declare war on the English, as Emperor Bonaparte desires.'

There were gasps and puzzled looks.

'Sire, this is—'

'Calm yourselves. I have taken the precaution of privily advising King George the Third of England that my declaration is in the nature of a form to satisfy Bonaparte only and that no offensive acts are contemplated against him.'

'You will proceed against British citizens, the merchants and factors, confiscate their property and—'

'I have been in consultation with my treasury officials. Full reparation will be afforded to those affected, provided they fall in with my motions.'

'A counterfeit war.'

'As will assure the emperor of the French of my best endeavour to agree to his demands. More than that, I have dispatched the noble Marquis of Marialva to Paris. He conveys my total subjection to the emperor's will, with the gift of a casket of diamonds.'

'Surrender?'

'It will buy us the time we need, Dom Rodrigo. In addition he is to offer the hand of Dom Pedro, Crown Prince of Portugal and my eldest son, to any princess of the Bonaparte family.'

Into a stunned silence Azevedo said evenly, 'There is no assurance that an armistice might be achieved in the short time remaining. Should we not take precautions – the defence of Lisbon, the military to take position?'

'I will do naught to antagonise Bonaparte. The military movement against us is to be expected. A war-like gesture to oblige us to feel his power when he makes his demands. There is no question that he seriously intends to threaten me or my throne, only to bring Portugal and its empire to his cause.'

'Then you shall do . . . nothing?'

Dom João looked offended. 'Not so. This very day preparations are in hand for my removal into the Ajuda Palace in Lisbon town,' he sniffed, 'where I might lie closer to the bosom of my people.'

Chapter 10

Captain Sir Thomas Kydd took his place warily. That Smith had ordered an 'all captains' so late in the day implied something was afoot: the admiral was not prone to excitements. Had it anything to do with the dispatch cutter that had arrived several hours ago?

'Gentlemen,' Smith said, leaning back in his chair languidly and smiling benignly. 'I trust I have not inconvenienced you at this time but I thought it meet to inform you of certain developments.' In the tense watchfulness he made play with a lace handkerchief, then continued, 'As they affect this squadron. I received a dispatch not an hour ago and in it were my orders. Gentlemen, Tsar Alexander has declared war on us.'

There was a stir around the table. Russia was about to join half a million soldiers to Bonaparte's legions and had a fleet in the Baltic as powerful as that of the British.

'You may consider anything wearing a Russian flag your legitimate prey.' The amiable smile disappeared. 'I don't have to tell you that this is a serious turn for us. Especially when

I've this day been advised of another. The Regent of Portugal, Dom João, has seen fit to bow to the Corsican and has in turn declared war against us.'

In the hard faces of the seasoned captains around the table there was now deep unease.

'This means that, as far as I know, for the first time in the glorious history of our isles there is an enemy under arms along the entire shore of Europe – from the Arctic Circle to Gibraltar. Napoleon Bonaparte has finally succeeded in turning everyone against us.'

His smile returned. 'But since when has England cowered from adversity? Europe lies under the tyrant's heel but we have the rest of the world. Let's help ourselves!' he added wolfishly.

Grins returned.

'In the matter of the Portuguese, how are we to proceed?' Thompson of *Foudroyant* wanted to know.

'As to a descent on their fleet? I would have thought nothing has changed. Should they feel disinclined to remove themselves from Bonaparte's grasp, we deal with them expeditiously.'

'Then, sir, may we be made aware of why are we not discussing the operation?' he added delicately.

'All in good time, sir.'

Kydd leaned forward. 'Sir, should we not think to bring off our people now?'

'Perhaps not yet.'

'May I know why?' Kydd asked, with an edge of impatience. There was a streak of theatricality in Smith that was most irritating.

Smith stretched and yawned. 'For the good reason that I believe this entire business a bore and distraction from the

35

larger war. Dom João's actions are perhaps, on the face of it, a rational move. He's saying that the French invasion of Portugal might be nothing more than Boney rattling his sabre, for even he would hesitate to devour a neutral country.'

'Sir. Bonaparte has the example of Copenhagen before him. I cannot believe it's in him to waste time in this way.'

'You think so? I would have thought it more reasonable for him to achieve his taking of Portugal comfortably, simply by a show of force, thereby bringing them straight into his camp and their ruler his puppet.'

'So Dom João is playing for time.'

'By his notions of strategy. He'll see how mistaken he is when the French walk into Lisbon and it's all over for him. Damn the man! If he'd take up our offer and sail for the Brazils there'd be none of this pootling about uselessly with a valuable battle fleet. As it is, the blockade must continue.'

Pellew of *Conqueror* intervened quietly: 'Nevertheless, sir, shall we not send away the transports with our people now, while we can?'

'No. For the first, there is no immediate necessity. For the second, they'll need escorting and I'm damned if I'm going to diminish my forces until I have to – I've few enough if Boney tries a sally from Rochefort. In any case, there's every reason to hope this affair will blow over, and sad loobies we'd look if we're seen to have panicked. Only when this Dom João has gone over *in toto* do we move, setting 'em on their way while we deal with their fleet.'

Kydd was guiltily relieved that he would not have to take Persephone Lockwood aboard just yet.

Smith picked up a silver bell and rang it. 'You'll all stay to drink to the tsar's damnation and confusion, hey?'

Chapter 11

The sailor stolidly held a lanthorn and waited while the diplomat came to himself. Lord Strangford woke groggily. 'Wha' is it?'

It was dark, rain hammering on the cabin deckhead, and the duty mate-of-the-watch showed no inclination to leave. 'Admiral Smith desires y' should join him.'

'Now? What o'clock is it?'

'One bell o' the middle watch, sir, which is to say, a half-hour after midnight.'

'Good God! I'm to be awakened at this time of night for—'

'An' asks you attend on him without delay.' He set down the lanthorn and held the swinging cot while the nobleman struggled out of it. A tousled valet appeared and the master's mate left.

'What's to do, my lord?' the servant asked sleepily.

'Damn it all to Hell! The admiral summons me – what he means by this I cannot know. Well, fetch my gown and slippers, you fool!'

* * *

In the great cabin just one candle glowed, illuminating the solitary figure of Smith, still in his sea rig.

He looked up as Strangford entered. 'I thank you for your attendance, my lord,' he said, in a dry tone. 'A trifle by way of developments that you will no doubt be interested in.'

'At this hour?'

'Quite so, considering the urgency of the business.'

'Well?'

'One of my sloops did take a Biscayman. In it was found a Paris newspaper only a day old and he thought to bring it to me.'

'You've wakened me to read the morning papers? You've a sad idea, sir, of the sources of information available to an ambassador!'

Smith smiled bleakly. 'Oh, but this is the *Moniteur*, Boney's own mouthpiece, which he cannot deny. It's official and at this moment is being read all over the continent. Pray cast your eye over it . . .'

He handed over the newspaper and watched for reaction.

'It says that "The House of Bragança has ceased to reign in Europe."'

'Well?'

Strangford frowned. 'Sir. The rantings of the braggart are of no—'

'You'll gratify me to an enormous degree,' Smith ground out, 'should you see your way to going ashore and waving this under the nose of your cretinous Dom João, yes?'

'For the purpose of . . .'

'To show the buffoon that Napoleon Bonaparte has gone on record to say his throne is about to become history!'

'Yes, well, as you do counsel,' Strangford said stiffly, 'tomorrow I shall—'

'My barge is manned and lies at your service this very minute,' Smith said cuttingly. 'I'd have thought it better to hear it first from us, with our renewed offer of escort to the Brazils, don't you?'

In the boat Strangford bristled. He was a peer of the realm and an ambassador and to be chivvied like a common sailor by a coxcomb was hard to take. The worst of it was that there was good sense in what Smith wanted. Now Bonaparte's intentions were clear there would be every chance to bring about a change of allegiance. The newspaper in his bosom would be the instrument of success – if he could play his part.

Apparently the regent had moved into the half-finished Ajuda Palace, its landing place not far along from the Belém Tower. As they touched at the rain-glistening stone steps there was no one to challenge them but neither was there any carriage. Doggedly, Strangford tramped up the hill towards the palace in the cold rain.

Astonished guards tried to dissuade him but, on the unanswerable pretext of bearing an urgent diplomatic communication, he was shown to a receiving room. A distracted chamberlain went for the regent who, after an interval, appeared in satin robes and slippers, blinking in perplexity.

'My lord Strangford, you cannot appear here. We are at war, sir.'

'Sire, I bear grave news for Portugal and its crown.'

'Oh?'

'I desire you read this.' He fumbled for the *Moniteur* and drew it out, damp and drooping.

Dom João took it, then gave an embarrassed smile. 'I do not have the French, my lord.'

39

'This is the *Moniteur*, the state organ of France. And in it we have a declaration by Napoleon Bonaparte that he means his invasion of your country to end with your deposition from the throne of Portugal.'

'It says that?'

'Unhappily it does, sire. "The House of Bragança has ceased to reign in Europe," it declares. His intention now is clear – he demands nothing less than the crown of Portugal for himself.'

With a stricken look, Dom João sank into a chair, wringing his hands. 'What shall I do?' he whispered. 'A council of state and—'

'There is no time for that. If you love your country there is only one course. You do deny him the crown by sailing to your welcoming colony, Brazil. He cannot seat another on the throne if it is removed to another place.'

'How then can I rule if all government and authority is here? The laws, records, histories . . .'

'That is easily solved. It is not the throne alone that is transported, but the instruments of administration in their entirety. Departments and divisions, with their records and accounts, your treasury, sacred articles of state—'

'This is not possible! Even—'

'It is more than possible, sire. You have a fleet of ships lying idle. They are stored and fitted for the voyage and, under our inviolable escort, will safely transport not only you and the royal family but the entire apparatus of rule. Your reign will continue uninterrupted but in another situation.'

'The entire administration of a nation to another world? I've never heard of such, no one has ever—'

With days before the vanguard of the French force

appeared on the hills above Lisbon, the chance was fast vanishing. 'It must be done, sir!'

'I will do it,' Dom João whispered, his voice breaking. 'It is my duty, is it not?'

'Well said, sire! Then may we say that—'

'A council of state will be summoned at dawn. It will be instructed to make preparations for the removal of the Portuguese state to Rio de Janeiro.'

'A very wise decision if I may say so, Príncipe. If there is anything we may do to assist . . .'

Chapter 12

Sidney Smith waited impatiently for his captains. 'I won't waste time. You're to know that the Regent of Portugal, Prince Dom João, has acceded to all our wishes. He intends to sail to the Brazils with the rest of the royal family and the Portuguese fleet.'

There was heartfelt relief around the table – a difficult and bloody operation against their own fleet had been avoided, and the prospect of the odium at yet another British assault on a neutral was laid to rest.

'Not only that,' Smith went on, 'the whole of their parliament and so forth is to be transported with them, such that the nation's rule may be continued out of reach of the Corsican. Our part – and let me be very clear on this – is to act in the character of escort. Not just to repel Boney's fleet, should they dispute the escape, but to make damned sure the prince keeps his word and doesn't end up in some Frenchy harbour.'

He nodded to his flag-captain, who produced charts and laid them on the table. 'Our dispositions are therefore as follows. We allow that the Portuguese have the honour to form escort on their monarch, their flag in *Príncipe Real*, 84. We take close station to windward and to leeward in good situation to intercept those desirous of leaving. This order of sailing is maintained until we reach Madeira.'

'When is it expected that—'

'Now. Junot is only some leagues beyond the hills, I'm told. They've run out of time. Your order pack is prepared, you're under sailing orders for perhaps two days hence. I should think it proper for our people to board the transports in the morning. Don't delay in this – we shall not linger for stragglers.'

He picked up his papers. 'We shall not reconvene before we sail. This is a straightforward operation. I see no difficulties.' Catching Kydd's eye, he finished crisply, '*Tyger* and *Viper* will not be needed on the voyage. After they've discharged their last duty to me they are free to return to England.'

There were murmurs of envy from the battleship captains but, with at least a dozen sail-of-the-line in company, the Portuguese needed fear no enemy.

'The duty, sir?' Kydd asked.

'*Viper* ranging south, *Tyger* to the north, you are to watch for any surprises that the French may throw to catch us as we sail. They've spies in the palace and, with Spanish ports only a day or so away, we take no chances.'

It was a prudent move: any small squadron including ships-of-the-line could cause havoc as the unwieldy armada formed up.

'Sir.'

'You'll sail immediately – you've not much time.'

Guiltily Kydd remembered. 'Oh, just one thing, sir. I have a lady I've promised passage to England. I'd like to send for her.'

43

Smith frowned in annoyance. 'What's that to me? I said immediately! Stand fast your promise, she goes with the others in a transport.'

There could be no arguing, and by this Kydd was neatly relieved of the necessity of her company.

Chapter 13

'You *must sign,* sire!' Louriçal pleaded in desperation, thrusting the pen towards the figure of Dom João, who did not respond, sitting with his head in his hands at his state desk.

The others stood silent, held by the unfolding drama. It was nothing less than the voluntary exile of a sovereign, who was abandoning his country and its citizens to their fate at the hands of an invading army.

'No. I will not.' The muffled words were more sobbed than spoken. 'My people – I cannot flee from them like a craven cur.'

Rodrigo intervened smoothly: 'They cannot all come, Highness. Do you not see? It is your duty to the crown to safeguard it. Only in this way—'

He was interrupted by a harsh bark from Azevedo. 'Junot and his troops are within a day of Santarem. If you do not act they will soon be here to seize your noble self and your family and take you in a cart to Paris!'

'They will see me, can't you understand? My good people

will watch their prince regent desert them . . . They will be angry, they will hate me!'

Louriçal came forward and, to the horror of the assembled nobles, stuffed the quill into his hand. 'Sign, sire. Now.'

Dom João looked up with a piteous expression, his eyes filling, then murmured brokenly, 'Very well. For the sake of my country.' His hand went down and the extravagant signature began to form. Suddenly he threw the pen to the floor and shot to his feet. 'I – I cannot! Please believe, I cannot.'

Quickly, Louriçal thrust behind him and forcefully jammed the chair into the back of his knees, causing him to collapse back into it, to a hiss of indrawn breath from around the room. 'Sire. Sign!'

Again the failed signature.

This time Louriçal was joined by Rodrigo and between them they guided the hand. It was signed.

'Sire, your duty is done,' he said crisply. 'Now let us do ours. Admiral, your plans, if you please.'

Almirante Dom Pedro was ready. 'As this scheme must be followed to the letter. Agreed?'

'As you will, sir.'

Quietly, he and foreign minister Azevedo had drawn up a list of those to be granted the benison of safety and exile. State dignitaries, the royal family, high bureaucrats – all were to be issued a numbered permit with details of ship and baggage allowed. Others – church functionaries, treasury officials, clerks, comptroller of the household and gentlemen of the bedchamber, servants, pages, pastry cooks – were meticulously allocated space, to a staggering number, in all, of some fourteen thousand.

A hum of incredulous murmuring set up at the scale of what was being contemplated.

There was more. The laws and records of the Portuguese nation, since the great days of the Discoverers and beyond, were to be crated and consigned to the hold in their entirety. Even the royal library of some sixty thousand volumes would be found a place.

Church silver and precious relics would be accorded particular reverence and plans were being drawn up to notarise the contents of the royal palaces of Mafra and Queluz with a view to their removal and shipping. The treasury would be emptied, as would every bank and repository – rapacious French looting of conquered countries was notorious.

The fleet would begin at once the task of victualling and watering for the long voyage and it was expected that this would soon be done, allowing an early departure.

Finally it was announced that the whole enterprise was to be concealed from the general population. Any disclosing these intentions would lose their place in the armada.

He finished, with a wry smile: 'And this whole only if the French oblige us by allowing us the days to execute it.'

At the Belém docks the situation rapidly turned into bedlam. Quiet and deserted while the English blockade had stopped all movement, now there was frantic activity – boats, carts, stores, endless casks of water, rope and spars.

Later in the day mysterious crates, numbered in code, were stacked on one side. Baggage left in heaps, drays arrived with full loads, and soon the waterfront was a jumble of all manner of items. Still more were unloaded.

The next morning, when rumour had it that within a day Junot would be on the hills overlooking Lisbon and contemplating his conquest, the tempo increased to a frenzy.

The carriages began arriving. Some of the occupants were

eager to be gone while others were reluctant and stood in small groups, looking back mournfully at the land that was no longer theirs. As if in sympathy a gentle rain began to fall, the sky leaden and bleak. The steep cobbled roads down from Lisbon's hills ran with water and the docks puddled quickly, soaking and muddying the piles of belongings and turning the scene into one of heart-breaking desolation.

Fearful crowds gathered, held back by bayonet-wielding soldiers. The onlookers gaped as carriage after carriage jostled for space by the quayside. The notion that a wholesale planned flight to the colonies of the prince regent, his government and nobility was simply too much to take in.

A procession of wagons and pack mules appeared on the dock road. Each was heaped with the wealth and effects from the royal palaces of Mafra and Queluz, hundreds of conveyances attended by pages and officials, watching over cutlery, priceless paintings, magnificent ornamentation, carpets and every species of luxury. In trunks and sacks sodden with rain, the accumulated riches of the Portuguese court were piled together for dispatch to the flagship.

The boats were now openly taking the fortunate out to the ships and the incredible truth began at last to dawn. Angry and frustrated, the populace stormed and battered at the carriages, in despair at their betrayal. As rumours spread there were shouts of rage, anguish and despondency. With the French so near their fate was now very clear.

Noble carriages stood empty, their footmen and servants no longer needed, unemployed. Baggage was looted, and as the last of the favoured hastened to board the boats, they left many of their belongings to the mob.

The final act was inevitable and infinitely melancholic.

Towards evening, as the rain worsened, an old carriage

driven by a single coachman in street clothes stopped at the edge of the crowd. The line of soldiers extended and enveloped it and out stepped Dom João, Regent of Portugal.

His face stiff with emotion he walked unsteadily forward, pausing only once to look back on his kingdom. The Belém waterfront was below the Ajuda Palace but it had a drawback: at low water the boarding steps were stranded above the tideline and no boat could approach.

In his last steps on the soil of Portugal he was to be debased further. A few planks across the tidal mud to the water's edge were his final path, leading out to a skiff light enough to approach, a dismal contrast to his usual rose-scattered progress through his realm. He stopped, took off his cocked hat and turned to the sullen crowd – was it to be a farewell speech, a stirring call to courage in adversity, a patriotic cry that would echo down the centuries?

The rain beat down balefully, plastering his hair in untidy streams. His hand moved in an ineffective gesture but the words did not come. Turning back, bowed and belittled, Dom João tottered out to the skiff.

Portugal now had no ruler, no leader, no future.

Chapter 14

*T*yger and *Viper* leaned to the keen south-westerly, working out to sea with doubled lookouts. Any enemy battle squadron would have them wheeling around and the escorting admiral warned to face about to meet them, but after ten leagues of brisk sailing it was clear there were no threats away to seaward. Parting company, *Viper* then made off to the south while *Tyger* angled in to the northern coast.

The bracing sailing conditions should have gladdened the heart of her captain, but Kydd was having an attack of conscience. Persephone Lockwood was now condemned to a Biscay crossing in a crowded, uncomfortable transport, a sordid and unworthy fate for a well-born lady. That he was obeying orders did not make the situation easier to square with his sense of what was right and proper, but what could he do?

He tried to put it out of his mind, but felt demeaned by having gloried in her absence from his ship. He forced himself to concentrate on the task at hand.

They had barely sighted the low blue-grey smudge of land

that was Portugal when a hail came from the masthead. '*Deck hooo!* Three sail, standing from suth'ard!'

'Bear down on 'em,' Kydd ordered. This direction meant they were not from the region they'd left and were thus probably friendly, but he was taking no chances.

They hove into view – a full-rigged vessel and two smaller barques in company, steadily heading north. Even before *Tyger* came up with them Kydd knew who they must be. A pair of transports and an escort, which he thought he could recognise.

It was *Belle Isle*, an old 64 with its odd downward-opening gun-ports. *Tyger* rounded to under her lee and Kydd hailed her quarterdeck: 'How goes the Portuguese fleet?'

'Still in a mill at the mouth of the Tagus,' came an answer. 'Should shake out a reef or two – French are in Lisbon b' now, I'd say.'

The transports, now hove to in obedience to *Belle Isle*'s signal hoists, wallowed uncomfortably in the long swell. Both were packed on deck with huddled figures and Kydd had a stab of sympathy at the knowledge of what they were enduring.

On a sudden impulse he lifted his speaking trumpet and blared, 'Do you have embarked a Miss Lockwood? I pledged her a passage in *Tyger* and would like to keep the promise.'

After a pause came the reply. 'No, we don't have the lady – but you're welcome to speak to the transports.'

Kydd threw up a hand in thanks and turned to the officer-of-the-watch. 'Away both cutters. Find out which one has a Miss Persephone Lockwood and bring her back with her baggage.'

The boats stroked smartly off, one to each transport, and he sent a messenger to Tysoe to prepare his bed-place for a lady.

He watched them each go alongside and wondered which would have her — but unaccountably both returned empty.

'Don't know of such a lady,' yelled up the first.

'Damn it, she'll be in one or the other. Did you make sure?'

'Cap'n swears she's not. He did ask about.'

The other's response was the same and Kydd felt a sudden unease. He knew that these were the only transports taken up by Smith for the transfer back to England and if she wasn't in either, then . . .

But there was nothing more he could do: he must get on with his mission.

Chapter 15

With a last friendly exchange, Kydd left *Belle Isle* and her charges and resumed his previous course, angling towards the land. His orders called for a single pass up the coast as far as Ferrol, making long boards out to sea to cross the sea lanes and back again in a zigzag. If nothing was spotted, he was then free to return to England.

It went without incident, an easy run in the increasingly lively south-westerly with no need for tacking about. But always there was the tense awareness that not only was Iberia a lee shore but in these more northerly latitudes it was a merciless and iron-bound one, with precipitous crags and stark headlands ceaselessly pounded by the North Atlantic. If a ship found itself in difficulties there it was likely to be brutally wrecked and end its life in a very short time. Not for nothing did the Spaniards call it Costa da Morte – the coast of death.

For *Tyger* there was no alternative but to close with the coast; the Spanish and French would take any risks to slip past the British blockade.

* * *

A day passed without a sighting, another, but on the third, nearly at the end of *Tyger*'s run, it all changed.

The legendary Cape Finisterre was a harsh peninsula pointing south, like a finger, and in its lee there was good anchoring. So near to finishing, Kydd was not about to cut corners and set the frigate into the bay beyond. Nothing.

The boatswain asked for a chance to set up the larboard shrouds after the long hours' straining in the brisk winds on the same tack and was granted his wish while *Tyger* lay to in the quiet of the lee side of Cape Finisterre, an appreciated respite from the constant buffeting of the Atlantic winds. Kydd went below, leaving the task to the watch-on-deck while he got on with his journal, bringing it up to date for his arrival in Portsmouth.

There was one subject he could not include as beneath notice: that he had left Persephone Lockwood on her own in the path of the advancing French.

Smith's casual consigning her to the transports was all very well, but what if she had taken him at his word and, believing he would return for her, had refused the transports? This would explain her absence when he'd sent the boats to enquire of her. Daughter of an admiral, it was within the bounds of credibility that this was what she had trusted in, and in the last anarchy and disorder she had been overlooked and left behind.

At that precise moment the French sacking of Lisbon must be well under way and . . .

Whichever way he looked at it, there was one unalterable fact. It was his fault. If he had not kept her from boarding earlier it would never have happened.

Appalled at the images rising, Kydd tried to rationalise that he'd made all reasonable arrangements to be expected of him, only to see them thwarted by his orders taking him away from Lisbon. If any were to be blamed surely it was Smith, who had given him the orders without making sure of Persephone Lockwood's passage out.

Lost in dark thoughts, he didn't hear the knock on the door and started at the sudden appearance of the midshipman messenger before him. 'Mr Bowden's respects an' he would be happy to see you on deck,' he stammered.

Kydd got to his feet and, thrusting his concerns aside, emerged on deck.

'Sir.' Bowden held up his hand for silence. Then, after a space, he asked quietly, 'Do you hear anything?'

Kydd concentrated. There was a subliminal rumble, more felt than heard. 'Guns?'

'What I thought, sir.'

They searched in all directions, seeing nothing, but then a seaman lookout cried, 'Smoke! I see smoke over yon hill!'

Where the peninsula was lowest at its neck, torn wreaths of light-grey – gunsmoke – were being carried up and over by the wind. It was coming from somewhere out of sight on the Atlantic side of the peninsula. And if this was an action, then logically one of the participants must be British – either punishing the enemy or in need of assistance. His duty was clear.

'Secure at the shrouds there. Get under way as soon as you may, Mr Joyce. Mr Bray, clear for action!'

Kydd swore at the delay but it needed tacking about at a respectful distance to double the louring heights of Finisterre before the far side passed into view.

Not more than a mile or two distant two ships were locked in combat. The larger, a frigate, was circling a smaller, a brig-sloop with her foremast down and helpless, her colours either struck or shot away. With its guns continuing to crash out mercilessly into the smaller vessel, the colours of the frigate were unmistakable: the tri-banded red and yellow of Spain.

A rush of anger came over Kydd: to persist in the destruction of a fallen foe was inhumane and beyond the rules of war. 'Lay us alongside the brute,' he rapped and raised his pocket glass.

A heavy frigate, thirty-eight or forty guns, with a typically more upright sternworks and more tightly curved beakhead. Probably out from Vigo or Corunna, implying a fresh crew and endurance. And, knowing that if injured it could easily fall back on a friendly port for repairs, it would be willing to take risks in any contest at arms.

Kydd's gaze shifted to the sloop. He realised it now to be an English brig-sloop of the same kind as *Teazer*, his much-loved first command. She was draped in fallen rigging and wreckage, floundering in the brisk seas. There were figures at work on the ruin and he thought he caught a hand waving in gratefulness.

Tyger had been seen by the enemy frigate, which warily changed its tacking to a wear, bringing its broadside to bear. Kydd was not fooled: at this range and with themselves bow on, it would be a waste of shot and he didn't think a senior frigate captain would stoop to the gesture.

He didn't. Widening his turning circle he hauled to the wind and made off directly out to sea, shortening to topsails as he went.

'Sir, y'r attention . . .' Joyce, the sailing master, pointed to an odd rust-coloured protrusion from the sea near the brig-sloop, much like a single canine tooth with the sea heaving whitely about it. 'La Carraca,' he murmured.

'The ratchet,' Dillon explained.

'Wha'?'

'I'm thinking he means a capstan pawl,' Brice offered. 'See how one side's curved and—'

'Never mind,' Kydd said tightly. It was obvious that the brig-sloop had been surprised by the frigate and had intelligently tried to place the rock between herself and a much superior enemy, and it explained why the frigate had so quickly made for the open ocean – sea room for a fight.

He would oblige.

'Snug to tops'ls and close as she can lie,' he ordered, glancing up at the sails as they were sheeted in, and they began to plunge after the Spaniard.

The two ships were now slashing out into the deep Atlantic a mile apart, *Tyger* comfortably to windward.

'A pity about the sloop, sir,' Bowden murmured.

Less than a mile offshore and dismasted, in the southwesterly she would inevitably be driven on to the cruel-hearted coast, the ship pounded to pieces and her company torn apart as they were flung by the breakers against the barnacled crags. It would have been a simple exercise in seamanship to pass a tow to bring the disabled vessel the short distance to round the cape and safely fetch the lee beyond for repair – but the harsh logic of war meant that it was out of the question while an enemy lay waiting to fall on them both.

Kydd's heart wrung with compassion, but the unknown sailors in her would know what the situation was and he hoped would take some last satisfaction in seeing *Tyger* in full chase of their murderer.

'Yes, Mr Bowden,' he said, in a low voice, 'but I'd wager they'll give it their all to get sail on and round the cape.'

He didn't believe it and sensed his second lieutenant didn't either.

Chapter 16

It was a hard beat. On the open ocean, winds blew harder and fiercer and the white-topped waves surged triumphantly towards them to explode against *Tyger*'s weather bow in thumps. The resulting shiver could be felt even as far aft as the quarterdeck, followed by the bowsprit tracing a wild arc through sky to sea in a dizzying pitch downwards.

The Spaniard was making heavy weather of it too, bursts of white constantly at its bows with colours flat as a board to the wind, lifting and smashing through the seas. The reality of the sheer malevolence of a thousand tons of menace radiated out, its reason for existence destruction and killing.

But it was *Tyger*'s kind of weather. Kydd could almost feel her throw off the massive seas as she shouldered her way into them, occasionally with an endearing shudder, like a dog emerging from the water. She carried her casks well down in the hold and was therefore stiff, returning quickly upright when bullied over and thus able to carry sail on for longer.

His eyes strayed down the deck, taking in the grand sight of his ship at her best in pursuit of the enemy.

Something made him move to the breast-rail at the forward end of the quarterdeck where he could look down on the rows of guns each side, manned and ready. The gun-ports were closed in deference to the seas and the gunners hunkered in companionable groups quite inured to the lively movement.

He saw Stirk sitting with his back wedged against a gun-carriage, obviously spinning a yarn to a rapt audience. He raised his head and caught Kydd's eye, giving a solemn wink before resuming his tale. With men like that, how was it possible to fail? His pre-action tensions subsided.

Tysoe came on deck, the wind whipping at his coat. He'd brought Kydd's foul-weather gear, which caused grins to break out on all sides.

'Knows what the weather's up to before you do, Mr Joyce,' Bowden chided playfully.

'I'd be a fool t' disagree, like,' the master admitted. 'It's a regular-going Atlantic blow a-boiling up, right enough.'

The western horizon had hardened against a backdrop of sullen blackness as the boreal forces balefully gathered, and a low drone like a maudlin piper heightened in the rigging.

'We should look to snugging down soon, I fears,' Joyce added.

In his heart Kydd knew he was right: he'd seen his share of the vicious storms the North Atlantic could conjure so quickly. But this was war: the first to shy away was running from the field of battle. Yet any talk of gun action in the movement from these seas was lunacy with a tempest about to break over them.

Soon it would be too dangerous to send men into the tops to reef sail – the time of decision was fast approaching.

The Spaniard showed no signs of resigning the field. In

59

these conditions any who took damage in the complexity of masts and rigging, however slight, stood a very good chance of not surviving the squalls that would soon be visited on them. He was relying on his superior size to stay the course for longer and *Tyger* would be obliged to follow suit at risk of her spars.

'Stand down from quarters, Mr Bray,' Kydd ordered. There would be no fighting in this blow.

And then, unexpectedly, the enemy fell off the wind, sheering around until it was headed directly away from *Tyger*.

'What the devil?' Was this a retreat, a fleeing from an inferior?

'Follow him!' Kydd snapped.

Then he noticed that in the manoeuvre the Spaniard was taking in reefs. He had blinked first – but intelligently – making it now a stern chase, and on this course luring Kydd into a ferocious coast that he must know far better, in conditions that favoured the larger ship.

With rising wind astern, *Tyger* was now awkwardly rearing and plunging as the following seas seethed past her, a wet and bruising ride.

'I mislike that boldering weather,' the master shouted against the wind's roar, pointing in its direction, where the darkness was split by lightning, startlingly vivid. This promised sharp squalls and punishing rain and would normally have them taking in sail – but caught up in the relentless logic of the chase neither pursued nor pursuer could afford to slacken speed.

Kydd rubbed his eyes after a dash of spray lashed across his face, and when he looked again, he saw the Spaniard's main topsail slowly begin to transform in shape from its usual square to an increasing triangle of absent canvas.

With a grim smile he understood. This was a goosewing, clewing up a lower corner of the big sail, gathering it inwards, a move as effective as reefs to reduce sail area and thus strain on the mast.

And he'd realised something else: its captain was trying him out – if Kydd followed suit, this would be an unspoken agreement to go further in mutual respect for a higher enemy, the weather. If he did not, it was simple enough to ease out the clewlines again.

'We'll do the same, Mr Joyce,' he ordered.

Soon after, the frigate's fore-topsail went the same way and Kydd followed. The effect was rapid and *Tyger*'s motion eased – they were out of immediate danger.

What was the plan of the unknown Spanish captain?

If they stayed on this course they would fetch the north-west tip of Spain beyond which lay the empty wastes of Biscay. It made sense, for Ferrol, Vigo and other ports there offered shelter and, no doubt, reinforcements. If that was so, there would be no conclusion, no fight. A pity, for he had a burning contempt for the man he'd seen firing into a helpless opponent, which must now be in her last hours against the rocks – he owed it to them to take destruction to this enemy.

There could well be a reckoning if the storm blew itself out, but this would take place up against the Coast of Death with the odds very much against *Tyger*. On the other hand, and probably the more likely, the Spaniard could still take the opportunity of scurrying into the nearest port.

The irony was that it didn't matter: the track would be exactly the same if it were to be an inshore encounter, losing the foe to a port refuge, or, as he was now free to do, make return passage to England.

Their position was of necessity dead-reckoning – 'deduced reckoning' from their speed through the water added to the surging impetus of the waves but subject to the south-setting Iberian current carrying them bodily and invisibly south. It was a supremely skilled art, and a conscientious navigator like Joyce would take the trouble after the event to back-calculate from his dead-reckoning positions what effects must have been present to make them raise landfall where they did.

As it was now, that skill was one of life and death: the south-westerly gale was taking them swiftly on and into the deadly rock-bound coast. At some point a decision had to be made and—

The thunder squall hit with a ferocious howl and a blinding curtain of freezing hail, coming swiftly out of the murk without warning.

The first savage blast caught *Tyger* on the larboard quarter. Even so it was enough to lay her over while the hail lashed the seamen mercilessly as they fought to throw off sheets and braces on the steeply sloping deck. With a deafening bang, quickly followed by another, two of the close-reefed topgallant sails blew out, strips of canvas instantly streaming to leeward. But with high sail now no longer levering her down, *Tyger* slowly rose again.

Clinging to a mizzen shroud, Kydd squinted up at the crazily arcing mastheads – as far as he could tell all spars were still in place, even if the remaining sails were banging and flogging as the wind direction chopped about, as so often in a fierce western ocean squall.

The bluster eased, *Tyger* shook herself and stubbornly resumed her course.

The Spaniard had seen her struck and had time to let fly

its own lines before it in turn was hit. That preserved its sails but they vanished as they were got in, and now both vessels were under reefed topsails facing what more the storm could bring.

They had not long to wait: behind the squalls the streaming gale was strengthening, flat and hard, filling the air with spume from torn-off wave-crests.

This was now a far more serious matter than the mere running down of an enemy.

Kydd staggered to where Joyce was standing, tightly gripping a line from aloft and squinting into the ragged wildness. 'Mr Joyce,' he bawled at the sailing master. 'By your best judgement, what's our position?'

The weather had turned against them and all thoughts of offensive action against the Spaniard had fled. Now their prime duty was survival. And this meant a decision – to scud before the wind with bare poles or lie a-try into the storm. The first gave them a small scope to steer where they wished, the second did not, but delayed their inevitable driving to leeward – into the Coast of Death.

It all hung on their position. If a half-decent lee could be found they could ride out the worst. Cape Finisterre would serve admirably, but this notorious seaboard was ill-charted. Most sensible mariners stood well out to sea as they passed and therefore charts needed only be sketchy and were not to be relied on close inshore.

Joyce did not reply for a long time, his usually jovial manner now deadly serious. The customary aids to navigation – a noon sighting, continual log readings, a hand-lead sounding – were denied to him. It was only the deep wisdom accrued in a lifetime at sea that was left, with the sum of the reflexive attentions he'd paid to their movements.

He looked Kydd full in the face. 'Sir Thomas, I'll not waste your time wi' fair words. On our outward board we didn't make our northing worth a spit, an' with the southerly current I doubts we're far off, say, forty-three 'n' three north and distant but a dozen miles or so the furthest.'

'Forty-three . . . then that puts us north of Vigo—'

'And south o' Corunna. Means there's no offshore anchorage I knows of to ride this out, none a-tall.'

The Iberian coast was known to be bold – steep to and deep water to within less than a mile, far too dangerous for foul-weather anchoring.

To scud in, hoping to find shelter among the clefted dark granite crags in these seas was inviting disaster; on the other hand, to lie to would only delay the inevitable. And just a dozen miles to leeward . . . The decision was impossible.

Then, in the drifting smother to leeward, the dread sight of the coast firmed. There were now vanishingly few alternatives – the veering westerly was pressing them relentlessly on to it, for with what sail they could show in this foul weather they could never find the manoeuvrability to claw off.

White faces turned to Kydd, waiting for the order that would mean deliverance – or death.

In a torment of doubt his eyes strayed to the fading shape of the Spaniard ahead.

Something was odd – and then it sank in: under what scraps of sail would stand, the frigate was heading directly for the ramparted coast, making no attempt to fight clear. 'Our friend knows a hidey-hole and he's making for it!' he blurted. 'Let him show us the way – and we'll join him!'

'Sir, once we're inshore we'll be—'

'I understand, Mr Joyce. For now we're to trust the Don

knows his own shores better than we do. Have you another plan?'

The coastline came on steadily through an air-blast thick with spindrift, the high crags sombre and lightless and with a tell-tale continuous band of white at its base.

In *Tyger* the frightful sight held them in an unspeaking thrall.

'I'm thinking we're at the other end o' the run of coast that starts wi' Cape Finisterre,' Joyce broke in doubtfully, against the gale's roar.

'What's there?' Kydd asked.

'Er, nothing as I knows of 'cept its called Cabo Touriñán. We generally keeps our offing and . . .'

Any half-competent navigator would do the same in these waters and the sailing master wasn't to be blamed if he had no knowledge of what lay close in.

The Spanish frigate sailed on, not deviating a degree from its track at about a mile or so off.

Kydd peered ahead of it, trying to get some idea of where it was on its way to but all that could be seen was the cliff-line lowering to a ragged headland nearly hidden by towering white explosions as the Atlantic seas pounded it with manic fury. Beyond was too obscured to make out.

Never in his years of service had he ever been in a situation like this – to be beholden to an enemy for salvation and the life of his ship and company. If it was a trick it was well done; he couldn't conceive of any last-minute moves that would see *Tyger* cast up on the rocks and he not, but all must be allowed to be possible.

Angling slightly, the Spanish frigate closed with the headland and disappeared into the welter of mist and spray beyond.

'He's rounding the point – there must be a bay or similar behind.'

If there was, the westerly would be cut off, as if by a knife, at masthead height as it blasted high over the cliffs. Time to be ready.

'I'll have both the best bower and small bower cables ranged and bent on as soon as you will.' The sheet anchor's cable was always permanently attached at sea and thus once around he would be in a position to deploy his anchors.

Kydd studied the wind-torn headland while he could through the mist and spray, then made up his mind. Like the Spaniard before him he held his course into the flying murk and, surprisingly quickly, was through into a bay as snug as could be desired.

He had no time to admire it for all his instincts told him to anchor while he could. With helm hard over, the battered *Tyger* was sent into the lee of the headland, and the sudden peace there.

Keeping well in, first one bower then the other was dropped, and under the grateful lee of the several-hundred-foot-high peninsula she rounded to her anchors. As he'd foreseen, the rushing surge of the Atlantic westerly around the point kept them parallel to the seething shore and at the same time well into the protective heights.

Taking a deep breath at their narrow escape, Kydd took stock. The bay was less than a mile across. At the far end he saw the Spaniard, not so nimble in his mooring and therefore further away from the precious lee but now snubbing to his anchors, no doubt appreciative of the respite, too.

And with darkness falling they would be riding out the storm together during the night hours. Each would be fearful of every break in the conditions that could see a swarm of boarders snatch the opportunity to overwhelm the other without a sea fight. It was going to be a long night. At some point during the next day the weather would inevitably ease sufficiently for sail to be spread – and the first to do so would fall on the other with blazing guns. Or have spars carry away and be driven on to the iron-hard rocks for its presumption.

Two bowers out – the big sheet anchor in reserve. It would be enough.

Without being told, Herne the boatswain had men aloft on repair, sending down the torn and tattered remnants of high sail and bending on their strongest storm canvas. When it came, the challenge would spare neither ship nor man.

Kydd did not leave the deck, watching the work go on while keeping his eye on the Spanish frigate, which was doing much as they. What was the other captain thinking at this moment? Did he still have the black malignancy in his heart that had let him hammer to ruin a hapless sloop?

Chapter 17

Kydd became aware that Bowden had come to stand beside him. 'A near-run thing, don't you think?' he murmured to his second lieutenant. 'And tomorrow—'

'Sir. I can't be sure but . . . I believe we're dragging anchors.'

Kydd swung around. 'What? Two bowers, still sound? Why do you say this?'

There had been no tell-tale thump and jerking of a severed cable falling away or an unusual swing to the other, and the anchor-watch on the fore-deck would certainly have seen or felt anything amiss.

'I've had my eye on that odd pinnacle of seaweed, its bearing more forward than it was.'

Kydd didn't hesitate. The seas here were far quieter but he was taking no chances. 'Nip below and get your sextant.'

Continued sightings showed the angle between the knot of weed and the foremast was closing. The ship was slowly but surely moving deeper into the bay. Bowden was right.

A chill wash of disbelief swept over Kydd. He hurried past the working seamen to the hawse where the anchor cable led out from the riding bitts down into the depths. He placed one foot on the thrumming taut cable. This was no parted rope and orphaned anchor. The other was the same – but it was just too much to believe that the tons weight of both anchors was being ploughed bodily through the seabed. It had to be . . .

'Mr Bray! Weigh the small bower.'

The first lieutenant looked at him in horror. To halve their hold on safety at a whim?

'At once, sir! Turn to both watches, if you must.'

Men were taken from their work to the capstan, puzzled and fearful, but hadn't Kydd just brought them through from a mortal lee shore?

In minutes the anchor came up. Kydd leaned over the beakhead rail, on edge as it emerged.

The dripping black iron of the great anchor broke surface. It rose higher out of the water until all was made plain: at the flukes was the betraying flash of bare metal where it had been scored and ground down. As well, the ends of the stock were worn and splintered – it hadn't had a chance to grip: the seabed was not mud or sand but bare rock.

Kydd let out his breath. Over untold thousands of years Atlantic storms like this battering the seaward side of the cape had surged around the point and scoured the seabed clean, leaving it denuded of the usual sand or mud. As a consequence they now faced a situation yet more dire than before.

Their choices were few. To do nothing would see them driven against the rocks of the inner bay to end as matchwood. To show sail and try for the open sea would plunge them back into the worst of the storm.

There were other contrivances they could try: to lash the

barrels of guns to the anchors to keep them down was one, but there was not time.

They had to make the break to the open sea, ready or not.

'Winds veering a touch northerly,' Joyce pronounced. The gale against them increased the danger of being embayed, never to get out.

Bleakly, Kydd took in the point of sudden transition from shelter behind the point to the raging violence beyond. It was a frightful chance with the odds that they'd leave their bones there for ever, but it was their only hope.

'We'll go out under stays'ls,' he ordered. 'Close-reefed jib, main topmast stays'l, mizzen – and a scrap of the driver.' These were all fore and aft sails and would allow them the closest to the wind that was possible.

There was no time to lose but Kydd chose to heave in his anchors rather than cut his cables and run. Who knew what last desperate scenes they would see?

Without their drag, *Tyger* swung off the wind but he was ready, and hoisting aft sails first brought her round, gathering way in the little bay before she met the blast. It would take her close to the Spaniard, who had apparently just discovered his own similar plight and was doing the same. Kydd snatched a glance – which of those figures on its quarterdeck was the captain?

He couldn't spare time to watch, for the moment of crisis would soon be upon them. Blessing his instinct to anchor close under the point, he had the width of the bay to gather speed in a sweeping curve before he punched into the waiting violence.

Willing *Tyger* on, he judged angles and directions and, when yards off the boundary, gave his orders.

The jib was doused and the driver held a-weather – and

70

then the tempest hit them with a blast so solid it sent the frigate staggering and heaving in protest. Sail off forward and the driver taut, she nobly turned to face it. Through slitted eyes in the stinging spray, Kydd gestured to raise the jib. It took up with a bang and, staysails rigid with effort, *Tyger* met the wind – and moved slowly out.

She had to weather the next point and pass it, clawing slowly along the coast as close to the wind as she could for the two or three miles to the final jagged headland, after which the coastline trended sharply eastwards and she could bear away at last.

As the point neared, black crags against the seething white appeared in stark reality and submerged not a hundred yards off, passing agonisingly slowly. Mesmerised, Kydd gazed at them until they fell away as the next bay opened up.

A hand clutched his arm. Bowden's face was grim as he pointed astern.

The Spaniard had made his play under the same staysails, but had met with a fatal flaw and was now going to pay for it.

Slower to anchor when they'd entered the bay he was closer to the point and therefore didn't have the advantage Kydd had brought to *Tyger* that had given her the mile width of the bay to pick up speed. It was now in perilous straits, closer still to the vicious shore and without enough way on, gathering a dismaying sag to leeward.

It couldn't go on. Even to the last they fought. More sail frenziedly hoisted to be instantly blown to ribbons. Anchors let go: one, two away . . .

The end when it came was heart-freezing to watch.

The bow touched first and, without a pause under the merciless gale, the frigate rotated about and at the same time heeled over and was held immobile. It was all the storm needed: in a victorious belabouring, the seas smashed continuously against the naked hull, bringing down first the foremast and then the main.

In the draping mass of black lines of rigging were moving figures. These anonymous dots were mariners, sailors the same as themselves, who would know they were in the last minutes of life.

Out and clinging to the hull they had no chance. Sluiced off effortlessly into the breakers, a scatter of black dots surging this way and that until the life was battered from them against the rock ledges, they disappeared one by one.

Kydd looked in vain on the grim heights above for survivors. There were none. All that was left was the carcass of the wreck, black and stark against the whiteness of the breakers.

He tore his gaze away. Their own prospect was grim: all it would need to join them was a blown-out sail, rudder carrying away or any one of the multitude of accidents that happened at sea.

Tyger plunged on, doggedly taking the seas on her bow in what seemed like an endless succession of giant hammer-blows but never wavering or falling away. British oak and skilled shipwrights had produced a vessel that could take even this wildness. Slowly leaving the tragic scene behind her, she finally won through – past the last foreland and into the broad sweep of the bay beyond.

It was over.

It was an odd voyage, homeward bound after only a week or two at sea, but after their close call there were few who did not feel a surge of warmth at the thought. Kydd, too, was glad to be on the way back. The concluding scenes of the death of the Spaniard had been depressing, despite the circumstances.

And he'd taken it on himself, when the storm had abated, to return to Lisbon on reconnaissance. The forts at the mouth of the Tagus had opened fire immediately, leaving no doubt that the Portuguese capital had been taken and his vague plan to land and search for Miss Lockwood was therefore hopeless.

He'd gone over the whole incident again: he had made the offer in good faith but had been foiled by the operational needs of the navy and thus, he told himself, he had no need to feel guilty. There was no other course than to put it behind him.

Passing Cape Finisterre on his way south, he had looked into the bay and seen the brig-sloop still afloat — just. By a masterly feat of seamanship, improvised sail had been spread forward and she'd clawed her way past the weathered crags into the safety of the lee beyond. She had endured the gale there, where *Tyger* had now found her, but in a sinking condition.

Her young commander had been effusive in his thanks and overwhelmed at learning who had brought deliverance, but Kydd was aware that this fine sailor was now without a ship, the crew he knew so well to be dispersed about the fleet, he to rot in the captains' room of the Admiralty as he begged for a command. Damn it, if he had any influence at that level he'd make sure the man was not forgotten.

73

Chapter 18

Back in Portsmouth Admiral Montagu apologised for the intrusion of the Lisbon affair into Kydd's existence and commiserated at the heavy weather, chuckling that it would certainly have preoccupied the Portuguese royal family at sea.

Then he poured Kydd a sherry and said affably, '*Tyger* in hand in the dockyard, nothing for you to do – a capital time to make visit to London, I believe!'

Kydd needed little urging and took his leave. But first he knew he had to settle the question of whether Persephone Lockwood had managed to find a place in some other returning vessel and made it safely back. It would have reached England well before the worst of the storm and he hoped she was now in the bosom of her family. There was only one way he'd find out for certain and that was to pay a visit to her home.

Admiral Sir Reginald Lockwood had been port admiral of Plymouth but had since retired to his estate in Sussex, conveniently on the way to London. Kydd wasn't looking forward to the encounter: the last time he'd faced the man whose daughter he'd spurned he'd been exiled to the Channel Islands Squadron. It was unlikely that he'd altered his views since.

The estate was modest but neat and well-tended. Kydd left Tysoe with the carriage out of sight, went to the front door and tugged the bell-rope.

'Captain Sir Thomas Kydd to call upon Admiral Lockwood,' he told the bored servant, who took his card without a word.

Kydd thought he heard raised voices in the long minutes that followed before the man returned.

'Sir Reginald will see you, Sir Thomas, but begs that it be a short visit on account of the early hour.'

Mid-morning? That was not the reason.

Lockwood stood in the small reception room, glowering and thin-lipped. 'Sir Thomas?' he rasped.

The years had not been kind to him: his eyes were sunken and the lines in his face deep and accentuated. He leaned slightly on a stick.

'Good day to you, sir. I hope I see you well?'

'What can you want, sir?'

The hatred was still there in the unblinking savage gaze.

'While passing I wished only to make my number, sir,' Kydd said, as lightly as he could.

'Well, you have now. I won't detain you any longer.'

'Your good wife, sir? Is she well?'

'She is in fine health, sir.'

'Um, your daughter is—'

'What is that to you, sir?' barked Lockwood. 'You can have no interest in Perseph— my daughter after her public indignity at your hands!'

'Sir, I merely desire to assure myself of her happiness and security. Is she—'

'Ha! She's not at this time, nor will ever be, at home to you, sir. Besides, she's not even in the country,' he finished with satisfaction.

A stab of apprehension went through Kydd. She hadn't returned. 'Oh. It's just that—'

'You've done me the honour of your visit, sir,' Lockwood said cuttingly, 'And now you'll want to be on your way. Good day to you, sir!'

Kydd took a breath, then said carefully, 'As I met her just two weeks ago, sir, and conceived it my duty to acquaint you of it.'

'You saw Persephone?' the admiral spluttered. 'How could you? She's in Sweden!'

'No, sir, it was in Lisbon that I saw her.'

'Lisbon!' Lockwood fell back a step. The flight of an entire royal family from one of the oldest capitals in Europe had been the talk of all England and the implications were plain.

Suddenly Lady Lockwood appeared from behind the screen, a look of horror on her face, her hands working. 'How was she?' she blurted.

Kydd bowed politely. This was not going to be pleasant but there was no other way to break the news. 'Madam, I can reassure you as to her soundness of health and condition when I spoke to her.'

'The French – there was an evacuation, I heard. Transports carrying them to Plymouth. She would have boarded one of those, surely,' Lockwood snapped.

'There was a deal of confusion, sir. And when I spoke to the transports at sea they had no knowledge of her,' he said carefully.

'You're telling me . . . that it's possible she's still there?' Lockwood said slowly.

There was a sudden shriek from Lady Lockwood. 'She's in Lisbon, where Napoleon's murderers are looting and plundering and— Oh, my God! My poor lamb! It's – it's—'

Lockwood snapped at the dithering footman, who helped the swooning woman to a couch, then turned sharply to Kydd. 'You were there?'

'Sir.'

'The French. Are they—'

'I was fired upon by the forts when I made motions off the Tagus. There is no doubt, the French have possession of Lisbon.'

'Yet you had chance to speak with her? Then pray tell, sir, why you did not have the common courtesy to ensure she had safe berthing in a transport out of there? Hey? Hey?'

'I did offer to take her in my ship, but operational requirements kept me at sea for this period and—'

'My child!' screeched Lady Lockwood, suddenly reviving. 'You left my child to Napoleon Bonaparte and his hordes! You brute! You wicked brute! Just because—'

'My dear,' the admiral said heavily, 'do be calm lest you bring on your vapours again.'

He breathed deeply, fixing Kydd with a look of intense loathing. 'And you, sir, while you glory once again in the unhappiness you have inflicted on this house, know that I will never suffer your presence here again. Do you hear me? Never!'

Chapter 19

The coach journey resumed and Kydd's thoughts turned to the past. To Rosalynd, that sweet country girl, so innocent and not of this world, taken from him so cruelly. Yet over time he'd come to believe that they'd never been meant to marry . . .

And was that true of Persephone Lockwood, who'd once smiled at him but now had set her face against him . . . wherever she was? It was a shocking thing that she'd been left but it had not been deliberate, as much the ill-fortune of war as it would have been for any other unfortunate caught up in the larger struggle.

Both were in the past, out of his life for good, and he resolved to get on with the business of living in the present and what lay in the immediate future for him. In his early thirties he'd achieved the heights of his profession: a knighthood, the King's personal approbation and a prime frigate to command. It had to be accepted that he'd reached the longed-for goal of every young and ambitious naval officer – precious distinction.

No longer need he worry that service out of sight of the powers-that-be would result in his being overlooked. It was only a couple of years ago he'd been in the Cape of Good Hope Squadron with Commodore Popham, both glumly contemplating a future rotting in a far-distant backwater. It had then been the fortune of war that had seen him a hero of Curaçao and in the public eye. Lately, the three-frigate action in the Baltic, followed by *Tyger*'s desperate struggle home, had caught the popular imagination and now, whether he liked it or not, he was one of the gods of the sea.

In naval terms he would never want for a ship – those heart-breaking hours of supplication in the waiting room at the Admiralty were only a memory and he could look forward to as much sea time as he chose.

As the coach rattled on through the charming green of Surrey he let his mind roam free.

What were his ambitions now? If he was honest, he was perfectly content with sea life at that moment. There was no finer thing this world could offer than to be captain of a crack frigate, and with all Europe under the tyrant's heel, he would not lack adventure, but sooner or later his seniority would be such that he would enter into an august role as captain of a ship of-the-line and his chances for further distinction would then be—

But there would be no need to crave this any longer! As a battleship captain he would steadily learn the ropes of tactics and strategy at the level of a fleet and – who knew? – in due course Captain Kydd might find himself chosen to take command of a squadron in the West Indies or another part of the world in some obscure act of empire. Commodore Sir Thomas flies his flag!

The island is seized – but at that point an enemy fleet is

sighted: he signals his squadron to form line-of-battle and a great action takes place. The Royal Navy is duly triumphant. He returns home to a grateful country and, as with so many sea heroes of the past, he is ennobled to an even higher order and takes a large estate in the country.

He'd spent his childhood within hailing distance of one such: the legendary Admiral Boscawen's Hatchlands. Would Guildford know another?

It was a warm thought but he knew the chances were slim. Not only to be a commodore at the right time and place but to have the French put to sea to make contest, which they did not seem inclined to do at this stage in the war.

As to full admiral – as with all post captains, if he lived long enough, he would be duly be-flagged . . . but would he have the vitality to relish it?

Who knew what the future would bring? All things pointed to the imperative of glorying in the present to the full. He had prize money, funds in the consols and, with the handsome sum from his Arctic furs salvage, need not fear penury. He was going to London as a celebrated figure. He would meet high people, mix in the best society and be applauded, entirely his own man to choose his friends as he pleased. And, damn it, he would! Whether it be weeks or months he would make the most of this time.

And then? Why, back to sea!

Kydd was brought to a start back from his musings when the coachman apologetically requested their destination. About to reply with the usual 'White Hart', he stopped. Why not the Albany where he could rouse out his old naval friend Edmund Bazely so they'd have a rare time together?

But he soon learned that Bazely was at sea. The coachman

helpfully suggested that, as a gent of respectable airs, he might consider lodgings more agreeable in the better sort of town, and in a short time Kydd was being welcomed into a Duke Street chambers on the Mayfair side of Wigmore Street.

The rental made him frown but the apartment was satisfyingly distinguished, the appointments far richer than he had ever known. He allowed Tysoe to fuss him into an armchair in the drawing room with a tincture of whisky and a copy of *The Times* while footmen were directed to move in his baggage.

He first needed to dash off a note by messenger to the Admiralty, informing them of his address; whatever they chose to do with him was up to them but, for now, his time was his own. He also sent word to Bazely to await his return.

Kydd sighed – he was Fortune's child and he meant to relish it.

Chapter 20

At eleven the next morning Kydd was considering what to do with his day when Tysoe brought in a card on a silver tray. 'A gentleman calls, Sir Thomas.'

He picked it up: 'The Honourable Peregrine Fookes. A Member of Parliament, no less. Do show him in.'

Kydd stood and settled his dress. This visit had to be in response to his note to the Admiralty – no one else knew yet that he was in Town.

A short and somewhat portly gentleman entered, bowing politely. 'Sir Thomas Kydd? An honour to meet you, sir.'

'Good in you to call, sir. Do take a chair.'

Fookes sat with a prim elegance. 'Do forgive me for the early hour, dear fellow,' he said, brushing invisible dust from his coat. '*Tempus fugit* we're obliged to say.'

Of an age with himself, Fookes had a genial, easy air. His attire was a determined effort at fashion but sadly let down by the stoutness of his figure.

'You're sent from the Admiralty?' Kydd asked innocently.

'Good God, no,' Fookes said, with a grimace. 'I'm to bid

you welcome to this great city and enquire if I can be of any assistance to you in your stay.'

'How so, sir?'

Fookes blinked and looked at him with amused puzzlement. 'As you are the hero of the day in course, Sir T. His Majesty's government do desire you be afforded the most fulsome respect in this—'

'I say again, why? A busy cove like you attending on a visitor like me? There must be quantities of the lesser sort you can spare.' Kydd was playing awkward but he wanted to know more of the emissary's masters and their expectations.

'You sailor-kind are direct speaking as always.' Fookes took out an ornamented snuff-box with a practised flourish. 'Do you mind?'

'If you must, sir.'

'Then in course I forebear. Sir T, know that your visit to the capital is entirely to the gratifying of the government of the day. It affords them the opportunity of publicly honouring a true son of the sea who—'

'Mr Fookes. Do grant that I have the intelligence to understand for what purpose I'm here. And be assured I shall endeavour to give satisfaction as I may.'

There was the barest hesitation before Fookes went on, 'Then know that a reception in your honour is proposed for two days hence – should you be at leisure to attend.'

'I should be delighted and humbled by the honour,' Kydd said neutrally.

'Hosted by the home secretary, Baron Hawkesbury, at White's, with quantities of guests of rank, whose names you will have heard mentioned. You have no objection to being seen in the company of same?'

Kydd smiled briefly. So that was it: a calculating gleam in

the eye betrayed the easy indolence of his visitor's manner. 'Forgive me for speaking plain, Mr Fookes, as I'm far out of soundings in these matters. Your presence here suggests to me that the affair is a political one and you are dispatched to ensure that I should not be an embarrassment in the article of manners or—'

'Why, Sir Thomas, this was not—'

'Mr Fookes. I shall be in London some small weeks. If I should be of service to the government within that time it were better *you* were plain with *me*. I'm a simple sea officer – to hob-a-nob with the quality to advance myself in society is not natural to me. Should you desire to gain my cooperation in whatsoever is planned, it were better you lay before me the pith of the matter, that I may decide how to act.'

There was a ghost of a smile. 'Then at your wish I will so be plain with you, sir. Your public comments at the Popham court martial were received by some in government with amusement, by others with alarm. If the Portland administration means to put you on display as an exemplar, how may they expect you to behave, yes?'

'Ah, that scribbler in the *True Briton*. Pray do not concern yourself on that account – the merest squib, obtained by guile. My lesson is learned.'

Fookes felt absent-mindedly in his waistcoat for his snuff-box, then, abashed, returned it and leaned back in his chair. 'I will be candid. By your manner I do believe you to be the veriest neophyte in the realm of the body politic.'

'I've no wish or ambition whatsoever to navigate in those waters, sir.'

'Sir T, if you are to make your *éclat* in the highest society, as you have every right and opportunity to do, then you will need to know the lie of the land – or is it to be the rocks and shoals? I know nothing of your family but I'd wager a bag of guineas that they're not of a landed description, who do imbibe the customs and lore of the ruling sort with their mother's milk.'

'Damn your impertinence, sir!' Kydd retorted. 'My origins are none of your business!'

'Rest your ire, sir. Our foreign secretary is the son of an actress, and I could name many others whose . . . start in life did not come with a silver spoon. But one's birth is no bar to advancement in these tremulous times. In fact, I do own to nothing but admiration for your achievings – and, if I dare remark it, your honesty of purpose in all.'

'Thank you,' Kydd said, still glowering. 'So what is it I must do, or not, as the case may be?'

'A matter of some delicacy needs must be discussed first.'

'Which I will not feel bound to answer.'

'Of course. You see, sir, you present as a mystery. While a man risen to fame in the public eye, nothing is known of you. You are a sea-beast of fabled nature.'

'Delicacy?'

'I bear down on the matter with all sails flying, sir. In this I am referring to your choice – that is to say, your inclination – to one or other of the interests now before the public.'

'I'm not sure I follow you.'

Fookes blinked. 'My, but you are a *rara avis*, Kydd.' He chuckled. 'Sir, I'm desiring to know your adhering to which cause – the Tory, the Whig or, Heaven forbid, the Radical. That is all.'

'That you may know if I'll dish your Tory government in my speech, which is why you're dispatched here.'

'Bless you, Sir Thomas, for a new-born innocent! Of course

this is why I'm here. In my circle, however, we phrase it a mite more fastidious as it were.'

'Then I'm sorry to disappoint, Fookes, but I've no interest in politicking. There is no cause to which I've sold my soul.'

'Extraordinary. But I do believe you, old fellow, although there are scads who would not.'

'If you would have me plight to a cause, then know there is one to which I've already pledged all.'

'Oh? Say away, Sir T – which is it to be?'

'The one to which I've taken solemn oath.'

'Yes?'

'Sir, I would have it known to all that I am the King's man! Does that satisfy at all?'

'Ha! As it would mortify Prinny and his set. Sir T, dear chap, do see if you can bear to be a Tory, there's a good fellow – simpler in the long run. You'll not warm to the Foxite heresies, and the Radicals are not of this world. Our clubs are of the first rank and the dining is Elysian. If you—'

'Fookes, old horse, as I've never said I'm interested in politicking,' Kydd said with a smile. Damn it, he was warming to the man.

'Politics? No one wishes you to dispute with those damn Whigs in the House, just be seen in Tory colours on occasion, of sound views, as it were. After all's said, it's they who are running your war for you, are they not?'

'I'll think on it. Now this reception . . .'

By the time Fookes took his leave, Kydd knew exactly where he stood.

As he'd suspected all along it was not the Admiralty but the Duke of Portland's ministry that wanted him, a hero of impeccable credentials, to stand with them in the storm that still raged over the morality of the Copenhagen expedition.

It had been reassuringly pointed out that he was not expected to play any part in the rancorous exchanges, still less express an opinion: a mere appearance was all that was asked of him.

Fookes had been revealed to him as a skilled political broker, himself Member of Parliament for Maldon North and holding the post of parliamentary under-secretary to the president of the Board of Trade, handily giving him the ear of the cabinet. Kydd recognised a character combining the utmost affability with a ruthless nerve, and suspected he was well-trusted to obtain results for his masters in the highest places.

A good friend, a dangerous enemy.

And he'd paid Kydd a warm compliment. In his description of the reception he'd been open and confiding about those to be seen there. The clever but principled Hawkesbury, a skilled manipulator, talked of and resented as a future prime minister; Castlereagh, gifted and dynamic but whose cold and distant manner had alienated so many; Perceval, the able and hard-working Chancellor of the Exchequer, unaccountably poor as a church mouse; others.

It seemed that Fookes had sensed Kydd to be honourable and true, his personal disclosures safe in his hands. Or was it that Kydd had no friends in higher places and was never a danger?

Chapter 21

Shaved within an inch of his life by a proud and dignified Tysoe, Kydd donned his full-dress uniform, resplendent in sash, star and medals. The gold lace of rank, glittering anchor-ciphered buttons, coat of the darkest blue and the contrasting white of his breeches made an outfit equal to any of the modish attire he'd seen – the saving grace of a uniform, where personal taste was never in question.

It was an occasion of a lifetime: he would be consorting with people at an elevation far removed from that of his peers, known only to them as names in the newspapers or Court Gazette – and all in honour of Sir Thomas Kydd!

The carriage was on time and at seven he left for White's, which he'd been told was the most prestigious and exclusive club in London, his senses heightened to a level they'd last been off Cape Finisterre. In a blur of exhilaration he waited as the carriage came to a stop outside the tall white stone building and a footman walked forward to hand him down.

He looked up. There were figures in the doorway, the flash of orders and decorations, movement. His heart bumped.

As he descended from the carriage hats were doffed and from within the muffled strains of 'See the Conqu'ring Hero Comes' struck up.

In a lurch of excitement he crossed the space as the figures moved inside and Fookes appeared to take his arm. 'The line!' he whispered.

Kydd was led into the bright interior and there was the reception line – all faces turned towards him, the sheer richness of their appearance an assault on the senses.

The first was the aristocratic, stiff-faced Hawkesbury.

'My lord, might I present the gallant Captain Sir Thomas Kydd of His Majesty's Navy?' Fookes murmured, and to Kydd, 'Sir Thomas, the Right Honourable the Lord Hawkesbury, home secretary to His Majesty's government.'

Bows were exchanged, Kydd aware of a sharp-eyed look of appraisal.

'Sir Thomas, you do us honour. I trust we have not intruded too much into your sea affairs?'

'Not at all, my lord. With *Tyger* lying at Portsmouth, my first lieutenant may be relied upon to keep her company active.'

Further polite words were exchanged and he was moved on to the next, a handsome, aloof man of patrician reserve and few words – the secretary of state for war, Viscount Castlereagh, who had sent in the bombardment fleet to Copenhagen.

Kydd managed a response to the polite abruptness and then it was on to another.

As the last in line was duly presented and spoken with, it dissolved and its members fell into conversation with each other. Kydd was neatly steered to a jovial fellow, who turned out to be an archbishop most taken with the navy, and then it was a slight, mischievous-eyed and soft-spoken man in Spartan black, and Kydd found himself talking of his experience in the past as a master of the King's Negroes to a keenly interested William Wilberforce.

'Gentlemen, if you please . . .'

A voice schooled in the raucous byplay of the House of Commons brought them to order.

'We are here assembled to do honour to the person of . . .' Hawkesbury's effortless delivery was received in respectful silence, and suddenly Kydd was there before them – and his speech fled from his mind.

'My lords, distinguished guests,' he stuttered. 'I am deeply honoured to stand before you . . .' He took a moment to gather his wits and, thankfully, the words came back. The modest acceptance of the recognition and a firm acknowledgement of his ship's company's valiant striving. A stern affirmation of the danger they stood under from the Corsican tyrant and the bravery of the British people under their king and Parliament in resisting him. To finish, a deeply sincere reminding that from where each found himself at that moment, to Napoleon Bonaparte in his palace, all that stood between them was the Royal Navy and its sea-worn ships.

It went down well, apparently. Vigorous applause rang in his ears and a circle of admirers quickly gathered around him.

'Clean done, Kydd, my friend,' Fookes acknowledged, as he handed him a glass of champagne. 'You'll do.'

Chapter 22

It was all very satisfying. To be at leisure in the capital while a public hero and knowing he'd done his duty quite as if he'd sailed against the enemy. No doubt there'd be one or two more appearances – already a massed parade in Horse Guards would see him up there on the podium, and he'd promised the Pensioners at the naval hospital in Greenwich a visit, which he knew would greatly please the old sailors.

And then back to *Tyger*. After a judicious sampling of the other pleasures on offer in the greatest city on earth, of course.

Tysoe clucked over the fall of his cravat as he prepared him for the afternoon, for four was a fashionable hour to be out. He rather thought he'd promenade in St James's Park and in the evening—

The front-door bell sounded, not once but twice, and when a footman answered he was briskly shouldered aside and a slightly dishevelled Bazely stormed in. The sloop commander and confirmed bachelor had a huge grin in place. 'What ho, the Grand Nob! So pleased to clap peepers on ye, old trout! Just back from the vasty deep – the Albany porter said as you'd called, an' your note told me where you're moored and . . .' He tailed off at the quality of the apartment, then went on, with exaggerated awe, 'So, Sir T is in a fair way of topping it the gent, so he is.'

'Bazely, sit yourself down and you're right gladly received. Tysoe, a snort o' the right kind for this guest and myself.'

Comfortably at length on a chaise-longue, Bazely lifted his glass and grinned at Kydd. 'As it does the heart good to see an honest mariner where he should be. My, but you've a few miles under y'r keel since last we were together in Town – and that wasn't so long ago b' my reckoning. Heard about how you took *Tyger* by the scruff an' shook out your mutineers – and then a three-frigate action to see if the rest were up to snuff.'

'Well, it was an entertainment to—'

'Don't deny it, Kydd! You're now a name in the land – and dishing y'r Admiralty enemies in proper fashion. Can't touch ye now!'

'That's as may be. Does seem a lot of pother for just doing my duty. Do you know I'm sent to London to be displayed like a mermaid fresh-caught as it obliges Portland's ministry?'

'Ha! In course I believe it of 'em. Rare chance for him – there's a drought o' heroes, these hard days.'

'They mustered a regular-going reception at White's, just for your friend, Bazely. Home secretary, Castlereagh, Wilberforce, all turning out for me.'

'High table indeed.'

'Ah, well, duty done now. Then it's back to *Tyger* and sea scran.'

'I think not, old horse.'

'Why not, pray?'

'They don't set a good sea officer and ship to idleness without they get good value. Mark m' words, they've tested y' mettle, and if they likes what they sees, there'll be more o' the same. Do hold y'self ready, m' boy.'

'Mmm. I'd more hoped to be let loose on the town, take my fill, if you catch my meaning.'

Bazely brightened. 'I do, and would bear a fist if I could – but what to set against what y'r high gentry is serving out?'

'A round of what answered before would be prime.'

'Well, I fancy I has ye to myself for a day or two yet before they exhibits you in St Paul's or some such. I'll get out o' this travelling rig an' then—'

'Then what?'

'If you could see your way to . . . but you being Mr Sea Hero might . . .'

'What are you a-wambling about?'

'A frien' of mine. Right sort o' cove and I'd like to see him set fair in a small matter as ye can help. In with your note in m' correspondence as I gets back from sea is an invitation to a party o' sorts in honour of his eldest daughter, she just betrothed. I know y' likes to sport the toe wi' pretty damsels, and as he's four more daughters and quantities of friends I'm sanguine ye'll not want for company.'

Chapter 23

K ydd suppressed the urge to ask how Bazely had come to make friends with Josiah Jenkin, the tea merchant, who'd made a comfortable fortune in the period after the American war, then invested in canal engineering. They were greeted warmly at the door of the impressive Portman Square townhouse, just north of Mayfair.

'Sir T, this is m' friend Jenkin, a business cove. Jenkin, I introduce Sir Thomas Kydd o' the Royal Navy, lately back from the high seas.'

The man bowed low and rose with a broad smile on his mature but kindly features. 'You do my house the greatest honour, sir, and at such a trifle of notice.'

Kydd bowed politely, ignoring the excited female faces at the windows. 'Sir, any request by my friend Edmund may not easily be denied,' he murmured.

In accordance with Bazely's desire he was arrayed in full dress uniform with sash and star while his friend wore evening attire.

'Well, then, and we will meet the others. Come in, sir, and be welcome!'

The faces disappeared. They passed through the hall and entered a lavishly appointed reception room to a decorous hush. Kydd paused gallantly and quickly took in the many charming, comely young ladies and not a few frowning men, all held in thrall under the blaze of rich chandeliers.

The happy couple were standing shyly together by the fire and Kydd crossed to them. At Jenkin's quiet introduction the girl bobbed a curtsey, too overcome to speak. Her betrothed stuttered inaudibly in open admiration. Kydd pronounced words of congratulation to each and bowed once more. Then, as if in release, the room broke into an excited buzz.

'Do meet Sir John, a capital fellow at four-in-hand. Why, I recall . . .'

But Kydd was thinking about the couple with a twinge of feeling. No more than a handful of years separated him and the young man – but what a vast gulf in their experiences of life! Yet this man was going on to happiness and fulfilment, children and roots at home, as nature intended, while he, for all his triumphs . . .

'. . . is Miss Darnley, and her sister Elizabeth.' Kydd managed a courtly acknowledgement while yet more young ladies approached in awe and trepidation. And these were not the fresh-faced innocents at the country balls of the past: here was all the beauty and fashion of London in attendance – and every one beseeching his attentions.

The heat was rising in the crowded room, which was alive with movement and talk.

An orchestra laid a few notes on the air and the hubbub subsided.

'The minuet! Pray take your partners for the minuet!' a bray-voiced master of ceremonies intoned.

Kydd stepped forward to lead out an overwhelmed Mrs

Jenkin, who wore enough diamonds to buy *Tyger* twice over. With stately movements they ceremoniously circled and bowed the graces before a wide circle of admirers.

When the next dance was called he retired for refreshment and was immediately besieged by what seemed to be most of the femininity on the floor. It was heady and he made play of consulting his dance card while composing himself. He was famous, moneyed, had a future and was at an eminence in the article of appearance and, dare he say it, handsome good looks. In short he must count himself one of the most eligible bachelors in Town.

Any one of these beauties would swoon to receive his addresses. If he chose, he could set in train the most agreeable process of selecting a bride for himself, a ravishing and exquisite Mrs Kydd – or should that be Lady Kydd?

Against the wall and above the perfectly coiffed bobbing heads, he saw the languid figure of Bazely who, catching his glance, raised his champagne in salute with a roguish grin. Kydd returned an angelic smile and turned to his audience. 'Well, now, and I'm persuaded I must favour none or all. I will stand up with each in her turn – who will it be for the first dance, pray?'

Chapter 24

After breakfast, as Kydd applied himself to the task of producing a polite note of thanks to the host of the previous evening, he couldn't help reviewing the numbers of elegant and personable beauties who had vied for his attention.

Annabelle Forsythe had quite taken his eye but, then, the younger Dashley with her – the laughing coquetry and play with her fan – had had an enchantment that was difficult to overlook. And the mysterious allure of the elder Mancour . . . It all added up to a most gratifying prospect for the future and there was no compelling reason why he should be hasty in the progress.

'The morning post, Sir Thomas.' Kydd's valet presented the tray.

On it was a single missive. 'Thank you, Tysoe. Do lay out my riding gear, there's a good fellow.'

Kydd slit the wafer and within found an invitation emblazoned with a crest that he recognised immediately: the Honourable East India Company. A dinner on Wednesday next at the London Tavern. No enclosed note indicating he would be a guest of honour and therefore no speech to prepare. A friendly gesture, no doubt. Kydd added it to the others on the mantelpiece for a decision later.

Before the hour was out, as if cued by an invisible stage director, Peregrine Fookes was admitted to his drawing room. 'Sir Thomas, and I trust I see you well?'

'In spirits, Fookes, in spirits.'

'Ah, "Prinker" to my intimates,' he pronounced, elegantly settling into an armchair and meticulously twitching at the snowy gush of his cravat.

'As shall be, Prinker. I'm to leave shortly for riding – do you wish to come?'

'Possibly. But more to the moment is my reason for visiting.'

'Oh?'

'A little bird told me you've received an interesting invitation to dinner.'

'I have. The East India Company, although I'm somewhat at a loss as to the reason for the honour.'

'You will be attending, of course.'

'Duty calls?'

'In a manner of speaking, old trout. You're not to know it, but this ain't your usual public gathering. Far from it. This is an occasion of the highest consequence, of the kind so desirous of a government wishing to test the temper of the people – which is to say, of course, no scions of nobility, no butterflies of society but, needs must, persons of standing and renown in industry and finance, makers of repute and, I dare say, those of an opposing persuasion.'

'You'll know who's attending.'

'The John Company directors will host and it is usual for the prime minister to take the chair and favoured members of his cabinet to sit in strategical places among the others, who will be from the Whig opposition, your captains of industry and similar. An intimate occasion, as will allow all men to converse freely.'

'All men.'

Fookes shuddered. 'The female of the species is delightful company in her place, dear fellow, but I do assure you the conversation will be on an entirely different plane.'

Kydd paused to digest what he'd heard. 'Then do tell, why in Hades am I invited to this grand gathering at all?'

'That is what I came to talk to you about. Kydd, you are nothing more than an ornament, a guest of distinction it is true, but no more than an interesting figure to leaven the company.'

Kydd gave a small smile.

'Yet the evening could not be of more importance to your person.'

'How so, Prinker?' Kydd asked carefully.

'You don't mind if I speak to you plainly, in the character of a friend, as it were?'

'Do, please. These are uncharted waters for me and I beg you'll set a course.'

'Then I'll lay it out for you. Your distinguished behaving at the reception has been well received, and this invitation is your reward. But do mark me well, dear friend. In this you are no hero to be honoured, merely a convenient celebrated guest. A reward, I say, for here you may meet and impress the highest in the land, should you choose it.'

'I see.'

'Many have emerged from the wilderness of obscurity to recognition in such circumstances.'

Kydd's interest was piqued. Was this how the famed Pellew,

a former frigate captain like himself, had come to prominence – and to his present role as commander-in-chief in the East Indies?

Fookes hesitated. 'Dear Kydd, don't take what I say as a criticism. Do know I'm drawn to you as a friend for your plain and natural humour, your direct speaking and fearless countenance. Such a wonderfully refreshing change from the usual denizens of Whitehall.'

'So do clap on sail and steer for the enemy, Prinker.'

'Then I will say it. There is a darker side to the business. Should you show contentious, touchy or shy, it will be in the worst possible arena. Your card will be marked, Kydd, don't doubt it. As one who it were better not to be favoured with the company of the elect. And then it will be too late. You will sink out of sight beneath the waves as it were, old boy. That's all.'

'I thank you for your candour, Prinker.'

What had not been said was that, by his very presence there, he would unavoidably be made privy to confidences and privileged information at the highest level. He was being trusted, and if he failed them the consequences would be dire.

The entire affair was intoxicating, incredible that he'd reached so far, so fast, but were sacrifices being demanded? Should he meekly toe the line the politicals had laid down – to mouth their dogma, the creed of the government of the day – or be his own man and stay staunch to what he himself held true?

By next Wednesday he would need to know where he stood.

Chapter 25

'My word, but this turtle soup exceeds any mortal expectations!' exclaimed the portly gentleman opposite, in a homely Birmingham accent. 'Damme if it ain't!'

Kydd lifted his spoon. The soup was perfection, its gelatinous green morsels a delight. 'As fine as ever I've had the good fortune to taste in all my sea service in the Caribbee,' he agreed.

The London Tavern was far more than its name suggested: a dining hall with Corinthian columns, a lofty vaulted ceiling and great chandeliers of dazzling brightness hanging low. From where he sat at the modest table he could see a dozen monumental portraits on the wall between extravagantly carved pilasters, and several balustraded galleries high up on the far side.

Although the table was alone in the vast hall, a sense of intimacy was preserved, for the gathering numbered less than a dozen and all other chandeliers were extinguished, save the ones that shone down from above.

In sudden panic Kydd glanced furtively down: his single-breasted white waistcoat had escaped decoration by soup, and with his black satin knee breeches safely under a napkin he was able to raise his head again in confidence, his composure returned.

He had the names of some although he'd not been introduced to them all: at the head of the table was the chairman of the East India Company, Charles Grant, who could well be the most powerful man there, effective ruler of the continent of India and custodian of the gigantic wealth it generated. At the other end sat a sadly diminished figure, in court attire of a previous age – but this was William Cavendish, Duke of Portland and England's prime minister, on his left the ambitious foreign secretary, George Canning.

Further down, a precise and careful individual was holding conversation with the respectful Canning. This was Hammond, chairman of the Stock Exchange and probably the only man in England in a position to bring down the government in a single day.

'Thomas Kydd, I haven't had the honour . . .' he dared, at the expansive man opposite enjoying his soup.

'Mine's the honour, Sir Thomas!' he said, with a civil inclination of the head. 'Matthew Boulton. May have heard o' the works we do in steam.'

Only vaguely aware of the engineering marvels draining coal mines and so forth, Kydd racked his brain frantically for something intelligent to answer. 'Sir, your wondrous inventions and engines will be remembered long after my own slight successes at sea are forgotten,' he came back, reflecting that while a speech might be a difficult thing to pronounce in public it had the princely advantage of being thought about before, rehearsed and therefore perfectly safe. Table talk was a split-second affair in which a foolish remark could never be retracted and might well damn him for all time.

'Nonsense, Kydd. Without we have brave young fellows such as you, Boney will be landed and it'll be all up wi' the kingdom and m' foundry both!'

They were interrupted as the prime minister got painfully to his feet. 'I do beg your respective pardons, gentlemen, as I've been called away – affairs of state,' he said, in a weak voice. 'Do continue your evening.'

Two footmen were on hand to help him away.

'Poor chap,' muttered the man on his left, as though addressing his claret.

'Oh? Why, pray?' Kydd said, without thinking.

The man turned his way, a sad smile touching his sensitive grey eyes. 'You're not to know, in course, but our premier be not long for this world. 'Tis not state affairs that call him away but rank mortality.'

He sipped at his glass, watching Canning smoothly shift into the vacant chair. Then, collecting himself, he turned back to Kydd with a polite gesture. 'Ah, William Astell, director of John Company – and all the world knows of Sir Thomas Kydd, dear fellow,' he added, laying a hand on his arm.

It was exhilarating to be in company such as this. Sitting on equal terms with a nabob of the fabled India trade and about to make light conversation . . .

'Sir, you cannot believe how many times I've seen an Indiaman from to seaward and been set to wondering how it is that you can make venture on such an argosy without you insure it at a punishing rate. How can this be possible?'

Astell looked at him with interest. 'Your concern does you credit, sir. I believe I will tell you.'

There was a brief pause as the haunch of venison appeared to general approbation, swiftly carved and served.

'Currant jelly? A capital accompaniment, I find.'

It was indeed, and Kydd set to on the fine dish while he was enlightened about the methods used by the City of London to take risks amounting to many millions each season. Capital markets primed to invest in the underwriting by Lloyds, instruments of bottomry and charters traded on the Stock Exchange, and with a peerless credit network across continents – it was an awe-inspiring revelation.

'And at the bottom of it – why can we routinely sustain an ocean voyage of six months at a steady three to five per cent?'

'Care as to costings?' Kydd hazarded.

'No, sir,' Astell said triumphantly. 'You, my dear fellow!'

'Er . . .'

'That is, the Royal Navy, as guards our ships and sea-lanes, and convoys even our greatest treasures to a safe harbour.'

'As is our duty to our country,' Kydd said carefully, 'not only for your worthy company, sir.'

'Well said, young man. Wine with you, sir.'

What a tale he had to tell Renzi, his noble friend! The youngest there by a significant margin and exchanging views with the highest in the land. Very aware of what Fookes had advised him, he'd been keyed up for anything but he seemed to have been accepted into this select group, all of whom knew each other. At the very least he could take away that he had not disgraced himself.

The man on his right appeared to have tired of his deep and involved conversation with his neighbour and Kydd turned to him politely. 'A splendid repast, sir, do you not think it?'

The man smiled thinly, aristocratic disdain not far distant in his look. 'Tolerable, tolerable. Sir, am I not speaking to

Sir Thomas Kydd, the noble mariner of Curaçao and Prussia both?'

'You are, sir.'

'Then, as a naval gentleman, do pray flatter us with your views of the late action in Copenhagen,' he said, loudly enough that several around looked up from their eating.

With a lurch of the heart he'd noticed too late the buff waistcoat and blue cutaway coat – as Fookes had warned him: the colours of the Whig party.

At the head of the table Canning sat suddenly upright, watching him, as unblinking as a snake.

The glow of the wine fell away and Kydd's mind scrambled for inspiration. 'Sir, and I do not believe we've been introduced?'

'Allow that I'm an interested party, is all,' the man said with a cynical smile.

'Give over, Charles.' It was Boulton opposite, who then confided to Kydd, 'That there's the Earl Grey, late out o' government and smarting for it.'

'And desiring Mr Kydd's views, if that is at all possible.'

Kydd tensed. Then came the icy discipline he'd last known when bearing down on the enemy. 'You shall have it, my lord. My view is . . .'

The entire table now was still.

'. . . that the Danes were cruelly mauled and suffered keenly, which circumstance I saw with my own eyes and sorrowed much after.'

A horrified gasp to one side and the hiss of indrawn breath tightened the atmosphere.

Grey gave a satisfied smile. 'Then a perfectly botched affair, is your—'

'As I'm persuaded was a grievous necessity forced on us

by the strategicals of the moment and therefore quite ines-capable,' Kydd finished tightly.

The aristocratic lips thinned. 'As I was first lord of the Admiralty in the last administration, you may safely leave the understanding of strategicals to me, Captain.'

But at the head of the table Canning, with glittering eyes on Kydd, was nodding slowly and, with various expressions of amusement or thoughtfulness, others gave an impression of silent approval.

Talk resumed.

A little later Astell leaned closer. 'I say, old bean, it crosses the mind that my club could welcome a little ginger at its dinners. You wouldn't consider to let me put you up as a member? Brooks's, that is.'

Chapter 26

Was there anything more desirable, congenial and satis-fying to the manly soul than a gentlemen's club? Kydd mused. He sat comfortably at leisure in a high-winged leather armchair flourishing a newspaper but too preoccupied to concentrate on it.

He'd been accepted without fuss. Proposed by an Honourable East India Company director and seconded by Mr Boulton, the hero of the hour had warranted no black-ball and the subscription of ten guineas was within hail of that expected in a wardroom of a ship-of-the-line.

The master had been firm about the rules – dinner promptly on the table at a quarter past four o'clock, the bill to be called always half past the hour of six, supper at a quarter before eleven. No gaming in the Eating Room, save 'tossing for the reckonings', under penalty of paying the bills of all those present. Dice money to be paid by members calling for them, and stakes at cards might never be borrowed from players or bystanders.

It was a top-rank club, venerable but with a pleasing air

of elegance tinged with loucheness, the old-fashioned grey-green walls lifted by red damask curtains crossed by gilt swags, with Venus, Bacchus and Cupid in prominent display.

It had been started as a political club for the Whigs, but these days it was quite the done thing to be a member both of Brooks's and White's, and the great – from the Duke of York to William Wilberforce, the Prince of Wales to Beau Brummell – were members of the same club as Kydd.

He hugged to himself that he could pass any one of them on the way to the huge barrel-vaulted Subscription Room or in one of the gaming rooms that he was free to frequent. There was no question: Thomas Kydd, one-time perruquier of Guildford, had reached the top!

'Kydd, old fellow – I see you well?'

He nearly dropped the newspaper but caught himself, elegantly folded it and put it to the side. It was the dilettante Granville, one of the first acquaintances he'd made at the club. 'Quite, old horse. And you?'

Granville eased a lorgnette from within his faultlessly cut waistcoat and polished it with a lace handkerchief. 'Thought I'd dash along to the Theatre Royal, take a peep at Mistress Nares leading in *The Devil Doth Call*. Care to come?'

'Sorry, old boy. Made the error of riding out this morning with Jeremy Ripon. The young blade is a damned fine whip and I'm to pay for it now with a hot tub, I believe.' He smothered a sigh as the man left, wondering whether instead to take up an alternative offer to sup at a new-found and much cried-up eating establishment given out by his new friend Robert Erskine, an urbane and unflappable barrister of note, but decided to spend the evening quietly in his lodgings, contemplating his new life.

To be a member of a decent club with fine friends was

to be on the inside of a cosy world of comfort and peace insulated from the bother and confusion of the outer pale. It was an existence of privilege and wealth but, dammit, hadn't he earned his place in it?

Chapter 27

He hadn't been long in his chambers when Tysoe urbanely announced a visitor. Was it his imagination or had the man put on airs since Kydd's rise in society?

It was Bazely.

'Haven't seen you in a dog's age, Kydd. Where've you been hiding – or is it that the Admiralty are working ye to death?' He took up his customary position, standing at the mantelpiece with a lazy smile.

'Er, not the Admiralty, dear chap. Prime minister is closer to the mark, poor fellow.'

'Poor?'

'When I saw him last he seemed ready to knock on death's door.'

Bazely gave Kydd a curious look. 'Moving in grand circles, then. Well, came to see if you're up for some roystering. I've a cove who desires to see something o' Astley's circus an' I thought to make it a party. Tomorrow eve?'

'Um, I'm desolated to find I've a supper engagement then.'

'Supper? We can find ye a supper after, f'r Heaven's sake!'

'With Rolly – that is, Roland Carlyle. After the opera.'

'Who?'

'The Earl of Leinster.'

'I see. Well, an' all, there's Tuesday. Can't miss this – Jem Belcher agin Tom Cribb over forty rounds. Wimbledon Common an' we share a coach. What about it, old boy?'

A twinge of guilt stole over Kydd. Although he'd never really taken to the sport and the spectacle of a prize-fight, his hesitation was more that he was finding his place among the high gentry gratifying to a degree and . . . 'Ah, Tuesday. Grieved to say it's a gaming rendezvous for me that night, Bazely.'

'Gaming?'

'Yes. Faro and hazard – at Brooks's.'

'Brooks's? Who's taking you along t' that grand pile, can I ask?'

'Er, well, I'm a member, old fellow.'

Bazely sat down, his face set. 'As I can understand, now.'

'Amazing how the time fills, why if I didn't—'

'No, Kydd, it won't fadge. You're not wanting to be seen with silly sailors any more is your meaning. Y' friends are all big nobs and politicals and they play different t' the rest of us.'

'Not at all! It's just that—'

'Another good sailorman and fighting captain gone soft on the world, lost to us. You think you're going back to sea, but you won't. The high life here is pulling you like a leash! You'll marry an heiress, set up your carriage in Mayfair and be damned to a hard life on the briny.'

'What? No, I'd rather—'

'Kydd. Whether you know it or not, y'r course is set. You can never take larboard and starboard tacks at the same time – you're either a sea creature who comes here a-rollicking on occasion, or you're a gooney coxcomb who thinks this is all there is to life. One thing's definite: you can't be both, cully. So ask yourself: which are you meant t' be?' He stood up and said, 'I leave you now, Kydd. Let you sort out what's best to do for y'self. Good day to you.'

Kydd felt a flare of anger. What did the man know of the fine circumstances he'd had the giddy fortune to find himself in? He'd every intention to take his fill, then return to *Tyger*, as any sea officer would.

But a thought of devastating allure was taking shape. He'd been accepted into the highest level of society on his own merits: what now was he going to do with it?

There were many naval officers who'd returned home from the sea with successes and honour, not to say prize money, and entered in upon society to savour the fruits of their actions while they were still of an age to relish it. Why not do the same?

He'd enough distinction to be honoured for it wherever he went, and with solid investments in consols at three and one half per cent, he need not fear want or privation. Why not quit the sea while he was on the crest – if he did go back, it could be to a waning career and he would then return a forgotten hero at the top of no one's invitation list.

On the other hand, if he moved on now, without delay, he would make more friends in the places that count, which could well lead to . . . even to politics, Member of Parliament, office! Or a small estate just outside London where he could live the life of a manor lord and . . .

To give up the life at sea that had shaped him and given him purpose. Could he do it?

Should he recognise it gratefully as the means that had allowed him to reach these glorious heights, and take his leave of it at the right time for the sake of his future?

Chapter 28

From the vine-covered balcony of the Portuguese *pousada*, Persephone Lockwood could see over dense-packed red-tiled roofs to the docks and, to the right, in a wan grey sea at the mouth of the Tagus, so many ships it seemed impossible they didn't bump into each other.

It was common knowledge that Dom João and his court had now boarded the vessels that were taking him into exile but they showed no sign of putting to sea. Probably something to do with the tides or the wind not fair. The docks were deserted; there were no traders left in Lisbon and any that had not secured passage out by now would be left to face the French. The transports had been warped out with their cargo of grateful British – thank goodness she was taking berth in a frigate. She hoped Captain Kydd wouldn't leave it too long before he came for her: the thought of Bonaparte's troops so close made her nervous.

'Do England have black cows, Dona?' asked the tousle-headed twelve-year-old boy. 'I love black cow ver' much.'

An orphan, he had served as tea-boy in a British wine exporter, picking up good English and an inordinate admiration for King George's realm, but now there was only one person left in his little world to whom he could talk about his favourite subject.

'Yes, Paolo, we have black cows in England,' she answered absently, gazing at the motionless ships. To seaward beyond the bar she could see the squadron, the bigger ships together and two frigates passing each other in an easy progress across the wide estuary. Which one was Kydd's ship? To her shame she remembered she hadn't even asked its name, so important to a sailor. Whatever it was she didn't really care: it was a means to salvation and she was not going to stir one yard beyond the door until she'd been called for.

The sound of raised voices came to her from the door, and before long the harassed landlady bobbed inside. 'A lady – want to see you,' she lisped, and beckoned in a fair-haired middle-aged woman.

'D-do you speak English?' the woman asked nervously.

An American.

'I do. I'm Miss Persephone Lockwood. Can I help you?'

'Thank the dear Lord,' the woman said, and collapsed into a chair. 'I'm sorry, but I've been hoofing it for hours trying to find any of my kind in this heathen place. And now I have!' she added, with a suddenly shy smile. 'I do hope you don't think it forward of me, Miss Lockwood.'

'You're not gone on one of the ships, er . . .?'

'Oh, forgive me.' She hauled herself laboriously to her feet. 'I'm forgetting my manners. Mrs Flora Bates of Boston, so pleased to meet you,' she said, with a gracious bob. 'My husband's in olives here and went on ahead but in all the moil I missed my own ship. I'm so frightened, my dear! We all know about that nasty Napoleon, and now his soldiers are coming here, and I can't think what to do!'

'You're an American, a neutral. You've nothing to fear.'

'I do! All my papers are in my baggage and that's been stolen. They'll think me a spy or – or something!'

'Rest your mind, Mrs Bates. As it happens, in a short while some sailors will come to take me to an English man-o'-war. I'm sure they won't mind another joining the party.'

'Oh, bless you! Bless you! So kind of you, Miss Lockwood! I never thought I'd—'

'Would you care for a cup of tea? I'm sure we won't have long to wait.'

At least the commotion and unrest were confined to the waterfront, where roaming packs of looters were ransacking what was left of abandoned luggage and effects, their faint cries reaching up the steep avenue to the *pousada*.

An hour passed, and another. In the tedium nerves continued to fray.

'Have you seen King George?' Paulo asked Mrs Bates.

'Whatever does the child mean?' she wondered.

There was near hysteria in the woman's manner and Persephone reached out to calm her. 'I rather think "Not yet" would satisfy, Mrs Bates,' she said, in a soothing tone, patting the other's knee.

'He has a golden carriage, pull by nine horses and—'

'That's enough for now, Paolo. Off you go!'

The evening shadows lengthened, and out in the harbour pretty lights spangled the mass of shipping that still lay there. Persephone knew that they would not sail at night in constricted waters, especially in such numbers, so now she and Mrs Bates would have to wait for morning – this was probably why Captain Kydd had let them stay on the land to the last. Considerate of him, but in the circumstances it had to be accounted a trial. Or was he selfishly minimising the time he'd have to give over his cabin?

She broke the news to Mrs Bates, who wept tears of frustration but turned her hand to arranging a makeshift bed.

'Don't worry,' Persephone said. 'The French are not close yet.'

'How do you know?'

'Why, there'd be first a big battle out in the hills to stop them, quantities of muskets and guns as we should hear. Now get a good sleep, my dear. Ships are always hard for we ladies to endure.'

Persephone retired to her own bed for there was no point in staying up. But sleep was slow in coming: every night noise seemed sinister and laden with menace.

At one point a rowdy, drunken group of men passed by in the narrow street at the back, their witless shouting going on and on until it slowly faded downhill.

Eventually drifting off fitfully, Persephone was surprised to wake to full daylight and a distraught Mrs Bates in paper curlers leaning over her, wringing her hands. 'They've gone!' she said, in a nervous whisper. 'The ships – they're not there!'

Gathering her wits, Persephone pulled a shawl around her shoulders and went to the window. At first her sleep-fuddled mind didn't take in the bare and empty anchorage.

Then, in an icy surge, the reality of their situation washed over her.

The exile fleet had sailed. All the ships, including the squadron and frigates, were nowhere to be seen.

She had been left.

'My, oh, my, what do we do now?' Mrs Bates wailed.

Persephone had to think.

It was inconceivable that Kydd had simply forgotten her – there had to be another explanation.

Perhaps the fleet had sailed at dawn and was only now out of sight below the horizon. Captain Kydd's ship was a frigate and she knew that these could be employed for escort. His duty would be to see the Portuguese fleet on its way; then he would turn back to Lisbon, take her aboard and sail for England.

It made sense and the cold dread retreated.

'We stay here and wait, of course.'

'We can't!'

'Mrs Bates. The frigate is returning to pick us up. Do you suppose we should not be here when they come for us?'

'What if it does not? We'll be left here to – to—' She broke off, weeping.

'We stay.'

'No! We must get away – anywhere, now!'

'And where do you propose we go? I'm returned from inland and am persuaded that no sensible person would flee into the interior. The sea is our natural path to freedom and we have only to wait for our rescue.'

'Please, please – let us leave, I beg of you, Miss Lockwood, before they get here.'

'Mrs Bates, you may choose to flee,' she said primly. 'I prefer to take the word of a gentleman and an officer of the Royal Navy and do await deliverance with trust and patience.' Then she added, 'Besides, have you heard our battle beginning? How can they be close by without there is a confrontation at arms?'

'How long?'

'I cannot know that, Mrs Bates. Now do let us prepare. Sailors do not appreciate overmuch baggage. I shall get together mine – quickly now, they may be here at any minute.'

Her bundle turned out to be dismayingly large. Ruthlessly she discarded her primrose evening gown, the feathered turban, the black satin slippers. But there was one thing she could not be parted from: her precious sketchbooks, from which she knew would arise in due course a magnificent study of decayed grandeur against bare mountains and an angry sky.

She packed them together and fastened them securely with string. This left little room for essentials but Captain Kydd would probably touch at Plymouth and therefore she'd be home the same day and able to—

Something was not right and it made her skin crawl.

Then she had it. There was an absolute stillness – no distant sounds of disorder, cart traffic, those myriad sounds that were the background to any city.

Silence.

In rising unease she hurried to the balcony and looked out. There was not a soul in sight.

It made no sense: if the local inhabitants had fled from a French advance why had they heard no firing, trumpet calls and similar?

Her tension communicated itself to Mrs Bates, who stood by in mute horror, not understanding.

'I don't know what's afoot, but perhaps we should be ready for a hasty departure,' Persephone said unsteadily. But what could they do – where could they go?

She hesitated in fretful indecision. If they left the *pousada* to go anywhere, they'd lose the chance of being found and taken off by the frigate. The risk was too great. They had to stay.

But in a little over an hour the decision was taken out of her hands. A fierce knocking pierced the quiet. Heart in her mouth Persephone heard the landlady scurry to the front door and her quavering voice ask something in Portuguese. The only reply she got was further banging.

The woman hurriedly withdrew to the back of the house and a commotion arose from the kitchen.

Then a male voice, harsh and insistent, cut through the landlady's shrill protests. It demanded food, wine and beds. Persephone's frozen mind had registered what was being said and that it was in French!

The landlady obviously didn't understand and tried English; then came sounds of men and equipment entering.

'They're here! Quickly, out of the side door,' Persephone hissed urgently.

She snatched up her sketchbooks and, gripping Mrs Bates's hand, dragged her out into the yard. She looked around frantically.

There! The donkey stalls.

They were empty, and the two women crouched together in the straw of the far one, Mrs Bates trembling pitiably.

'Wh-what can w-we do?' she whispered.

'Be very quiet, if you please, Mrs Bates.' Persephone desperately needed time to think.

The uncanny silence: it must have been decided not to resist, to allow the French to enter without a fight – no battle, no firing. The population had simply bolted themselves indoors until it was over.

And if the *pousada* was going to be a billet for French soldiers of occupation, they would be discovered very soon. They had to get away – but where?

With no Portuguese, little idea of where anything was in

the country and conspicuously in foreign dress, they would stand little chance. And if they—

A sudden explosion of straw beside them nearly paralysed her with fright and then a pair of bright eyes and wide smile emerged. It was Paolo.

'Hah! You hide from the *soldados franceses,* I think!' he whispered.

'You wicked child, you frightened us half to death,' gasped Mrs Bates.

'Paolo. We need to run away,' Persephone said. 'Will you help us?'

'What, now?'

'Yes. Will you?'

'If they catch me, they will beat me.'

Inspiration came just in time. 'Oh. I didn't think drummer boys were frightened.'

'Drummer boy?'

'If you can help us get to England I will speak to the colonel of the regiment to have you enlisted.' If boys younger than he went to sea, surely the army would take him at his age.

'Really? You not play me the fool?' His wide eyes told her she'd hit home.

'Yes. A uniform of red and gold, a tall hat with a big badge on it and drumsticks of your own.'

'Yes! Yes! I will.' The eyes shone. 'What do I have to do?'

'Your duties will be those of interpreter,' she answered quickly. 'Asking the way, er, and so forth.'

'I have a map,' he blurted. 'Shall I get it?'

'Yes, please – but be careful!'

'Those poxy *francês* don't scare me,' he said scornfully, and made off through a hole at the back of the stall.

Chapter 29

Paulo was back quickly with a carefully torn out sheet from his school atlas, a small-scale map of Portugal.

Persephone studied it feverishly. Here was a river, there the Spanish border, and over to the left was Lisboa – Lisbon. Names of places were densely printed but meant little to her. Added to which her knowledge of navigation was hopeless: she hadn't even an idea of how to orient the map properly.

But it was a map, a kind of land-chart. Forcing her mind to coolness she pored over it again. To the south was the Tagus river and beyond that were untold miles – leading to nowhere but the end of land again.

To the west was the empty ocean; to the east the mountainous interior of Portugal – but that was where the French had come from.

It left only the north.

And there at the top edge of the map was the border – Spain, the enemy.

In despair her eyes darted over it, looking for anything

– something. And nearly at this top part she saw a name she recognised: Oporto. Her father had an arrangement with one of the big English merchants there for the importation of the finest port for the dockyard and wardrooms of the fleet. 'There!' she said brightly. 'We're going to Oporto.' If the French were lunging for Lisbon there was a good chance they'd leave invading further places until later.

'Oh dear. Is it a long way?'

'Not far, Mrs Bates,' she said firmly. 'We shall—'

The back door of the *pousada* squeaked.

Quaking they dropped down out of sight.

There was no sound or movement.

After a moment Persephone dared a quick look through the slats of the stall. Outside a soldier was tamping a long clay pipe. He was a young man, unshaven and in a uniform not much better than rags, his toes visible in what was left of his boots.

Persephone felt thrilled and fearful at the same time. She'd seen what few in England had: one of Napoleon Bonaparte's actual veterans in the flesh! And so close. She put her finger to her lips and held her other arm protectively around Paolo. Daring another look, she saw that the soldier was leaning against the wall with his eyes shut, the pipe drooping and unlit. He was clearly exhausted. No doubt the French column had been driven mercilessly towards Lisbon hoping to trap the royal family before they made their escape.

There was a chance to get away while the troops lay in weariness. They had to do it – now!

The young soldier pulled himself upright, turned and pissed noisily against the wall before shuffling inside.

Persephone thought furiously. To get past any sentry they had to be in local garb, and pass as Portuguese women. They would need money, not only for lodging on the way but for any transport they could hire . . . and what else to keep them for countless miles?

'Paolo. I want you to go inside and get me . . .'

He was soon back with what she'd asked for: her saddle bag with its funds, along with two dresses and wet-weather cloaks from the landlady's wardrobe. The woman had fled.

'It easy – soldiers snore like pigs,' he boasted.

The two women looked anxiously at each other. Persephone was now in a coarse mustard-coloured wool skirt and loose white top with a green shawl covering her head. Mrs Bates wore a similar disguise. Paolo had found a wide-brimmed straw hat to go with his tattered red waistcoat and shapeless brown jacket. A pair of baskets to carry their bundles and all was prepared.

Now it was time to leave, Persephone felt overwhelmed. She was about to quit the safety of their hiding place and boldly step out into frightful danger. She gulped. When they opened the back gate into the outside world, which turning should they take for Oporto?

But she had a plan: the precious map displayed every town and village. All she had to do was join the dots to Oporto and at each one tell Paolo to ask the way to the next. No need for a compass, navigation – just go from one to another until they arrived.

It steadied her and she consulted the map for the first objective. 'Paolo. Which way to, um, Mafra?'

The lad pointed confidently in one direction.

'You will lead us. Everyone ready?'

Heart pounding, Persephone moved out into the yard and scuttled to the gate. The other two followed closely behind.

She pulled, and it opened with a deafening *screeeak*. She was through into a narrow alleyway, gloomy and smelling of rubbish but mercifully deserted. 'Quickly!' she urged, remembering to close the gate after her. With this step forward into the unknown there could be no going back.

'You say I lead!' Paolo said importantly, and pushed to the front, then stepped off in a smart march, imaginary drumsticks rattling a jolly beat.

The alley led to a cross street, the houses quaint and of another time.

A woman came out of one and, without a glance in their direction, hurried off. Their disguise was working! As they pressed on, more people emerged but they had other things on their mind and passed them by without a word, two ladies with baskets and a child – what could be less threatening?

They toiled up a steep hill between drab townhouses and, over the crest, came upon an aqueduct. It was long and had curious pointed arches.

Paolo noticed Persephone's interest. 'We always go this way – is faster,' he explained. They found a path in the bushes beside the great structure and struck off across the valley.

It was hard going but the undergrowth hid them and gave her time to ponder.

The worst thing that could happen was that the French would stop them. Their lack of Portuguese and any apparent reason to be heading out of Lisbon would be cause enough to seize them and she had no doubt about their fate at the hands of the soldiery. It would go hard with little Paolo: found assisting the English he'd be shown no mercy. She resolved that if they were stopped she'd tell him to run for his life – rough soldiers wouldn't demean themselves by chasing a boy.

The Portuguese themselves, abandoned by the British, would have little sympathy and might well turn them over for reward.

At the bottom of the valley, with the aqueduct soaring above them, they rested, fatigued and aching. Paolo started to fidget and Persephone set him to fashioning stout walking staffs. All too soon there was nothing for it but to press on up the other side of the valley. At the top there were a few mean houses with squawking chickens and surprised faces but then they joined the road, a substantial straight highway, leading on into the countryside.

'Estrada Real, Dona,' Paolo said proudly. 'To Mafra.'

His explanation caused her fears to rise again. This was the royal road to Mafra, the highway to Dom João's royal palace, and it passed belief that the French were not at that very moment ransacking the palace for the all the treasures and finery they could find within. She said nothing and they trudged on wearily. The map's scale was meaningless and she had no idea how far ahead it lay, let alone Oporto. In this world of fright and pain there was only one burning imperative: one foot in front of the other, on and on, until the end.

Paolo followed doggedly, dragging his feet, his small figure bent. Persephone's heart went out to him as she waited for him to catch up. When he reached them he managed a weak smile.

Mrs Bates was swaying with weariness.

They couldn't go on – but to lie down was to give up.

The road was deserted but suddenly they heard a piercing squeal behind them. Shocked rigid, Persephone waited in near panic to see what had caused it.

It turned out to be a farm cart pulled by a single horse with an old man loosely at the reins, steadily screeching along with dry axles. It drew near. He looked at them in astonishment and halted sharply when Paolo threw himself in its path, waving his arms. There was an exchange in excitable Portuguese, then Paolo bowed grandly and invited the women to haul themselves up into the cart: they had won themselves a ride all the way to Mafra along the royal road. He lowered his voice to explain that he'd told the farmer they were fearful of the French and wanted to leave Lisbon. And that the ladies were shy about speaking to strange men and desired only to rest.

They needed no urging: the cart was empty but for three barrels of olives tied to the side, and they lay down in a delirium of exhaustion on a folded canvas cover. It was impossible to sleep with the deafening squeal under them but they did not care. They were at rest and on their way to the next dot on the map.

Paolo happily joined the man on the driving seat.

The day was drawing to a close when the cart lurched to a standstill. The old man said something to Paulo and pointed to a shabbier road that forked to the right. The lad translated: the royal road led on to the palace and the smaller to the town of Mafra only a mile or two further down.

They left the farmer to take his olives on to the palace. Paolo told them that the wheels were left deliberately ungreased so the appalling sound of their progress could be heard by carts out of sight around precipitous mountain tracks.

Chapter 30

It was excruciating to walk again but ahead there would surely be a *pousada* for weary travellers, a bowl of soup and—

Unnoticed by the trio in their weariness four armed French soldiers had spread out in front of them, their sergeant with folded arms smiling cynically. Persephone sensed more behind. It was all over for them. In a rush she remembered the promise she'd made to herself. 'Paolo! Run – run away as hard as you can!'

The child didn't move, staring at the French soldiers. Suddenly he let out a howl and threw himself at Persephone, clutching her skirt and crying out in terror, screaming inconsolably.

Mrs Bates dropped her basket and stood paralysed.

The sergeant hesitated, then moved forward, making pacifying gestures, but Paolo's screams only became louder and the man halted with a frown. In hoarse French he called out, 'Stop that child bawling, for God's sake!'

Persephone feigned incomprehension.

'Tell him he's quite safe. Frenchmen don't make war on infants!'
She shook her head mutely.

Exasperated, he swore and looked around. 'Anyone know Portuguese? Someone tell the stupid woman . . . No, let 'em pass. Get them and their noise out of m' sight.'

Hardly daring to breathe Persephone shepherded her little party away with as much dignity as she could muster but safely around the corner she buried her face in her hands.

She had to pull herself together. The town was not far ahead and there they had new challenges. 'Well done, Paolo,' she told the boy, who beamed. They owed their escape to the lad's quick thinking.

Around the next bend was the beginnings of a street and on the left the unmistakable vision of a *pousada*, two-storeyed and of faded grandeur. The three entered and headed towards a shabby desk. A man jumped to his feet and looked at them in astonishment. Had he recognised them as being in disguise? Fearing the man would betray them to the French, Persephone faltered in dismay.

'Leave this to me, dear,' Mrs Bates said, with sudden determination, taking her arm and pulling her forward.

'We are Americans,' she said loudly. 'You savvy, no?'

'I spik. You are United States?'

'Mrs Bates, my sister here. We're in Lisbon, the French come, we don't like what they do. We come away. If you have rooms as are fit for ladies, we stay – if not we go somewhere else. Compree?'

'I hear. Ver' good lodgings – this place ver' grand. Er, *a criança?*' he asked hesitantly.

'The boy? He gets a separate bed,' Mrs Bates replied firmly.

In their rooms it needed only to be decided which came first – a hot tub, a vast dinner or cool sheets . . .

The morning brought even better tidings. When the Regent had abandoned the Mafra Palace, it had been comprehensively cleared of its contents to be stored aboard ship for the convenience of the court in exile. The French had come and, finding an empty shell, left quickly to fall back on Lisbon. If Persephone and her little party moved fast, there was every chance they could get through and away.

Aching, swollen limbs promised a grim and painful journey ahead before they could feel safe, but they took heart at what they next heard.

The *pousada* was deserted. The high-spending clientele from the city, merchants and courtiers, were not coming any more to Mafra now that the royal family had left. Therefore they had at their disposal its wealth of transport assets at a mere trifle of the former price. Would the ladies like a sedan chair, one on either side of a mule or possibly a horse litter was to be preferred? Regrettably carriages would not answer beyond the royal highway on the roads to come, but on the other hand they would draw unwelcome attention to the travellers.

Horses: wiry, compact ponies that could be relied on to pick their way over mountain passes, patient and enduring. A pack-horse for their bundles – now with additions procured for them by the innkeeper: warm brown cloaks, cheese and wine, a loaf of corn and rye bread. Paolo would ride two-up in turns with the women. Persephone counted the *cruzada*s carefully from their little hoard and they mounted, Mrs Bates a little precarious with Paolo, and Persephone somewhat doubtful of her mouse-grey working horse after the splendid mounts she'd grown up with in England.

Obidos was the next dot on their little map but Paolo had never been further than Mafra and could say nothing about it. After a few miles they lapsed into a companionable quiet as the horses clopped on towards the distant edge of land and sky.

To each side the prospect was always the same: poor country, stony soil, with unvarying fields of Indian corn, olives and vines but there, always in the far background, a vista of craggy, rumpled mountains tinted between grey and purple as the light changed. The journey would be slow and uncomfortable over the rutted and holed road, little more than a track, but the one thing that made it all bearable was that every mile took them further from the invading army . . . and a mile nearer deliverance.

Chapter 31

Many days later the little band, weary beyond conceiving, stood together in the heights above Oporto. There was no rejoicing for it was so unreal, seeming as much a delusion as being suddenly confronted by the man in the moon. They'd seen much – from the distant and ethereal sight of a Moorish castle at an eminence to the intricacies of a cork tree as they sheltered under it in the rain. A long stone causeway across an endless morass, narrow mountain tracks over which they'd passed, hearts in mouths, then on to valleys plunging far below. An ancient bridge of twenty-seven arches, oil-mills and long, straggling villages.

The most poignant of all were the crosses planted at odd places by the roadside. These, Paolo had explained, were put there by villagers who'd come to bury those who had not survived their journey or had been robbed and murdered to leave their bones there for ever.

Once, Persephone had decided to press on through a village in the hope they could make the next before dark – two dots achieved instead of one. They had been benighted, compelled to call a halt and lie huddled together under their cloaks on the stony ground, shivering and frightened, a wide-eyed Paolo between them.

The hardest time was their last night. Caught by an evening shower they'd crowded into a *pousada* to find it full of sullen, sodden travellers who made it impossible for them to get near the only fireplace. Their bed that night was dank straw on the floor of the cellar and their supper a pipkin of weak gruel.

In these final days Persephone had been hoarding their last *cruzada*s, fearful they would run out of money and be left starving. They had been forced to travel on foot, sustained in their suffering only by the promise of the near mythical Oporto close by.

And now, heaven be thanked, they were there.

Persephone had kept to herself a dull ache of fear that had stayed with her over the last days: that in the absence of British ships the French had thought to send a squadron north to occupy Oporto. If they had, there was most surely nowhere else for them to go.

From their high vantage-point, they peered into the long, clefted harbour. Everything seemed normal enough – busy strings of hoys and barges, substantial ships mid-stream working cargo, boats criss-crossing – but at this distance she could see no flags, no indication of friend or enemy. The only way to lay her fears to rest – or not – would be to get to the harbourside. But in their state, after making their way down the steep sides they would never be able to labour back up.

As in a dream they left the skyline by the long zigzag road and gradually descended until, quite abruptly, they were above the big wine godowns packed along the waterfront, open sail-barges before them crammed with barrels and men working industriously – the very picture of the ordinary and routine.

They were met by a side road and then a tavern.

It was in full swing – and something made her pause. Then she heard it:

> 'Scrub the mud off the dead man's face,
> An' haul, or ye'll be damned;
> For there blows some cold nor'westers, on
> The banks of Newf'n'land!'

In a tidal wave of relief she knew they'd done it.

They'd reached Oporto before the French!

Gulping with emotion, she calmed herself and entered the tavern.

The singing and happy babble tailed away as, in astonishment, all eyes turned to the apparition.

'I desire to be shown the establishment of an English port shipper, if you please.'

'Why, yes, ma'am,' an old sailor nearby said, rising hastily and touching his forelock. 'It's just yonder, is all.'

A little later they were sitting in comfortable chairs in the office of Mr Holroyd, senior comptroller, who was aghast at what he saw before him. 'From Lisbon? Overland? Miss Lockwood, I'm distressed and overcome with the thought of what you must have endured! If there's anything at all I can do for you, then . . .'

'Sir. As of this moment I can conceive of no greater service than that you should allow us passage to England.'

Chapter 32

Outside number 101 the Strand, Kydd looked up and saw the sign: Ackermann's Print Shop, an establishment warmly recommended for the vigour and quality of its wares. He entered and enquired about purchasing a set of contemporary prints suitable for framing as a gift for his sister.

'Certainly, sir. You'll be interested, then, in consulting this very tome, new arrived in the shop. It's setting the town a-talking.' The man handed a sizeable bound volume to Kydd. 'Our *Microcosm of London.*'

Kydd leafed through the collection of pictures portraying life in the metropolis, from Billingsgate Market to the interior of an asylum, all done with remarkable detail and feeling.

'Rowlandson and Pugin,' the man said loftily. 'As each may be purchased individually for a trifle.'

Behind him the door opened as a customer entered.

'Excuse me for a moment, sir.'

Kydd was happy to be left with the compilation, impressed with the ingenuity of the artists in bringing out the conceit of each tableau.

He heard the customer addressed and a cool woman's voice answer. No, it couldn't be! He turned and saw a poised, handsome figure in the latest fashion, a Pomona green bonnet and matching redingote over a delicate white high-waisted sprigged muslin gown.

She noticed his look and glanced at him – and, with a shock, he saw that this indeed was no other than Persephone Lockwood. 'Um, Miss Lockwood, my duty,' he managed with a civil bow, scrambling to find something to say that was neither banal nor foolish.

With a barest bob, she replied, 'Sir Thomas, this is my cousin Clarinda,' indicating a younger woman next to her. Shyly he was accorded a deeper curtsey.

'A pleasure to meet you. That is, the both of you, of course!'

'Quite. You are well, Sir Thomas?'

'Thank you, yes. And you? Er, but I heard you were not on the transports—'

'No, I was not. I was too long waiting to be taken off for my frigate's berth and was overtaken by the French.'

Kydd reddened. 'As was not in my power to fulfil, Miss Lockwood. But if you had neither, then—'

'I was obliged to walk, sir. To Oporto.'

Through the French lines? Not knowing the language and . . . 'A formidable journey, Miss Lockwood. Are you now recovered, might we say?' He was unable to begin to imagine what it must have been like for a lone English gentlewoman abroad in the interior of Portugal.

'I am, sir.'

'There will be those who will be delighted with your safe return. Your parents and . . .?'

'My husband? I am not married, sir, if that is your meaning.'

'Oh, I didn't mean to imply . . .' Kydd tailed off.

'Not yet, that is to say,' Persephone Lockwood added.

'Yes, of course.'

'Your wife – is she in health?'

Kydd stiffened. Was she playing with him? Then he realised that the last she had known of his previous attachment was his leaving to be married to Rosalynd, and the accidental death of some common country girl would not have meant anything at the time. 'I have never married, Miss Lockwood. The one with whom I once had an understanding was taken from me by an accident.'

A tiny flicker crossed her features. 'I'm sorry to hear it,' she replied evenly.

'You're staying in London long?'

'It is the Season, Sir Thomas,' she said coldly. 'I shall bid you goodbye, sir.'

He was left standing while his thoughts settled.

That she'd been spared was a relief; that it had all been by her own pluck and initiative was impressive – that she'd not felt inclined to share the experience less so. Was it that she held it against him? Did she despise him, even? And the defensive 'not yet' about being married. Did this mean she was shortly to make a formal commitment?

There was no question that she was now a remarkable beauty, a woman whose natural comeliness, informed by character and individuality, set her at the first rank.

For the first time since coming into his eminence he felt unworthy, diminished. He knew this was foolish – he had no need any more to make allowances for himself – but whoever ended with Persephone Lockwood on his arm would be a fortunate man indeed.

Chapter 33

'So glad you could come, old bean.' Jeremy Ripon beamed, patting Kydd on the knee. The coach, swaying and rumbling over the green Surrey countryside, was on its way to Epsom. Kydd was looking forward to the thundering hoofs and visceral excitement of a first-class meet: just what was needed to lift his mood. 'Your first time?'

'At Epsom, yes, Jerry. Tell me, how's the course run?'

'Ah. Today's big 'un is a five-hundred-guinea purse over a mile four furlongs. Simple enough run – a horseshoe course, up one prong, and I mean up, and down t'other.'

'Up?'

'They say it's a hundred feet in half a mile the horses face, but then after rounding a sharpish Tattenham Corner it's down-hill all the way to a finish. And that makes for damn fine racing. Fastest-paced in the world, is Epsom's finishing straight.'

Kydd tried to focus on what his friend was saying but he couldn't get Persephone Lockwood out of his mind. When he thought of the pretty young things flocking around him, her strength of character was very appealing, and her indifference to his fame and public attentions was refreshing. If he'd met the woman without the burden of the past, perhaps things might have been different . . .

Ripon gave him a quizzical look. 'Some top sportsmen'll have horses running. You'll see the Duke o' Cumberland – he's entered Caledonian, I've heard. Such a sprinter as never you've seen. And the crafty old Bobby Shafto has his Sapphire mounted by Sam Chifney as we hold to be the chief of all horse jockeys. It'll be a rare day!'

Kydd nodded and came to a resolution: the only course to take was to cast the woman out of his mind and enjoy the race day. 'So, what mount will your money be on, Jerry?'

They talked of breeds and bloodlines, silks and courses, and the knowledgeable Ripon, no mean whip himself, kept Kydd entertained until they joined others converging on the little town on the Downs where it seemed all the fancy and mobility of England were going to the races. Carriages of nobles jostled with pony trap, post-chaise and donkey-cart in an excited concourse about the race track.

At the cry of 'Member! Member!' the throng reluctantly parted to let them through and into the paddock where handicapping was in public preparation. With some difficulty they finally got through to the members' enclosure.

'Over there – the cove with the black hat. That's your Duke of Cumberland.' A richly but conservatively dressed figure was leaning on an ivory stick, an aristocratic frown on his dark features, observing procedures closely as the required measurement was done.

'Ha! Watch this,' Ripon said.

An official stepped up with a measuring rod. 'Handicap is b' size in Epsom,' Ripon confided. 'He's to discover the height o' the beast.'

The rod was placed against the horse's withers and immediately the animal's rear end dropped into a slight squat. Ripon laughed loudly, and scattered jeers in the crowd beyond the rails showed that it had not been missed there either.

'Wha'?'

'The Duke tells his stable hands to touch, then thwack his mount. This teaches him that a tap on the rear is to be feared and he shies down.'

It was not lost either on the other owner, a shorter, handsome man in a buff leather and plush riding dress. With folded arms and a look of scorn he waited for the measuring, and when it was done, his own horse did exactly the same thing.

The crowd roared its delight. Caledonian and Sapphire would be carrying equal weight.

'Which do you favour, Jerry, old sport?' drawled a languid figure with lace cuffs, appearing next to them.

To Kydd the two horses looked alike: lean thoroughbreds gleaming with condition and lines unbelievably sleek close to.

'I've a feel it's going to be Bobby's day, Pincher. Oh, and this is m' friend Kydd.'

'Sapphire? Then I've fifty cobbs says you're going to rue it.'

'Fifty? If you'll make it a hundred you're on, old fish. Kydd?'

'Ah, I'll go five on Sapphire.'

'Five?' They looked at Kydd in puzzlement.

'As I've not seen the nags run,' he said hastily.

They had a fine view of the track from high in the members' stand at the finishing post, packed with nobility and gentry, and Kydd revelled in the heady atmosphere of excitement and tension. Below them the greater mass of spectators pressed up to the rail in feverish anticipation.

Ripon took out a small spyglass and trained it on the opposite side of the course, the start. 'They're lining up . . . Under orders . . . They're off!'

The crowd roared, pressing against the rail. A mile and a half – less than four minutes' running.

'And it's Caledonian by a neck . . . No, he's doing better . . . He's out in front, the villain!'

The gaggle of horses came into full view as they tightened into Tattenham Corner, and when they opened into the final straight, bedlam erupted.

Even without Ripon's glass Kydd could see the purple silk of the duke's mount in front by a margin but now the downhill gradient told and the horses flew, frenzied drumming of their hoofs emerging even above the crowd's roar, coming towards them in an unforgettable spectacle of man and horse flying to a finish.

With just two furlongs to go, Chifney on Sapphire turned into a crazed man, thrashing his horse in a frenzied passion. The maddened beast bolted forward, taking Caledonian, and into the lead. The clamour was deafening as the climactic thundering of hoofs approached and passed the finishing line, Sapphire a clear winner.

It had been a great race and Kydd looked down on the seething crowd below, his cup full.

They were beginning to disperse and individuals could be made out. Extraordinarily it seemed that every class of society from noble to gypsy was mixing freely together in high good humour. On one side there was a noisy coven of country girls, and on the other, a decorous group in the dress of fashion, a beau with a striking figure of a woman on his arm, discoursing agreeably with a gentleman who held a cane and—

'Give me your glass!' Kydd demanded abruptly.

Surprised, Ripon brought it out and handed it to him.

With long practice won at sea he quickly had a close-up image in focus. It was Persephone. By her side – and taking her arm – a man dressed faultlessly in a dark blue coat, snowy white shirt and cravat, was in earnest converse with her father, Admiral Lockwood. That had to be her mother next to him.

They broke into good-natured laughter at some sally, Persephone happily looking up into his eyes, clearly enjoying his company.

Kydd lowered the glass. So, she had an attachment. As she was perfectly entitled, of course.

He raised the telescope again. The man was fashionably willowy, his bearing gracious and elegant and with all the natural authority of rank. Probably a young noble, perhaps with prospects of inheriting one day, a fine catch for a mere daughter of an admiral.

He lowered the glass. The sight had stung.

Chapter 34

'Your amiability in the article of appearances is well remarked, Kydd,' Fookes purred. 'Just the ticket for these dire times.'

They stood together in the vestibule of the grand Kensington Lodge, the venue for Countess Grafton's gathering, a *fête* to which it appeared all the fashion of London had come.

'No presentations, no speeches, just show confident and tranquil.'

'As if Boney doesn't own all Europe end to end.'

'Just so. And ill-bred as I am,' Fookes said, plucking an invisible hair from his sleeve, 'I can't help but observe that your opportunity to make acquaintance with the comeliest maids is enviable in the extreme. Some might tell it that you'll have your pick of 'em, you devil.'

Kydd hid his amusement. Yet if he failed to land a fair lady this season it would be a very odd thing.

The great room was packed with humanity: candlelight glitter of jewellery on pale skin, hair plumes and spangled dresses mingling with buckskin, cravats and extravagantly polished riding boots. Laughing faces, coy glances, roving looks.

'There's someone you must meet,' Fookes said, spotting an individual in the crowd. 'Come over, Kydd – it's the treasurer of the Navy as was. Bound to want to see you, m' friend.'

The one at the highest level of the chain of authority that stretched from his ship's weekly accounts to the faceless spectres with god-like powers, who could summon even an admiral to explain himself. Kydd rather doubted he would want to make his acquaintance, but as far as he was aware his yard-arm was clear and he was ready to do his duty.

He was led to a man in a tobacco-coloured coat and rumpled waistcoat, his hair tousled and face lined with dissipation, sitting on one of the few sofas along the wall surrounded by a circle of admirers.

'Sir, I bring you the hero of the hour, none other than Kydd of the *Tyger*!'

The man hiccuped as his gaze swivelled to Kydd, his wine slopping. 'What was that, Prinker? Mr Tiger? A fine name, sir, damn fine name!'

'Sir Thomas, this is Mr Sheridan, he whose parliamentary prose is nonpareil but which is nevertheless exceeded by his perfection in the art of the theatre.'

Kydd bowed politely, then realised that this Sheridan must be none other than the Richard Brinsley Sheridan, whose plays were celebrated the world over. 'My honour, sir,' he said sincerely. 'As I near wept at your *Glorious First of June*, so true to the day.'

'A mere trifle of the time. Not *The School for Scandal* then, Mr Tiger? Or *The Rivals* as shall stir you?'

Fookes intervened gently: 'Richard, this is Sir Thomas Kydd. His ship is the *Tyger* of whose gallant deeds you may have heard.'

Sheridan gave an oddly sheepish smile and lifted his glass in salute. 'So I have, you villain. Well, Kid it is. Not Tiger – but, then, for a dashing frigate captain that would suit you a gallows deal better, I'm persuaded.' There was a titter of approval from the mainly feminine circle around him.

'Or should it be a more manly tagging – Captain Hawser Trunnion comes to mind . . . or perhaps Tom Toughknot? I could do a lot with that. Or Rough Tom Topsail, scourge of corsairs? Methinks Christopher Crosstrees too tame . . . Should you more like Bob Binnacle? Tomkin Trident?'

'We have to take our leave of you now, Richard. Come on, Tiger.'

Kydd hesitated, but if he was going to be anointed with a nickname it could hardly have come from a better source. At a discreet distance he asked, 'You said treasurer of the navy?'

'Indeed. In post up to a year or so back.'

They moved on, Fookes acknowledging passing acquaintances and steering Kydd to a small group, the man with a shrewd and penetrating glance with what must be his wife and daughter, the latter a dazzling beauty with a flawless complexion and a plunging neckline.

'Sir Thomas, do meet the Honourable Mr Percy Houghton, a most valuable member of foxhounds who nevertheless finds time to attend cabinet in the character of secretary.'

Houghton bowed, his manner faultlessly urbane.

'Mrs Houghton.' A respectful bob. 'And Miss Georgiana Houghton.' A deeper gesture. When she rose and met Kydd's eyes the look from under the long eyelashes was unreadable.

There was polite discourse during which Kydd learned that not only did Miss Georgiana adore dancing but by coincidence she would be at the Mansion House ball the following Thursday. Would Sir Thomas be attending by any chance?

He was shortly whisked away but Fookes was intercepted by a footman who whispered a message. 'Ah, dear fellow, I'm called away for a spell. Do see if you can find your friends and I'll be back in a short while.'

Kydd looked about him – there were none he knew nearby so he eased through the crush, making his way slowly to the far end where it appeared a little less crowded.

And then he saw them: Persephone – and the man she had been with at the races.

Should he move on? Something held him but then her head turned. She caught sight of him and started in surprise.

The man noticed her look and threw a quizzical glance at Kydd before asking her something.

The couple moved towards him.

'Charles, may I introduce Sir Thomas Kydd? Sir Thomas, the Honourable Charles Pountney.'

Kydd gave a stiff bow. 'My pleasure to make your acquaintance, sir.'

'Likewise. Kydd – I can't seem to place the name.' The tone was an effortless patrician drawl and Kydd's hackles rose. 'Pray where's your estate at all, sir?'

'My estate? Shall we say out on the briny wilds, sir?'

'Briny . . . Oh, you mean you're a species of mariner. Persephone, my dear, you know this gentleman?'

'Sir Thomas is a naval officer, Charles. As daughter of an admiral, it were hard for me to avoid an acquaintance.'

Kydd smouldered but bit back his reply.

'I see. Then you're one of those stout fellows who are

keeping Bonaparte at bay for us. An honour it is to be sure to know you, sir. I really cannot conceive where the country would be without you're floating about with all your guns primed and so forth.' Any sincerity in his words was buried under a languid manner and his affectation of raising his eyebrows while looking down his nose at the speaker.

Persephone was in high good looks, wearing a dazzling white satin gown and yellow robe, and a turban with white ostrich feathers, but her air was cool and distant.

'So Pountney is a landed gentleman?' He deliberately directed the question to her.

'Charles is the eldest son of the Viscount of Carlisle, Sir Thomas.' The tone was cutting and it hurt, but not as much as the amused glances she and Pountney had exchanged.

'In the north, then,' he blurted, for something to say.

'Carlisle is in the north, old fellow, but the family seat is in Shrewsbury,' Pountney explained, as if to a child. His attire was exquisite: from the elegance of a snow-white starched cravat to the skin-tight buckskin pantaloons it showed him to be at the first rank of fashion and put Kydd's garments to the blush.

'So you've known each other some time, then.' Again to Persephone.

'A little while,' she answered primly, then laid her arm on Pountney's and, smiling up at him, said, 'He's going to take me to the Royal Academy exhibition on Thursday, aren't you, Charles?'

'Count on it, my dear.'

She beamed at him, then turned to Kydd. 'Well, we really must be getting along, Sir Thomas, quantities of people to meet. Goodbye.'

It shouldn't have affected him but it did. She was of the

past, and not only that: she was about to be married and start a family and . . . Where was this all leading? If he had no feelings for her, how could the evening's scene have touched him? If it had, did it mean he still carried a torch for her?

That was nonsense. He was older, his world experience vastly greater, and he had his choice of many. Why should he still be hankering after a youthful episode?

A small inner voice came back: there must have been something of her there as she had been in the past that had reached out to him. Was it unreasonable to suppose that the same attraction was still at work?

Of one thing he was very sure. He burned with a single-minded hatred of Charles Pountney. The instinctive aristo-cratic assumption of superiority, the well-bred mannerisms and obvious wealth brought back memories of forelock-tugging to the squires and landed gentry of Guildford in his youth. Here was a prime example of the breed, supercilious, arrogant and haughty, born to lord it over honest folk, never to stand tall as a man. How could Persephone bring herself to be at the side of a fop like that?

Kydd choked back his rage and tried to dismiss the whole thing, but it wouldn't go away.

He drew himself up. He couldn't, and wouldn't, let it spoil his time of triumph and place in the sun – and, indeed, should he not be thinking about a match for himself?

Yes! With savage glee it came to him: a way to get back at Pountney in his own coin and at the same time better his own prospects in the matrimonial stakes.

He'd take advantage of his time in London to turn himself from a provincial bumpkin to a blade at the top of fashion, the kind of vision he'd seen draw gasps of admiration in

Hyde Park, whether at the reins of a high-perch phaeton or taking the air, men stepping aside in respect and homage, ladies openly smitten.

And then perhaps he would idly venture to the Royal Academy on Thursday next – who knew who might be there to be confounded by his transfiguration?

It would not be easy but he knew a man who could help.

Chapter 35

Fookes looked pleased to be called on for advice. 'Of course, dear fellow. Say away – what's on your mind?' He signalled to a passing waiter for their glasses to be refreshed. 'Gambling? Is it to be turf or baize think I, knowing your—'

'Prinker. I'm a simple sailor but if I'm to navigate in these waters I've a yen to be rigged like a good 'un. I mean, a man o' fashion, can go anywhere, not be slighted in company. Now, I've always thought you a right fine figure, knows your buckle from your topknot. How should I proceed?'

Fookes frowned but was clearly enjoying being asked. 'Well, now, and it depends on what grade of the *ton* you aspire to, dear fellow,' he murmured, then cocked his head and looked at Kydd with an amused smile. 'As this would not be in any way connected to the lady I saw you with at the *fête*?'

'Of course not!'

'Handsome woman,' he reflected, watching Kydd for reaction, then went on, 'Miss Lockwood, wasn't it?'

'It was, but I really don't—'

'Not as if she comes from a family of note.'

'You know them?'

'I have an acquaintance with them. An only daughter, but they've just a small pile in Sussex, and she cannot look to being settled with more than a thousand or so. One of the family was groom of the stole around the year three, and her mother was a lady-in-waiting at St James's Palace before she married.' He rubbed his chin. 'Spirited lass, though – will stand for no nonsense from the beaux and much given to dashing off to wild places. I'm supposing she's seeing the need to wed and bring forth – after all she'd be north of, what, twenty-seven? Scored well with her match, I'd say.'

'Oh?'

'Pountney. Ancestor did well in the 'forty-five, stood fast against Bonnie Prince Charlie, and the second George showed his gratitude in lands. The viscount is an old goat but he's not long for this world and, as eldest, Charles stands to take up a fair-sized demesne, castle and such. As I said, she did main well to land the fellow.'

Kydd heard it all bleakly. Then into his mind stole her never-to-be-forgotten words from those years ago: that she would never wed except for love. Did she then hold such a feeling for the man? For her sake, he knew he should be pleased that things had turned out so felicitously for her. But why Pountney? An idle sprig of aristocracy with not even character enough to make a lubberly waister. The resentment bubbled up again. She could have him, but he'd get his own back on the coxcomb by showing her what a real man could look like, with all the advantages of art and fashion behind him.

'That's as may be, Prinker, but my intention is to make something of myself as I'd be proud of. What do you think?'

'Ah. A fop you are not, neither a fribble, still less a pink.

Tiger, with your figure I rather fancy you as a Corinthian, old chap.'

'So?'

'A fellow who is a full head in front of all others in the matter of looks and body, a master of the manly sports.'

'Is this the highest rank of the *ton*?'

'Um, not at this moment, I'm obliged to say. That honour belongs to the dandy, a species that values wit and learning along with due attention to fashion.'

'I'll be a dandy, I believe.'

Fookes leaned back, brow furrowed. 'I wonder if you know what you're asking, my good friend. It requires a discipline of appearance and manner that must be learned, and this only from the gifted.'

'Who?'

'"Who" you may well say. Many strive to be an exquisite of the breed but few are anointed. The greatest of these is George Brummell, a one we call "Beau", and know he is a member of this very club.'

'That's my man.'

Fookes assumed a pained expression. 'Er, he is to be accounted more a princeling than a mere mortal, Tiger. We may pay court, but never may we command his services.'

'Ah.'

'Yet we may begin your elevation with a pilgrimage to his temple, there to imbibe his wisdom. I shall arrange it.'

Two mornings later they were admitted to number four Chesterfield Street, Mayfair, by a blank-faced valet, who conducted them up a narrow staircase to a modest upper floor, placing them in a small ante-room with two other men who avoided Kydd's eye.

After an unconscionable wait the valet came out of a side room and bowed. 'Mr Brummell is receiving visitors now.'

To Kydd's utter surprise, instead of a drawing room they were ushered into a spacious dressing room set about with mirrors of every kind, basins, potion bottles and all manner of apparatus chased in silver, most of which Kydd could not put a name to.

A tall, fair gentleman was standing in his underwear before a dressing table, fastidiously studying his reflection in the looking-glass this way and that. 'I rather think the Oriental,' he pronounced finally, and turned to greet his visitors. 'Gentlemen,' he said, with a lordly bow, and beckoned imperiously for his valet.

'We're going to watch a man dress?' Kydd whispered awkwardly to Fookes.

'Be patient, old boy, and you'll learn much.'

The shirt was produced. Faultlessly ironed, and of a purity of whiteness that was breathtaking, it was eased on over a camisole.

'Fine linen and country washing, it must always answer,' Brummell threw at them.

Next were the pantaloons. Buff-coloured buckskin, they were worried on by the valet until they made a creaseless encasing of the lower limbs with straps under the arch of the foot to preserve their line.

'If people turn to look at you in the street, you are not well dressed, but either too stiff, too tight or too fashionable,' Brummell pronounced.

'Watch this,' muttered Fookes.

A collar was brought and fixed to the shirt. But what a collar! It was stiff, heroic in size and completely hid the head.

While rigid in this position the valet bore in a yard or two of the finest muslin, starched to perfection. It was brought twice around the neck and, in an agony of care, was finished with a knot, exquisite and perfectly symmetrical. The collar was folded down over it, with Brummell gazing upward. Then, gently bringing down his head with slow side to side movements of the jaw, he settled the creation and peered into the glass in judgement.

Incredibly he snatched at it, tearing it free. 'An abominable failure! Bring another.'

It took two more tries until the result was reluctantly accepted and the remainder of the ceremony could proceed.

A buff waistcoat was snugly fitted, after which came Hessian boots, which required the best part of twenty minutes to haul on. Their deep, lustrous black gleam was so dazzling that someone dared ask the secret.

'Well, sir,' Brummell said lazily, 'you know, I never use aught but the froth of the best champagne.' It left Kydd speechless.

A dark blue coat was brought. Double-breasted, with plain brass buttons polished to a discreet sheen, it was frogged with silk and an immaculate fit – long, elegant and quite without any ornament whatsoever.

His round beaver hat and silver-tipped stick were offered. He twirled about once or twice before the full-length looking-glass with an expression of boredom, yet the picture of delicacy and sophistication.

Kydd was left with much to think on.

'Damn hard work,' he muttered, as they walked slowly back to the club. 'And costing a pretty sum!'

But he was not satisfied. Even if this was the pinnacle of fashion there was one glaring objection: the finished article with all its understated grandeur was nothing more than the fashionable Pountney affected.

It wasn't an equal in refinement to the man Kydd wanted – he had to be visibly, significantly superior.

'Prinker, I want more. Do you know of any . . .?'

Chapter 36

Fookes was equal to the demand, and the next day saw Kydd stepping out with one Byng Roscoe, an exemplar of the fancy, arrayed in all the furbelows and accessories necessary for the rank, to Kydd's eyes satisfyingly *élevé* over the austere Brummell.

'The tailor first, Tiger, my fine fellow. Mr Schweitzer will be no end pleased to see you. Such a fine figure to adorn – it'll be pure pleasure for the man.'

The old-fashioned interior of the establishment enfolded Kydd in its musty embrace as the elder Schweitzer stepped forward approvingly. 'Sir will know that His Highness the Prince of Wales favours us with his custom. Will Sir then place himself in our hands in all trust?'

As opinions were expressed, then various cutters and finishers summoned to applaud the judgements, Kydd felt he was being admired like a prime side of beef.

'Very well. We begin.'

But Kydd's years before the mast had left him with strong

muscle definition and a deep chest – what was wanted were more willowy, rakish proportions.

It would appear therefore that Sir would require a corset. The humiliation did not stop there: his sturdy leg muscles that showed to such advantage in knee-breeches were an embarrassment in pantaloons, at least in sheer deerskin leather. The experienced Schweitzer had the answer: figure-hugging styling that was so tight he could hardly totter but which gave a perfectly admirable curve.

The tail-coat was easier. Olive green superfine, in an exaggerated cut, short in front with overlong tails and buttons of pure silver. The only way to wear it was for a valet to work at the sleeves until it encased the arm leaving it a rigid claw.

The tailor left to his task, it was the bootmaker next.

At the premises at the corner of Piccadilly and St James's Street it seemed that none but George Hoby himself might be trusted. Some time later Kydd settled on an order for a pair of the finest Hessian boots – not plain but for him nobly tasselled.

Roscoe beamed. 'Not as if we're finished, Joyous Spirit.'

Legions of seamstresses were engaged on shirt and neck-cloth while collars and kerchiefs were put in train to suit.

A decorative watch fob was found and a hickory walking-stick chased in silver was added to the purchases. After a visit to the hatmaker to acquire a tall beaver with a wickedly curved narrow brim, Roscoe allowed himself moderately content.

The final essential was a snuff-box of suitable *éclat*. It was apparently necessary to learn exquisiteness in the art of snuff-taking. Kydd rebelled but was mollified to learn that it was not absolutely required to take snuff, the mere appearance of so doing was enough. The lid would be flicked up with the thumb of the left hand while the right hand selected a pinch to place on the back of the left, the index finger having closed it in a flowery gesture, a handkerchief flicking away the imaginary result after inhaling.

One by one the articles of apparel were delivered. A chastened Tysoe was set the task of mastering their intricacies and, perilously close to Thursday, Kydd was ready to face the world.

As soon as he stepped out on the street, at the fashionable hour of four, he knew he'd achieved his purpose. Heads swivelled, ladies clutched arms and stared at him as he walked past with an expression of perfect indifference and superiority, even if it was more of a totter in the fiercely hugging pantaloons and with the ridiculously high collar, which made it impossible to take notice of any to the side.

But with a fierce glee he knew he held Pountney to a finish.

Chapter 37

The Royal Academy of Art's new rooms in Somerset House were crowded, which was to be expected on Exhibition Day and therefore Persephone was patient, waiting with Charles for entrance to be granted to what promised to be the most important showing of the year.

A shilling apiece entitled them to mount the steep, winding staircase to the exhibition room on the top floor where they joined a throng of patrons and disciples. It was an impressive sight, so many paintings closely interlocked and rising together to the lofty thirty foot skylights, all four walls closely covered.

They moved into the concourse.

'Is there any you would wish to see first, my dear?' Pountney enquired solicitously, his hand at her back possessively shepherding her forward.

She had a preference but now was not the time to confide it. 'There's a new Turner, I've heard,' she answered. That odd but gifted painter she'd seen once. Anything fresh from his brush was bound to be interesting. They strolled along until they saw it, high on the wall and the centre of attention.

She studied it keenly. *The Trout Stream* – bucolically spacious and suggestive, near two-thirds dominated by rearing, subtly tinted clouds. She let it enter in on her consciousness but concluded that to her it was neither romantically calling nor dramatic, and in its inexactness it held a troubling element she could not quite put her finger on.

Nearby was a hearty country scene, rural folk in every kind of rustic enjoyment outside a tavern. *The Village Holiday*, a well-applauded outing for David Wilkie, complete with the moralising figures of a drunken farmer and his dog, perhaps intentionally harking back to eighteenth-century certainties.

'Now there's a daubing I can like. Straightforward – tells it like it is.'

Charles was never going to be an adept or a romantic, but that was not what men were. She tried not to show her impatience but this was a day that held so much significance for her. Casually she edged towards the left corner. A little above eye-level, stark beside Grecian-robe-clad noble ladies in sylvan glades, hung a much more satisfying work, agreeably already attracting a knot of admirers.

A Valley for Weeping – a broad and powerful view of a craggy glen in the shadow of storm-driven clouds in a suspenseful aura of dread and mystery. In the bottom right-hand corner of the oil was a tiny 'PL'. 'Oh, how does that move you, Charles?' she asked innocently.

He consulted his guide and straightened. 'Polonius Loxley. Not sure I know the name.'

Squinting closely, he pronounced, 'The fellow's too fierce for my taste. Look at those great storm clouds about to break, all the steep mountains. Makes me feel uncomfortable – not our English countryside at all. Wonder where he's taken it from.'

Stung, she retorted, 'I rather think the pass of Glencoe, Charles. The title . . .?'

They moved on. Would it be her mission to bring him to a sensibility of the arts by some means after they were married, or . . .?

She looked upward at the higher compositions, searching for new talent that would be blossoming, new styles setting a modish fashion and—

'I do beg pardon, sir,' she exclaimed, and bobbed to the gentleman she had accidentally collided with.

It was a dandy, the preposterous high collar and indecently tight doeskin pantaloons, the hair piled forward in a caricature of a Roman emperor. She caught his eye in apology – and, to her speechless astonishment, she recognised him.

'I say, don't we know you?' Pountney got in first. 'Aren't you, um, that navy fellow?'

His startled gaze took Kydd in from head to toe. His own dress was impeccably tailored in discreet homage to Brummell and, in its clean, unadorned simplicity, contrasted wildly with Kydd's ostentation.

'A pleasure to see you again, Miss Lockwood,' Kydd said, with a stiff bow, which unfortunately ended in an undignified totter. 'And you, er, Pountney, is it not?'

Persephone, struck dumb at the apparition, could only nod.

'Rattling fine show, I believe,' Kydd said, in lordly tones.

This was never the Captain Kydd she knew! 'Why, yes, er . . .'

A gaudily decorated snuff-box came out and, in a clever

but artless display, it was opened, snuff liberally spread and duly taken, a silk handkerchief flourished to disperse the residue.

'Then does anything strike the eye, Miss Lockwood?' Kydd enquired, with exquisite disdain.

'Um, the new Turner is interesting,' she said, finally finding her tongue.

'Oh.' Kydd strained to turn but was obliged to rotate to take in the prospect, looking blankly for a Turner.

'On the wall,' Pountney said archly. When Kydd stiffly glanced about, he added loudly, pointing, 'Over there, old bean.'

'Of course,' Kydd replied loftily. 'As all the world can tell a Turner.'

The man shook his head in wonder and flashed a private look of amused bewilderment at Persephone, who frowned. Whatever had caused Kydd to display publicly to such extreme, he was still – had been – a distinguished sea captain and did not deserve such contempt.

'Sir Thomas, I'd be much obliged for your opinion on this new artist,' she said encouragingly, and firmly led the way to her painting.

Kydd stepped back to view it and, in something like his old way, said, 'I like it. The fellow's got a passion and it shows. Gives it, er, a life that those others don't have. Not as if it's as good as your Turner, o' course,' he hastened to add.

'Why, thank you, Sir Thomas,' she said, with a shy smile.

Completely floored by her change of mood, he managed an awkward bow, but Pountney intervened, taking her arm: 'We must be off now, my dear. The Mountjoys?'

They left together – but as they moved off Persephone

could not resist a last look back, a nameless feeling pricking her eyes and bringing a lump to her throat.

What had happened to Kydd? Had he got in with the wrong set, lured by the titillations and sins of the capital? Where was he trying to go?

Chapter 38

He'd failed. Kydd was in the very forefront of fashion but Pountney had done all but laugh at him. Those in the street had stopped to admire his progress and Byng had assured him of a welcome wherever men of taste and distinction might gather. But where it mattered most, he had lost the contest.

But there was one precious remembrance: Persephone Lockwood had spoken with him, asked his opinion. And as they'd moved away, she'd thrown a look back that had had him transfixed. What could it have meant?

Of one thing he was certain: there was no woman he'd ever encountered who was as dazzlingly beautiful, accomplished and intelligent. She had now become the centre of his thoughts – and it was all for naught, for she was about to be wed to another and he had no right to intrude.

But what had that last look implied? Sorrow at what he'd seemed to have become, an idle dissolute of some kind? Whatever it was, it now had no meaning. She was not for him.

He drank the whisky in one, slapped down the glass and stared bleakly at the fire.

'Sir?' Tysoe edged into his vision. He was carrying Kydd's cast-off finery. 'Will this be needed tomorrow, at all?'

'Wha'? No, it won't. Get rid of it, there's a good fellow.'

Tysoe's instant blank-faced compliance nearly brought a smile.

Kydd knew he was not cut out to be a fashion god, and if he never saw a square inch of starch again, it would be too soon.

His man returned a little later with the silver tray. 'A message. Just delivered, Sir Thomas.'

He recognised the bold hand on the outside at once. Cecilia. With rising feeling he tore it open.

My very dearest Thomas,

In the wilds of Wiltshire we've only just heard you're in London for the Season. I know you're in such demand by your adoring public but do say you'll be able to see us! It would be such fun, for it's a shame you've so seldom the time between your battles to take your pleasures of the capital. We've just arrived, so please tell us when you're at leisure and we'll have dinner together, just as the old times!

In haste,
Your loving sister
Cecilia

What could be better calculated to raise the spirits! He dashed off a quick acceptance and sent it by messenger to the address enclosed, which he knew to be the Farndon townhouse in Mayfair. Within a short time a delighted reply was returned, offering a repast that very evening.

Chapter 39

'My darling brother!' Cecilia squealed, hugging Kydd and planting a kiss on his forehead. 'It's been ages!'

It had been only a month or two since their return from Copenhagen in *Tyger* but he knew what she meant. Various sea adventures had ensured that they had not had time together in the excitement of London since those brittle, febrile days before Trafalgar, but then she had not been married to his closest friend Nicholas Renzi, now the Earl of Farndon.

'Nicholas! So pleasing to see you, so well-found as it were.'

Kydd had no knowledge, neither did he wish to pry, of the clandestine activities at the highest level of state that had left his friend so affected by his recent experiences. But it warmed his heart to see him in fine fettle again.

'And yourself, old horse, the sea hero and cynosure of all eyes – are you not yet sated by their attentions?'

The meal was intimate and superbly presented, the dark-jowled butler Jago silently in the background, watchful and attentive.

Kydd recounted in humorous detail his deploying as a convenient victor by the Tory government; the friendships he'd made at high table as a result; his insights into politicking – but also the satisfactions of eminence; membership of Brooks's, first-name terms with ministers and industrialists, society invitations by the score.

'Oh, Thomas! I'm so glad for you,' Cecilia sighed, 'as it's only what you deserve. The prime minister! Whoever would have thought it?'

Renzi reserved his observations for when the cloth was drawn and the trio left alone by the servants.

'Dear brother, I do exult in your advance in the public eye. Kydd of the *Tyger* should know no less.'

'It's all a flim-flam, really, Nicholas. But I own it's a very agreeable fate.'

'Your pardon, dear fellow, but do I detect a certain satisfaction, not to say complacency?'

Kydd gave a wry smile. His friend had always been able to see through him. 'True enough, as I'm finding it a mort effortful to see myself back to the worriments of weekly accounts and powder standings.'

Renzi regarded him soberly. 'As you must, brother. Yet I give you that you've reached a fork in your highway of life.'

'What do you mean, Nicholas?'

'You'll know that your present situation you owe to your recent triumphs at sea. You may well understand that this tide of adulation will, in time, ebb. Therefore you have before you a quandary, a dilemma. Do you return to sea, out of the sight of your present admirers and at the risk of descent into anonymity – or cultivate these same to the end that you achieve a different eminence in what answers to society ashore?'

'I . . . I can't make reply, Nicholas. To leave the sea is unbearable, but I've a future to consider. Should I now give ear to the politicals . . .'

'Quite. I would wish I could bear good counsel, but it's not within my being to dictate your time to come. It is for you alone to decide.'

'He stays with the sea, won't you, Thomas?' Cecilia was in no doubt of his calling.

'Cec, it's not so easy.' He avoided her eye, fiddling with a walnut. 'You see, I find this high life a fine thing for a man, and, well, I, er—'

'There's a woman at the bottom of it. Aren't I in the right of it, Thomas?' she broke in shrewdly.

'No!' Kydd blurted. Then he conceded, 'There may have been, but not now. Excepting there could be, should I chance upon the right sort.'

'I knew it!' Cecilia laughed delightedly. 'A lady in siege of your affections. You'll tell us about her and we'll give you our opinion,' she added.

'Damn it, Cec, it's not like that!'

She looked at him curiously. 'So – complications. Interesting. Should you share it with us we may be of service to you in the article of decisions, my dear.'

Kydd reddened. 'It's private. And finished. I don't want to talk any more of it.'

'You may—' Renzi began, but was cut off by Cecilia who'd sensed something.

'No, Nicholas. Leave him be, my love.'

In the quiet Kydd stared into the fire, trying to quell his thoughts. A clock ticked loudly into the stillness and then, without warning, there came a welling of emotion.

'Thomas?'

'It's as you said, sis. A woman.' He gulped. 'The most beautiful I've ever known. And so accomplished and clever – I never thought . . .' He tailed off, eyes bright and unseeing.

'She spurned you?' Cecilia asked softly, her hand on his knee.

'I didn't realise . . .'

'My poor dear brother. To be—'

'She's promised to another. But I . . . I think she likes me.'

'Oh? How can you know this?'

'She . . . she looked at me.'

Renzi blinked. 'Dear fellow, if—'

'Do be quiet, Nicholas. I know perfectly well what he's saying. This is a serious matter. Thomas, you will tell me how the lady stands in the matter of obligations, understandings, if you will.'

'She's not of a high family but has attracted an – an admirer, elder son of a viscount, whom she's accepted and is freely seen in public with.'

'No betrothal notice in the newspapers?'

'Not yet, but she intends to wed.'

'Then why are you so cast down? There's still time to win her, Thomas! Go out and—'

'It's Persephone Lockwood.'

Cecilia stiffened. 'P-Persephone Lockwood? The same as you . . .?'

'Aye, sis.'

She shot to her feet, staring at him for a long space, then paced quickly about the room. 'This is entirely different. You've hurt her the once and you're contemplating the same again.'

'No, I'm not, Cec. I said as I'm to let her go, forget her.'

'That's not the point,' she said cuttingly. 'She's engaged

169

your affections and now you're in a tizz, wanting us to give blessing on your advances.'

'No! I'll not see her again, this I vow.'

'If we're going to help you in your suit, we need to hear from you on this one question. Thomas, how is it that you've fallen for her anew? How can this be a different affair from what passed that time? Do think hard on it before you tell us.'

Strangely, it was easy to answer. 'I was young then, a sailor who knew nothing of ladies. She was a wonderful, high and noble creature and I . . . I thought I could not suit her in station and prospects and . . . and she'd tire of me. All those manners and civility, it would be a hard beat to windward for me, Cec. And then at breakfast all that severe politeness and so on, grievous hard to bear day by day. I didn't think I could be a good husband for her and ended with . . . with one I knew would not tax me so.'

'And now you've grown up and can perceive her qualities.'

Kydd bridled. 'I've seen more than a slice of the world since then, yes.'

'Well, we must accept that you're sincere in your admiration.'

'I never said—'

'Do you love her?'

Kydd rocked back, shaken at the sudden challenge. It was a painful thing to face. 'Yes,' he finally whispered. 'I do. God help me, but I do.'

'Bless you, dear Thomas,' Cecilia said softly, brushing away a tear. 'You've told us now, so we must see what can be done.'

'I don't—'

'Dear brother. Allow that I know you rather more than I

should admit. You're a fearless warrior of the sea, and if you've been laid low by a woman, she must have touched your heart in a very extraordinary way or you wouldn't be in this state. You love her, Thomas, and that's that.'

'Cec, I . . .' He was staring at the fire.

'So you'll never be happy again without you have her at your side.'

He looked up, his face empty of expression. 'That's as it may, but it cannot be.'

'Cannot be? Of course it—'

'She's made her choice and it would be very wrong of me – morally wrong – to come between them, to interfere, Cec. This is why—'

'Tosh and nonsense, Thomas! Have you declared your feelings to her, to let her know you're a prospect? I'd wager you haven't!'

'Leave the man alone, Cecilia,' Renzi protested. 'He's taken aboard a cartload and—'

'No, I will not! Men are such sillies when it comes to affairs of the heart. How will she know Thomas is available to her else?'

Kydd gave a small smile. 'Cec, this is not to be considered, believe me. Not only did I turn my back on her those years past but not a month ago I met her in Portugal of all places.'

'Really? And how is this?'

'Well, in short, sis, she must hold against me what was past for she was as cold as a fish fresh-caught. And then, well, an unlucky thing happened. As the French made their descent on Lisbon I promised her a passage out in *Tyger*. I was sent away to seaward and couldn't do it, and the squadron admiral must have forgotten my telling him of her and she was left.'

'You mean . . . to the French?' Cecilia whispered, appalled.

'Just so. But she was a game 'un – she made her way overland to Oporto. Can you conceive of it? A well-born lady, riding donkeys and such out in that wild country and never a complaint to me.'

'Then you saw her again?'

'Only a brace of weeks ago. And . . .' He took a deep breath and explained what had happened, how his feelings had changed. 'She's her own life to lead now, Cec. I can't—'

'Listen to me, Thomas. Do you desire her hand or not?'

'I do with all my heart. But—'

Cecilia went on, 'She's had a lot to get over, true, but she's of an age to look to her future, to be safely wed to the best prospect in sight. And she's done well – very well. A noble-man's son who stands to inherit. And you were nowhere in sight – until now.' She bit her lip in concentration then pronounced, 'What we have to do is remedy this. Place you at an eminence above this Pountney.'

'He's of noble blood, Cec. How—'

'A woman desires spirit and ambition, not to say character and intelligence, always above mere station,' she said, with a warm glance at Renzi, who had the grace to blush. 'To put you at a clear distance above your rival, that she may perceive you as the superior.'

'You mean hobnobbing with the prime minister, that sort of thing?'

'Not at all. Anyone can top it the political, but it's more success in society that counts. Who you're seen with, your friends and acquaintances. Thomas, you're in the same clubs and at the same racecourses and so forth as your Pountney. What is needed is for you to be seen by her at a prominence that he himself can't possibly aspire to.'

'Cec, what can you mean?'

'You must make yourself friends with the Prince of Wales.'

It nearly took his breath away. 'Prinny? You don't know what you're asking – he chooses his friends and they're all—'

'He's to be found at all the highest affairs of consequence, and if you're seen there with him she'll know what circle of society is yours.'

'Ha! And just how do I go about it? Will you introduce me?'

'Farndon and I are not privy to that company,' Cecilia said primly, 'else we should.'

'Then . . . ?'

'It crosses my mind that there is another who would relish your friendship, your feats of arms at sea being so applauded.'

'Who?'

'His brother, the Duke of Clarence. Who you'll recollect was in the navy before the war and never ceases to remind people of it. He's very close to Prinny, I'm told, and if you were to make his acquaintance I'm certain you'll be seeing the Prince of Wales before very long.'

With a growing hope Kydd realised it was not impossible. In the fleet William was still talked of – a strict and insensitive captain with service in the American war, whose nautical talents were tacitly admitted to be slim. At the outbreak of war he'd been hurriedly promoted away from sea and had gone to live with his mistress in the country.

If he could get alongside the man navy-fashion and chew over old times . . . Yes, it could work.

'A fine notion,' he allowed. 'You've a headpiece to be proud of, sis!'

Chapter 40

Fookes was on form, returning from the games room with a smug expression. 'As our Jeremy has been fleeced by a master,' he crowed. 'Faro. There's only one way to play it – to win!'

Kydd waited patiently for the passing stream of congratulations to ebb and laid down his paper. 'Prinker, old chap. Do you think I've done my duty well enough? Tell me true.'

'You have, dear fellow. Be assured the powers-that-be are well pleased with you. If this is to say you're pining for the briny deep, I see no reason why you shouldn't return to your wooden world when you wish it.'

'Ah. First there's a matter I want to discuss with you, my friend. Advice and that kind of thing.'

'Rattle on, old bean. I'm in a good mood tonight.'

Kydd glanced around but they were safely alone together in their leather armchairs by the fire. 'It's a mort embarrassing to talk about it, but you've been so obliging to me before and—'

'She's refused you.'

'I – I beg your pardon?'

'Nothing plainer, Kydd, my friend. Why else would a sturdy sea captain tog up like a fopling save he wants to impress some object of his affections? What else would have you miss the grand meet at the Downs? And Rolly's little evening with the ladies? Has to be, although why any lass would turn down the prize I see before me for a mere viscount's son is past my ken.'

Kydd gave a small grin. There was no hiding anything from this man. 'It's not as if she refused me, Prinker.'

'Miss Lockwood? You're not going to tell me you've not yet paid your ardent addresses to the wench? You're leaving it a trifle late, I fear.'

'There's . . . complications, Prinker.'

'Aren't there always? Tell away, my friend.'

'We have a past that's turned her away from me. I can't even be noticed while she's with Pountney, and I have to do something to catch her eye.'

'What have you in mind, old horse?' Fookes effortlessly took a pinch of snuff.

'I want to be seen in Prinny's set.'

Fookes raised an eyebrow. 'Not as if this might be commanded, my friend.'

'I have a plan.'

After Kydd had explained, Fookes leaned back in admiration. 'A splendid lay, if I might be permitted to remark. If I can be of small service, do say.'

'Thank you, Prinker.'

'You've not met our sailor prince?'

'No, before my time in service.'

'A few words. He's long left the navy, but you'd never know it. Likes to shock the ladies with salty yarns, that sort

175

of thing. A mite coarse, he's never going to be an ornament to society but he idolises his brother. Some think him slow-witted but he's not to be scorned. You'll find him bluff and direct but well-meaning, a decent kind of cove – I think you'll get on. He's lived with his dolly, Mrs Jordan, for fifteen years or more and there are quantities of FitzClarences. His official residence is at St James's Palace, but they live out at Bushy Park, and do know she's not to be received in society.'

Fookes reflected further. 'To get you noticed won't be so hard a thing – there's a levee you'll want to attend at which you will be introduced as Kydd of the *Tyger* and you can engage with him how you will. Your object is to charm the fellow into appearing at an intimate soirée you happen to be giving, the details of which you may leave to me. Will that do?'

Chapter 41

E ven in his full dress uniform and sword, his splendid
sash and star, Kydd felt outdone by the trappings of
court and retinue. In the glitter and circumstance of the
Throne Room gentlemen of the household were in the blazing
gold and scarlet of ancient medieval costume, and, in age-old
measured cadence, chivalric honours were rendered to the
highest punctilio.

It was near overwhelming but he held himself with a noble
bearing, for was he not a knight of the realm and present
by right?

In the respectful hush, he waited for an equerry to prepare
him. Standing below the canopied throne with its richly
embroidered footstool he could make out the receiving party:
two sons of King George III, Prince Augustus, Duke of
Sussex, and Prince William, Duke of Clarence. They were
closely attended by courtiers.

The princes were in polite conversation with those introduced; others yet to be honoured waited elegantly in expec-
tation.

The equerry came up to him, murmuring politely as he was conveyed to the royal group.

After a small exchange with the Duke of Sussex, Kydd was introduced to Prince William.

'Your Royal Highness, might I be permitted to present Sir Thomas Kydd of His Britannic Majesty's Royal Navy?'

Kydd swept down in a graceful bow and his eyes rose to meet those of a genial, thick-set man in court dress, wearing an old-fashioned naval sword, instantly recognisable as the Duke of Clarence from Fookes's previous divulging of his nickname – Coconut.

'Why, Sir Thomas, and it's a damn fine thing to see you here!' he exclaimed, with obvious sincerity. 'Your victories are spoken of in the warmest terms throughout the land and I give you all homage for your laurels.'

'Thank you, Your Royal Highness. As it was my ship's company that made it possible.'

'Just so, just so, Captain. It was always my practice to give firm guidance to my seamen that they'll know their duty when facing the enemy.'

'My recent service in the Caribbean allows me say that your own service in the American war there is still remembered, and in fact there are one or two articles of discipline in your order books that I have taken the liberty of including in my own *Tyger* orders.'

'Really? Aha! Then I can say I've played some part in your triumphs, sir!'

'Indeed,' Kydd said, with an acknowledging bow.

'I've not been so active in naval service lately, but do understand, Sir Thomas, as a fellow sailor I've a ready sense of what you faced. Would that I could hear the full yarn some day!' he added regretfully.

It was the perfect opportunity.

'I hardly dare say it, but I'm having an evening at Brooks's for friends who wish that very thing. It may be a roysterous occasion but, if you feel inclined to do me the honour of attending, you'll be right welcome, sir.'

''Pon my soul, and I think I will!'

Chapter 42

Kydd's powerful baritone rang out over the convivial hubbub in the snug clubroom, drawing admiring glances from those who hadn't thought it possible that a celebrated warrior could find it in him to dare a sea song before such company.

He was pleased with himself: this was an old ballad learned for the occasion that would have been sung in wardrooms of the middle-aged Duke of Clarence's day. He was rewarded by the sight of the man, red-faced and beating time with his glass, wine slopping down his satin waistcoat and following him in a hoarse voice, entirely out of tune.

'*While our salt water walls, so begird us about,*
And our cruisers, and bruisers, keep good looking out,
What force need old England to fear can offend her
From France, or from Spain, or a Popish Pretender?
So, Huzzah! to King George, boys; long, long may he reign,
By the right of old England, long lord of the main!'

He sat down to much applause, not least of which was from Fookes, whose look of surprise and delight was gratifying to see. The bishop was chortling and the barrister, Erskine, was trying his best to encourage his napkin to dance a hornpipe on the table.

It could only be accounted a great success. He'd modestly told his sea tale and the many toasts resulting had done much to bring about the hearty and comradely mood he was after, and now, with a perilous upset of tablecloth and dishes, Prince William lurched to his feet.

'M' lords an' gennelmen. All of you! I give you Sir T-Thomas K-Kydd, who's done s' much for his country an' flag. We raise our glasses in honour t' you, sir!'

There was no holding back the full-throated response, and it brought a flush of pride, tinged with guilt that the entire occasion had been planned with a purpose.

The duke sat down abruptly and leaned across the table. 'W-wine with you, sir!'

They clinked glasses, and in a happy fuddle out came the words that Kydd had been waiting for.

'You're a jolly d-dog, Kydd. Haven't enjoyed m'self s' much for a donkey's age. You know, I'm going to ask you along to meet m' eldest brother. He's not navy, but he's a military cove and likes a right dimber sort as can raise a wind. You'll come?'

Chapter 43

'As I'd never have smoked it,' Fookes said, in awe, as the carriage ground over the cobblestones. 'A braw sea officer with a singing voice!'

'Not so strange, Prinker. Should you venture on the fo'c'sle of a dog-watch you'd hear some fine enough voices, the men in spirit.'

'Ha! But not from the throat of any sailor who stalks the halls of Brooks's. Never happened afore!' He chuckled, then assumed a serious expression. 'It would be amiss of me not to give fair warning of what you're contemplating.

'Prinny is surrounded by flatterers and leeches and you may believe that you'll be closely scrutinised. If you're in with the Duke of Clarence it will help mightily, but be prepared to be yourself. The fellow may be a prodigious spendthrift and coxcomb but he warms to the natural man and always stands by his friends. And call him always by his title. Only by small children and handsome ladies does he suffer to be called "Prinny".

'You'll need staying power – they're a hard-drinking lot

and can put away a regiment's allowance in a night. If you can stay the course you'll be respected but, for God's sake, leave the gambling to those with the head for it – and the rhino. I don't know how much you've made in prize money but there's a fair chance you could lose the whole lot in a single night.

'And he's not one to fear. Far from it – he's a gladsome host and is charming and generous, but if you try his patience and get on the wrong side of him he's like to be merciless.'

'Thank you, Prinker. I'll steer a tight course, be sure of it.'

Their destination was Carlton House, which Kydd knew was the town residence of the Prince of Wales and a scandal of extravagance, a mansion three times the cost of a fitted-out first-rate ship-of-the-line. For all that, it had to be reckoned that it had a diplomatic role in the receiving by the king's heir of the most eminent state visitors.

Their carriage drew up at the long, porticoed front of the mansion.

As they moved into the foyer there was an impression of limitless splendour, and in the anteroom, velvet and satin, gold damask and antique paintings in vast frames.

'I leave you now, stout son of Neptune,' Fookes murmured. 'Good fortune attend you, m' friend.'

'Prinker – aren't you staying?' Kydd asked, in not a little apprehension.

'Not I – you're the guest of another. Adieu!'

Kydd had not long to wait: word had been passed and Prince William hurried out. 'So good to see you, Tiger. Do step inboard, shipmate!'

With relief he saw that the prince was in fashionable evening dress rather than uniform – by now he wore his own rarely, on ceremonial occasions only, and was dressed similarly.

'Your Royal Highness. Kind in you.'

'He's a mort engaged,' Clarence huffed, as they made their way quickly through several rooms, each in an entirely different décor and theme. 'Having a right famous tussle with Barry – that's not the Hellgate Barrymore, his brother Newgate. Um, that is Augustus, o' course,' he prattled.

Fisticuffs? In his own house?

'Five-card loo – and they're both in deep. You're a wagering man, Tiger?'

'Not as one should say,' Kydd replied cautiously.

'Stout fellow! Seen too many ruined as will tempt me to the dice.'

They emerged into a tall, circular room set about with gaming tables, around which groups of players sat or hovered. The focus of attention was on a large table in the centre, brilliantly lit by a low chandelier above it. Eight sat, with more than a dozen standing behind in attitudes of drunken eagerness, watching the card-play.

There was no mistaking the Prince of Wales. Portly and florid, the First Gentleman of Europe leaned intently over the table as the cards were dealt. He was coat-less and wore a dazzling blue satin waistcoat embroidered with silver and gold motifs.

Talk lessened as the cards were picked up. There was a deathly hush as each of the players consulted their hand.

Opposite the prince sat a thin, long-faced man with an absurd amount of personal adornment, his expression cynical and controlled, presumably 'Newgate' Barrymore.

'Well?' demanded the Prince of Wales, loudly.

The others remained silent, watchful, as the object of his

demand continued coolly to appraise his cards. The untidy pool of counters before the dealer was sizeable and he was clearly in no hurry to call.

'Play.'

A sigh from the spectators went up.

'Seven hundred guineas on the table, Highness,' whispered one to Kydd's host who, in concern, drew closer, standing behind his brother.

With little interest in card games Kydd remained where he was, but he was conscious of the animal tension and animosity. He was here as he wanted, about to be introduced to the heir to the throne, but the scene was alien, not of his reality.

'Pass.'

Two more threw in their hands as the rounds went by. Another three, until only the prince and Barrymore were left.

The five cards were dealt to each and the Prince of Wales shielded his hand before peering at it blearily.

'Head the trick!' whispered the Duke of Clarence, hoarsely.

He was ignored and the pile of counters grew.

Then it was time.

The Prince of Wales, with a snort of satisfaction, slapped down the ace of spades.

With a calculated pause, Barrymore's eyes flicked over the table. Then, with his gaze fixed on the prince's card, he placed another firmly over it and leaned back, expressionless.

The knave of clubs. The highest card possible in Lanterloo.

'Trumped by Pam!' blurted the Prince of Wales, in disgust. 'Dear God.' He groaned. 'I've been looed all night. Take your beastly gains, Newgate, and choke on 'em.' He slumped in his chair and looked up at his brother. 'Oh, hello, Clarence.

Didn't see you there. I'm famished. Care for a morsel of pie?'

'I would. Sir, I'd wish to present Sir Thomas Kydd, captain of the *Tyger*.'

'Oh? Pleased t' see you,' he responded wearily, a flicked glance and wave of the hand the only sign he'd been noticed.

'Of Curaçao, and as lately fought three frigates to a stand off Prussia.'

'I see.' A fat hand tried to stifle a yawn. 'I need food. Are the kitchens still good for a bite of supper, do you think?'

There was a respectful scattering of the onlookers as he lurched to his feet and stretched extravagantly. 'Come on, then. Bring y' friend, if you like.'

In a much smaller and darkly furnished room a large mahogany sideboard was spread with an extravagant array of cold dishes: a raised giblet pie, plovers' eggs in aspic, potted beef, a Marasquino jelly, fruit tarts, a mayonnaise of lobster, cheeses, baskets of pastries, custards and more.

The Duke of Clarence beckoned Kydd to follow him to the Prince of Wales's table, one of three set with gold cutlery and French porcelain.

'What did you say his name was?' the Prince of Wales mumbled, through his food.

'We call him Tiger, on account of—'

'Evening, Tiger. This is McMahon, my man o' business.' A quick nod and shrewd glance came from a sardonic individual next to him. 'Stafford, Tavistock, Smyth.' He continued around the table in a bored voice, evoking cautious responses from each. 'Light along that lobster, won't someone?'

The Duke of Clarence tried again. 'Wales, this is Kydd of the *Tyger*,' he said earnestly. 'You must have read about him in the *Gazette*, surely.'

'Oh, did I? You must have seen a bit o' service then, Tiger.' He reached for another plover's egg, discreetly offered by a hovering footman on a silver platter. 'Tell me about it.'

It was quite plain that it was the last thing he desired and a dull burn began building in Kydd but, given the stakes of the evening, he began, 'Your Royal Highness. Service, yes – leagues beyond counting of the great salt sea but nary a mermaid sighted.'

It brought a flash of curiosity, the watery grey eyes briefly swivelling his way.

'Naval service, he means Tiger,' the Duke of Clarence urged.

'Why, yes, I've had my share,' Kydd said. The Nile, Trafalgar – there were few with his record of hard fighting. 'And I most remember . . .'

There was barely a flicker of interest. This night there was perhaps a minute or two to establish himself as a character or be cast aside from this circle.

'. . . I most remember my adventures as a young lieutenant. When I and a midshipman signalled to the fleet – using naught but a lady's bodice, a yellow shirt and a frilly shawl. I do allow it proved of some utility in the taking of Minorca in the last war.'

'What's this?' demanded the Prince of Wales, bemused.

Kydd recounted the tale with much warm personal detail and was rewarded by a bark of appreciation and a look of dawning interest. 'But, then, naval service does bring strange entertainment at times, is not this the case, sir?'

The Duke of Clarence, gratified to be included, chuckled fruitily. 'Yes, indeed, Tiger. As midshipman I always took my rats grilled, never roasted. What was your—'

He was ignored. 'Tell on, then, Tiger,' Kydd was ordered.

'Ah. There's the time before Trafalgar in the Med when my particular friend, now the Earl of Farndon, took away ship's boats over the land of Ancient Greece to the other side, to dish the French in their vile plot by dressing up in motley as Russians. Most put out of countenance, the villains.'

This time the table paid agreeable attention. It was no more than yarns he would bring out in the wardroom at sea but it was clear that in this gathering they were pleasingly novel and diverting.

A deprecating and light-hearted account of the siege of Acre followed, his visit to the harem of the Pasha Djezzar, whom they called the Butcher, and the victorious conclusion that saw Napoleon Bonaparte beaten for the first time on land, and that by English seamen, a fact patently new to them.

The supper was finished and the cloth drawn but none showed inclination to leave.

Port and Madeira were brought and the Duke of Clarence announced to all, 'My good friend Tiger is a man o' shining parts. Should we ply him well with grog he'll tip us a song. None of your pawky shoreside ditties but a good round sea song!'

'Can he, b' God? Then I believe your sailor friend should sing for his supper, don't you?'

There was acclamation from the others and a smug superiority on Prince William's face as he sat back.

Kydd was appalled. In these august surroundings, a mansion of state and before the future King of England? 'Do excuse me, Your Royal Highness. I really cannot, speaking for so long and—'

'Sing! Sing!' The Prince of Wales thumped the table, others one by one joining heartily in the loud chant. 'Sing! Sing! Sing!'

Kydd got to his feet, mind racing, not helped by the liberal quaffing that had been urged on him. The safe, stern calls to duty of the public sea ballads would not do here and the more full-blooded rousing seamen's refrains were far too raunchy.

So . . .

> '*Come all ye jolly sailors bold*
> *Whose hearts are cast in honour's mould;*
> *While English glory I unfold*
> *Huzza for the* Arethusa!
> *She is a frigate tight and brave*
> *As ever stemm'd the dashing wave . . .*'

He launched into the driving strains of the old fore-bitter with real feeling, for in a flood of unreality he'd caught a glimpse of himself as a young seaman listening to it for the first time, open-mouthed and moved by its simple, loyal sentiments. How then could he ever have foreseen this moment, here, in this company, the callow wig-maker of Guildford . . .

It pricked his eye and, perhaps noticing, the room fell silent as he brought it to a finish.

'Bravo, bravo!' The thunderous applause broke over him and he sat down, abashed.

'More! More!'

A brandy glass obscenely full was pushed into his hands and he took a gulp, the spreading fire steadying him.

The Duke of Clarence stood up, swaying, and began in a tuneless bellow a lewd foremast favourite. He was howled down but Kydd blinked back his surprise. Well, if this was what they wanted . . .

Head swimming, he took it up, and after the first few stanzas the entire table joined in the refrain in a riot of noise and good fellowship.

The evening had to end: he was beginning to totter. He sat down suddenly.

Through fuddled ears he heard the Prince of Wales utter generous words of thanks and turn to demand a snifter before retiring.

'Is this wise do you think, Your Royal Highness?' McMahon said tightly. 'We're off to Yarmouth tomorrow to see in the North Sea Squadron. The royal yacht, sir?'

'Ha! You're forgetting, Chinks! I've Viking blood in m' royal ancestry. I never get sea-sick!'

'As I understand, sir, but—'

'Besides, I'm taking m' sea-dog friend here, sees I steer a straight course. Ain't that so, Tiger?'

Chapter 44

Fookes and Kydd stared in disbelief as they descended from the coach. The last third of the encircling stone pier at Margate was tumbled in ruin. No vessel could approach for peril of the litter of stones over which the sea swashed carelessly.

The royal yacht would therefore not be coming alongside. Kydd looked out to where she lay at her moorings. Not much bigger than his old *Teazer*, she was, however, ship-rigged, three-masted, but looking oddly shorn as she crossed no yards above her topsails. This was not the King's new *Royal Sovereign* but another, *Royal Charlotte*, built for a previous King George. She had high and stately stern-windows, an astonishing abundance of gilt and filigree and, with a considerable freeboard, her lines were antique and spoke of a far less austere age.

The mayor in his chain of office approached with outstretched hand. 'Gentlemen.'

It was a fine occasion for Margate, and the stands that had been erected outside the Droits Office were already crowded.

'The pier?' asked Kydd.

'Storm earlier in the year. Temporary inconvenience only.'

He lies, thought Kydd, cynically. The loss of safe harbour for the London coal trade must be a continuing catastrophe for the little town. But it didn't seem to dampen the enthusiasm of the local folk, who were gathering loyally to greet the Prince of Wales with bunting and ribbons fluttering gaily. A military band stood by, waiting patiently, veiling an army of flunkeys and baggage assembled behind.

Kydd was led to one side to await the arrival of the prince.

The band suddenly burst into life: the entourage had been sighted turning into the end of the street and they energetically thumped and fifed to rising cheers from the spectators.

Open-topped, the first carriage carried the Prince of Wales in full view, graciously acknowledging the crowd. The splendid vehicle came to a halt and he descended, assisted by a military officer in elaborate frogging. The prince was in a grotesque parody of an admiral's uniform, all deep blue and scarlet, encrusted with orders and decorations. On his head was an enormous black bicorne, which he doffed amiably to the wildly cheering crowd.

He looked around, the signal for the yacht party to come together. Kydd knew better than to have worn uniform and, in plain but well-cut dress, joined them.

'What? Not in your blues, Tiger?' the prince cried.

'As I would not want to be noticed, Your Royal Highness,' he answered, with an elegant bow.

'You're too modest, m' friend. Let's get aboard, then.' With a gracious sweeping bow to the throng, he turned and made his way towards the pier.

It was, as Kydd had feared, not possible to bring the yacht

alongside and allow the usual decorous boarding up a brow. A ceremonial barge under oars lay off.

The lieutenant brought it in hesitantly until the bowman could jump to the makeshift planked low jetty.

McMahon, the prince's aide, pushed past Kydd and, with a superior smile, made to enter the boat to be the one to hand down the prince. Like a raw midshipman, he committed the cardinal sin of first standing on the gunwale before stepping in, causing the boat to roll alarmingly. With a cry he ended on the bottom boards in a tangle of legs and sword.

The prince drew back in dismay.

Kydd moved forward. With a beaming smile, he confided, 'He does not bow to the custom of the sea, Your Royal Highness. I will convey it to you directly, sir. In every ship and boat when it is built, for good fortune a golden coin is placed at its keel. We do well to acknowledge this and place our trust in it, stepping directly from the land into its keeping.'

In one easy movement he swung a foot from the little jetty directly on to the centreline of the craft above its keel, which, of course, remained perfectly still, then brought the other foot in to it.

'You see, sir?' He held up his arms as to a child.

The prince hesitated, then awkwardly did the same, declaring, 'There, Chinks! You see? This is how to do it.'

Kydd didn't want any courtiers following to spoil his moment and snapped, 'Bear off forrard, out oars!'

The lieutenant looked at him accusingly, but Kydd took no notice.

'Give way larboard, hold water starboard . . . give way together,' he rapped, and the boat made its way through the small craft towards the royal yacht.

'Lot to learn in a sea life,' the Prince of Wales acknowledged, lifting his hat to his public lining the shore and waving furiously. 'But I do believe that it's in me to make quite a fair sailor, should I have the time, don't you think?'

The yacht had rigged an elaborate bosun's chair and the prince was hoisted ceremoniously aboard, pipes twittering, a formal party waiting for him on the quarterdeck.

Kydd came in over the bulwark as he had done so many times in *Teazer* and joined them.

'Ah, Tiger, this is our captain, Mr Sankey. Sir, this is Sir Thomas Kydd, whom you must know of.'

Sankey was an elderly, careful gentleman, with an oddly soft voice. 'Of course, Your Royal Highness. Do be welcome in *Charlotte*, sir. We are doubly honoured.'

'A fine vessel to command, sir,' Kydd offered. This brought no reply but the sadness around the seamed eyes told everything. To be standing before a much younger and famous frigate captain of public renown – there was an unimaginably wide gulf between them and the ships they commanded.

Kydd tried to find something more to say and looked around approvingly. The decks were blindingly scoured, the whips and halliards not merely brought to a point but a royal blue ribbon was threaded through each end. The standing lines from aloft were faultlessly tarred, black and lustrous, and the sails ready bent to the yards were each furled, with the bunt taken neatly over the yard in a pleasing pig's ear, the gaskets ornately plaited.

But the paint on the bulwarks was thick – up to a quarter-inch of layering, over half a century of industrious primping by idle sailors, and he doubted whether the top-masts had once been sent down. The gear was well-maintained, though, and he had no doubt about the seaworthiness of the grand old yacht.

'And finely kept, sir!' he managed. Sankey gave an inclination of his head – both knew what was passing between them.

The entourage crowded aboard, careful to leave the prince to his conversations, and Kydd became aware that the ship's company, bizarrely outfitted in harlequin costume and silently padding along the decks about their business, had eyes only on himself. His reputation must now have spread to every ship in the fleet – he'd never have trouble manning a frigate again.

But he was contemplating retiring on his laurels at the top his fame. The gentle heave of the deck and the familiar fragrance of Stockholm tar and oiled canvas brought a poignant stab.

'Well, Sankey, and we're ready for the off, are we?'

'Er, we are, Your Royal Highness. Wind's brisk and fair from the west, but . . .' The old captain fidgeted nervously.

'Well, are we?'

'*Piper* and *Weazel* have not shown, sir,' he replied, in embarrassment

'Whatever does he mean?' the prince said in irritation, turning to Kydd.

'I rather think he refers to our escort, sir. Is this right, Captain?'

'It is. Two sloops o' war. We cannot proceed without we have navy escort, Your Royal Highness.'

'Where are the damned ships, then? I want to be back in time for Cheltenham, sir! Send for them at once.'

'Um, that's not so easy done, sir. They must have improper orders and could be waiting for us upriver at Deptford or lying in the Downs. They'll tumble to it soon and then they'll be with us. I counsel we lie at anchor a day or two more—'

'Damned impertinence! Didn't you hear what I said? I need to be back prompt and quick. See to it, sir! I'm going below.'

'Yes, Your Royal Highness.'

Kydd waited until he was out of sight, then went to the elderly captain. 'Not as if you can do anything, I believe, sir.'

The man flashed him a look of wry gratitude. 'A hard thing,' he replied quietly. 'The escort carries the Trinity pilot and always leads the way, ours only to follow. If I'm obliged to proceed alone it'll be without proper charts and so forth, and that I'm not ready to risk.'

Kydd nodded in sympathy. 'At least we're mainly to the east'd of the Thames swatchways. Only have to make Black Deep to avoid Margate Sands, and then it's the East Swin north to the Naze and clear sailing.'

Sankey bristled. 'Are you putting yourself forward as a pilot, Sir Thomas?'

'No, but lately with the North Sea Squadron and earlier the Nore, these are not strange waters for me.' There was no need to point out that the last was as a master's mate caught up in the great Nore mutiny.

It was plain that Sankey was locked in indecision: he was right to advise patience, for as soon as the escort arrived they could be on their way; to send boats in different directions to seek out the errant sloops would be seen as doing something but at the cost of delaying in wait for the other to return.

Kydd was glad the decision was not his.

The Prince of Wales stumped out on deck and demanded they sail at once.

Stiff-faced, Sankey sent the hands to unmoor while Kydd stood back politely.

It was intriguing: every order was carried out in perfect silence by men in soft-soled shoes and without direction. No petty officer roaring and swearing, the boatswain hailing the tops in a voice of thunder or the first lieutenant bellowing at the fo'c'slemen. These men, older than the usual and no doubt grateful for their soft berths, were nonetheless agile and quick to obey.

A cast to starboard and *Charlotte* paid off handily as sail tumbled down and was braced around to meet the lively breeze. Before long she was bowling along with the wind astern on her way to round the North East Spit of the Margate Sands, and with lines precisely belayed, sea watches were set and the age-old routines of the outward-bounder were in motion.

For Kydd it was curious to be a passenger, to have no purpose in the progress of a ship. He resisted the urge to cross to the wheel where the quartermaster had the conn, as Sankey stood by him, his face rigid and resentful.

Soon the distinctive hills and nestling town faded to a blue-grey and then only an empty horizon was left.

'Er, a cracking fine pace,' muttered Fookes, hanging on grimly to a line from aloft.

'Tolerable,' Kydd replied. A frigate with topgallants and royals abroad would by now be leaving this old lady well astern.

He sniffed the wind. This westerly was fair for Yarmouth and gaining strength. The passage would be a pleasant and, in some ways, piquant experience.

'When will we get there, do y' think?' Fookes held his hat tightly under his arm and the streaming wind blew his hair horizontally. 'It's a touch too frisky for me out here, Tiger.'

He was able to assure the landlubber that it was some

hours only to cross the wide estuary, then sail north to intercept the line of latitude the North Sea Squadron would be using to run down their westing to Yarmouth Roads.

Unconvinced, Fookes decided to get below out of the 'gale', others of the entourage doing likewise. Kydd remained on deck, unwilling to leave the fine sight of the brimming seascape. Unexpectedly he was joined by Sankey, who stood next to him, irresolute. 'A fair wind for Yarmouth,' Kydd said encouragingly.

'As it may be, but I'm going to clear the Kentish Knock before shaping in for the Swin,' he said truculently, as though expecting Kydd to contradict him.

'The safer course.'

It would mean standing out to sea for considerably longer to clear the last of the banks and shoals at the mouth of the great river instead of threading through them but, as he hadn't the comfort of a pilot, Kydd could understand.

'And on the ebb . . .' At this state of tide there was less water over the ever-shifting shoals.

'Quite.' He stood for a few more minutes, then stumped back to the wheel.

For a little while longer Kydd took his fill of bracing salt-laced air before reluctantly going below.

Chapter 45

'Clean done, sir,' Kydd, now back on deck enthused to Sankey. 'Dead reckoning and you raise the Naze in one!'

The masthead lookout had confirmed sighting the unmistakable Naze Tower, and the old captain eased visibly. 'I'm sanguine we're now clear o' the Gunfleet and are in with the King's Channel. I believe I'll keep abreast the land to round the Ness, then all plain sail to Yarmouth Roads.'

Kydd said nothing. They were now where they should have been if they'd gone direct but he felt for the man: without the reassurance of hallowed routine and having the heir to England's throne on board, he'd achieved a workmanlike transit safely to this place.

'Odd. Nothing much about, is there?' he wondered aloud. This was the main sea highway from the north to London and there should have been a steady stream of Newcastle colliers and other vessels on their way to feed the insatiable maw of the capital. But as far as he could see there was only one or two sail in sight in both directions.

Then he realised this would be the case if they'd arrived

soon after the passing of a coastal convoy or the passage of a naval vessel of size attracting an informal gaggle of sail.

Sankey gave the order and, bracing around, the ship took up to a quartering breeze north-eastward. The sailors had little to do but stand back and allow the yacht to make Yarmouth on one board. For the passengers it was disagreeable to be on deck as the increasing westerly was slapping driven waves into her beam and, despite the high freeboard, an occasional dash of spray soaked the unwary.

'*Deck hooooo!* I mislike the two sail t' weather!'

Sankey whirled on his midshipman messenger. 'Get aloft and send that man down to explain himself! This instant, sir!'

An irritated Sankey told Kydd, 'In a royal yacht sightings are never bawled out promiscuous from the masthead, at peril of incurring His Royal Highness's annoyance. My orders specifically state that—'

But before he could finish Kydd had sprung into the lower shrouds and demanded the officer-of-the-watch's telescope.

It was passed up and, bracing it against the thick rope, Kydd trained it inshore. At first he couldn't make out anything but two pale blurs, but when he adjusted the focus they leaped into view. Not two but three – and what he saw chilled him: a large schooner and a pair of smaller luggers, three-masted.

He knew the breed and they weren't English. Without question these were enemy: French or Dutch, waiting to snap up any lone merchantman on the east coast without the wit to sail in company.

He'd heard of the trick from Brice, who'd served in these waters. The desolate marshy lowland about the Colne estuary a dozen miles to the south was out of sight of the shipping lanes and protected from curious eyes by miles of marshland. It made an ideal skulking place for privateers as they could not be seen from seaward of the Gunfleet Sands where any naval patrols would be confined as they kept watch and ward in the King's Channel.

Kydd dropped to the deck and, avoiding curious eyes, went to Sankey. 'A word, if I may.'

'What is it, Sir Thomas?' the man said, frowning in impatience.

'You should know, sir, you have a brace or more of enemy privateers off to weather. Should they take it in their heads to put us to the chase, I'm not sanguine we can survive.'

'Nonsense,' Sankey said peevishly, his face suddenly pale. 'They wouldn't dare!'

Kydd knew to them this was an old-fashioned ship without company, and on the prowl they'd be fools to pass up the prospect of an easy kill.

A vision rose up of the worst of outcomes: triumphant privateersmen swarming over the bulwarks and discovering they'd taken in prize the King of England's heir. What would Bonaparte not give them in reward?

And *Royal Charlotte* would end her days a tyrant's trophy to put on display to all nations the hollowness of Britannia's claim to rule the seas.

'Hands to the braces!' Sankey blurted.

'May I be told your course of action, sir?' Kydd asked carefully. He had no right to demand an answer, having only as much authority aboard as any other passenger.

'I'd be obliged to you, Sir Thomas, to leave me to my own quarterdeck.' Sankey turned his back and the conversation was over.

Squinting against the far-off shore Kydd could see the three now with the naked eye. They were maintaining their course parallel with the coast and showed no sign of altering their heading.

Sankey glanced down to the binnacle and ordered, 'Helm down, steer nor' nor' west.'

Kydd grimaced. The fool was going to cut ahead of the threat and make for Harwich and the small naval presence there. 'Sir. I desire you hear me,' he said quietly, plucking the man's sleeve.

'What can you mean, sir? I am captain of this vessel and I will brook no interference with my actions from any man!'

'You are heading for Harwich.' Kydd dropped his voice. 'Sir. I will put it plainly. I'm as well acquainted with war as you are with princes and I tell you now, sir, that those privateers are quite able to overwhelm us. And—'

'We're armed with ten six-pounders!'

'They will work together. I've seen them. They're fore 'n' aft rigged and will come in from ahead or astern and grapple while you're just thinking about reloading. They've twice as many fighters as we and there's no hope for it, sir!'

'Harwich is less'n two hours' sail!'

'To windward! Through them – which we can never hope to do.'

'They'll hear our guns and—'

'When they first see us alter for Harwich they'll gratefully wait for us to fall into their hands. We'll be taken well before they wake up in Harwich.' Kydd glanced shoreward. 'They've seen us. Brailing up – they're waiting for us, as I said.'

Sankey hesitated. 'I will not have my command overborne, Sir Thomas.' The words were dull and had the ring of desperation.

'Neither should you, sir. I wish only to act as pilot – a war pilot, if you will.'

Sankey came to a decision. 'Very well. Your advice?'

'Put over your helm, and with as much sail as you can put abroad, stretch out to seaward.'

'But—'

'It will buy us time at the very least and while we're well to suth'ard of the North Sea Squadron line of latitude it's not impossible we'll come up with an outlying frigate.'

There was a heavy silence. Kydd added, 'And I'd think it very necessary to keep the knowledge of what is afoot from the prince and his retainers – whatever the ending of this affair, if it becomes public that you've hazarded England's next king then I believe you would gladly welcome the Tower as a refuge.'

Sankey gulped. 'That is well observed, sir. The seamen may never speak out of station and my officers will be told to keep their counsel. But when His Royal Highness sees us laying the land astern . . .'

'Let us worry of things as they come. Do you put up your helm, sir.'

The old yacht paid off before the wind and, in the hard streaming airs from abaft, wallowed around to seaward. The following seas lifted her stern and began launching her forward in an exuberant rhythm, her spread courses full and bellying.

Almost immediately the privateers shook out sail and fell in for the chase.

The change in motion brought the Prince of Wales up on deck in consternation, his hair blowing in all directions.

'What's afoot, sir? We're going in a different direction. Why is this? I demand to know! Tiger, what's happening?'

'Oh, it's the wind, sir. Save your gracious presence, the winds are not to be commanded by mere mortals and I fear we must make a leg out to sea to give us room to round Orford Ness. Over there, sir.' He pointed into the wind's eye.

'Humph. Well, it's damn uncomfortable at a table with the cards sliding all ahoo. I'll be glad when we're in from this horrid gale.' He sniffed the hardening breeze and left abruptly.

'Stuns'ls – I must have stuns'ls,' Sankey muttered. Conferring with the boatswain revealed that there were precious few aboard who'd ever seen one rigged and these were quickly formed into a party to set them as they could.

Kydd concentrated on their pursuers. The big schooner was spilling wind to keep with the luggers but there was now no doubt – they were the quarry and all could be lost and damned by one unseamanlike mistake. So much hung on so unfit a ship and crew.

The two lieutenants were unsure in the tension and Kydd took to standing next to them, prompting quietly.

One stunsail caught and was sheeted in but the yard was out of balance until the other could be set. It took longer as the impromptu party struggled with the canvas – and this was only the pair at the main course. There would have to be another pair at the topsails, then the whole repeated on the fore.

Now some miles astern the privateers were steering arrow-straight for them, end-on an impossible target even if they mounted chase guns. They obviously planned to overhaul and take *Charlotte* on both sides.

In the open sea the big driving sails of a square-rigger could normally be relied on to lay any for-and-after well back into their wake, but for comfort's sake the old yacht was bald-headed: she did not spread topgallants or royals above her topsails. Robbed of this advantage, it could be only a matter of time before they were caught and taken.

The prospect brought a cold knot to Kydd's stomach.

'Damme, what's going on now, Tiger?' The Prince of Wales had been disturbed by the characteristic wallow brought on by the stunsails at the extremity of the yards. He looked about at the welter of seas – the ship was passing through the Roughs, choppy seas thrown up by uneven sandwaves not twenty feet below their keel.

Kydd could see real disquiet in his glance: they were out of sight of land, where the elements reigned unchecked, no doubt a fearful experience for him. If ever he learned what the true situation was . . .

'What are those fellows doing?' he cried, pointing to the privateers. 'They're going after us!'

'Why, sir, and so they should,' Kydd said, then allowed a look of embarrassment to come over him. 'I do confess you've caught us out, Your Royal Highness.'

'Tiger, explain yourself, sir!'

'Your Royal Highness. Sir, the big one is the, er, *Saucy Sue*. She's with, um, *Cock o' the Morning* and *Jack the Lad* and we're in a wager. First to lay Yarmouth Light abeam, and I've a hundred guineas on us to win!'

'Have you, b' God! How are we doing?' All traces of apprehension disappeared, replaced by an avid interest.

'Sir, as you may see, we're well ahead but those knaves have been pulling up on us and we now spread all sail to check 'em. Looks like a close race to me!'

'Ha! Come on the *Charlotte*!' The prince chortled, 'Show us some breeding, now!'

Despite the blustering wind and occasional dashes of spray,

he stayed with Kydd, watching the drama of the distant craft slowly but surely pulling them in and frowning at the incomprehensible acrobatics of the men in their rigging.

'Captain Sankey!' he called importantly.

'Your Royal Highness?'

'A guinea a man should we cross the line first.'

'Sir.' He shot a glance of helplessness at Kydd before bowing in acknowledgement.

'Let me know if there's any change in the field, Tiger.' The Prince of Wales then went below, wet but satisfied.

Chapter 46

At length, with barely a mile separating *Charlotte* and her pursuers, Kydd called Sankey aside. 'I fear we must now decide, sir,' he said, in a low voice.

'How so, sir?'

'In fine, do we fight or yield? The time is nearly upon us.'

'We fight, in course!'

'At risk of the life of the Prince of Wales? Without we have confidence in a smart finish to the enemy this is not to be contemplated. You have six-pounders only, I believe.'

'In number, ten.'

In these seas gun-play was chancy indeed – it would imply a close-quarters engagement, which was the very thing they had to avoid.

'Let me see them.'

They were on the main-deck below; five a side. With a sinking heart Kydd noted the spotless black finish – and the blocked touch-holes. And these were of another age, no pierced cascabel to take the breeching rope against recoil and, worse, not fitted for gun-locks, needing an old port-fire smouldering match to fire them.

'Powder, shot?'

'Should be plenty – we've never used any.'

The report came back: plenty of powder, but this was low-grade scaling powder used in salutes. As to shot, unhappily these were rusted into their lockers and were being chiselled free as they spoke.

'Captain Sankey. I gravely fear there is nothing to be done. We may stand on for an hour or so in the hope that we meet with the squadron but then to avoid unnecessary bloodshed we must lay down our arms, sir.'

'How can I? *How can I?*' the man ground out. 'To be known in history as the captain who yielded up the person of—'

'I understand you,' Kydd said sharply. 'Then we have a mere hour to reflect on the consequences.'

He turned on his heel and looked back down their wake at the chase. There was now a vanishingly small chance of getting away. In fact their only advantage was . . .

It could work – it must work!

He paced back to Sankey. 'Sir. I have a plan.'

Sankey's haggard face lit up. 'You have, Sir Thomas? If there's anything . . .'

'Pray close up all hands for some pretty seamanship, sir, and if I might take the conn?'

Much depended on the cupidity of the unknown corsair leader, who would not want to damage his future prize with overmuch cannonading – and the fact that Kydd knew just how a privateer went about making a kill.

He stood by the wheel, nodding to the quartermaster. 'Two men at the wheel, and when I order, you act instantly.'

It was all in the timing and there was not going to be a

second chance. Crisply he issued the rest of his orders, then calmly stood, arms folded, waiting for the right moment. At least the prince was below at his cards safely out of the way.

Long minutes followed. Yard by yard the two luggers, sails board-taut, inexorably closed the gap, now only a few hundred yards off. Still not yet time . . . closer, closer – and then came what he was waiting for. They separated slightly with the obvious intent of laying them aboard one on each side. Perfect!

From the bow of one, then the other, a gun cracked out – the universal demand to heave to.

Kydd gave his orders.

In a frantic bucketing the yacht came around, a wild rolling as the men at the braces furiously kept pace with their dizzying turn. Astern the two luggers were thrown into confusion as they tried to make sense of what was happening.

Charlotte's bowsprit tracked their turn until he had the nearer lugger precisely ahead as if meaning to skewer it with the big spar.

'Ease her – well!' Kydd snapped.

Sankey gripped a downhaul and stared at Kydd in horror.

They plunged nearer and nearer but, in her crew's puzzlement, the lugger had left it too late. In a chorus of screams, shouting and a terrible splintering, the high sides of the royal yacht lumbered down on the slightly built vessel, smashing and disintegrating, snatching and dousing the sails, leaving the wreckage to pass in a deafening screaking down their side.

'Hard over – I'm taking the other!'

The second lugger, mesmerised by events, had put about but *Charlotte* already had good way on and remorselessly caught the unfortunate craft on her quarter – with the same result.

'Tiger! *What are you doing?* Why is . . .?' The Prince of Wales, standing at the companionway, was near beside himself with pop-eyed shock.

Kydd hadn't the time to attend to him, but mercifully the schooner began wheeling away, clearly stunned by the sudden turn of events. A gun fired from it, then another two but in the melee the balls were lost somewhere overhead.

There would be no more trouble from it as there were survivors to pick up.

'Tiger! Tell me, *pleeeease!*' implored the prince.

Kydd took a deep breath, then said lightly, 'Your Royal Highness, I thought you were below. Well, those two rascals contrived to take our wind when staying about, a clear breach of the rules of racing as you'll admit. They didn't give way to us and paid the price. They're naturally going to appeal to the clerk of the course – that was signified by all the firing – but there's no question that the ruling will go our way.'

'Well, and I stand flummoxed!' the prince gasped in relief. 'I had no idea – you sailors play a deep game, no quarter given. I can only give you joy at your purse of guineas, sir!'

Chapter 47

'You didn't have to come, Prinker.' Kydd chuckled. It was singular to observe the arch-metropolitan Fookes strolling about the gaudy tents and trappings of a country fair.

'I wouldn't miss it for worlds, dear fellow.' He looked down in exasperation at the mud that disfigured his faultlessly polished Hessian boots and sighed. 'Besides, this be a place of distinction and fashion today, as should not be scorned.'

It was costing them both twenty guineas to be there, the annual ox-fair at Richmond Park – a royal estate turned over to the charitable hosting of a public fair, funded by the subscriptions of the great and good on parade for all to see.

Two king's deer would be roasted but that was not what had brought the two men to Richmond. It had been Fookes's idea to bring about the one thing that Kydd ardently desired: revenge upon the person of the Honourable Charles Pountney.

Kydd was arrayed in impeccable morning dress with an ebony cane swinging carelessly, his gleamingly buffed beaver-skin hat with its wicked curve and just a peep of lace at his cuffs. Men made way for him and he caught more than a few flashes of admiration from their ladies.

As if in common consent the swirling crowd began to draw in from the far parts of the field to the grand marquee, for this was the high point of the day – the prize-giving for gurning and the greasy-pole climbing – and where those of the ordinary sort could come and freely ogle the high-born, and they in turn display their position and wealth.

People were coalescing in a broad semicircle, in front a discreet gathering of those of rank, who would be meeting the host of honour.

He manoeuvred carefully. As he'd known he would, Pountney had made sure of his attendance and took his place in the line as high as he'd dared – and there beside him was Persephone, a wrenching vision of beauty and cool-ness. Clarinda stood to one side. Kydd eased his way to the front of the crowd just behind the pair, watching the play of polite intercourse between them, quite oblivious of his presence.

A sudden ripple of excitement swept over the crowd and eyes craned to see. A carriage drawn by four matched greys drew up, its coat of arms clear and bold.

With much ceremony the Prince of Wales descended, giving a civil bow to the awed gathering and moving to the head of the line to begin his duties as royal host.

With a murmured greeting here, polite remarks on a lady's attire there, he progressed down the line – Kydd sensed the tension in Pountney's rigid pose as the prince neared. He was counting on being recognised in the crowd and acknowl-edged in front of Pountney, but now he was not so sure. It was taking a long time, the greetings attentive and considerate – there was every chance that he'd be overlooked in the masses and if that were the case he'd better slink away before they caught sight of him.

The prince reached the couple before them and gravely intoned words of welcome – Pountney tensed for his great moment and . . .

'Be damned to it! Tiger, for God's sake! What are you doing there?' The Prince of Wales, ignoring Pountney completely, left the line and beckoned Kydd to join him. 'You'll stay for the ox-roast, old friend, won't you? And I can promise you a confection after as will tempt the angels!' He beamed. 'But before that, shall we not lift a brimmer to King Neptune? Wouldn't be right for you to forget your true fealty, only as you're standing on land!' Suddenly recollecting himself he turned back to the line, bowing in general to them. 'Later, later,' he rumbled apologetically. 'At the prizes, perhaps.'

They walked off together and Kydd felt only a fierce exultation – even if he would give anything to look back, just once.

With a wicked expression on her face, Clarinda sipped her ratafia. 'You're really taken by him, aren't you?'

Persephone glanced around before she answered, but Charles was still away somewhere, pursuing the Marquess of Granby. 'Nonsense, Clarinda dear,' she said, with a toss of her head, 'Nothing could be further from my mind. The man is odious and faithless. I'd rather be shackled hand and foot than have to pay my addresses to such a one.'

'He's every inch a man, you must give him that.'

'As it may be. I didn't look.'

'Prinny thinks him a friend. Did you see how they went off together?'

'I can hardly think that a recommendation, my dear.'

Clarinda toyed with her glass. 'A sea captain. How romantic – I heard tell how he's sailed to the South Seas and North Pole both, each time bringing back a sackful of Spanish treasure. And a hero, a sir, and—'

'I don't want to hear any more about that man from you or anyone!'

'I'm sorry you feel so, Persephone. You're so alike, really. Handsome, strong-willed, a touch of the dashing – not to be compared to your boring Charles, my dear.'

'Clarinda. Let me speak directly. There is nothing on this earth would move me to risk losing my chance at a good marriage. All this talk is nonsense and has no purpose. We are to be wed shortly and that's that. Must I make it plainer?'

Chapter 48

Covent Garden Theatre was aglow with light and noise. In the pit rowdy elements were at work and, adding to the din, women with oranges and sweetmeats walked the aisles crying their wares. The orchestra increased the bedlam as they tuned up. Above it all, the warning bell sounded for patrons to take their places and Persephone hastened to find theirs.

It had not been possible to obtain good seats. The theatre had quickly sold out as this promised to be a high point of the season – the legendary Sarah Siddons as Volumnia in Shakespeare's *Coriolanus* in a classical production by Kemble. Persephone didn't care where they sat: the infrequent outings of the famed actress meant that if Persephone was going to see her, now had to be the time.

The gallery was boisterous, full of chattering people of all classes. Next to her Charles sniffed audibly in disdain. He was no theatre-goer and she knew he was humouring her but she was determined to enjoy the great tragedy. Above the uproar the orchestra began playing, which served to moderate the pandemonium, and after twenty minutes or so, the audience was settling down.

The music ceased and an expectant hush spread, all eyes on the stage.

From between the curtains an actor in Elizabethan costume stepped out and, flourishing a mock vellum, declared a ringing verse prologue into the void. Unexpectedly he stopped mid-stanza and, in slow-motion, executed an elaborate bow to his left, which he held motionless.

The audience as one turned in excitement to the royal box and saw King George himself and his queen entering it. They scrambled to their feet in respect and he stood for a moment to acknowledge the ringing cheers from all, the good-hearted and loyal shouts. The old King was popular with his people and it was known he was partial to good theatre.

The actor took up his lines and the performance resumed.

Persephone knew the play. *Coriolanus* was a bloody tale set in Rome after the Tarquins – the Volscian conquerors, the hapless women, the eponymous hero's expulsion from the city of his birth and now his march against it, the strident demands and piteous entreaties of the fallen women. It was powerful and engrossing, precisely what she needed to take her mind off the destabilising events of recent days.

Beside her, Charles fidgeted. Persephone sighed. He was no romantic but, under her gentle guidance, he too would come to adore these jewels of the human experience.

'What's that fellow up to, at all?' he whispered, plucking her sleeve.

'Sssh! He's saying rule by the people is letting crows peck at eagles and . . . Never mind, I'll tell you later,' she ended abruptly, her eyes never leaving the stage.

Sarah Siddons was throwing herself into her role as the mother of Coriolanus, in heartrending drama pleading with him to spare Rome from destruction while—

'Good God! Did you see . . .?'

'Do be quiet, Charles,' she said in a fierce whisper. 'This is important!'

'*It is!* There – up in the royal box. I'd never have reckoned on it – he's in with the King and the princes!'

'What are you talking about?' she said crossly, but glanced away from the stage for a moment.

'Your ridiculous sailor friend, up there lording it over we groundlings, the wretch!'

Persephone looked up in disbelief – and there, in the second row behind the King, and quite at his ease between the Duke of Clarence and the Prince of Wales, was none other than Sir Thomas Kydd.

Chapter 49

The maid had been sent to bed, and in the stillness of the night, Persephone unlocked the secret drawer in her bureau and drew out her precious journal. Setting the single candle with pen and ink on the writing surface she sat down slowly, trying to collect her thoughts.

Her feelings about Charles were unchanged. He was gentle, considerate, in every way an admirable prospect, and she knew she was fortunate to have him as suitor. She was not actually besotted with him but, then, she was no longer a child and was old enough to know that this didn't happen in the real world. In fact, if she thought about it, nearly every one of her friends had ended in arranged marriages and many had later sought solace with lovers. She was fortunate enough to be able to make choice of her husband and Charles was handsome, kind and would, before long, be titled.

It had all seemed so straightforward.

She was nearing thirty. She had to recognise that it was well past time she was married, and she had no desire to be left an old maid. She had her man – and she must love him a little, or why had she missed him so terribly when she was escaping in Portugal?

And then out of nowhere this apparition from her past. Thomas Kydd. To stir her just as he had then – what did it mean?

She remembered his shy, uncultured and endearing directness, but now he was an entirely different man. Bold, fearless and well-spoken, at the forefront of fashion, he was quite unaffected by his fame and honours. That he was now moving in royal circles meant far less to her than it did to Charles – it was what it said about the man himself that made her pause. Kydd had risen entirely by his own efforts through society to its pinnacle. Without connections or patronage, he'd reached up for what he wanted and succeeded.

The realisation rocked her. She'd greatly underestimated his character, misread him completely – and didn't know him any more.

What must he think of her now? But, then, that didn't matter, did it?

Stealing over her, like a warm zephyr in a rose-garden, came another realisation. The time at the Royal Academy, when he'd bumped into them in those ridiculous dandified trappings: it had been so out of keeping with who she knew he was that he must have dressed so for a reason. And the only one that fitted was that he wanted to impress a lady . . . Herself.

Which meant, of course, that he still had feelings for her sufficient to goad him to such lengths.

She thought about the times they had met, seeking signs or hints of his true feeling. Lisbon didn't count: they had both been defensive. At the print shop she had been deliberately cold, and at the Kensington Lodge *fête* he had been awkward and affected. By her?

And then the embarrassment at the gallery.

It couldn't be coincidence – his glances at her had always lingered . . . The man was taken with her.

Other thoughts crowded in. This was madness. As a soon-to-be-bride, she had no right to be thinking such things. Her duty was to Charles, and if she was to be married it would be with a whole heart – that she owed him.

Yet . . .

She picked up her pen and after a long moment began writing.

Today came into my life a terrible shadow. I cannot sleep for what it means to me, my future. Pity me in my doubting, for today I have discovered that my heart is split in twain, by two who lay claim to me and I know not how to act! Am I to be wed to the wrong man and allow the other to slip from me for ever? Or . . .

A sudden bleakness invaded.

There was one thing she'd overlooked that made the whole affair nothing much more than a cruel mockery. Kydd might once have been attracted to her but the man was moving on quickly to a higher destiny. He'd shown no interest in her at the ox-fair before he was whisked away by the Prince of Wales, not even glanced back, and there, high up in the royal box, she hadn't seen him once look her way.

It was clear he'd tired of her and now, with the pick of London society at his feet, he would find another.

Her eyes pricked. What in Heaven's name was she going to do now?

Chapter 50

K ydd accepted his whisky from Tysoe, and bade him retire. He wanted to be alone with his thoughts.

It was such irony that Prinny had asked him to the theatre that evening to be in company with the King, who'd been very obliging in his remarks towards his eldest son's distinguished guest. The invitation had come out of the blue: he had not planned and plotted for it beforehand.

And she had been there, with Pountney, among the common folk. He had seen her immediately but felt embarrassment at the great social distance between them and had given no sign that he had noticed her.

It was, of course, a complete and crushing victory over Pountney, who could never hope to move in such circles, let alone claim royal friendships. It was over, and he had triumphed. But had he really?

He had won – and lost. He had tried everything to catch her eye and, apart from civil words at the Royal Academy, bestowed in some sort of pity, she had ignored him.

He had faithfully carried through all that Cecilia had suggested but it hadn't answered.

Should he now resign himself to seeing Persephone married off, get over the clamping despair and move on with life? If he could come up with nothing else to put himself forward, then for the sake of sanity and self-respect, wasn't that what he should be doing?

In the morning he was no further ahead. And in the cold light of day there was nothing but to admit that he was in love with the wrong woman. It would take time, an unthinkable gulf of desolation, but he would get over her – he had to.

Listlessly he prepared for the day.

No appointments, no invitations.

Should he look up Bazely, make his peace with that bluff and honest mariner, rejoin the human race, find solace in roystering?

In a black depression he heard Tysoe answer the door to the morning post. A single letter. Would this offer deliverance from his devils?

His spirits fell. It was from St James's Palace, the Prince of Wales again. The last thing he wanted was to face the wearing round of gluttony and self-indulgence, endure the constant swirl of sycophants and rivals about the royal presence.

Kydd picked it up and slit the seal.

It was not from the prince – it was from an aide, a hurried scrawl, begging that Sir Thomas would grant a particular favour at this short notice. Captain Sankey of the royal yacht was regrettably indisposed, at the very time he was needed to take the *Royal Charlotte* to pick up the prince in Harwich after His Royal Highness had made visit to the army in Colchester.

The prince was known to trust only the captain but, in view of his friendship with Kydd, would Kydd consider standing in for this one short voyage? Escorts could in this case be relied upon and, as token of respect and thanks, it would be quite in order to bring along a small party of guests.

Reply by return would much oblige.

Kydd did not need to think about it. Of course he would. An east-coast chop would go far in dispelling his dark mood and he rather looked forward to the trip.

He sent off a quick reply, promising to be at Deptford stairs at the appointed time, then remembered the offer to bring guests.

Who? Did Prinker have any he'd like to favour?

Then an idea swelled and blossomed, impossible to check. For the very first time, it was in his power to have Persephone before him, obliged to be civil, constrained to make converse with the captain, to answer him . . . to be near him.

Within the hour he took delivery of some special stationery and began to write.

'See this gets there at once!' he snapped at a waiting messenger.

But after it had gone the ferment of excitement ebbed.

Without a doubt Pountney would jump at the chance of being in close company with the Prince of Wales and would take Persephone to witness his glory – but then Kydd asked himself, was it wise for him to see her, so close, and in company with her intended?

It was too late now – in a way it would be a farewell to a part of his life that, for as long as he lived, he'd never be able to forget.

Chapter 51

'B e damned to it, and I've an invitation to the royal yacht – look at this!' Pountney flourished the expensively textured card.

In the chocolate house, patrons looked around in polite astonishment. He turned and smiled an apology but continued to hold the card with its coat-of-arms casually in plain view.

Persephone took it. 'Oh, it says, "The Honourable Charles Pountney and party". Am I then invited, do you think?' Her spirits rose. It would be an agreeable diversion: bracing sea breezes always exhilarated her.

'I would imagine so. In any event you shall be coming. I demand it by right of my future intended.'

She smiled dutifully and read on. 'It doesn't say where we're going, and—'

Then she noticed something: the signature below was apparently that of no other than . . . Acting Captain Sir Thomas Kydd.

It was impossible.

'Ah. Charles, I – I rather think not this time,' she said

faintly. 'Out on the water . . . truly, I can't. You go, please.'

'Persephone, you will do your duty and accompany me. To be seen, accompanied by my future bride, with His Royal Highness is a social coup not to be denied me.'

'Oh, please understand. I really don't wish to—'

'You will come, and that's that.' He added pompously, 'And, mark my words, the sea air will do you good, my dear. You've been out of spirits lately, I've noticed.'

It was only later that Persephone saw it as an opportunity in disguise. What better way to put behind her these foolish fancies than to see Kydd for what he really was – a simple sailor?

Chapter 52

Royal Charlotte was alive with activity, securing for sea, and the lieutenant greeted Charles and Persephone at the brow as Clarinda followed behind. 'Captain Kydd sends his compliments and begs to say he is occupied for the moment and will see you in a short while.'

Seamen were summoned to bring aboard their baggage and they were left standing together, gazing up at the maze of rigging, the men going out on the yard to throw off gaskets and still more ranging lines along the deck, all in silence and with no fuss.

'Um, where is the Prince of Wales, pray?'

'We sail directly to Harwich to convey him back to London, sir.'

'Humph. Well, we'll go below, keep out of your way. Come, Persephone.'

But she had made out Kydd, aft on the quarterdeck. He was standing legs a-brace, in sea uniform without stars and decorations, looking perfectly at home on the deck of a ship, the first time she had seen him so.

'Oh, I'll stay, Charles. This is so exciting, a ship putting to sea outward bound. I'm going to watch – will you?'

'I've no interest in the work of the common sailor, my dear. Don't be long,' he admonished her, and escorted Clarinda below.

Despite herself Persephone felt a guilty thrill as she looked aft, but then pulled herself up short. She was here to find reasons to dismiss the man from her thoughts, not admire him.

She had a notion of how a ship worked. The yacht was alongside the wharf and would need to be warped out mid-stream by boats before she could set her sails and proceed down-river to the sea. In the open Persephone would be out of the way until they made sail and then it would be unsafe to be on deck, with all its straining ropes and flogging blocks.

A blare of orders floated forward as the lieutenant sent men to their stations.

The brow was let go and lines on their bridle were sent up to the fo'c'sle. Three large boats lay off, waiting with the other end of the tow.

Sharp commands, then mooring ropes were cast off the bollards ashore to splash into the muddy river, then being hauled in hand over hand.

Persephone stole another look. Kydd had moved from his solitary place by the taffrail to the wheel where a group of men had collected. Every so often he would speak to the lieutenant who would snap orders or dispatch messengers at the run while he stood in lordly isolation.

Her eye caught a seaman snatching down the big ensign aft and, realising what it meant, looked behind her. Between the ship and the stone wharf a widening canyon of water was opening up: they were legally at sea.

More men leaped to the shrouds, mounting in swift, lithe

movements to the tops where they spread out along the yards ready to loose sail.

Surprisingly quickly they were a hundred yards or so out and a volley of orders carried forward. A bluff petty officer loomed up beside her. 'Not a good place t' be, miss. We's going to be workin' hard here soon. Why don't ye fall aft, out o' the way like?'

If she wanted to see the theatre of departing there was no other alternative. It had to be the quarterdeck. She edged her way along the side of the ship, avoiding sailors and trying to keep out of sight of the captain, whose eyes were following the activity aloft. She stopped right aft, no more than ten feet behind him.

'Let go 'n' loose!' Kydd ordered crisply.

Instantly sail blossomed at the yards. On deck men ran away with lines and a stamping of feet.

More orders volleyed, the boatswain urging seamen at their tasks.

As if by magic the yacht was now sliding through the water and making for the first bend in the Thames. The wind was coming from behind so they had a fair passage out, and for that she was thankful, if only for Kydd's sake.

There was no slackening in tension. This was the busiest sea highway in the world and it took the utmost concentration to avoid collision or, worse, a stranding for all the world to jeer at. She knew she was witnessing sea professionalism of the highest order.

Slowly the river widened and countryside replaced the ramshackle waterfront of the city. At each bend there was work at the braces to bring the yards around, all the time the stately progress of the yacht, assured and steady.

Without warning Kydd turned about as if to check their

wake and caught sight of her. Heart bumping, she remained still, unsure what to do.

He hesitated, then crossed to her, doffing his hat, his eyes unreadable. 'Miss Lockwood. An honour to have you aboard.'

Close to, in his well-worn naval uniform, the face looked hard, the authority in its lines formidable.

Nevertheless she returned his gaze defiantly. 'Our thanks for your invitation, Sir Thomas.'

He said nothing, his eyes not softening.

She faltered, the pleasantry on her lips unsaid.

After a long moment he spoke, his expression still set, severe, his words low and difficult to catch. 'We're opening Gravesend Reach. You'll remark Tilbury Fort to larboard.'

There'd been no change in his features, no amiable easing. Her heart sank. The man wanted nothing better than to be rid of her embarrassing presence.

Near them two seamen teased out lines from a block on the driver boom above them, then padded away. She glanced at the odd white edifice. 'Ah. So we're above twenty miles from London Bridge then, sir.'

There was no reply and she obstinately faced away, as if observing the passing scenery, now so flat and uninteresting.

A cry came from the group about the wheel and Kydd straightened, as if in relief. 'Do excuse me, Miss Lockwood. I find I'm required.'

She watched him go. The determined stride, the men's obvious respect . . . Her eyes stung. It was not working out as she had hoped – the man was every inch a sea king, not in the least a homely sailor.

And clearly he was not interested in her.

But she wouldn't leave – she couldn't, for she was determined to see it through.

A grubby collier ahead slewed carelessly into their path. Kydd went to the side and bellowed at the craft in salty language. This was the real man, not the affable fop in a London club.

He did not look back at her.

The Thames widened still further, the prospect of drear grey flatness of mud and marsh reaching deep into her soul. Then it was the Yantlet at the seaward extent of the river, Sheerness and Sheppey to the right, a dull mud-grey expanse of sea opening up ahead.

They hove to in a slight chop for their escort to form up, two sloops with the Trinity pilot on board.

The first and then the other fell into line ahead, leading the way into the maze of swatchways she had known as a little girl when her father had been serving at Sheerness dockyard. The waves grew as they reached the open sea, and with it the lift and heave of the deck she had always thought of as the eagerness of a ship to be away from the cloying land.

Stubbornly she stayed, knowing in her heart she'd never see Kydd again – she couldn't.

Charles emerged hesitantly from the companionway. He paused, looking about suspiciously, then saw her at the taff-rail. 'Ah. Persephone, my dear. Have you had your fill of the jolly sights of the sea?'

'Never my fill, Charles,' she whispered.

'What was that? Anyway, what are you doing here? It's much more exciting at the front, the waves coming at you and such. Let's go and watch – come on!'

He motioned her eagerly forward, and she went with him, as she knew she must. Passing seamen at their tasks, they

230

moved by the men at the wheel and then Kydd. The watch-on-deck, coiling down lines, looked at them curiously as they headed for the big spearing bowsprit.

Kydd watched them, his heart of stone. It was all over. He'd had his chance, the one he'd prayed for, to have her before him – alone – to say anything he desired to her, and he'd ruined it, struck dumb, like a gawky schoolboy, by her breathless beauty and grace. And later, remembering her presence too late after he had saltily seen off the collier, too embarrassed to look back.

She'd been distant, awkward, but what could be expected from a woman whose husband-to-be was with her in the yacht?

It had been a stupid mistake, inviting her. He'd only been reminded of what he would never have. Depression returned, darker than before.

The sooner he could escape the hurt the better. He was tempted to signal 'More sail' to the escorts but thought better of it: some sort of blow was on its way.

Shaping around into Black Deep to where the North Sea beckoned, the surge was now longer and steeper and the old *Charlotte* took them more on the weather bow with a twist and heave. He glanced down at the compass, then up to the sloop next ahead.

'Steer small, blast your eyes!' he growled to the man at the wheel. The quartermaster looked up in surprise but duly passed on the admonishment to the hapless man.

Chapter 53

'Damn it – can't he keep the boat in a straight line?' Pountney grumbled, wiping his streaming face clear of spray. He clung to a rope for the deck was slippery and wet but he continued obstinately to look out ahead.

Persephone had ducked below the line of bulwarks and escaped the worst but knew better than to give advice. Their exciting rush over the waves had now turned into a spirited smash through them, and for those with unproven sea legs, it was a trial.

'I'm going below,' he snapped at length. 'Come on.'

She didn't argue and followed him to the hatchway. He stopped at the dark opening, staring down, his hands working on the handrails.

'No, I'm not,' he said thickly, and backed out.

Hesitating, he looked around wildly. 'Feel sick.' He gulped and staggered up the deck to the ship's side – to weather.

'Charles, no – the other side,' she urged quickly, trying to get him to go to leeward.

'Leave me alone,' he snarled, shaking her off. 'Can't you see I'm s-sick?'

He painfully made it to the higher side and retched help-lessly.

In an instant the brisk winds did their work and he was smeared in vomit. With an expiring groan he flopped to the deck, slithering down it to fetch up in the lee scuppers where he lay quietly moaning.

She'd seen what was coming and avoided it but now she went to him. 'Charles, dear. I'm so sorry for you. Some people are more affected by seasickness than others. There's no shame in it.'

He groaned weakly.

'Is there anything I can do for you?'

He said something that she didn't catch in the swash of sea and leaned closer to hear. 'What was that, dear?'

'B-bugger off, you b-bitch!'

In a storm of feeling she got to her feet, rage roaring through her.

Instinctively she hauled herself aft – towards the quarter-deck . . . to Kydd.

He saw her coming and went to her, a look of the utmost concern transforming his face. 'Miss Lockwood, you're not . . . That is to say, are you seasick at all?'

Through a wild roaring in her ears, she heard herself blurt, 'No, not at all! Never – I'm enjoying it!'

Kydd took in her shining eyes, her tense body limned by the wind . . . and melted. A shy smile appeared, widened. 'It's a rare thing, wonderful – always touches my soul and . . .'

He tailed off and she leaned closer to hear. Immediately he snapped rigid, the unreadable hardness clamping back. For a fleeting moment she had glimpsed the man she'd fallen for those years before – and her heart wrung with grief for what might have been.

And there was nothing more she could do.

She should leave, now. Yet . . .

Stubbornly she faced away into the wind so he couldn't see her face. She stood there, erect and proud. Kydd did not leave, and stood equally silent.

From forward came the muffled tone of the ship's bell – *ting-ting, ting-ting*.

The helmsman's relief arrived and there were quiet words of hand-over, the lieutenant taking report from the watch-on-deck. She heard it all. To her ears there was a nameless feeling of security about a ship at sea: the timeless routines and disciplines, the calm certainty that always, in every hour of day and night, there were those who had watch over them and whose bounden duty was to be guardian angels over their little world. Each trustfully answering to the one above them – until at the very summit there stood alone one who looked down on all their being: the captain. Instinctively she turned to Kydd.

As if released from a spell he asked, 'Miss Lockwood. Would you care to see about the ship?'

The words were stiff and formal but she didn't hesitate. 'That's so kind in you, Sir Thomas. But would it not take you from your duties?' She spoke as lightly as she could.

'L'tenant – you have the ship,' rapped Kydd and, with an awkward bow to her, gestured forward.

They left the blank-faced sailors and walked down the moving deck. She stumbled, and suddenly found she had taken his arm in quite the most natural way in the world.

But the touch was of fire, which turned her arm to a rigid claw.

234

Kydd was saying something about the weather rigging, the dead-eye lanyards, but in the wind she couldn't hear: a team of bulls would not have been enough to persuade her to lean closer.

They reached the forward hatchway. Pountney was still in the lee scuppers, now joined by others, but at this moment nothing on earth would have taken her from the side of Thomas Kydd.

Below was the seamen's mess-deck, neat and spotless. Along the ship's side she saw the sailors' ditty-bags of belongings sway in unison, the mess-tables, with a wooden kid below, and, interspersed between them, the gleaming black of guns.

'It's where the seamen live. This is their quarters,' Kydd said. She noticed that he'd taken off his cocked hat and tucked it under his arm. 'It's private, really, and I shouldn't be here.' He flashed her an apologetic smile.

Three off-watch sailors at a table watched them warily but made no move to acknowledge their presence. It was a close community, as she had always known it to be but had never seen. Her father had not allowed her to venture to this part of ship but here she could sense that the seamen would develop close bonds of friendship and trust, loyalty and pride.

In a sudden rush of guilt she recalled that Kydd had told her those years ago that he himself was from their number, a pressed man, in fact, who had come to love the sea. He must know intimately of this world within a world, a state of society that could never come alive and endure on the uncaring land.

What sort of man could have risen from this and achieved what he had, to take to himself honours and distinction, fame and glory, yet stay modest and true?

Returning on deck, they reached the open space overtopped by the ship's boats. Then it was down a small ladder – she accepted his hand – and facing forward was the galley. The cook looked up in surprise from his coppers. His mates stood defensively about him. 'Carry on, please,' Kydd said, his hat again under his arm. He took her to the all-purpose oven, a surprisingly large iron-grey construction with attachments and spits in dizzying confusion. 'Do tell Miss Lockwood how we cope at sea in the article of cooking,' he asked the cook, who creased in pleasure as he demonstrated each one.

They emerged on deck, her heart full.

After passing the boatswain and his mates at work re-reeving a line, and a respectful noticing of their captain, they descended down the after companionway to quite another world.

First, the wardroom, stained mahogany and brass on all sides, a polished commensal wine cask at the deckhead, the whole lined by cabin doors. She barely heard Kydd's description of wardroom life, the comfort of a free-swaying cot in a blow, the close brotherhood that even a captain had no right to enter.

And under the poop-deck, the spreading magnificence of the chief cabin, the Prince of Wales's dining room. All ebony, silver and a small fortune in ornaments and paintings.

It was breathtaking, formidable – but so alien to the sturdy plainness of the sea world she had just seen.

Kydd guided her past the table to the stern-windows. Light streamed in with a sparkle and splash of gaiety but she saw only the ship's wake, stretching away to the horizon in a straight line that disappeared into the hazy distance. A lump in her throat caught her unawares as she realised this could be a metaphor for her life, a featureless progression from the distant past without deviating into an endless future where—

Suddenly she felt herself swung about to face Kydd. He was trying to say something, but it came out hoarsely, broken.

His hands gripped her. It hurt – she couldn't resist but he was choking in an effort to speak. Then, in what seemed like slow-motion, he drew her to him and kissed her, savagely, hopelessly. Shocked, she tensed but then responded, eagerly seeking his lips, a tide of passion seizing her in a flood of need.

They drew apart. He still held her, his eyes wild and staring – then he brutally pulled away, his hands falling from her arms in release.

'I – I'm sorry. S-so terribly sorry, Miss Lockwood. I really don't know . . . It was unforgivable of me. I . . . I . . .'

She swayed.

One thing hammered at her: it had been wrong, terribly wrong. What she had done was unfair to both men and could never be forgiven. Even if she . . .

With a sob she ran from the cabin.

Chapter 54

Kydd stood stiff and upright on the quarterdeck as the Prince of Wales and his entourage noisily made their way down the brow after his successful army ceremonials. On the foreshore, carriages were drawn up but no crowds had gathered: sea voyaging did not lend itself to precise estimates of arrival.

After them the passengers descended.

First, the Honourable Charles Pountney on his own, in haste, as if wanting to throw off a bad dream.

His coach clattered off with a hasty flourish of whips and was soon gone.

Then Miss Lockwood, pale but calm, boarded a waiting hackney carriage with Clarinda. She did so without a backward glance and kept to herself while her baggage was loaded. It ground off until it, too, was lost to sight.

Kydd stood alone on his quarterdeck.

Persephone Lockwood kept her composure all the way to the London mansion the Lockwoods had taken for the

Season, a mindless enduring. Clarinda was at a loss to understand what had happened but did not press matters and bade her a tearful farewell at the door to her own family's home.

Dinner was a brittle affair, Persephone warding off her mother's suspicions with a tale of a dreadful storm that had quite undone her. Her father wanted details but she pleaded fatigue and retired early.

Dismissing the maid, she sat on the bed, staring into nothing, feeling the torrent of emotion build until it climaxed in a tearing spasm of tears. She flopped down, giving herself over to the onslaught of feeling. She cried herself to sleep, too torn with grief and pain to think, to rationalise. It was more than she could bear.

In the morning when she awoke nothing had changed. What had passed had passed. In a way the fact that nothing could be done steadied her and she took care with her appearance before she went down to breakfast.

'Do you feel better, dear?' her mother asked, with more than a hint of asperity. She wanted answers – why had Persephone returned in such a state, how had she behaved before the Prince of Wales, what was afoot with Charles?

She diverted the questions but her father's shrewd expression told her she needed to come up with an explanation that satisfied.

Later, as they walked in the park, Clarinda's frightened look of incomprehension betrayed her confusion, but Persephone was not going to let a soul know of her torment.

Charles had behaved badly, and by the time the voyage was over they had stopped speaking to each other. It was too late for him: she knew with a terrible certainty that she could never spend her life with such a man. Whatever her mother said, she would never marry him.

It left a storm of questions but there was one that demanded an answer above all others, if only to steady her course into the future.

Kydd had presumed on her. But the kiss had been passionate, intense, consuming.

What had he meant by it? Was it lust at close quarters or a vengeful fling? Did he have another he was betraying? Why had he been so hard and repelling before?

She had to know, and the sooner it was over the better.

It hardened into a resolve and before they reached the children's pond she knew what she had to do. A bold and decisive act, never to be contemplated by a lone woman, but it had to be done.

'Clarinda. Do please accompany me. I believe that I must visit someone.'

The door was answered by a dignified servant, who seemed puzzled by her request at this early hour to make visit on Sir Thomas.

They were shown into a well-appointed drawing room and, in the tense stillness, waited together for some minutes.

Kydd appeared at the double door and stopped, frozen in shock.

His eyes were rimmed by dark pits – did this mean . . .?

'Miss Lockwood. I . . . I . . .'

'Clarinda. Do leave us, if you please. I've some private business with Sir Thomas as cannot be disturbed.'

A steely determination filled her to the exclusion of all else, and the words came out colder than she would have liked but this was something that had to be seen through to the end, here and now.

Clarinda left with a single imploring glance, ushered away by the servant, who seemed to have sensed the gravity of the scene.

'Sir Thomas. Let me be brief,' Persephone opened strongly. 'I apologise for this importunate visit but I vow I will have answers, sir.'

Kydd's eyes never left her face, his hands bunched by his side in mute helplessness.

'And I will be blunt. Sir, you made trespass on my person and I will know what it means.'

He made no effort at reply, his gaze still fixed on her.

'If you have an understanding with another this can only stand as the act of a poltroon, a rank—'

'I love you,' he croaked. 'Before God I can't help it, but I love you!'

She froze – the words rang in her ears, like the sudden pealing of church bells, dispelling the so recent darkness in an overwhelming rush of insane hope.

'You're promised but, as Heaven stands witness, I can't stop myself. Forgive me, for I—'

Tears came – in a hot, stinging surge that had her running to him. 'Dear love, my sweet love – there's only one in this world that I want – I need,' she cried, through her tears. She threw her arms around him and held him in an embrace that was crushing, that had no room for the rest of existence, her body shaking with the raging tempest that was coursing through her.

At last they pulled apart, trembling with the violence of the moment.

'You're not . . .?'

'No, my dearest love, all that's finished now,' she said shakily, trying to smile amid tears of happiness.

She found a handkerchief and dabbed her eyes, then tenderly wiped away his tears too.

Together they sat on the couch, hand in hand.

'What happens now?' he said, in a voice of wonder and awe.

She leaned over and kissed him with the utmost tenderness, then withdrew her hands to sit pointedly apart. 'I rather think we have an understanding, don't you, Sir Thomas?'

Kydd rose to his feet and crossed to the mantelpiece, smoothing his clothing. With a quick conspiratorial flash at her, he rang the silver bell. 'Ah, Tysoe. We have concluded our business, um, satisfactorily. Would you kindly inform Miss Clarinda?'

Fearfully Clarinda came around the door, seeing Persephone sitting primly in an armchair, Kydd standing nonchalantly at the mantelpiece.

'Thank you for your patience, Clarinda. We have now finished our—'

'Persephone – you didn't really?' she gasped, her face abruptly transformed by a dawning smile of huge delight. 'The captain – tell me true, did you . . .?'

'Clarinda, I don't know what you're talking about,' Persephone said severely.

'You've accepted him, haven't you?' she squealed, her hands clasping. 'I can see it! How wonderful – I've always said that—'

It was no use – Persephone went to her and they hugged, afterwards with much flourishing of handkerchiefs to dab sparkling eyes.

'Please, I beg you, Clarinda, don't tell a soul.'

'I won't! I won't! Oh, how marvellous – I'm first to know!'

'You promised!'

'Yes, yes! But when . . .?'

'You must allow that we should be granted time to consider our position.'

Kydd watched them with bursting happiness and pride, then said, 'My dear, there's one who in all the world I'd like to tell before all else.'

Chapter 55

Cecilia came to the door, incredulous, and saw them standing outside, hand in hand. 'You . . . you . . . you're together! At last – I'd nearly given up all hope! Oh, Thomas . . .' She threw her arms about her brother, weeping in delight. 'Dear Thomas, you don't know how happy this makes me. I give you and Miss Lockwood joy of your uniting, much joy!'

Renzi stepped forward from behind her with a fond smile. 'So you will be spliced at last, dear fellow. And may it be a long one,' he said, repeating the age-old sailor's benediction. His handshake was strong and heartfelt.

'It's been a devil's age since we saw you last, Miss Lockwood. And that was when . . .'

'I fear my good parents have not changed, Lady Farndon.'

'Cecilia, please, my dear. And may we call you Persephone?'

They were soon at their ease in the Blue Velvet Room.

'Now, tell me, what plans have been made? Do say if there's anything at all we can do.'

Persephone smiled wistfully. 'Before this hour I was having

my grave doubts of your brother's intentions. It's all been . . . rather unforeseen, if you understand.'

'Then it were better we begin. For the first I'd think that . . .'

Kydd shot a look of resignation at Persephone, who returned a warm and patient smile. Cecilia was taking charge and that was that.

The chief need was to preserve reputations. From this day on, the town mansion of the Earl of Farndon would be Persephone's haven in these troubling times, the countess being so obliging with her sympathy. That Kydd was to visit his good friend the earl at the same time could only be accounted a coincidence and not to be remarked. Later, when the engagement was announced there would be no need for such subterfuges.

There was the whole delicate question of disengagement from previous attachments and then, after a decent interval, the revealing of a new.

After this—

'Cec, I do think Persephone has a good haul on the particulars. What she craves most is a mort o' sea room, see to the main heads of the matter, that sort of thing. And, er, talk it with me as we may lay a course together,' he finished, with a sheepish smile.

'Dear Thomas, of course! I understand. You'll want to be with her. Well, we can soon arrange that. This room is yours while you may! Come, Nicholas, we'll leave you in peace to do your talking.'

They were alone.

Kydd moved to sit by her side and reached for her hands. 'My very dearest, darling Persephone. How can I—'

She disengaged herself gently but firmly. 'My love. I'm

resolved we shall enter in on life as one with never a stain or reproach on our conduct. And . . . you'll believe I've much to think on, dear Thomas.'

'Of course, dear love.'

'Then you'll know I must act as is honourable in the matter of Charles. He is to be told this hour.'

'Your note will say—'

'I will see him. This he is owed.'

In a little under an hour she was back – pale-faced but composed.

Kydd kept silent, watchful, concerned.

Finally she spoke. 'Do you know how much you hurt me when you did the same?' she asked, in a brittle voice, her face averted.

'It was one of the hardest things I've ever done.'

She buried her face in her hands and wept silently for long minutes.

Then she looked up and smiled through her tears. 'And here I am, taking you to myself. I should be taken to Bedlam, I do swear!'

Gently, lovingly, they talked, healing the hurt of years, discovering, revealing.

'That time with the Marquess of Bloomsbury and Mama knew you as a penniless sailor, you with your common speaking. Then the foreign secretary steps in to make your acquaintance and she's thrown all in a tizz. We never heard of anything else for a week. How did you contrive it at all?'

'It was Nicholas's doing, of course. A rattling fine fellow in anything of a blow, is he. I must tell you about the time . . .'

'Shall we take tea now, my cherubs?' Cecilia said happily, craning around the door.

Afterwards, Persephone excused herself. 'I must now do my duty to my father and mother about Charles. It will be a hard thing for Mama – she's so set on a society wedding for her only daughter – and Father . . .'

Chapter 56

'Do stand still, Thomas. It's hard enough as it is . . .'

Persephone put down her pencil in exasperation. It really wasn't his fault, she had to concede. Standing absolutely still in a valiant pose for so long must be trying for an active man. The real frustration was of her own making: to capture the essence of the natural dignity of his modest heroism and the near-Grecian expression of his masculinity, she was reaching deep into her well-springs of creation and it wasn't quite enough.

She bit her lip with impatience. How could she bring out what she wanted?

It was now three weeks after her rejection of Charles.

'Thomas, I think we must talk.'

'Ah, yes, Seph,' Kydd said, stretching in relief and flopping into an armchair. 'Say away, m' dear.'

'I do believe it time to make arrangements.'

'Um, which?'

'To announce our engagement, in course.'

Kydd's slow smile broadened and he leaned forward to kiss her hand.

She accepted gracefully but went on in a practical tone, 'As I despise our meeting in this way and would wish the freedom to go abroad together where we may.'

And let the world know that Sir Thomas Kydd was now hers.

'In *The Times*,' he said.

'And the *Gazette*.'

'Who will do, er . . .?'

'I will draw it up, and you will place it with the publishers.'

Kydd sat back in a happy daze. It was the final, irrevocable step: once publicly engaged there was no turning back. In a matter of months the woman by his side would be Mrs Kydd – or, more rightly, Lady Kydd.

'I thought the usual six months before we're wed,' she went on, in the same matter-of-fact manner, infuriatingly practical as he'd learned was her way. 'And the occasion to be in St George's, which Mother adores, with—'

'Seph, there's one thing you've fore-reached on.'

'Oh?'

'Should I not in the first instance make my addresses to your father?'

'It would be for the best.' She sighed. 'As I'm vexed beyond endurance by Mama's importuning.'

Chapter 57

'What is it, my dear? Whatever is the matter that it needs your father to hear you?' Lady Lockwood grumbled. 'He's busy at this time, as you very well know, Persephone.'

She held her ground. 'Mama, it is important, I promise you.'

'Very well, I'll call him down.'

Her father came, leaning painfully on his stick. 'So I'm here, Persephone,' he growled. 'What is this great matter that I must turn out so precipitate?'

Persephone took a deep breath, standing demurely before them with her hands clasped together in front. 'Mother, Father, I wish you might meet the man I will marry.'

There was a moment's incredulous hush and her mother burst out, 'You – you're in jest, surely my child! We've heard nothing of—'

'He waits in the carriage outside.'

'Your mother's right, Persephone. Without I am consulted, there can be no question of—'

'He comes today to seek my hand, Father. Do hear him.'

'This is all damned irregular, Persephone. Have I met the fellow? How can I make a deciding without I know his family, his prospects and so forth?'

'You do know him, Father.'

'Oh? You don't mean the younger Fotheringham? How exciting! If you—'

'No, Mama. I will fetch him for you directly. Now, Papa, do I have your promise you'll hear him fairly, without prejudice, as we must say?'

Admiral Lockwood reluctantly gave gruff agreement. 'You have my word.'

She left and, in a short while, returned, a figure behind her. Once in the door she moved to one side and Kydd stepped forward with an elegant bow.

Lady Lockwood took one horrified look and fell to loud wailing, clinging to her husband.

'Good God!' exploded the admiral. 'Is this your conceiving of a joke, Persephone?'

'Tell her, Reginald! My nerves can't stand it!'

His face was suffused with anger, fingers writhing on his stick. 'I've told this – this knave I'll not have him under my roof! Get out, sir! Get out! This instant, before I—'

Persephone moved to stand beside Kydd. She took his hand and, in a cool but determined tone, said, 'Father. Knave or no, this is the man I shall marry and no other.'

It brought on fresh bawling from her mother but something of her certainty must have penetrated her father. 'Do control yourself, m'dear,' he threw irritably at his wife. He fixed his daughter with a look of great intensity. 'Now listen to me, Persephone. I am in deadly earnest – and I demand you will swear to me here and now to my face that you do truly and sincerely love this man, that he does not have some evil hold on your affections, some – some—'

'Papa, I do! We have had our misunderstandings in the past, but have found our lives and love come together in a way . . . You must understand, Papa, please!'

Lady Lockwood collapsed full-length on the sofa, weeping inconsolably into her handkerchief.

'Should I forbid this union, what then?'

'Then I shall be broken-hearted, Father,' Persephone said, in a small voice, 'but I will still marry him.'

He turned away, eyes unseeing, face working. Then he faced her again, his countenance stony.

Eventually he spoke, slowly and deliberately. 'I will not stand in your way, Persephone. I love you too much to deny you and can only trust you know the consequences of what you're contemplating.'

She threw her arms around him. 'Thank you, dearest Papa. You've made me so happy.'

A sudden howl came from the sofa. 'Reginald – how could you? Our poor daughter, whatever will happen to her? My God, it's not to be borne!'

'My dear, she's of an age now and has made her decision. We must respect it.'

Then he turned to Kydd, his stick tapping, and thrust his face full into Kydd's. In a low voice of infinite menace, he ground out, 'And if in any wise you do bring hurt to my daughter again, believe me that I'll see you roast in the furthest corner of Hell! Do you understand me, sir?'

Chapter 58

Fookes bounded in, his chubby features wreathed with good humour.

He waved *The Times* at Kydd, chortling, 'You sly dog – wondered why we haven't had sight o' your fine figurehead here at the club! An autumn wedding, then.'

'As it says, Prinker, although I'm still betwaddled by the whole thing. A married man – me!'

Fookes sat in the best armchair, thrusting his legs out and cocking an eye at his friend. 'A son of the sea, putting down roots? Happened before, old fellow.'

'Yes, but—'

'Have you given thought to your future, Tiger? I mean, being useful in the longer term as it were.'

'Not really, no time.' He was uncomfortably aware that a decision as to whether to retire from the sea would soon have to be made.

'I've a suggestion,' Fookes continued.

'Oh? Fire away, then.'

'You're an active sort of fellow and I can't see you sitting on your hands for too long. Why not do a bit more for your country – like serving before the mast . . . in Parliament?'

'What? Prinker, are you saying as I should stand as a Member of the House of Commons?'

'Why not? In battle you've the courage of a lion, it'll be the same firing broadsides at the opposition. The House sore needs fearless coves who'll hold 'em to account, stand up for what's good and decent. A right true sort like you would be an ornament on the benches, believe me.'

Kydd sat back and let it sink in. He'd not been keen on the idea before but his life course now looked very different. Once he had retired from the navy, the cut and thrust of lively debate appealed.

'I'll think on it.' And the more he did so, the more enticing it appeared. While already on a rising tide of recognition and distinction in the highest quarters, who knew where it could take him?

'If you're in the Tory interest, there's a seat waiting, old bean.'

'And I'll need to speak with Persephone, o' course.'

Then it penetrated that he was being offered a rotten borough – a safe seat of a relict village that had a mere handful of pliant voters safely returning a Member of Parliament. It was the way it was done for many but he wanted no part of it. 'Thank you, Prinker, but I'd rather contest it in the proper way.'

Fookes raised an eyebrow. 'If you desire it so, Tiger. It'll cost you dear but I'll have a word with the sec and see if we can help.'

With rising feeling Kydd recognised that Sir Thomas and Lady Kydd could shortly be setting out on a path that—

Fookes cut through his thoughts. 'Oh, just a formality,

naturally, but the commissioners will need to be assured that you're a respectable gent and so forth. Which is why I ask in all delicacy if you have land at all, an estate tucked away somewhere, perhaps.'

'Er, not as we might say.'

'Sadly, until you do we cannot entertain the idea of a candidacy. Do see if you can lay hands on one, dear fellow – in the amount of some hundreds should suffice.'

A landed estate. It would take all he had in consols, his prize-money account and salvage on the Russian furs, but this was an investment in the future – his and Persephone's.

'I'll see to it.'

'Capital. Candidly I would think you'd walk away with a seat, so exposed to the public eye – they love a hero, do John Bull and his dog. Offhand, I seem to remember there's a by-election looming in the Potteries or some such. Do you want me to . . .?'

Chapter 59

'I'd think you'd be a splendid figure in Parliament, Thomas, and I'd be very proud of you. Do you not think it, Clarinda?'

The park still bore signs of a frost and it crunched underfoot as they tramped along companionably.

'Dear Persephone – I'll need your help.'

'Of course.'

'To find an estate to satisfy the commissioners – but more worrisome than that, to please a wife.'

'A lady cleaves to her husband,' she replied sweetly, 'whatever estate he is in. Do you have a preference at all, Thomas?'

In fact he did, one that had stayed with him in the years since, as a master's mate and caught up in the great mutiny, he'd made a clandestine landing on the Devon coast and headed inland. A village on the post road to London that was so pretty and peaceful it had haunted him ever since as the England of his remembering when times had been dire. Now to be considering placing his being there was a beguiling and intoxicating thought.

'Ah, not too close to London. In the country. I value romantic beauty above all, don't you, Miss Lockwood?'

'Well, Sir Thomas, and that would be the way to steal a woman's heart. Can there be some far patch of the sublime that tempts you?'

Ivybridge was as enchanting as he remembered – the crystal River Erme bubbling over mossy rocks, the houses near hidden by a profusion of chestnut and oaks, the old bridge – and the peace and stillness.

They stayed at the London Inn, its warm taint of beer on sawdust wafting out from the taphouse bringing back memories that he shared. In the evening they strolled with Clarinda along the lovely little road next to the Erme where stood the sturdy mansion Corinthia that he'd passed so long ago and envied its inhabitants.

Friendly folk at the inn were keen to tell of the local gossip in their warm, round Devon burr, but Kydd knew what he wanted. He had mustered his accounts and had a figure. With a twinge he had passed over the thought of buying something like Corinthia for what he needed was land – a respectably sized house and tenant farmers who'd provide the several hundreds of income required.

With his means there was no chance of securing an estate within close distance of London but here in the country there was.

By morning he had four possibilities but one stood out before the others.

They rode out on horseback, for a time along the banks of the Erme before taking the road heading around the foothills of the moors and into the enfolding embrace of a wooded valley, sheltered and smelling richly of forest loam.

Then quite unexpectedly there was a bend in the road and a street, with a cluster of houses lining it, an attractive pond and broad green. Combe Tavy.

They dismounted at the single inn, their arrival stirring interest from passing village folk, several of whom stopped to stare. While the ladies refreshed themselves after the journey Kydd took an ale – the sparkling moorland water giving it a singular freshness.

Leaving a buzz of speculation behind, he collected Persephone and Clarinda and they took a side road that wound through orchards and steep sheep pasture, then on higher, until it stopped outside a substantial dwelling. On one side of the gatehouse arch bronze letters with the patina of generations spelled out 'Knowle Manor'.

'Shall we?' Kydd said, and spurred his mount through the archway towards the mansion. It was near covered with ivy, but enough remained visible for them to take in the tawny brick walls, diamond mullioned windows and tall decorated chimneys, which all told of another age. A weathercock was sadly askew over a central tower and the gardens were lost to undergrowth, signs of neglect and age everywhere.

Behind the house other buildings were difficult to make out – stables, barns, a smithy? From one chimney a thin spiral of smoke ascended.

Kydd dismounted and looked about, discouraged, but when he turned to speak to Persephone he saw she was standing next to her horse gazing up at the old manor house with a faraway expression, rapt.

'How enchanting!' she breathed. 'So . . . mysterious. Secrets and memories from time out of mind. And, Thomas, just sleeping and waiting these centuries – for us!'

Kydd smiled, his disappointment quite overcome by her

ardour. 'Shall we go in? There's someone at home, I see.'

The bell-pull produced no response so he wielded the heavy lion-head knocker.

They were answered not from within but by a figure emerging from the side of the house; an old but firmly upright man in country smock and gaiters, clutching a hay-fork. He glared at them suspiciously. 'What's thee want, then?'

Kydd told him he'd heard of the availability of the property and wished to see it for himself, its prospects for improvement and so forth.

The man introduced himself as Mr Appleby and confirmed that the manor estate was indeed for sale. The owner had emigrated to Canada some two years previously and had instructed that the proceeds be remitted to him there, but few had shown interest in this secluded location. Was Kydd considering the purchase of the six tenancies and Combe Tavy holdings that the ancient manor held still?

The answer satisfied the old man and they were led around the back to enter by the kitchen, the imposing front door having been sealed shut some time ago. They were introduced to a flustered Mrs Appleby, who showed them about the mansion.

It was dusty, creaking, and most rooms were empty, but the manor hall, with its ancestral fixtures, minstrel's gallery and enormous fireplace, had Persephone clasping her hands in joy.

A musty odour hung about much of the mansion and outside only one of the stables was in use, the barn long since shuttered. Appleby was at pains to point out that there had been no funds expended on upkeep since the departure of the owner. It was clear that it would take some time and money to bring the quaint old place to any semblance of homeliness . . . On the other hand, Knowle Manor was within reach of Kydd's means and fulfilled the parliamentary requirement. And Ivybridge was not an hour away, where the London post road passed conveniently by.

Kydd felt a rising tide of elation. Was this going to be where he and Persephone would spend their lives together?

Chapter 60

The last miles from Stoke-on-Trent were dreary and tedious: an industrial landscape of unrelieved monotony. Rolling hills carpeted with endless towns, each the same slate-grey and grimed brick. Countless odd bottle-shaped chimneys issued dun-coloured smoke to merge into an unresisting sky.

Kydd tried to keep up spirits with conversation but this foray into the north was turning into a trying time. As women always did, Persephone and Clarinda found things to talk about, leaving him to stare morosely from the coach windows.

At last Bursley was announced. Stiff and sore, they descended into an inn courtyard. 'No welcoming party for the next Member of Parliament for Bursley North?' Persephone said, with mock asperity. 'A sad omission, I'm obliged to say.'

But, alerted by the horn of the mail coach, Fookes came to greet them. 'My dear, so long,' he purred, with a low bow to Persephone, who returned a polite bob.

Kydd stretched elaborately. 'So, Prinker. We're here.'

'You are indeed. This is the Dog and Whistle and you may call it home for the nonce. All's in train, we set to immediately.'

Kydd's room was the best at the inn and to be headquarters for the upcoming contest. The table was cleared and he was sat down, Persephone and Clarinda to one side. It was a very different Fookes who took charge, crisp and purposeful. 'As we agreed, I'm your election agent. I'll give you the lie as shall see you cruise to a well-earned victory, so long as you'll do as I advise.'

'I'm in your hands, Prinker.'

'Good. It's a by-election following the decease of old Fenton. Two candidates – you in the Tory interest and one Billy Meakin for the opposition. He's much put out, incidentally, as he trusted he'd be unopposed, but we've gone and brought in a prime cockerel to stand against him.'

'Go on.'

'Shouldn't be too much of a showing from them. He's a coarse enough gullion, manufacturer of tiles, done well but has never been out of the Potteries in his life. You talk the bigger picture, he'll never be able to stand against you.'

'How's it to be run at all?'

'The fun begins tomorrow. The mayor o' Bursley will call for nominations at the town hall. You two present yourselves and he calls for a show of hands. If enough of the crowd like what they see of you, it'll all be over, you'll be returned as the new Member, saves further expense. Clear?'

'That's all?'

'Probably. It'll go your way, fear not, Tiger. You'll want to work on your speech, then?'

But as news of his arrival spread, a stream of well-wishers appeared, each of whom had to be flattered and humoured. And in between, not being a great one for words, Kydd sat scowling blackly at his paper, waiting for inspiration to strike. Evening brought an increasingly raucous gathering in the rooms below where his supporters were milling. Every so often he was called down by Fookes, to appear to thunderous acclaim and toast the cause in rich brown ale, which did nothing for his concentration.

Kydd spent a restless night with careless shouting in the street and occasional bursts of jollity spilling out from the tavern. He woke blearily to Fookes's firm shaking.

'Voting's at ten at the town hall. Ready?'

By nine it was clear that he was not going to walk away with the seat. The crowd about Bursley town hall was in the mood for an argument with their shouts of 'Bursley and Meakin', but Fookes was unperturbed. From the side streets came a triumphant thumping of drums and into view erupted a much larger ragged horde, which converged on the hall.

None too gently, the parish constables kept the two groups separated. Kydd mounted the steps to the balcony where the mayor stood importantly in his chain of office. For the first time he saw his opponent. Red-faced and burly, he glared suspiciously at Kydd, then scornfully looked away, waving to the crowd, which responded with a roar.

Feeling more than a little self-conscious, Kydd did the same, bringing an instant and much louder clamour.

The mayor nodded to them both, then spoke to the town crier, who advanced to the balustrade and swung his bell mightily, with no effect on the din below. For minutes more he kept it up, then, in a stentorian bellow, called, 'Pray silence for his worship the mayor!' repeated several times until the commotion died away.

'Gentlemen, brother electors of the ancient borough of Bursley. We are met here today for the purpose of . . .' Apart from individual cat-calls he was heard through until he came to the meat of the matter. 'Therefore I call upon any here who would nominate a candidate for the seat of Bursley North to step forward and make your plea.'

A thin-faced clerkly man moved quickly and, addressing the crowd for longer than the mayor had, declaimed his admiration for the person of William Meakin, until the booing and jeers rendered him inaudible. The mayor held up his hand in acknowledgement and motioned Fookes to take his place.

In a practised motion he bounded forward and, in quick, thrusting shouts, put out that Sir Thomas Kydd, the most famous sea captain of the age, was doing Bursley the greatest honour by representing them in the Parliament of Great Britain and deserved their full support. Any man who thought otherwise could only be a poltroon or French agitator.

It was met by a frenzy of delight only a little shot through with the outraged shouts of the opposition.

Then Meakin was ushered forward.

His was an angry speech: the manufactory owners in the Potteries, blind in their slavish obedience to the government line, needed a thrashing to bring them to their senses and he was just the man to do it. Unemployment on all sides while profits of such outrageous amounts were being made demanded action. And if elected he, Billy Meakin, would be up on his feet in Parliament all day and every day on their behalf and never rest until each man had a full belly.

'How much do yez pay y'r own, then, Billy?' came one cat-call, quickly followed by others. Sensing an easy victory, his opponents drowned him out in laughter and jeering.

And then it was Kydd's turn. He moved to the balustrade, looking down on the unruly mob, which quietened as if in awe of a knighted hero. At the back he caught sight of

Persephone, who waved frantically at him. It was not what was wanted for the calm collecting of his thoughts.

'Gentlemen of Bursley. I'm not used to pretty words or your rousing speech so I'll keep it short.' There were a few shouts, indistinct in the gathering crowd, which petered out quickly. He pressed on.

'I ask you this one thing. Raise your eyes, look out to where your fair land meets the sky. Go further – and you'll come to the sea. And what's on the other side of the waves? Why, the rest of the world – where every nation is in arms against us. Every one! Any burden or worry that's riding you now is nothing compared to this.'

He let it sink in. 'You stand here today in liberty only because England is strong and can defend you and yours. I promise to you that in Parliament I'll not rest until I see her stronger still. All I ask is that you put me there to do the job.'

In a joyous shout the crowd erupted, cheering and screeching, while Kydd, pink with embarrassment, waved an acknowledgement. He stepped back, meeting Meakin's venomous glare with a modest smile.

The mayor announced importantly, 'I call upon the meeting now to elect a new Member of Parliament for Bursley North.'

There was little doubt: a sea of hands arose for Kydd in a good-humoured roar but for Meakin there was only a desultory showing.

'I therefore declare—'

'Hold!' rasped Meakin. 'I stands on m' rights and demands a poll!'

The mayor looked around helplessly and a committee man whispered something to him.

'Very well. A poll – in this place five days hence.'

265

Chapter 61

The committee for the electing of Sir Thomas Kydd met that evening in the snug of the Dog and Whistle. 'He's quite within his rights, the villain,' Fookes conceded. 'And now we're all to the further expense of a contest. It'll take a lot of work,' he warned. 'As we should start now.'

The voters of Bursley borough paid scot and lot, which placed them at a degree above the common pot-walloper, but would still need encouragement to cast their vote in the right cause. To this end an army of supporters was mustered.

The ladies were set to a furious sewing of blue cockades, sprays and banners while men were dispatched in all directions for other purposes that it appeared Kydd need not be troubled about, and then it was the dinners and banquets. From pies and beer to hog roasts, with lavish attention to drink, the object was to outdo the opposition.

Soon rival parades were pounding the streets, motley bands of drums and horns in the lead turning the town into a bedlam of excitement. At the taverns riotous supporters overflowed into the roads, fights broke out between rivals, and shopkeepers shuttered themselves in.

Kydd was taken to the Modford pottery where he gravely inspected the works, shocked at what he found: the hellish heat of the kilns, the ragged children running their tasks, the nauseating stench of colouring vats. A vast spread was turned on for the artisans, clerks and toilers at which his speech was heard politely enough but, judging by the glassy-eyed stares, would not be remembered.

And then there was the canvassing – tramping depressing streets, to beg for votes from those with no notion of the world that lay beyond their ken, was a trial.

Persephone and Clarinda went out together, proudly wearing the favour of the blues but returned much subdued after what they'd seen in the mean houses and alleys.

Polling day came round all too quickly.

A husting was erected by the town hall, a temporary pavilion to shelter the officials and provide a platform for speech-giving.

The crowd that seethed around it was looking for some ready entertainment.

'Kydd a-main!' The cry went up, the shouts frenzied and hoarse. This was met instantly by 'Bursley and Meakin!'

Pandemonium broke out. Fist-fights sent the ladies scurrying and in the confusion pickpockets got to work.

The mayor puffed his way up the steps. 'In the matter of a contest for the seat of Bursley North, I here declare polling now open!'

Meakin took one side of the platform to begin a speech but was drowned out by drunken shouts, and Kydd from his side fared no better, quite unable to make himself heard.

A determined surge of early voters mounted the steps to cast their ballot.

'Name!' the poll-taker demanded of the first, opening his book importantly. Round him were scrutineers of both parties, waiting for the vote. The name was entered in and then the vital question, 'Jacob Marley, how is your ballot cast?'

'Why, Sir Thomas, o' course!' There was an instant howl of contempt and damnation from the Meakin camp as the man hurried away to collect his due at the taphouse.

The morning wore on, the tide of advantage running this way and that.

'Don't much like the way it's going,' grumbled a harassed Fookes. 'As we should be ahead more than we are. High time we got serious.'

Soon every alehouse, grog-shop and tavern was packed to the rafters with joyously rioting supporters.

On the following day the result was announced.

'I, Richard Field, returning officer for the Barnsley North constituency, declare that the total number of votes given to each candidate was as follows . . .' When they were read out, Kydd's was a poor showing. Then Field declared, 'And I therefore give public notice that William Meakin be duly elected as the Member of Parliament for Barnsley North.'

As Meakin was chaired away by a triumphant gang, Fookes scratched his head ruefully. 'I should have smoked it, the gutter rat that Meakin is.'

Kydd, his thoughts in a turmoil, heard why he'd lost. 'Carted in a high load of best ale from Burton and let it run.'

This didn't seem to be any more than Fookes had been doing in entertaining the voters and Kydd asked the obvious question.

'Well, he doesn't give it to his crew, no. It all goes to your brave boys,' he said bitterly. 'Why? Simple. By the end of the night there's none left standing who'll make it to the poll the next day to vote in your cause.'

Kydd wasn't satisfied: with his own eyes he'd seen some who'd cheered him to the rafters meekly place their vote with Meakin. He stopped one of them. 'I'd take it kindly if you'd tell me why you voted for my opponent, sir.'

The man smiled awkwardly. 'Why, sir, and there's no mystery there. It's m' plain duty – you're doing a grand job out there on the sea, keepin' us all safe like. I vote for you, I take ye away from all that. And Meakin, he's a shab right enough but he knows the Potteries, savin' your honour's presence, morc'n you.'

It might have come as a let-down but to Kydd it was a guilty relief – this was not what he should be doing with his life. He stole a look at Persephone and saw from her knowing smile that she shared his conclusion.

Chapter 62

Suddenly awakened in his sea-cabin Kydd sensed that his cot's gentle, rhythmic sway had changed into a more fretful working – either *Tyger* had altered course or the weather had taken a turn for the worse.

He lay there, pulling his thoughts together. Their course would not have varied – he had personally laid down its northward-bound track to round Ushant in this fair south-westerly and enter the Channel later in the morning, and as to the other, his invariable night order was to be woken at any shift in weather conditions.

For several more minutes he remained abed, ears straining for any clue – shouted orders, men running on the deck above, anything to explain it. But there was nothing beyond the thump and swash of the ship's progress and the comfortable creaks from deep within *Tyger*'s bowels that he knew so well.

It was no good: he landed lightly on the deck and peeped out of his cabin door aft to the stern-windows of the great cabin. The first light of day was stealing in and, through the salt-encrusted panes, he saw an expanse of hurrying Biscay seas pale and cold in the morning light. He paused, searching out wave patterns that would reveal the direction of the swell. There it was – coming in a point or two off the quarter, more or less as it had been before.

It was a mystery that had to be resolved. He dressed quickly, snatching up his grego against the chill morning breeze, and went on deck.

What he saw stopped him cold. Away out to larboard, manifest even beyond the horizon, was a cloud mass stretching across his entire vision. Dark, crepuscular, it was a sullen, spreading menace that, even as he looked, seemed to reach across towards them. He knew what it was – quite unlike a North Atlantic storm, this was a concentrated core of fury the like of which he'd last seen in the Caribbean, even down to the same dull green and copper tinge on its underside and the fringe of white at its base.

It was incomprehensible. The barometer had been at a steady twenty-eight and a half inches for the last several days – how had this situation crept up on them? Then he recalled the shocking way it had plummeted in just hours the last time he'd been caught up in a hurricano. But here, on the other side of the Atlantic?

He stalked up to the wheel where the first lieutenant was on watch.

'Mr Bray, what's all that to wind'd, pray?'

Others of the watch were standing near, still and silent.

Bray glanced out to larboard, then back. 'Looks very like a storm, sir.' The voice was strange, stiff and wooden.

'Well, be damned to it, and why wasn't I given a shake?'

His first lieutenant simply looked at him.

Was he drunk? Bray?

Kydd swallowed his annoyance for there were far more serious matters to attend to now.

With another glance at the ugly threat to weather he made up his mind. They had to outrun the monster, get out of its path. The trouble was that they would soon be pinned against a lee shore, the rock-bound coast of France; the only possible course therefore was either to the south, Gibraltar and the Mediterranean, or north through Biscay.

Something in him rebelled at the unfairness of it all and defiantly he chose the harder – to go for the north. Where darling Persephone waited for him!

'All hands on deck, Mr Bray,' he snapped. 'We've much to do.'

Bray continued his empty stare.

'Damn you, sir!' he roared. 'You're dismissed the deck, d'ye hear me? Mate-o'-the-watch – pipe all hands this instant!'

Maynard lifted the boatswain's call to his lips and turned to face Kydd.

'Well? Get on with it, man.'

The third lieutenant was at the hatchway, watching.

'Mr Brice! Get here at once. The watch-on-deck is in liquor. We've a right blow a-weather and I'm turning up the hands.'

Slowly, as in a trance, Brice came up to him.

'Did you hear me, sir?' Kydd spluttered. 'Take charge – all hands on deck!'

Brice looked at him oddly – then quite deliberately turned his back and went forward.

Speechless, Kydd could only let him go.

He rounded on the watch, all of them remaining as they were, unmoving, wordless. 'Is everyone mad? Maynard, pipe all hands – now!'

The master's mate lowered the call and, with a look of

great sadness directed straight at him, turned and followed Brice.

'Are you all insane? This is mutiny, and you'll answer for it, I swear!'

Bray came alive – but only to shoot him an expression of the utmost contempt before he, too, turned his back and left.

'Mutiny!' Kydd roared after them. 'You'll swing for it, all of you!'

One by one the seamen turned away and left, leaving him choking with rage.

'Do ye hear me, you worthless scum? Come back, do your duty by me or I'll . . . I'll . . .'

The last to leave was Tobias Stirk, whose face was stony, despising, before he turned his back and followed the others.

Kydd woke in a sweat in the darkness, his heart hammering, the dream still half with him, tearing at his sanity. Sitting up, he willed the shadows to go and then lay back, shaken.

What did it mean? Was it a warning or a farewell?

Chapter 63

The next day Kydd allowed Tysoe to fuss over him and decided to catch up on some reading, let his mind settle. The election business was now over, thankfully, nobody among his friends at the club particularly surprised at the outcome.

Persephone had taken it all in a remarkably relaxed manner and was with her mother discussing wedding plans.

Work on the Knowle Manor estate would begin when he'd had time to review his finances and spare some days to go down to get it started.

Tysoe entered apologetically with his silver tray. 'A message, sir.'

Kydd took it. No cipher or expensive paper, just a simple folded note, unsealed.

'Delivered by a ragamuffin youngster,' Tysoe added, as if to furnish Kydd with an excuse for ignoring it.

It was brief, the calligraphy perfectly formed but without individuality, much like a teacher's.

Dear Sir Thomas,

Do forgive my writing to you so importunately but I beg that you will grant me a short interview at your convenience. You will appreciate that the matter I believe is important enough for me to trespass upon your privacy in this way.

Your servant, sir

Mrs S. Martin

He didn't know any Mrs Martin that he recalled – but could she be a petitioner of some kind from the election? If so, he would have to disabuse her that he was any more involved with politics.

'Sir, the child waits, an answer is expected. Shall I . . .?'

Kydd quickly scrawled on the back to the effect that he found himself free to see her at three that afternoon. Five or ten minutes should conclude the business.

At the appointed hour there was a timid knock on the door and Kydd heard Tysoe answer it.

His valet entered with a vexed frown. 'Sir, Mrs Martin,' he said in a low voice. 'But I beg to observe that she does not appear to be entirely of the genteel sort.'

'Show her in,' Kydd answered, puzzled. The quality of her writing belied Tysoe's observation.

The woman entered diffidently and stood in the doorway.

Kydd rose to greet her. 'Do take a seat, Mrs Martin.'

She was slender and dressed in a clean but faded blue dress, the shoes plain, her bonnet trimmed with the bare minimum of ribbon. Of an age with Kydd, it was difficult to read her character, for she kept her face cast down and sat rigid.

'Now then, Mrs Martin. Do please state your business. I

regret I'm unable to spare you more than a little time as I've much to do.'

She hesitated, then looked up into his eyes. 'Then you don't recognise me . . . Thomas?' she said gently, her voice low.

Taken aback, Kydd could only stare at her. A woman with attractive features, near elfin, her large eyes framed prettily with auburn hair, high cheekbones and generously curved lips.

And a nose that was unusually recurved with— 'Sarah . . . that is, Miss Bullivant,' he said at last.

It was an incredible gulf of years that separated Sir Thomas Kydd and a young sailor on a world-girdling voyage in Macao, the other side of the world, but it had come back to him.

'Yes,' she said, with a shy smile. 'You remembered.'

It had been a passionate but cruelly short affair and he'd not seen her since his ship had sailed, leaving her alone, desperately sobbing.

He'd been young – too young, and with eyes on the next horizon.

'Ah, yes, Miss Bullivant – that is, Mrs Martin. I do remember.' He swallowed, trying vainly to think of something to say to such a visitation from the past.

'So do I,' she said, and looked down modestly.

'Are you, um, well?' he asked.

'Thank you, sir, yes.'

Her accent was strangely attractive, lilting in an exotic way. A silence hung.

'You came on an important matter?' he prompted.

She blushed and a slow smile spread. 'Sir Thomas, you will think it dreadfully impertinent of me . . . but if you could just the once come to tea with us I'd be so very honoured!'

He caught the 'us' – this would be her husband, Mr Martin, therefore it would be quite proper to call and, besides, did he not owe her something?

'To tea. I do believe I will, Mrs Martin.'

She beamed with delight. 'That's so kind in you, sir. When shall be convenient to you?'

Arrangements settled, the smile slipped a little. 'I . . . I do ask pardon, sir, that our lodgings are not so fashionable, that is to say are humble indeed for a gentleman of your—'

'Nonsense!' Kydd interrupted. 'I never pay mind to the trappings – it's character that counts.'

That she was in reduced circumstances was very plain but she had not taken advantage of the acquaintance or shown any resentment at what was past – it would be nothing more than an afternoon of reminiscing about Macao.

'Thank you, sir.' Her face lit up again. 'And for the occasion I shall make some little dumplings as Ah Lee cooked for us – do you remember how fluffy she had them?'

Chapter 64

Kydd dressed in the plainest garb he could, left his beaver hat and stick behind and hired a common hackney coach to make his arrival. The driver pursed his lips and threw him a sharp look when he gave the address.

Kydd soon found why: their route took them deep into South London, to Southwark, where the streets were ancient, mean and filthy. They persevered into the warren until they reached their destination, Horsemonger Lane, pulling up in front of a line of decaying tenements.

Stepping down from the coach in dismay, Kydd turned to the jarvey. 'Do wait for me if you will. I need to check that—'

'No, cully, more'n it's worth for me t' linger here. I'll have me fare now, then.'

Left on his own, Kydd looked about helplessly for the right address; it cost him a penny for an urchin to show him the squalid alley that led there and, with sinking heart, he knocked on the door.

It was opened quickly by Mrs Martin, her face alight with pleasure. 'Oh, you're so welcome, sir! Do come in.'

Inside it was clean and neat, but small, dim and crowded with articles of furniture.

He knew better than to expect a drawing room and took a seat at the kitchen table, gaily decorated with fresh flowers – his heart wrung at the thought of her spending her hard-earned coin on them.

'Can I offer you some refreshment, Thomas? Do you mind if I call you that? It's so much easier to say.'

'If you let me call you Sarah, Mrs Martin.'

She looked happily across at him while she took a chair opposite. 'I'd never have thought it! You've done so well, Thomas. I couldn't believe it when the sailors told me that you were just the same sailor-boy that, well, was in Macao.'

'The sailors?'

'Oh, on the ship. I'm not long in England. We came from China only a short while ago and they knew of you.' She gave a wistful smile. 'After all these years I suppose really I'm a stranger to England – fancy that.'

'Is Mr Martin here? I'd like to meet him, Sarah.'

'Some tea? I brought some prime *heung pin* back with me – it reminds me so much of China.' She dabbed her eye and smiled bravely. 'It's been such a change, coming back here – but, then, we mustn't talk about me all the time. Do tell me how you became a sea captain from an ordinary sailor. It must have been an enormous adventure.'

It was hard to take. Their circumstances: so unspeakably different, yet diverging from the same distant point in time and converging again – to this.

'You've lived in Macao all the time?'

'Yes. It hasn't been so easy for me, as I was dismissed by Mr Tsoi and left on my own. But kind Honrar Nuñez – you remember him? He took me in as a housekeeper and assistant at the orphanage. I've lived there ever since – the Chinese children are so much better behaved, little angels some.'

So that was the accent. She'd been living and working in China all those years where she'd seldom ever hear her native tongue.

'Your parents, were they not alarmed at your absence?'

'They died of the fever quite some years ago. It was why I decided to stay in Macao. There, I had a much larger family.' She looked away suddenly, snatching out a handkerchief to muffle a sob. 'And then just three months ago the old man died and I was turned out by the sisters.'

Kydd shook his head wordlessly. A return to a harsh and friendless England that had no meaning for her.

'Mr Martin? Did he not—'

'There is no Mr Martin,' she said, in a small voice, looking down at the table.

'No?'

'A name only. To conceal my condition.'

'I don't understand.'

'I was with child. This was why I was dismissed by Tsoi *saang*.'

'So all the time—'

'Let's not talk about it any more, Thomas, I beg.'

She offered a small plate of dumplings. 'These are my *cha siu bao*. Would you like to try one?'

'Sarah. I want to give you some money and you must promise—'

'No!' she flared. 'Do you take me for a fallen woman, deserving of charity? My circumstances now are not good, I grant you, but by my own efforts I will succeed. I will!' Her eyes glistened.

Kydd was torn with admiration and pity. 'What of your

child? Can you not . . .' He tailed off when she suddenly got up and faced away, rigid and silent.

After a long moment she spoke, but in a low, controlled voice, still facing away. 'Thomas. I beseech you – don't be angry with me.'

'Angry?' Kydd said, bewildered. 'How can I be angry with you?'

'My son. I call him Taai Hoi Yan.' The voice was now calmer. 'Great Sea Traveller. His proper name is Thomas, after you.'

With a ringing sense of inevitability rising like a tidal wave about to fall over him, he heard her finish. 'After all, he's yours as well. Your son, Thomas.' She turned to him with a shy, warm smile. 'He's in the other room – shall I call him?'

Held to a numbness by what must come, Kydd braced himself.

The door opened and Sarah ushered in a boy, pale-faced and painfully thin, the same large eyes and retroussé nose, but with Kydd's raven hair.

'*Hai nei-kei papa, Hoi Yan,*' she said tenderly, gesturing at him.

Kydd, stunned, could only manage a feeble 'How are you, little fellow?'

The child buried his face in her apron, whimpering.

'He's very shy,' she said defensively, 'and doesn't know English very well yet. He'll be used to you in time.'

'I-in time?'

'You will come to visit us, Thomas, surely. Say you will – it's very hard to be here on my own. Please do!'

A storm of emotion broke as he left, inchoate thoughts invading, jostling, demanding, in a tempest of feeling that left him trembling. After all these years he was a father. Proud and self-sufficient, Sarah had made no demands on him, only asking that he visited, as he could not in all kindness refuse.

If ever Persephone found out she would be mortified – he could never let that happen, but at the same time it could not be denied that the mother of his son had rights, too.

Kydd spent the next two days in a ferment of indecision.

Then, unsure and hesitant, he visited again, this time with carefully chosen gifts, not too costly as to beg refusal.

'Oh, Thomas! So sweet of you! But you must not – we have what we need.'

'Sarah, you must let me—'

'No, that won't do, dear Thomas. I will not be an object of charity, you know that.'

'But—'

'In my position it can only mean the one thing and this I will not have.'

'I understand,' Kydd said weakly.

She regarded him with her penetrating eyes. 'There is something.'

'Anything,' he found himself saying.

'I've asked and found out about you,' she said demurely.

'Oh?'

'Thomas, you're not married. If *we* were, it would solve everything, wouldn't it?'

Chapter 65

Kydd cursed and swore. Just when he needed him, Renzi had taken to his carriage and was back on his estate in Wiltshire. Of all in the world, his dearest friend was the only one he could confide in. He had been there with him in Macao, knew Sarah, and it was his cool, logical and considered advice he yearned for now.

After the briefest hesitation Kydd took post-chaise to Eskdale Hall.

Renzi greeted him warmly. 'Brother! So good to see you, but from London? Are you yet satiated with—'

'Nicholas. I burn to talk with you. Can we . . .?'

Cecilia hurried up to them. 'Thomas! Such a surprise – that you esteem our company of more account than your grand friends! How long will you stay?'

'Sis, I ask no more than a walk in the grounds with Nicholas.'

Renzi touched her arm. 'Dear Cecilia, would you grant us this for a space?'

They strolled together down the cultivated sward leading to the river meadows while Kydd marshalled his thoughts.

'Nicholas.'

'Yes, old fellow.'

'I have a problem.'

'So I surmise.'

'Which I'd be for ever beholden to you should you give me a steer.'

Renzi sensed the intensity of Kydd's manner. 'As I'd do my utmost to achieve, my dear friend.'

'Do you recall Macao, in *Artemis* frigate in the year 'ninety-four?'

Renzi nodded, and in a rush Kydd laid out the situation. 'Nicholas, what must I do?'

Renzi paced on, head down. 'In view of your current engagement I can think of no more serious circumstance,' he said finally. 'It is in itself sufficient grounds to break off the understanding, I fear. And the damage to your reputation will be severe should that happen for such a reason.'

'I know,' Kydd said miserably. 'But I feel for the woman so.'

'It is much to your credit that you do, but that's as may be. I ask you to conceive of the righteous infamy that would attend popular discovery of the indiscretion. In the level of society that you now inhabit these matters are dealt with rapidly and out of the public eye. This is the problem we must now address.'

'And Persephone – if she . . .'

'Quite. You have a pretty problem at hand, dear fellow.'

They paced on in silence. Then Renzi stopped. 'It's of no utility to debate possibilities without we have certainties. I will help you in this as far as I'm able, m' friend. For now, I suggest you consider the possibility that the woman is not who she says she is, that she practises a fraud upon you, knowing of your fortune.'

'No, Nicholas, I'm sure it's Sarah,' Kydd said miserably. 'Besides, she's never made claim on me for anything, not even to embarrass me, and—'

'Nevertheless, I desire you should think of an intimate detail of your . . . relationship that only the lady concerned could be sensible of. If she does not know it, we have our answer.'

'Yes, Nicholas,' Kydd agreed meekly.

'And within small days I shall conclude my business here and join you in London.' Renzi's face was set with a deep frown. 'This is a most serious affair, brother.'

Kydd looked up and down the mean streets before hurriedly drawing on some old clothes and a battered felt hat in a side alley. He hastened to Horsemonger Lane and, with a glance about, knocked on the door.

'Why, Thomas – what's this that you're wearing such old clothes?' Sarah said, in an exasperated tone.

'Oh, I thought it would come on to rain and I didn't want to spoil my new coat. How is, um, Hoi Yan?'

They sat down to a simple repast. The meal proceeded, the boy not saying a word, unable to take his eyes off Kydd. With a thrill of dread, of finality, he realised that in the next few minutes he would learn if the child was in truth his.

He'd thought about his vital question long and hard.

Waiting for the right moment, Kydd said casually, 'Do you know there's a pagoda in Kew Gardens? I remember the old one in Macao – do you?'

She stopped immediately and gazed across at him with a soft and unbearably private look, then extended both her hands to squeeze his.

'Of course I do, my dear Thomas. It was where we . . .'

Her eyes strayed to the boy and returned to his in bashful acknowledgement. 'I've never forgotten that night, my darling, and never will.'

Kydd reddened and slowly withdrew his hands.

'My sweet sailor-boy, I'm so glad I found you after all these years. And I've been giving thought to our future. I know it will be hard for you but it will be for the best. A little church wedding will be all I desire and we'll live somewhere there's no sea to tease you. I do think for both our sakes we should not long delay, don't you?'

Kydd managed to divert the conversation but as soon as the meal ended he made his excuses and went out into the night, shocked and unnerved. His recent world of perfection and promise had comprehensively unravelled.

He was so preoccupied in care that the sudden scurrying of a figure in the shadows went quite unnoticed.

Chapter 66

Renzi was on his own as Cecilia had remained in Wiltshire to deal with outstanding business. He listened to Kydd with great seriousness, then said, 'I see. So we must accept that she is in earnest. A dilemma it is for us, dear fellow.'

'Dear Nicholas, I've always known you as a straight-talking cove, a friend to morals and decent conduct. May I be told of your perceiving of my position?'

'And I know you to be fearless in your standing for the right in all things, my friend.' Renzi paused. 'I must ask you some questions, the first – do you love Persephone?'

'With all my heart!'

'The second – do you love Sarah?'

'I – I cannot say yes.'

'She is the mother of your child. Yet if you marry her, you will break the heart of two. If you marry Persephone it will be but one.'

Kydd recoiled, then said thickly, 'At times your logic can be damned cruel, Nicholas.'

'I haven't finished. If you take Persephone and she discovers this situation you are trying to conceal from her, it will destroy her. Are you willing to take this risk to indulge your own desire?'

'I . . . I . . .'

'If it is Sarah, you will have satisfied the morals of the case but will leave Persephone relict. She will be desolated, but she's beautiful and talented and will not lack suitors. Therefore the elements of the situation dictate that you should accept the other.'

Kydd went grey. 'That is fairly said, Nicholas – and hard, grievous hard. I don't know as I can—'

'Then think on this. Should you fail to do so, Sarah is in a position – one of revenge or spite, I do not know her – such that she can destroy your prospects with Persephone and you will then have caused a complete three-sided tragedy. My dear friend, the choice is yours to make.'

Kydd fell back, paralysed by the irreconcilable.

Renzi softened. 'Brother,' he said gently. 'I see before me the nation's foremost frigate captain, he who has defied the enemy's malice on so many occasions, laid low by circumstances not of his making. There is one last option. Go now, offer a settlement in lieu to any amount, if only to buy time.'

'She is honourable and determined and will never hear of it.'

'Nevertheless, it is our last hope. Excepting one, which you will leave with me.'

'Nicholas?'

'We each have our part to play – suffer me to follow mine.'

Chapter 67

Persephone was pleased with herself, dabbing content-
edly with her brush at the limned figure sitting on the
rock.

At last she'd captured something of Kydd's heroic character; all it had taken was subtly to alter the angle of the
light falling on his figure from the low glowering sun beyond
him. It was one of her best paintings.

'Miss Persephone, the admiral asks you attend him in his
study.'

'Tell him I will be with him presently.'

The maid bobbed, but would not leave. 'He desires you
go to him now, miss.'

This was odd: usually she was left in peace in her little
studio, her father out of respect, her mother from lack of
interest. She found some rag and cleaned her fingers,
wondering what it was that was so pressing a matter.

He was sitting at his desk, and turned abruptly to face her
as she entered. 'Shut the door, my child,' he said, in a low
voice.

Something in his manner clutched at her heart. She sat on the single chair in front of him. 'Persephone. There is no easy way for me to tell you this, but I must.'

'Papa? Is it . . .?'

'It will cause you much hurt that I would spare you – the Lord knows if it were in my power I would cast it aside and leave you untouched.'

'Father, if you must tell me something, I would rather be told directly.'

'It concerns Captain Kydd. You must be aware of my views upon his character and thus I have taken extreme care to verify what I'm about to inform you of him.'

'Father, I will wed him. There is nothing you can tell me that will alter that. Nothing, sir!'

'Then hear this, child. It was reported to me that he lives a double life. Double, I say! In his public aspect he consorts with the Prince of Wales and his disreputable crew but in his private being he . . . he keeps a mistress. One he's been with since he was a common seaman no less, and whom we must believe he cares for beyond the usual.'

'No! This is not possible! He'd never do that! Father, you've been tricked!' she burst out.

There was a gleam of triumph in the admiral's expression as he went on remorselessly, 'Not so, Persephone. I have proof. This is no scurrilous tale for I've taken steps to prove it beyond all question. Child, he leaves his lodgings under cover of night – in disguise – and flies to his woman, returning before dawn. This I have from an entirely reliable source.'

A chill of unreality stole over her. This was not the Kydd who'd breathed so transparently sincere words of love and adoration to her . . . or was it?

'I cannot believe you, Father. I know him as—'

'I can prove it to you now, if that is your wish.'

The certainty in his voice struck a cold dread deep into her soul. 'If you can, sir.'

'Very well.' He lifted a silver bell and rang it. Noiselessly, a figure entered, dark-featured and repellent. 'This man is a runner I sent after your Captain Kydd.'

'You had him followed?' she cried in indignation.

'As well I did, my dear. Do tell Miss Persephone what you observed, fellow.'

The man extracted a paper and recited from it, his words sepulchral and damning. He'd followed Kydd twice to the same address in Southwark and there seen him spend hours within. He'd been on each occasion farewelled by a creature who had readily admitted her long acquaintance with the subject and even – he begged pardon of Miss Lockwood – had with her issue of the same, a boy.

'Thank you. You may leave. There – I take no satisfaction in subjecting you to this pain, my dear, but you can see how necessary it is for you to be told before it becomes all too late.'

Persephone felt herself on the brink of madness but held to sanity by the slenderest thread of hopes – that it could not be true, that the runner had been mistaken in the dark, the woman a poor relation or some such.

'Yes, Papa. I can see that,' she said faintly. 'And I must consider my situation.' Excusing herself, she fled to her bedroom to confront the horror of it all.

If, God forbid, it was true, she would be sharing married life with another, the mother of his child. And even worse – what if he was in fact one of those men who needed women like a drug? She knew nothing of those kind so how could she ever be expected to recognise one? A storm of emotion threatened to break and she steadied herself at the last moment with a resolve to prove it was not true.

That night a nondescript two-wheeler lay quietly in the dark at the end of the street where Kydd had his lodging. In it was a lady cloaked and hidden, waiting.

Persephone nearly missed the hurried and furtive individual who came out from the door, but it was a figure that was unmistakable to her. Dressed in clothes of the common folk, Kydd looked this way and that, then walked quickly around the corner of the street.

'Follow!' she ordered.

The two-wheeler ambled off in time for her to see Kydd get into a hackney coach, which moved smartly away. They picked up speed and followed across the river into the maze of pitiful rookeries in Southwark and finally to Horsemonger Lane. They stopped well back – she had with her a pair of opera glasses and through them could see plainly as Kydd descended, paid off the coach and hurried down a mean alley to a door, looking suspiciously about as he did so.

Then she saw it open – it was not at the right angle to make out who it was that answered but Kydd plunged inside as though he'd been impatiently waiting all day for the reunion.

Heart weeping in sorrow she endured until he emerged.

And there in the doorway, a woman, with a child, taking farewell in a way that could not be described in any other way than as affectionate.

The agony was unbearable. Blinded by tears, she choked on her anguish, racking sobs consuming her, relentless and cruel.

The jarvey, concerned, leaned down. 'Where to, miss?'

She couldn't speak at first and then blurted, 'Anywhere – I don't care, anywhere!'

Chapter 68

'Nicholas, I'm grieved to say she would have nothing of it. Only a union will answer, and that soon.'

Renzi gravely heard him out. 'Then your last recourse may be said to have failed.'

Kydd's head drooped. 'I'm on a lee shore to all this'n,' he said, his voice muffled. 'As it's set fair to rob me of my wits.'

'Then I feel it best to send for a brandy.'

Kydd didn't seem to hear. 'What was that?' he asked.

'Oh, a reasonable precaution.'

'Nicholas, damn you, you're not making sense!'

'In the case you should lose your intellects entirely after my information is passed.'

'My God, but you try me sore sometimes, Nicholas.'

'Then you do not wish to hear it?'

At Kydd's dangerous look he continued hastily, 'You're aware that in my position with the government I have resources of an arcane, not to say secretive nature?'

'I'd be a sad looby if I didn't conclude that after our adventures,' Kydd answered sarcastically.

'Well, in this case they were not needed.'

'I'm pleased to hear it.'

'Just a common, sordid instance of criminality of the basest kind.'

'Nicholas, I'm tired and ragged. Another time, I beg.'

'Requiring the services only of my inestimable man, Jago.'

Kydd stood up suddenly. 'I've heard some catblash in my time but now's not the time to top it! I have to go now and—'

'Your Sarah. She nearly got away with it, you know.'

He sat down equally as abruptly. 'What are you saying?'

'I sent Jago to make enquiry of her. He can be quite persuasive when he needs to be, a most valuable asset.'

'And?'

'He was able to determine that she is indeed the woman you knew in Macao – you were right in those particulars.'

'I see.'

'But that is all that is true.'

'Are you saying . . .?'

'I am, brother. She's never a selfless orphan-house keeper, still less an innocent. And has been living in England these past eight years, in loose consort with the felonry, particularly one John Grundy, no stranger to the buffer's nab. Together they plotted their lay, which was to entrap and bleed you dry.'

Kydd slumped back in disbelief. 'Sarah? This can't be true.'

'The pair are notorious, dear fellow.'

'And . . . the child?'

'Hired for the occasion, as was the ken in Horsemonger Lane.'

'So . . .'

'So you are entirely free of the succubus, brother. It leaves only your desire to be known as to the fate of the woman.'

Faint with the wash of shock Kydd could only stutter, 'Leave the wretch be – but knowing she's found out, by God!'

The brandy did its work and he calmed.

'And now?' Renzi asked gently.

'Nicholas – there's only one thing that I want to do at this moment,' he said unsteadily.

'Oh?'

'This very hour lay eyes on my dearest Persephone that the world's set to rights at last.'

Chapter 69

Kydd dropped easily from the carriage with a light heart, went to the door and tugged at the bell-pull. For some reason the admiral's house was still and quiet and, disturbingly, the curtains were drawn across every window.

It was some minutes before the door was answered by a maid, not the footman. She took one look at Kydd and fell back, eyes wide. Her hand flew to her mouth.

'Who is it, you foolish girl?' called Admiral Lockwood, from behind her, and Kydd could hear an ill-tempered tapping of his stick.

He appeared at the door.

'Sir, I—'

The man recoiled as if Kydd had assaulted him. Then, with a screech of rage, he brought up his stick to strike at Kydd but without its support he fell sideways. His wig was knocked off and he writhed on the floor, clutching helplessly at Kydd.

Struck dumb, Kydd froze.

A pair of manservants hurried forward to lift the admiral to his feet. In a paroxysm of fury, he shouted incoherently.

There was no sign of either Persephone or her mother, but her cousin hurriedly appeared at the commotion.

'Miss Clarinda, pray tell me what's to-do? Why is—'

Tight-lipped, she pulled him aside. 'I'm glad you came, Sir Thomas,' she said icily. 'It enables me to tell you to your face what I think of you, sir!'

Kydd was utterly bewildered. What on earth was going on?

Clarinda continued in a hissing tone, 'I despise and loathe you to the very depths of my being, sir!'

'B-but—'

'And wish you in Hell this very moment.'

Kydd stiffened. 'I believe I'm entitled to an explanation of your conduct, Miss Clarinda.'

'I doubt you're truly in ignorance of what you've done to Persephone, sir!' She drew herself up. 'That dalliance with your trollop in Southwark was discovered by her father, who informed her of it. She wouldn't think it of you, poor lamb, but followed you – and found it to be the truth.'

Her eyes glittered with tears. 'That night very late she departed this house and has not been seen since.' A sob escaped before she could continue. 'She left me a note: she was broken-hearted and could not bear it. At the last she said . . . she said . . . she was going on a long journey and no one should trouble to look for her.'

Kydd staggered. 'What?'

Clarinda looked directly into his eyes. 'If you haven't the wit to understand what she meant by that, you vile creature,' she ground out, 'know that men are dragging the canal this very hour. Sir, I suggest that you be gone and no longer torment us by your presence.'

'But I came to—'

'Go, sir!' she spat.

Chapter 70

Through the whisky there was one thing Kydd clung to – that it could not be true. Her vitality, spirit, the incomparably lovely creature that was Persephone could *not* be gone from the world. It just could not be, and he refused to believe it. The pain was intense for he'd brought suffering to her, albeit unintentionally, and that was unforgivable.

He fought his grief at the knowledge that, whatever happened now, he would never see her again. And he vowed he would never marry, however long he lived.

Tysoe hovered, clearly distressed, finding excuses to be near. Another whisky dulled the cruel reality.

Kydd stared into the distance, trying fuzzily to focus on the whys of it all when his thoughts were broken into by a thunder of knocking on the door.

'Tell 'em to go away, there's a good fellow,' he slurred to Tysoe.

He heard strident voices and three men burst in.

Kydd scrambled to his feet, trying to throw off his fuddled

stupor, and immediately recognised Pountney among them. 'What the devil?'

'I'm sorry, Sir Thomas, these gentlemen would not be denied,' Tysoe apologised.

Pountney was breathing hard and threw Kydd an angry, accusing stare. He was holding a newspaper and shook it in the air. 'I've just seen this – you're engaged to Persephone Lockwood!' he blustered. 'To her!'

Kydd held his tongue. It would take very little to trigger a lethal madness in him.

'You damned villain – you took her away from me! D'you hear?'

'Steady, Charles, old boy,' hissed one of his friends, putting out a restraining hand. 'You don't want to cause trouble with this man, now do you?'

Pountney threw off the hand. 'You enticed her from me, gave her false promises or . . . or worse.'

Kydd came back: 'A lady might be trusted to place her favours where she will. If she finds him not man enough . . .'

'What are you saying, you vile dog?' Pountney said, with rising heat. 'I'll not be cuckolded by a common sailor!'

Kydd swayed, teetering on the edge, goaded to unreason by what he'd so recently lost.

Pountney sneered, 'Ah, yes. I know where you come from, Kydd! A jack tar, a base-born tarpaulin fit for nothing but—'

He never saw Kydd's fist coming. With the bitterness and frustration exploding inside him, the blow drove straight and true. Slammed backwards, Pountney landed in a huddle on the floor. His friends went to him and looked up at Kydd, horrified.

'He's out for the count,' one murmured.

Kydd took no satisfaction in it. 'Put him on the sofa,' he

said dully, and sat down again, pouring a fresh whisky. The man was an imbecile to think to come and taunt him. Or was it something else? It didn't matter really. He had deeper things to concern him.

There was no answer – he had to find ways to accept what had happened or slide into madness and ruin.

'Tysoe – get these . . . gentlemen a drink,' he called.

There was no response. 'Tysoe! Did you hear me?'

'He went out,' one of Pountney's companions said blankly.

Went out? Kydd glowered at his whisky, a nameless resentment building at the world.

Not long afterwards Tysoe returned, accompanied by Renzi. Both were breathless.

'Hello, old bean,' Kydd slurred. 'Come to join the party?'

Renzi took one look at the situation and hustled him into the next room. 'Get coffee, Tysoe. Black and plenty of it.'

He waited until Kydd had downed several cups. Then, very slowly and in a flat voice, he outlined the position that Kydd must now recognise he was in.

It was potentially fatal. Among gentlemen a blow received was an intolerable insult. Unlike hot words that could be retracted with an apology, to be struck with malice before witnesses was a contumely that had no redress other than to seek satisfaction in an encounter. If Pountney chose to, he could call Kydd out, and the next time they met it would be with pistols on a lonely heath.

'He never would, the shicer,' Kydd muttered.

'Pountney's been out twice. Why should he decline now in front of his friends? He must, or be thought craven before a man at arms. This is a deadly serious matter and I beg you will take it as such.'

The coffee was doing its work, but when Pountney came

to, would he press for satisfaction? Kydd had no doubts about his own conduct in a duel – he'd faced worse, but lives could be ended simply because of a moment of hot-tempered lashing out.

Muffled groaning came from next door and Kydd and Renzi returned.

Pountney was sitting in a chair, eyes closed, being fussed over by his friends.

'How is he?' Kydd asked.

The eyes flicked open. 'You struck me, sir!'

'An ill-considered act, which Sir Thomas regrets,' Renzi got in.

'Who's he?' one asked, and an introduction was quickly made.

Ignoring Renzi, Pountney went on, 'Before witnesses, by God!'

There was the rub: those same witnesses would be in a position to attest to any response by a principal that in any way impinged on their honour. The next moments would decide the affair.

Pountney felt his jaw and grimaced. 'To strike a gentleman is not to be borne.' He fixed Kydd with a glower of barely concealed hatred. 'Sir, I shall be seeking satisfaction in the matter. What do you say to that?'

'Sir, you will act as you may. It's of no consequence to me.'

'Then, sir, you shall hear from me directly. Good day to you.'

'So. It'll be a meeting then, Nicholas.' Kydd was light-headed with drink and defiance but it was ebbing fast.

Renzi didn't speak for some time, then said quietly, 'I don't think you realise the consequences of this hour, dear fellow. A formal challenge is to be expected, and you must reply. It's not too late for a comprehensive apology, perhaps citing over-indulgence, the hour?'

'Never. If I walk away from the bastard he'll spend the rest of his days crowing over how his reputation was too much for a knighted hero. I'll stand in this, I believe.'

'Then there will be an encounter. You know, of course, that in these enlightened times any fatality occurring as a result of a duel constitutes murder? Should you down your man it will undoubtedly be seen as a military man taking unfair advantage of his deadly skills. No jury would acquit you.'

'It won't come to that, Nicholas. A duel is to show you can face fire – pistols are too unreliable at range, as all boarders know.'

'I fancy a rather different form of the weapon will be met with in this instance. The duelling pistol is a work of great art and precision and, you may accept, might be relied upon to deliver a mortal stroke at a distance.'

'Very well.'

'And to the result. Should either of you be carried lifeless from the field it will be the scandal of the age. There will be—'

'Stow it, Nicholas. I'll not show craven.'

Renzi saw there was no softening in the hard features. 'Then in sorrow I do offer my services as your second.'

'Thank you.'

'To do what I can in order to effect a reconciliation.'

'I understand,' Kydd said sombrely.

Chapter 71

The challenge came at an early hour in the morning. Stiffly phrased, it left no room for doubt that a mere apology would be insufficient to remove the stain upon Pountney's honour, and that a meeting was expected under the rules of the Code Duello.

Renzi studied it gravely. 'This is then the cartel, brother. I must ask – what is your desire in this?'

'To stand.'

'Very well. I shall approach his seconds to define conditions. To you lies the choice of weapon – I advise accepting a duelling pistol else you suffer an intolerable disadvantage – and the ground. His is the distance and the terms of satisfaction.'

'Terms of . . .?'

'Shall you exchange but one shot, or will it be *à l'outrance*.'

'Which being . . .'

'Fire until one of you falls mortally wounded.'

'I see.'

'For all that, the usual is a single shot at seven yards and honour satisfied. The form of address will vary – a pacing outward until the signal is given, a counted time at rest. These details will be known to you before. It is for we seconds to agree the formalities.'

Kydd knew the dry, precise listing of the details by his friend hid his care and anxiety but, strangely, it steadied him. Renzi would see to it that only the strictest fair play would be seen, and though Kydd had never witnessed a duel he was in the best possible hands.

Renzi sat down and composed the acceptance, which was sent off promptly.

Kydd was held in the grip of unreality. In a short while he would be taking the ground and facing an individual who held sufficient malice in his heart that he was prepared to kill him in cold blood. Did he have the same intention?

Renzi was called away before noon to consult Pountney's seconds, and he was left alone with his thoughts.

Cecilia was still in Wiltshire and Persephone would never know of it. Should he be struck down, neither of them could come to his side. And should he not be putting his affairs in order, supposing he . . .?

In a flood, just like a wave on the beach returning, came the knowledge that it didn't really matter: he now had none in this life who depended on him, who would be left forlorn and alone by his passing. A lump grew in his throat as he thought of Cecilia and Renzi, their intimacy together in marriage, a condition he'd thought would be his and now never would.

He was resigned. Whatever fate was in store so be it.

Chapter 72

The carriage rattled across the old timber Fulham Bridge, the toll-keeper asleep in his booth at this early hour.

The knot in Kydd's stomach tightened. Across the Thames on the other side was Putney Heath and the duelling ground.

Beside him sat Renzi, grave and unspeaking, the lines in his face deep and severe. Opposite was the surgeon Bates, doing all he could to avoid catching his eye and, next to him, Tysoe. He'd been quietly but doggedly insistent that he should attend and had come as Kydd's other second. All four were sombrely attired in black.

The day had broken grey, cheerless and, in the stillness of dawn, had a numbing chill. Kydd drew his cloak tighter – it would not do to be seen trembling.

They passed the sleeping village of Putney, dogs barking the only disturbance, then left the highway for a modest trail into the woods.

Would Persephone ever know of this morning – if she were alive, that was? He crushed the thought – she *was*, somewhere, and that conviction he would faithfully carry with him for the rest of his life . . . which could be ended in less than an hour.

It was to be a formal affair: at nine yards, the signal a dropped handkerchief. To three shots if satisfaction was not attained, being held to be the effusion of blood. Discretion in the matter of public knowledge to be observed at all times.

The trees thinned and, after following a wide curve, the coach drew up in a clearing. On the other side was another vehicle, its occupants standing by it, unmoving, waiting.

Kydd stepped down and, in accordance with custom, faced about while Renzi walked up to the mid-point between them to meet the challenger's seconds.

'My principal avers that this affair is most regrettable,' Renzi opened, 'and does offer anything within his power to bring it to an honourable conclusion without the necessity of bloodshed.'

At a dignified pace the second turned about and marched over to Pountney, arrayed in a frogged green coat and tasselled boots. The murmuring of words between them was brief and the answer was quickly returned.

'Nothing but prostration to the knees to beg pardon will satisfy – and before witnesses.' The man's expression was a studied blankness as he delivered the preposterous demand.

Nevertheless, bound by his duty, Renzi returned to Kydd.

As he mouthed his refusal he knew that could be the very last word on earth he uttered.

Renzi returned to Pountney's second. 'My principal has consulted his honour and finds he cannot accede to the demand.'

'Then the business must proceed, sir.'

A gentleman's sword was thrust into the grassy sward and the required distance measured out to another sword.

'To your marks, gentlemen.'

Kydd took his place, standing loosely. Thirty feet away Pountney sauntered up to his mark, casually removing his silk gloves and never once taking his eyes off Kydd's. Even across the distance a malevolence radiated out, a visceral force that hammered at his senses. This man was an experienced duellist and therefore would be making no mistake in the encounter.

The seconds met in the middle. An elaborately ornamented wooden case was brought: the weapons. They were offered first to Renzi, who inspected them both. Expensive, damascened and chased in silver, there was a lethal beauty in the oiled blued steel of the dedicated duelling pistols. Long-barrelled, with a hair trigger and dispart sights to fire true, these were consummate killing pieces.

Without a word, Renzi began loading one, taking the utmost pains with wad and charge, inspecting the ball closely before ramming it firmly home. Pountney's second did the same. When they were satisfied they yielded the pistols up to the surgeon.

'Sir?' Renzi duly turned his back. As challenged, his would be the choice; a deadly decision but scrupulously fair.

'The left one, sir.'

He was presented with the weapon and, with measured tread, carried it to Kydd and handed it to him with a bow.

Kydd took it, feeling its finely balanced heft, the indifferent chill touch of its oiled steel.

It was time.

Turning side-on, he lowered his pistol to point to the ground. He took the opportunity to unobtrusively sight down it – it was a perfectly tuned weapon and gave an instinctual sight picture, but it was still a pistol, even with its superior performance. The next time he sighted, it would be trained on Pountney – and the only rational course would be to aim for the chest, the beating heart – a killing shot.

He looked up to see Pountney readying in the same way until he stood motionless, pistol by his side, his gaze unwaveringly on him.

'Gentlemen – cock your weapons.'

A curious floating sensation calmed Kydd, as though he were an outer being viewing the world through his own eyes. He saw the seconds draw back, Renzi's white face turned towards him, the surgeon to one side, his medicine chest open, the gleam of steel instruments clearly visible.

The hammer came back with a light snicking of steel, first to half, then full cock.

Conscious of his heart thudding, Kydd concentrated on the handkerchief. It was slowly raised and held at full arm's length where it hung limply in the still, cold air.

Then it fell.

Kydd swept up the pistol and, in a frozen moment, saw the foresight align on the figure and as distant powder smoke blossomed, his finger curled around the trigger and the pistol bucked in his hand. Almost at the same instant there was the vicious *whuuup* of a ball past his head. A heartbeat later, a rush of elation – he'd come through to the other side!

Lowering the pistol he fought down the shaking of a reaction. Pountney still stood – his mind had recorded however that he'd staggered slightly, his ball apparently nicking him in the clothing.

Breathing deeply, he waited for the formalities to conclude as the seconds met in a huddle.

It had been an experience but the cold analysis of his battle-trained mind told him several things. First, that such a piece was considerably more precise than a boarding pistol, without question a formidable weapon. Second, that Pountney had undoubtedly aimed for his head – and that he was a hardened duellist. Moments before firing, he'd leaned forward to bend his head over his body in a bow shape, reducing his frontal area down by five or six inches and at the same time minimising exposure of his vitals with his sighting arm.

All that was now over but the seconds were taking their time.

Then Renzi came over to him, his expression wooden. 'I'm to inform you that in accordance with the terms of this meeting the Honourable Charles Pountney insists on a second shot, the first having produced no result.'

Numb, Kydd handed over his pistol.

Reloading complete, they faced each other again. But it had given Kydd time to consider his move. There was a chink in Pountney's firing position: the armpit. With the accuracy of these pistols it made a better aiming point than a general body shot and would be a sure settler, if at the cost of a fractionally longer aiming.

The handkerchief was raised and steadied.

It dropped.

Kydd brought up the pistol and sighted. Before it settled, Pountney's pistol gouted smoke – but in his haste the ball missed.

Kydd was left with his finger on the trigger, his sights still on the helpless form of the man, a hair's breadth from touching it off. All the rules would agree that Pountney should now stand and take Kydd's shot, but something in Kydd revolted against the cold-blooded kill and he deliberately fired wide, into the turf.

That should be full and fair satisfaction for any man and Kydd drew a shuddering breath.

Oddly there were angry cries and seconds came running. What was going on?

'Sir, you deloped!' a red-faced individual cried, stalking up to him.

Renzi hastened to interpose himself but Kydd was at a loss as to what was going on. 'Delope?'

His friend, face ashen, said sombrely, 'A barbaric notion. That to fire aside is to cast the other as an unworthy opponent and therefore an insult upon his honour.'

Before he could explain further Renzi was summarily taken aside but was back within minutes, his face tight.

'I'm bound to inform you that your opponent invokes the Code Duello in the matter of deloping and demands a third shot, as is provided for in the terms of the meeting.'

Kydd held his fury in check. This time he would go for a kill – it would be a service to rid the world of such a toad.

He looked down the distance at the stiff figure and coldly measured his aim – the four-inch square where his ball would finish the business.

The pistols were returned, his hand feeling the almost soft satin of the blued steel, the intricate lock-work ready and obedient to do its work at his bidding.

After his last hurried shot, Pountney would take his time over this one – and so would he.

The handkerchief rose for the third time – and dropped.

His pistol came up and the sights immediately found their target . . . and before gun-smoke could gout from the far pistol and with no remorse whatsoever Kydd squeezed the trigger.

And with only a sullen click and stray spark the gun stayed silent.

A misfire!

He slowly lowered the pistol with a deepening apprehension, for he knew the rules. A misfire counted as a shot – and therefore he must remain at a stand and present his body for a return fire.

A principled opponent would relinquish the advantage but that wouldn't be Pountney's way.

Sure enough the muzzle of his gun wavered at the realisation of his advantage, steadied as his bow-like posture unbent, but then it moved, slowly traversing Kydd's body up and down as if seeking his vitals.

Kydd's skin crawled with unbearable anticipation, his mind frozen on the one reality: that in the next second he would be sent out of this world.

The distant muzzle stopped, pitilessly trained directly at his head. A heartbeat – and then gun-smoke.

And then . . . nothing.

Chapter 73

The world swam into focus reluctantly, the dim whirl of colour and returning sensation taking hold more insistently, but bringing a heaving nausea with it. Kydd was conscious of hands supporting him as he retched helplessly to the side, a near unendurable shaft of pain in the side of his head stabbing in as he leaned over.

'He'll do,' he heard a gruff voice above him pronounce.

He lay back again, his mind scrabbling for a foothold in the vertiginous daze. Then another voice came, low and concerned: 'Lie still, brother. You've taken a chip in the headpiece as would give a bear pause.'

Kydd opened his eyes, letting in the world. 'Nicholas,' he answered weakly. 'It's you.'

'The last time I looked, old fellow, yes.'

Another figure appeared. 'Thought we'd lost you, Tiger. Please don't do it again.'

'You have my vow on it, Prinker.'

Memories returned, reality taking form.

'Pountney?'

'Packed his bags and gone to his lair,' Fookes answered, with contempt. 'Keeping a mort quiet about calling out a public hero. Now, you should really have given me a tootle that he's up to his old games – we've a way with his sort.'

Renzi helped him to some broth. 'As I'm mightily relieved I'm not to take evil news to Cecilia. She'd never let me hear the end of it.'

Kydd levered himself up on his elbows. 'News – has anyone word of Persephone?'

'None,' Renzi said uncomfortably. 'I rather think you should consider she's . . .'

Kydd rolled to one side, wincing at the spasm of pain it brought but it was nothing to the wave of bleakness settling on him.

By nightfall he was sitting in a chair, allowing Tysoe to clean and dress his wound.

The ball had clipped the side of his head, an injury he'd seen often in battle and he knew what to expect. Some days of pain and discomfort but where a head wound was not fatal the skin tended to heal quickly. What he felt about Pountney was fading; he despised the man but at the same time it was his own lack of control under drink that had led to this.

His mind shied away from confrontation with his loss: the grief was too recent.

Two days later a terse letter from the Admiralty arrived, desiring Kydd to resume the command of his ship forthwith or tender reasons in writing if he should be unable.

He passed it to Renzi. 'Do you think . . .?'

'Undoubtedly,' his friend replied. 'There's been no public disclosure but there have been rumours. I rather think your

315

days topping it the society lion are herewith summarily concluded.'

So it was going to be a return to the simplicity and stern duty of a man-o'-war, so greatly in contrast to his life at the highest. But in a rush of feeling he felt in his bowels that nothing could be better suited to the healing of a soul.

Chapter 74

A week later Kydd posted down to Portsmouth with his sea gear. The familiar countryside passed and then they were rattling down the last miles of the London road and on to Portsea Island. He took rooms at the George, and shortly afterwards made his number with the port admiral.

'Ah, yes, Sir Thomas. I hear you made quite a showing – entirely to your credit, of course.'

'Sir.'

'Yet I have to tell you that I have orders for you to rejoin the North Sea Squadron with the greatest dispatch. You've been missed, I believe.'

'Kind in you to say so, sir.'

'Well, with all dispatch – I won't delay you.'

So his dawn encounter was not to be noticed. It made it easier, of course.

Tyger was lying at anchor at Spithead – he'd seen her from Portsdown Hill, her sturdy bulldog lines unmistakable even over such a distance and he yearned for her enfolding embrace in quite the same way as any foremast hand after a punishing spree ashore. It would be the best medicine possible.

He'd sent word of his arrival and precisely at ten the next day his barge touched at the sally port, the yellow and black striped jerseys of the Tygers recognisable from any distance.

'Very pleased to see you again, Sir Thomas.' It was touching to hear Bowden so patently sincere in his greeting, as were the warm grins on the faces of his coxswain Halgren and the boat's crew.

'As I am, to see *Tyger* and her company,' he replied, almost in a whisper, and stepped into the boat.

'It's been very quiet since you left, sir,' Bowden said, with a boyish smile. 'We heard you were seen with the king and the Prince of Wales both. Did you—'

'Yes, I did. Perhaps later.'

Sensing something the young lieutenant subsided.

It seemed that no word of his meeting on the heath had reached *Tyger*, which was as well – no curiosity, no explanations. He was piped aboard with due ceremony and a side party of size quite beyond that required for a post-captain. On the inboard end was the first lieutenant. 'Could I say how delighted we are to see you back aboard, Sir Thomas?' he boomed, giving an instinctive little bow, which was just as touching as the other greetings had been. 'And am I the first to congratulate you upon the occasion of your engagement? We were so pleased to read that—'

Kydd froze and the polite words tailed off. 'Thank you, Mr Bray. Your words are well-meant, I'm sure.'

He went below, leaving puzzled murmuring behind him. His cabin was as he remembered it, neat and clean as a new pin, sparkling spring sunshine coming through to dapple the deck-head above. Yet it brought little joy and no diminishing of the desolation in his soul.

As token of their pleasure at his return the gunroom invited him to dinner, but it was not a success. The effort of being congenial was beyond him and he knew he was poor company. His curt admission at the outset that the engagement was at an end for reasons that need not concern them had ensured a joyless occasion.

Kydd retired from the dinner early and went to his cabin, the wound still throbbing under its artful concealing of wavy hair. It was not working as he'd hoped – the slight but live heave of the deck, which had always touched him before with the promise of the open sea, had a melancholy in it that spoke of the ebbing of hope, of life.

A light tap at the door, and Dillon entered. He quickly took in Kydd's mood. 'Oh, I didn't mean to disturb you at all, sir.'

'No, come in, Edward. I do beg pardon to be such a drabble-tail tonight before your mess-mates. I'm a little out of sorts, I do confess.'

'There's no need for apologies, Sir Thomas,' Dillon replied awkwardly. 'As Lord Farndon was good enough to inform me of the reason.'

'What was that?' Kydd snapped, suddenly defensive.

'Er, he saw fit to send me in the strictest confidence a letter outlining your late travails as would—'

'He told you what, pray?' Kydd said dangerously.

'Recognising the grievous effect on you of the loss of your intended, he desired me—'

'He had no right to do so!' Kydd exploded. 'None at all, the damned shab!'

'He desired me to watch over you as I may, that—'

319

'He dares to tell you this?'

'Sir Thomas, I believe he's right to do so. Sooner or later you'll have to confront that she is . . . that is, she may well be no longer with us and then—'

'No! No, I tell you! How can you or your poxy tribe know she's dead?' Kydd snarled. 'I won't have it! Do y' hear, sir?' His voice rose to an ugly shout. 'I won't have it – and be buggered to you and all your slivey crew who say she is!'

Dillon remained silent, waiting for the storm to pass. 'I understand, Sir Thomas. Please believe, I understand,' he said quietly.

Kydd breathed deeply several times and forced himself to a calm. 'Edward. That was uncalled for, and I do crave pardon. You see, it's . . . it's all I have to hold to,' he went on huskily. 'It's all been so sudden – all of it.'

Noiselessly Dillon left the cabin. There was nothing any man could do for Sir Thomas Kydd aboard *Tyger* but leave him to find peace in his own way.

The gunroom had lingered over their last drinks and was in a buzz of comment and opinion about their captain. They barely noticed Dillon return. He resumed his chair but then reached for a glass and rapped it sharply for attention. 'Gentlemen. I would have you listen carefully to what I say.'

He looked about the table significantly. 'I see you are at a stand to fathom what's happened to our captain. My position of confidence has placed me in a position to know and I believe it to be in the best interests of the ship to share this with you – but on the strict understanding it goes no further and you give no indication to his person that you are aware of certain facts.'

Letting it sink in, he continued, 'While in London, he lost his heart to a beautiful woman. This led to an engagement of a public nature, but very recently he was confronted by a situation to which he responded in the most gentlemanly way but which in the event was misconstrued. As a result the lady withdrew from the public gaze and is to be accounted lost to Sir Thomas.'

'Doesn't explain why—'

'If I tell you that the woman in all probability has done away with herself you will understand more of what guilt, grief and the torment of not knowing her end he labours under.'

In the shocked silence Dillon went on, 'He believes she is alive, somewhere not known to man. Gentlemen, it were a mercy not to take this away from him.'

Chapter 75

'And I can't say as I'm other than delighted to see *Tyger* back with us, Kydd. Doesn't Shakespeare say something about one having a valiant heart that lets you keep good sleep at night, or some such twaddle? A cigar? Took 'em from a saucy Dutchman a week or so ago.'

'Thank you, sir, no.'

Admiral Russell was in good humour and gave a lazy smile, tinged with puzzlement. 'Well, you're here – what am I to make of it? A direction from their lordships sent at the run that you're to be employed upon such service as you are peculiarly fitted for. Most irregular. You haven't run afoul o' the beggars?'

'I can't think how, sir.'

'You seem a little t' weather, Kydd. It's not that you're pining after the ladies at court, the life of a sybarite? I've heard you quite charmed the politicals and Prinny both – yes, I have my sources, old fellow.'

'No, sir, I'm not,' Kydd said woodenly.

Russell paused, trying to make him out, then tapped absent-mindedly on the desk with a pencil. 'So, I'm to send you on some harum-scarum affair without I know why. And this not the season for any gallivanting – we've a quiet enough blockade on the Hollanders, and Ganteaume's frightful sortie now finished, there's not much excitement to be met with in my command as I can offer you.' He sighed. 'The best I can come up with is Gothenburg. Ice in the Baltic is breaking up – we can expect mischief of some kind when the Danes wake up after the winter, but saving that . . .'

'Sir.'

'Cheer up, m' boy. The sea air will see you purged of whatever ails ye. Tarry a while over a cup and I'll have orders readied for *Tyger*.'

The orders were straightforward enough: to lie at Gothenburg and gather intelligence from the British consul. Should word of trouble emerge, Kydd should place himself across the Kattegat, the entrance to the Baltic, to counter the threat and send his accompanying sloop to alert the squadron. If none, he was to wait a week before returning to station to resume blockade duties.

Chapter 76

The winds were northerlies, foul for the Skaw and Gothenburg, and *Tyger* made a slow passage, a wearisome staying about in the fresh breeze until fifty-eight degrees of latitude was reached to allow them to put up the helm and bear away for the Swedish coast.

Picking up the Vinga light, they anchored in Gothenburg roads as they had done those times before, lying off the myriad flat, uninteresting rocky islands.

Kydd boarded *Wasp* for onward passage into the city. The brig-rigged sixteen-gun sloop was not unlike his beloved *Teazer*, but that only deepened his sadness, for it was while in her command that he had first met Persephone.

The sloop's captain was Langton, a middle-aged commander, whose careful manner and evident awe of Kydd made conversation hard going. The pilot caught something of this and retreated from his usual banter while the men on deck moved about in uncanny silence, awkwardness radiating out with Kydd at its heart.

* * *

The consul seemed confused at Kydd's request for intelligence.

'Cap'n, I don't at all have any news as will interest the likes o' you. Trade gossip, currency exchange, your mad king, Gustavus, but naught of the French or the Danes, bless 'em.'

'Nothing as would alarm?'

'Why, no. Too early in the season. Should there be?'

So, there would be no distracting, no action, merely a week at anchor in idleness and then back to the blockade.

The days passed slowly.

Liberty ashore was not taken up by many: they had spent their means in the month or so in Portsmouth and now idled listlessly on board, the officers subdued by the knowledge of the private suffering endured behind the closed door of the great cabin aft.

One morning at daybreak Kydd rose for his practice of taking a turn about the upper deck.

As was usual he was not 'noticed' by the watch and paced slowly along until he was clear of the main-mast shrouds, where a good view of the broad seascape was open to him.

There was nothing special about this wan grey Scandinavian foreday but for some reason his senses were uncannily acute – the scent of brine, the soft buffet of the morning zephyr, the rhythmic tapping of lines from aloft against the mast.

He drank in the sensations with appreciation – then came a dawning realisation. These were all outside his being: he was now beginning to take notice of things beyond his shell of grief, to find comfort in the trappings of life, the unacknowledged elements that were in truth the flavours of living.

Even while his heart was sick within him, he would perform his rightful duty to the ship and her crew. This he owed them, the ship's company whose trust was in their captain, their leader. They had a right to expect his attention, his devotion, as they would in turn repay to their ship.

He was aware that the pain was no longer so raw. Things were slipping inexorably into the past. It was time to move forward, into what life was able to offer him now.

He felt better. Raising his gaze, he took in the grand sweep of deck to the bowsprit that was *Tyger* – she was a first-rank frigate of the breed and it was granted to him to be her captain. How could he remain locked away from her martial enchantment?

As though a burden had been lifted, he stepped out, then saw a young seaman on the main hatch working an eye splice with marlinspike and whipping twine. 'Not that way, lad,' he said kindly, taking it from the astonished youngster. 'You're making it hard for yourself. A twist against the lay and it does invite the strand in, so.' He demonstrated with an easy motion and gave it back.

'Th-thank you, sir,' the youth stuttered.

Kydd moved on, oblivious to the significant looks being exchanged aft.

Later in the morning the pace livened with a hail on deck. 'Boat *ahoooy!*'

It was a not a naval craft coming off the shore or one of the usual bumboats but more of a yacht. It rounded to with an unnecessary flourish and it was soon evident that it was the consul, who was seeking an immediate interview with Kydd.

'I've a news for you, Cap'n, as should please ye. Friends o' mine – no need f'r names – have just told me as there's a convoy to sail up the Danish coast from Esbjerg. No one knows where it's bound.'

'A convoy?' Kydd said in surprise.

'Not as if it can stand beside our Baltic trade – four merchant jacks and an escort.'

Kydd's interest quickened. It was no threat but was certainly prey. 'Where's it off to, do you think – what cargo?'

'Don't know anything o' that. Just as it's more'n a mort curious, don't you think?'

It made little sense – an escorted convoy of only four ships and coast-hugging up the Jutland peninsula? That implied a valuable freighting but on its way to where?

Kydd's orders did not include ignoring potential prizes but, more to the point, anything being risked like that had to be looked into, if only for peace of mind.

For the first time in a long while he felt a quickening of the pulse at the scent of action.

'Throw out *Wasp*'s pennants,' he said, noticing the sudden grins on deck and unable to suppress a tight smile himself.

As the consul's boat made its way back, Kydd took Langton down to his cabin. 'A pretty mystery, Captain,' he opened, the North Sea chart spread out before him. A nearly land-locked sea, it had only three points of exit: the Channel, the Baltic and the far north.

Where the convoy could be heading was not at all obvious. The Channel was too well patrolled and guarded, the Baltic still choked with ice. This left the north, but what destinations in the vast wastes of the North Atlantic or the Arctic regions were there?

'All we can say is that they're headed up the coast towards us.' He gave a small smile. 'Any suggestions?'

'Has to be Oslo, sir. The Danes rule Norway but now it's cut adrift from them. They hunger after their timber and iron so this is a species of trade payment being made.'

That would take the convoy on past the Skaw, the tip of Denmark, and across the sixty-mile strait between the two countries, less than a day's sail. It could be – but for one thing: traditional foes of the Danes, the Swedish had a coast-line reaching nearly the whole way up the Skagerrak between it and Norway. 'The Swedes would never let 'em by.'

'Kristiansand?' Langton offered.

'Hmm. I'd think it to be the most likely,' Kydd ruminated. 'It makes sense if they're trying to get across before we arrive for the Baltic thaw – except that they didn't reckon on us looking into here before our time.'

It was a straightforward matter to set up an interception. Close in with the Danish coast, the convoy had to make their crossing from one of two points – the Skaw itself or the shortest distance, a near-overnight dash from Hirtshals on the north-west coast of Jutland.

Kydd outlined the plan to his officers. 'My guess is that it's Hirtshals. We sail this hour. *Tyger* to lay off nine miles out of sight and *Wasp* to scout inshore. When sighted, *Tyger* will put down the escorts while *Wasp* delays the merchantmen. Clear?'

That night Kydd slept as he hadn't for a long time.

Chapter 77

The coast of Denmark under their lee, low, sandy and featureless, the two men-o'-war began their watch. It would be a day at most if the convoy had sailed, according to the information, and conditions would be ideal – they'd be boxed in against the coast, and then a sympathetic prize court in Gothenburg . . .

But well into the second day it was obvious that they'd miscalculated or been fooled. Either there was no convoy or they had taken their departure for Norway earlier – Hantsholm further south, perhaps?

The only rational course was to stand out into the Skagerrak and search along a line connecting the two. Failing that, give up the chase and return to Gothenburg.

Strung out abeam at masthead sight of each other, *Tyger* and *Wasp* set sail and, within hours, had the answer. A humble British timber drogher out of Hull bound for Sweden on sighting them made much of wanting to speak, and when Kydd closed, the merchant master hailed him excitedly. He was sure the navy would want to know: a half-day's sail away a crowd of ships was heading close-hauled westwards. He'd counted them: four merchant ships and an escort – a heavy frigate and three sloops-of-war.

It turned everything on its head – a frigate and other vessels were clearly more than the convoy was worth, but the sting was in the course it was taking. These ships were not going to Norway, they were headed out to the open sea. And with such force in the escort it was most certainly up to no good. There was no question now of returning to Gothenburg – their presence had to be explained and the threat met.

Kydd felt a stab of foreboding. Their reported track was to the west where there was nothing but the coast of Britain. If they intended to round Scotland into the empty Atlantic, they'd be sailing north-west to clear the Orkneys – which were headed directly west.

There was one reason that fitted: that it was a raiding party or some covert force to be landed on the wild shores of the Scottish Highlands, where they'd never be discovered before their mischief was done. It had happened before, in Wales, and, but for the incompetence of the enemy commander, it could have been a serious blow, the forerunner of an invasion.

That would explain the strong escort, ships enough to carry troops for a sizeable landing that could be relied upon to overwhelm the local militia.

To fly south to warn the North Sea Squadron would give the enemy all the time it needed to complete their mission. Should he follow them and send *Wasp* to alert the squadron? However, only the two of them working together would have any chance of locating the chase in this limitless expanse of sea.

It was a tough decision, arguably against orders, not to

send warning to the squadron, but this was not a straight stern chase. Into the wind the enemy might be well over on the other tack and therefore out of sight.

It would be a standard frigate search: in a wide zigzag centred on a line touching the northern tip of Scotland, in case the true destination was further on – Ireland.

They were on their own and could not call for help, but there was a very slight chance they might meet one of the gallant little band of cutters and sloops out of Leith, sailing in all weathers on distant patrol. Just one of their number could carry an urgent alert to the North Sea Squadron.

Tyger and *Wasp* lay over under full sail as they began their hunt, an exhilarating charge with the seas creaming at the forefoot and lines thrumming in the fresh breeze. A leg of twenty-five miles full and bye on opposite tacks, stay about and the next leg on the other, a sighting rendezvous every four hours.

Kydd was counting on his superior speed and handling to make up distance on the enemy, knowing that they also would be tacking into the fresh westerly, but with only a couple of days' sailing to overhaul their quarry it was going to be chancy.

There was no way he could endure working on the long overdue papers in his cabin. This would be a chase straining every nerve and his place was on deck. The streaming wind tautened every rope and hardened each sail: it was a headlong race that could only be his to lose.

It had to be admitted, it was neatly done: well in with the Danish coast and out of sight, then a sudden lunge westward of only a few days. It was their bad luck that *Tyger* had been at hand.

Yet here they were, the Scottish coast barely a half-day away and still no sighting.

Chapter 78

It was time to make some hard decisions.

Kydd spread out their charts on the cabin table. Sparse in detail they spoke of a rugged, wild shore that no ship would approach unless they had to, and the north of Scotland was notorious for its weather – shrieking gales even in summertime, fogs and hail the year round.

Then he had an inspiration. 'Ask Mr Brice to step down here.'

His third lieutenant entered warily. 'You wanted to see me, sir?'

'You've served in these waters, I believe, Mr Brice.' His record showed small ship service in the Baltic convoy trade, and the hard lessons in seamanship he'd learned there had made him possibly the best foul-weather seaman aboard.

'Sir.'

'I'm wanting some advice.'

'Sir.' For some reason the man's posture shifted from one of circumspection to a more defensive stance.

'You know we're on the tail of an enemy force as can

cause us much grief where it lands. Have you any ideas in the matter?'

After a long hesitation Brice answered. 'The length o' coast north of the Moray Firth is in the lee of the westerlies and might be attractive . . . but there they'd know we have our armed brigs and unrated craft out of Invergordon and similar as could bring with them their big brothers from Leith. These could fall on 'em the same day.'

'Please go on, Mr Brice.'

'South o' the firth it's too inhabited to let 'em land in peace with the army too close.'

'Yes?'

'So if I had to place money on it, then I'd say . . . 't would be the other side – Ireland.'

It made sense.

Brice hadn't finished. 'And there's a way we'd know for sure.'

'Do stand on, sir.'

'South o' Dunbeath the shore is steep-to, the Highlands come down to the sea. They never can land there. We need go no more'n thirty miles to the south, and if they're not sighted then . . .'

'Thank you, Mr Brice,' Kydd said warmly. 'If they're not seen it must be Ireland. You know this coast well, then?'

Oddly, the defensiveness came back in full measure, his look of blank inscrutability puzzling.

Duncansby Head, with its unmistakable twin conical sea-stack sentinels, the extreme north-eastern tip of Scotland, was raised later in the morning and the two ships shaped course for the run south, the continuing westerly ensuring they could close with the coastline in no danger of being driven ashore.

At daybreak they made rendezvous there once more – and with their answer. No convoy, no ships. The enemy were therefore on their way to Ireland, somewhere at sea out of sight to the north.

Kydd turned to his third lieutenant. 'Mr Brice. We've time to make up. The quickest passage around?'

Again the enigmatic defensiveness. 'There's only the one, sir. The near fifty-mile space a'tween the Orkneys and the Shetlands. I much doubt they'll want to go further, around south of the Faeroes, extra distance, a current against 'em.'

'I see.' This was where the Armada of Drake's time had struggled past to reach the Atlantic.

Kydd traced the enemy captain's plan with his mind's eye. Into the wind he'd take advantage of a long larboard tack, then put about to make his rounding of Scotland in the form of a long triangle that could reach Ireland on the same board. The apex would be well north but it would have the sovereign merit of being both sure and safe for a convoy of merchant ships.

It would also make their own task harder for how could they know when the unknown captain would decide to put over his helm and make his run?

Kydd's alternatives were reducing one by one: to make chase with the hope of bringing them to battle – or slip away and make every effort to reach Ireland to warn the defences? Instinct told him to run them down and settle everything in the fires of combat but cooler thought made him realise that the chances of interception were now slim.

His gaze refocused on the chart. 'Mr Brice. I note that there's a passage – a narrow one I'll grant you – between your Orkneys and the mainland. Should we slip through, we'll be able to follow the base of the enemy's triangle, shortening the distance by an agreeable margin.'

The more he considered it, the better it looked – it could even be they would be in place to trap the south-tracking ships as they came, a gratifying conclusion.

'What do you think?'

Brice stiffened. 'I really don't think it a good idea, Sir Thomas.' His voice was strained, on edge.

'Oh – why not, pray?'

'The passage . . . it's too dangerous.'

'The chart does not say so.'

'Sir, this is the Pentland Firth. It's strewn with islands and reefs and . . . and tide rips that are great and terrible.'

'Are you saying it's impassable, Mr Brice?'

'I say as I cannot help you, sir, if you choose to risk it.'

'Hmm. A lot to be gained should we win through.'

The man became strangely fidgety, then mumbled, 'Sir, I have to be back on deck, my duty.'

'Very well, Mr Brice. You've been helpful. Ask the master to attend on me if you will.'

The sailing master came promptly, as if expecting a summons.

'Mr Brice tells me that the Pentland Firth is not to be passed. Is this your understanding?'

'Not as who's to say, sir. Why, I remember in *Stentor* brig, we made passage from the west in, when was it?, last days o' the American war or was it—'

'So you have knowledge of it, Mr Joyce?'

'I were only a master's mate at the time. In them days it was—'

'Are you confident to take us through?'

'Ah, well, as I was about to say, it all depends on the

weather. Can be calm as you please an' you'll sail along at a spankin' pace but if it goes agin you, why, I'd not like our chances, even in a fair-sized barky as ours.'

'We're not far off Duncansby Head. We can start our passage very soon.'

'Well, it ain't so easy as I'd say, sir.' He scratched his hair in vexation. 'It's the tides, y' see, sir. Go sliding through east, then slack and off to the west. And at a rate o' knots to make ye stare. Nine, ten – more.'

This was as fast as they could manage in a brisk fair wind – and all to stay in the same place.

'Heard tell they once logged a sixteen-knot race off of the Swilkies.'

'And it reverses with the tide?'

'Aye. Just as fast in the opposite direction, see.'

It was no wonder Brice was cautious.

Joyce picked up on his theme. 'An' if these tides come up agin the wind, then that's when it starts to get ugly, like. Seas kicked up as high as y' main-yard and if ye're caught in them, you'll be shakin' hands with Davy Jones himself afore the hour's out.'

'*You* got through.'

'We came from the west, wi' the wind astern – and it was a prettier day than this 'un. Sir.'

Kydd's hopes fell away. 'You know what we're about, Mr Joyce. We're the only ones who can thwart their mischief and we haven't a chance of that if we go around the Orkneys. Knowing that, would you take us into it?'

'Um, I'd like to – bigod, I'd like to, but . . .'

'Very well, I understand you, Mr Joyce,' Kydd muttered. 'We'll go the long way, then.'

'If you had one wi' the local knowledge, why, then it would

be a different basket o' fish. They knows the tide times and quiet places to tuck away in if it gets roaratorious, t' wait it out, killick down. I knew one old man who—'

'Thank you, Mr Joyce.'

The master apologetically made his exit and left Kydd with his thoughts.

The stakes were high: not simply prize-taking but what might be a pre-invasion diversionary landing with all that this implied – and no risk was too great to head it off.

By his decision to chase after the convoy he'd thrown away his chance of sending warning. It meant that if he followed in a forlorn chase he'd almost certainly not catch them – but if he left now to alert the Irish defences he'd be compelled to take the same course as they but trailing them, a futility.

They had to get through – it was imperative. But how? Local knowledge? Land a boat and search out one who knew both the sea and a frigate's capability and vulnerabilities? Ludicrously unlikely.

There was one last resort.

Chapter 79

'Clear lower deck, Mr Bray. All hands lay aft.'
  Tyger's ship's company crowded together, agog to know what such an order breaking into their sea routine meant.

Kydd stood by the wheel, the seamen in a disciplined mass forward, his officers aft, behind him.

'Tygers. You don't need me to tell you what we're about. Those ships we're chasing are sailing to fall on our land to do it harm and we're the only ones to know it. We've a chance to even up the chase – but only if we can thrust through this passage and get ahead of them. What I'm asking – is there any man aboard who knows this place, can assist the sailing master to make transit safely?'

He was aware of their astonished looks – safe navigation was an officer's job and Kydd was asking them for a steer.

'Come, now. There must be some who've made passage or—'

'Sir.' It came from one of the fo'c'slemen, a seasoned old able seaman whom Kydd knew to be steady and reliable.

'Come here, Holm, and tell me what you can.'

The man approached, whipping off his shapeless woollen cap. 'Sir. I knows naught o' the passage, but I knows one who does, an' I'm main puzzled why he don't step forward.'

'Oh? Who is this man?'

'He's standin' right behind you, sir. L'tenant Brice, sir.'

Kydd wheeled about in astonishment.

'I don't know what this man's talking about,' Brice responded quickly – but his pale face betrayed discomfort.

'Ask 'im about the old *Montrose*, back in 'ninety-three. See if'n it helps his memory, like.'

'Sir!' Brice blurted, 'I'll not be taunted by a foremast jack. It's intolerable! Sir, I – I . . .'

But Holm would not be overawed, standing firm with a lopsided smile.

'Carry on the men, please,' Kydd ordered, adding, 'and my cabin at once, Mr Brice.'

'Now, sir. What does this all mean, and I will have an answer.'

Brice stood mute, his hat held in a crushing grip.

'Well? Should I ask Holm, or will you . . ?'

'*Montrose*. A long time ago.' Ashen, he spoke in a voice so low it was barely audible.

'Go on.'

'I wasn't always in the navy. Once I was a young mate – in *Montrose*. Full-rigged, a general trader out o' Liverpool, Wicken her captain.'

Kydd saw it was costing the man a lot. 'Yes?'

'One voyage, returning from Hamburg in porcelain. Cap'n Wicken has a rival, another ship. Has to go north-about but he knows that I grew up on Hoy, Lyness. He asks me if we can make it through in the face of a fresh westerly. I had m' doubts but knew if we caught the tides right we could ride the currents. He says as how, damn it, this gives him a chance and he'll take it whatever.'

'And then . . .?'

'A wind out o' the west, current piling in from the east, they meet together in a fearsome rip. We clears Muckle Skerry on the ebb and we're well in when I see the whole firth is alive with white water ahead right across to Tor Ness. We can't go back against a twelve-knot current so I tells him to go south-about Stroma, avoid the Swilkies and we've a hope.'

'Did you?'

His face haggard with memories, Brice answered, 'No, sir, we didn't. Caught by a murderous back-eddy – without steerage way we took the rocks way south o' the point.' He gulped, but went on doggedly, 'No hope for it, it's bold, steep-to thereabouts. Can't get up, we stays with the wreck. All night.'

'A terrible time you had, Mr Brice,' Kydd said gently.

'I was found by fishermen in the morning, only one left alive.'

He stared unseeing into the distance. 'Sole survivor. The only one. I've lived with this all my days, can't forget it. Ever.'

So that was what had been behind the close-mouthed, taciturn officer he had come to value for his skilled and natural seamanship.

'Then I joined the navy as an able seaman and was placed on the quarterdeck by Captain Pierce, *Triumph*, and I've never come back here since that time. That's all, sir.'

Kydd wished he could reach out to him, say the things that sailors do to those who have suffered at the hands of the sea yet had tenaciously continued in their profession – but, of course, as captain he couldn't.

It made what his duty demanded he say next so much the

harder. 'Mr Brice. I'm greatly in sympathy with you in your ordeal, please believe me.'

'Thank you, sir.'

'Which puts me in some difficulty. You are the only one aboard who has reliable knowledge of this part of the world. I asked you before if you can help us but . . .'

'Sir.'

'Do recollect our country lies under peril from this enemy force. Only we can prevent it. Can you not . . .?'

Brice remained silent, his face a mask.

'And may I speak freely? If you conn us through to a successful conclusion, you will have laid any ghosts you may still have – well and truly.'

Tyger's third lieutenant held still and rigid.

'I cannot and will not order you to do this thing but do consider before you refuse again.'

It was a cruel and extreme pressure he was putting the man under but the circumstances were merciless. 'If it helps, know that all responsibility is mine and mine alone. I take advice but the accountability is mine. You shall be held blameless in the event—'

'No!' Brice said thickly. 'You know how to shame a man, sir. I'll take us in, but you understand as well as I that it's upon my word that we sail on – to ruin or safe harbour both. It's I that lives with the consequences.'

'Mr Brice, we comprehend each other – and here's my hand on it that I know how to honour a brave man.' It was done.

The sailing master was called and planning for the passage put in train.

'A vexatious thing, your tide races, Mr Brice,' Joyce agreed.

Kydd stood back as they worked it out – the hardened

old shellback with the experience of years and the man with the precious knowledge of how to outwit these fierce seas.

The point was well made that there were no tide tables for this remote fastness, and therefore they stood fair to be headed or worse by the turn of the ebb.

Brice was equal to it: high water here was exactly two hours and five minutes behind Inverness, a known location, and therefore they could know the tide state directly.

Another anxiety was that if they were confronted by the same phenomenon as *Montrose* what would be the prudent course? Presumably to lay Muckle Skerry well to the northward instead.

As more concerns were brought up and dealt with, Kydd's confidence firmed. They'd do it!

Chapter 80

After a sweeping curve to the eastward *Tyger* and *Wasp* were aligned. They would pass between the crags of the Orkney islands to the right and the mainland of Scotland to the left – barely five miles apart. And in the precise centre, the ugly dark fangs of the Pentland Skerries, now the focus of a seething whiteness.

'We wait for the tide to turn – head in on the ebb when it's west-going,' Brice said, in a detached, almost indifferent manner.

Kydd understood: with wind and a furious tide-race against them, like now, they'd never make headway. He nodded and asked, 'What of *Wasp*? Should we detach her for the longer passage north-about?'

Brice gave a tiny smile. 'She's handier than we, and'll do better closer inshore.'

Sails trimmed to allow them just enough to stem the racing tide, *Tyger* stood by for her time of trial.

'Weather's a-boldering,' Joyce offered, standing with the tight group around the wheel.

'Aye,' said Brice, eyeing the sky ahead. Low, driving scud, a study in depressing grey, from silvered to leaden.

'Nor'-west,' Joyce added. Barely fair enough for a taut clawing through. 'Backs a mite an' we've got trouble.'

'Or veers and we've our slant,' Kydd said neutrally.

'That's not our worry,' Brice said soberly. 'It's if'n this wind freshens more. Then we'll see the whole firth in a torment as it strikes against the tide-race.'

Nobody uttered a word, the mental picture only too vivid of a ship thrown through by an unstoppable current, meeting seas and wind dead against them in a maelstrom of violence.

Taking out his fob watch, Brice said offhandedly, 'The current's now with us, I believe. We go in.'

Kydd gave the orders, and with Brice at the conn, *Tyger* took the wind and placed her bowsprit on Muckle Skerry, the low, scraggy island a mile ahead, tortured with white that lay across their path.

Abruptly, without a word, Brice swung up into the weather shrouds and methodically climbed to the maintop where he could be seen gazing fixedly ahead.

Returning on deck he went to Kydd. 'It's my duty to tell you that this westerly is in a grievous moil with the tides. Sir, I cannot see that we can win through.'

In the appalled quiet, he added softly, 'Sir, I'm sorry, I truly am.'

Kydd slumped in defeat. 'Never mind, Mr Brice. You did your best.'

He turned to the master. 'Mr Joyce, we'll wear ship and go back. We've lost the race.'

As he looked out at the hurry of waters, now in meaningless heaping and confusion, he felt a hand on his arm. It was Brice. 'Sir. There's something.'

'Do tell it, sir.'

'This you see is the Outer Sound o' the firth. There is another, Inner Sound, a'tween Stroma and the Scottish shore. Smaller, more restricted and dangerous – but the tides are lesser in vehemence and if we take it, we're past the Swilkies and the main surge. The wind's shifted – veering more to the nor'-nor'-westerly – and can see us through.'

'What are the perils, pray?'

'It calls for us riding the ebb into the sound – as is only a mile or so wide. Once in there's no turning back.'

'Any other?'

'All is in the timing. We've a few hours left to be through, else the tide turns and we'd be cast ashore in a trice. And at the far end waits the Merry Men.'

'I beg your pardon?'

'It's said that if a ship sees the Merry Men o' Mey dancing it's the last thing they'll see on this earth. The greatest and fiercest of all the tide-races, it's death to ships to be caught in it, whatever their size. At the right time it's quiet and playful, at the wrong it's vengeful and unmerciful.'

'When is the wrong time, then?'

'It grieves me to say it, but on the ebb, which we must use to get through.'

'So . . .?'

'As I said, sir, it's the timing. We can't challenge it on the ebb, the flood will take us back where we've come. Sir, we have to arrive at precisely slack water between the two.'

'That's a gallows deal hard to swallow, Mr Brice,' Kydd said slowly. To venture *Tyger* and every man aboard her on the word of a man who'd lost a ship before . . . but he soon came to a decision. 'This is war. We're paid to take risks – and this is one. Brace about, Mr Joyce – we're on our way.'

With Stroma firming in the distance *Tyger* joined the seething rush of waters off Duncansby Head and, hard up by the wind, found herself impelled by an invisible hand – directly towards the mile-wide gap.

'Can't steady her!' cried the helmsman in alarm, the wheel spinning in his hands. Kydd realised quickly that the mass of water in which the frigate sailed was itself moving faster and therefore they'd lost steerage way, slewing perilously this way and that.

Brice was as calm as before. 'Snug her down. Use bear-off spars and steer by sail.' He was suggesting they take in or show canvas fore and aft to lever her bodily back on course.

A lieutenant was sent to the headsails and men stood by with tackles to the driver boom aft.

In the tense atmosphere Brice coolly pointed out a cluster of wind-swept houses just visible through the mists of spume to larboard. 'There you are, gentlemen. John o' Groats, as is the furthest point in our islands you can reach without you get your feet wet.'

Kydd glanced at the dwellings. It was inconceivable how people could live in peace so close to the ship-killing waters raging within sight of their drawing-room windows.

'And to starboard – there's pirate gold in the Orkneys. The haunt of Captain Gow and his bloody crew,' Brice added.

No one would be drawn: there was too much theatre in the present, for Stroma was nearer – much nearer. Their speed over the ground must be breathtaking. The master raised his sextant and began rapping bearings to Maynard, his mate, while seamen watched fearfully the passing rock shore, so close.

'I don't care for the seas over the point,' Brice murmured, motioning ahead.

'Your Merry Men.'

'They're dancing.'

Even at half a mile distance, the tossing white frenzy of seas torn asunder was spreading broadly from the point across their entire vision, a monstrous barrier, and they were shooting headlong towards it.

'We're too early, the ebb's still surging – we'll never get through that.' Without looking at Kydd Brice bellowed forward, 'Clear away the larboard bower. Helm down – dowse the driver, all sail off her.'

He measured with his eye, then bawled, 'Let go forward!'

The anchor plunged down and the cable tautened immediately, bringing *Tyger* to a restless stop, her bows swiftly coming around to stem the current. They were shockingly close in under the land but Kydd said nothing until it was done, then asked, 'Are we safe?'

'For now. This is the Ness o' Quoys, the only place where back eddies cancel the tide.' Brice appeared strained and weary but continued to look out warily over the rushing waters, occasionally taking out his fob watch.

For the best part of an hour *Tyger* snubbed at her anchor until Brice was satisfied. 'Now the last and worst peril,' he said absently, almost as if talking to himself. 'Sail on aft until we're with the current,' he said, his gaze on Stroma, not the rocky shoreline so near.

Kydd understood: it was there, across the water, that he had lost his ship, his shipmates and nearly his soul. And now he was doing it again.

The after sail rotated the ship around her anchor until more could be spread as the anchor was won and they were under way again – the last mile.

As the point neared it was as if a miracle had been

commanded. The frothing waves and broken seas were falling and unaccountably the roaring white breakers were on the move, out to sea where the entire surface of the sound was in an agitated ferment.

With freshening winds now hard and flat from the north-north-west they forged ahead. Brice moved to stand by the helm where two men were working together, tightly grasping the spokes.

'Larboard two points.'

The sailors obeyed but Kydd's anxiety increased when he saw that this was taking them much too close inshore. 'Belay that!' he barked suddenly, but Brice countered with an urgent 'Hold your course!'

The helmsmen looked in bewilderment at Kydd, who bit his lip, then snapped, 'Mr Brice has the ship.'

The point, with its oddly shaped pedestal of rock, came closer, the aura of its deadly reality clamping in on them all.

'Mr Brice – you do know what you're doing?' Kydd said tightly.

'You've ten, twelve fathoms under your keel.'

'If we—'

'This is a clear lead through – we can't do it else.' The voice was low, taut.

From the tumble of rock at the tip of the point out a hundred yards or so there was a strange calm – a balance between opposing masses of water that would hold until the dying ebb turned into a strengthening flow.

But Brice was taking it frighteningly close – Kydd turned to give him a warning glance and stopped in shock. The man was visibly shaking, the whites of his eyes showing.

'Do we . . .' Kydd began, but tailed off – he was not reaching him.

Less than the length of the ship directly to larboard, the rocks with their kelp and limpets showed in all their pitiless detail as they passed, wetly gleaming from the careless swash and heave of the seas, a nightmarish vision for any deep-sea mariner.

Without fuss, and in an unnatural silence *Tyger* passed the point, then through the stretch of calm, out into the open sea, the choppy firth welcoming them finally into its embrace.

With a shuddering sigh Kydd went to Brice. 'Sir, I give you all honour and gratitude for what you've done this day. *Tyger* owes you much, I believe, and your country more.'

For a long moment his third lieutenant stared at him. Then he straightened and gave a boyish smile. 'We're through, Sir Thomas, and naught ahead but Cape Wrath . . .'

Chapter 81

Kydd had his point of interception worked out: any self-respecting shipmaster rounding the Orkneys with a fair wind for Ireland would not think to stray far from a direct course around the Butt of Lewis and on south. *Tyger* and *Wasp* would straddle this at the fifty-ninth line of latitude and await a fateful rendezvous.

They reached it in hours, well within the time expected for the slower ships of the convoy, and settled down to their vigil, expecting at any moment to see the sails of their chase loom above the horizon to the north.

But as they lurked in ambush there was a startling development. A bluff dogger returning to Stornaway from the fishing grounds on the brisk winds readily admitted to a sighting that set them a puzzler. The ruddy-faced skipper hailing up to *Tyger*'s quarterdeck in the broadest Scottish swore on his mother's grave that, far from shaping course for Ireland, the convoy was now firmly tracking out into the empty Atlantic.

Why were they wasting time making a wide sweep around

before descending on their objective? There was no reason to do so but then, on the other hand, what were they up to heading westward? There was no enemy territory in that direction, and if the Caribbean was their destination, they would surely take the trade-wind passage curving across the south.

For Kydd it was back to a stew of uncertainty. Should they stay where they were to intercept the convoy – or believe the fisherman and go after them into the trackless ocean?

The man's honest weather-beaten fisher-folk appearance swayed him. There was nothing to be gained in lying and his description of the ships was exact: he must have seen them. Only a day away to the north and heading west – in this boisterous north-westerly they could come up on them within a very short time. If they moved now.

'Make to *Wasp* – form line of search on this bearing, west-nor'-west.'

He would give it five days. If in that time they had no success he would stand down the chase.

On only the second day Kydd was wakened urgently. In the early dawn *Wasp* had come flying downwind and signalled, 'Enemy in sight!'

'Where away?' Kydd hailed the figure on the sloop's quarterdeck as she neared, rising and falling sharply with a considerable Atlantic Ocean swell.

'Should be forty-two miles to the west by now, close-hauled on the starboard tack, course west b' north,' bawled back Langton. 'As told to us, a heavy frigate and three sloops, four merchantmen.'

They were still steadily making their way west, away from the British Isles and, indeed, Europe.

'So let's have 'em,' Kydd bellowed back. 'As we've got the legs on them. We place ourselves athwart their track, in the eye of the weather.'

Joyce was ready with his slate.

'So we head west b' south five hours, and with an hour west-nor'-west they should be in sight.'

There was a wave of acknowledgement.

'Leave the frigate to me. You're to worry the sloops without you let 'em box you in.'

Another wave.

'Do not approach the merchant jacks – they're probably full o' troops as would give any boarders a warm welcome.'

'Aye, Sir Thomas. Good fortune to you, sir.'

Kydd raised an arm in farewell and the two ships diverged on to their final closing line.

They raised the convoy in the early afternoon. Pale smudges against the line of the horizon growing in size as they bore down on it.

Kydd soon had his telescope up, bracing with his left elbow pressing into the chest and his right hand manipulating the eyepiece.

It was an untidy gaggle – none of the discipline of the columns and rows of a British convoy. The frigate was a big one, a 38 or 40, and moving protectively out to the convoy van. And its colours: French. What the devil were they about? With a quickening of his pulse Kydd took in the scene. The central gaggle were the merchant ships. On their beam to weather were two of the sloops, the third to leeward and the frigate rightly in the van where she could fall back to protect the convoy, should *Wasp* prove a threat.

It was going to be a hard fight, odds of two to one, and if *Tyger* was winged *Wasp* could not save her.

They took up positions ahead, criss-crossing as they waited for the enemy frigate to advance and for Kydd to get a sense of the mettle of the captain he was facing. The ship was a heavy frigate, like the *Révolutionnaire* class of forty-gun, fine-lined racers that could be relied on to catch *Tyger* in anything like a fair wind. If he was to prevail in this battle Kydd knew it would be only by seamanship and skill at arms.

He could depend on Langton. Mature, considered, he would look to prudent opportunities that did not require *Tyger* to come to his aid. There'd be no need of badgering signals or encouragement: he knew what to do.

Falling back, Langton manoeuvred to get at the lone leeward sloop. The press of ships was such that the pair to weather would be prevented from firing and would need to fall back to go around the convoy, then make up the distance – and to claw back to their weather position would be hard going.

Kydd watched the frigate's actions in response with grim joy. Its white creaming forefoot brightened: it was making a charge against *Tyger*. The captain was in the grip of the Gallic sense of honour – it was beneath him to do anything other than go against the biggest opponent in the field.

Kydd would take the more practical and effective course: first to cripple and put out of the fight the lesser, for then with only one to deal with, with no divided attack, victory over the convoy would be simple. 'Bear away three points to leeward,' he ordered.

Tyger eased away from close-hauled to full and bye on a diverging course away from the convoy. As she took up Kydd noticed, with growing satisfaction, that Langton's bold move had been rewarded by the downing of the main topmast of his antagonist, which was crippled and falling away astern of the convoy.

It did not affect the frigate, which was now in full pursuit of *Tyger*. The two sped on, the other captain no doubt thinking that Kydd was clearing the field for a classic frigate duel. He had no intention of obliging him.

'Clear away the aft chase guns, Mr Bray.'

Two nine-pounders on the quarterdeck to play on their pursuer. Unlikely to amount to much, for in these seas accuracy would be difficult, but it would make things uncomfortable for the Frenchman, who on this point of sailing was virtually defenceless.

One of the sloops to weather had dropped down to the convoy and was trying hard to make up the distance to reach the unprotected near side of the convoy – where *Wasp* lay patiently in wait.

Kydd grinned. It was exhilarating slashing through the Atlantic rollers on a predatory mission, *Tyger* the lethal fighting machine at his command and giving of her best in a chase that was of such consequence to his country. With a start of surprise he realised he was passing content – more than content, he was revelling in the part he was playing in the drama: there could be no better. The Prince of Wales, his club, and the formalities of polite society were countless leagues behind him. This was what it was to be a man!

He was mending, healing. He would never forget Persephone or lose the hurt, but it was now no longer eating into his soul.

The pursuing frigate finally woke up to the situation. It put over its helm and swung towards the convoy but Kydd was ready and conformed immediately, the two ships wearing as one, the pursuit transformed into a race before the wind back to the convoy.

Kydd knew that the other captain would be berating himself

for leaving the convoy unprotected and his fury would be directed at *Wasp*, even now exchanging fire with the sloop, which, if Langton succeeded with it in the same way, would transform the situation seriously.

They reached the first of the merchantmen but Kydd had other ideas. At the last moment he bore up for the weather side of the convoy. Taken by surprise and not knowing what it meant, the enemy frigate captain fatally delayed and they were now on opposite sides of the crowding merchantmen.

The single sloop to weather must have known its fate before *Tyger* reached it, but there was little it could do – to abandon its post and the convoy, or do its duty to stay and take *Tyger*'s broadside.

It chose the latter and Kydd duly obliged with a thunder of guns into it, their martial slam and reek of gun-smoke gratifying to the senses after so long.

The stricken vessel fell away but the reckoning was about to be paid.

As the convoy cleared past, the frigate would be poised to wreak a terrible revenge. Langton had too much sense to be trapped by it and had sheered away – he could not come to their assistance even if he was foolish enough to try.

It was now going to be a close-range smashing where the Frenchman's superior size and number of guns would tell. Who knew how it might end?

The last ships passed. To Kydd's astonishment, this left an empty sea. He stood open-mouthed in amazement: out to leeward the frigate was under full sail and with it the remaining sloop. Their course was taking them ever further away – they were fleeing!

Kydd looked around for *Wasp*. Having seen the situation she had quickly gone to the head of the convoy and brought them to a stop, four ships hove to, no doubt raging at the disgraceful betrayal and little inclined to surrender.

Tyger joined her and Kydd hailed Langton. 'Do you board the first while under the guns of *Tyger*, if you please. Take possession and cause the soldiers to throw their weapons in the sea under penalty of being fired into at close range by *Tyger*.'

He watched a boat launch from *Wasp* and head towards the closest, the figure of Langton easily recognisable. Then he noticed that each of the ships wore the red flag and white cross of Denmark.

'What the devil? Taking Danish troops across the Atlantic? Nothing makes sense today,' he murmured.

The ships were sea-worn and shabby and, oddly, had no soldiers crowding up to see what was going on. As prizes they would be mean picking.

The mystery deepened when Langton went up the side and was met only by a few figures, none of whom was in any kind of military uniform. He disappeared below by the fore-hatch but was back on deck within minutes, losing no time to board his boat, which pulled strongly to *Tyger*.

Langton cupped his hands and shouted up, 'Sir Thomas, all is not as it seems. I beg you will return with me to the Dansker.'

Kydd quickly joined him in the boat with a wary Halgren.

As they made for the vessel, Langton explained. 'Nary a soldier nor piece of military kit did I see, sir. Cargo – a most contemptible lading. Grain, tin pots, clothing of the lower sort, cheap books and, um, a pianoforte.'

'Defended by as many men-o'-war? This is rank madness. There's more to it than we're seeing. Did he say where he's bound?'

'Wouldn't talk to me, sir. Demands he speak with the English admiral.'

Kydd's experienced eye took in much as he stepped on the deck of the Dane. The hairy, frayed ropes coming down from aloft, the grey of age in timbers not oiled or varnished, the sullen, bitter expressions on the faces of the few work-hardened seamen – and the dull stench of bilge.

'Captain Sir Thomas Kydd,' introduced Langton.

The Danish captain came forward and acknowledged Kydd with a short bow. 'Sir, you's in charge?'

'I am, sir. And whom do I address?'

'Kaptajn Groos, Danske ship *Kierteminde*. Sir, ve must speak.'

They went below to the tiny cabin and sat alone together.

'Well, Captain Groos, I'd be pleased if you'd be so good as to tell me what the devil is going on, sir.'

The hard, weathered features tightened. 'You vill make we prize, *nej?*'

'It is customary, sir. You will be taken to a port in the British Isles and, if it is any concern of yours, I can assure you that all your men will be well treated.'

The man's head drooped and then he looked up, something like despair and pleading coming over his face. 'Cap'ten. We're us both *sofolk*, the common sea dog, you say. We rather fight th' sea, not each other.'

'Sir, I cannot hear of any arrangement as contravenes the—'

Doggedly Groos went on: 'Sir, hear me. These ship, they go to a place o' hunger and death, misery an' hopeless. Where they been suffering for s' long that—'

'Sir. Where are you bound?'

'Iceland.'

Instantly Kydd had the puzzle solved. This was a Danish

colony and, like any other around the world, the war had cut them off completely from the motherland by the effectiveness of British sea-power.

Hunger and death? It didn't take much imagination to conceive of conditions in a country of the far north living on the edge, where trade had been wiped out, the rich fishing harvest left to rot while the inhabitants yearned for sustenance, the basics of living.

'Our convoy, our ships, these all are private, b' subscription. The burghers of Copenhagen even in their own distress think of their brethren in Iceland, s' far away. They give their only coin, their means . . .'

Kydd was moved. He had witnessed first-hand the terrible results of the British bombardment of that city, and now to find that its people had still the humanity to think of their colony . . . But it made no difference. The pitiless logic of war left no course other than the one he was duty-bound to follow. 'My sincere condolences, Captain, but I have to tell you there can be no change in my orders. Your ships are prize-of-war and will go to England. I'm sorry.'

The light died in the man's eyes and he slumped back with the bleakness of defeat. 'Do your duty, then, Cap'ten.'

Kydd rose to go, but then asked, 'You were escorted by Frenchmen. What does this mean?'

'Ha! Th' *ubrugelige kujoner*,' he spat venomously. 'They say they are comrades, will protect we all. They run – now they decide for them Iceland is not worth a fighting.'

'Go on,' Kydd said carefully, sensing there was more to it than that.

'Not the people, they don' care. They want to take the land, build fort, make the ship harbour. This they use to haf nest for corsair, privateer to attack your ships.'

In an instant the stakes had changed. If there was any chance of such a move it would have catastrophic consequences to the Atlantic trade routes and Britain's survival – and he needed to know more. 'Captain Groos – are they already in Iceland? Are they building now?' Kydd asked urgently.

'Who knows? I don' – nobody does,' he answered bitterly. 'No Danish ship fool enough to try to reach there past you. An' now I vill never know neither.'

Shaken, Kydd realised that, with this threat hanging over him, there was only one thing he could do now – go to Iceland and see for himself. And that meant . . . 'Sir, you may just have saved your voyage and people both.'

'I'm not understand.'

'I will make agreement with you. Pilot my ship safely through Iceland waters and I'll release your ships and cargo to your folk ashore, provided no military stores are included. A bargain?'

Chapter 82

'You're looking thoughtful, Mr Dillon. What's on your mind?' Kydd forked another mutton cutlet, and followed it with a taste of a rather good claret that Tysoe had had the foresight to tuck away before they sailed.

'I have my regrets, sir.'

'Oh?'

'That so marvellous a spectacle will not be granted to Lord Farndon.'

There were knowing smiles around the table. Renzi and his eccentricities were still held in fond memory, it seemed.

'Why, what marvels are these, pray?'

None present had ever seen anything of their destination as the Danes had always jealously guarded their colony from outside influence, allowing trade only in Danish vessels.

'Iceland – a land both of fire and water. Volcanoes beyond counting and rivers of ice a hundred miles from side to side.'

'Good grief, Dillon. How do you know this?' Bray asked.

'A traveller by name of Horrebow made visit in the last age and his book made an impression on me as a young fellow that stays with me to this day.'

'Do tell us something of the place,' Kydd encouraged. 'As all I know is, for fishing it can't be beat.'

'Ah, there's one thing I heard as'll curl y' whiskers, gennelmen,' Joyce interrupted importantly.

'What's that, then?'

'All yon volcanoes, they's still a-going. The whole island's made o' this black stuff, twisted up into mountains and worse.'

'What worse?'

'Skerries. Rocks awash as will tear the heart out of any stout ship, an' they says new rocks are thrown up all the time. B'gob, even new islands! Why, I heard—'

'Mr Joyce, you forget we have a thorough-going pilot to take us, even if he tells us the name of the capital of the place is Wrecky-vik. Do stand on, Mr Dillon. What of the natives?'

'Iceland was settled long ago by the Vikings and their Valkyries, fierce and beastly folk, but since ground down by grievous poverty. The Laki volcano in 'eighty-three was a frightful thing – half the livestock destroyed and a quarter of the population by starvation. A proud people, though – no lords and ladies for them, all the same and as can vote equally in a parliament older than ours. And literature to wonder at – the great Skallagrímsson is to be recommended.'

'An interesting place indeed. Were it not for one thing.'
'Sir?'

'If the French are there we're in for a fight. This is no sight-seeing, and even if they're not, the Danes may have forts and such as will give us pause. We're promised landfall tomorrow. Let us trust there will be a satisfactory conclusion to the day.'

'There. Vestmannaeyjar.' Groos was with Kydd on *Tyger*'s quarterdeck pointing to a precipitous island that was the first close sight of land that could be considered Iceland – the vast white glow of the Vatnajökull glacier from far to seaward did not count.

'Ve pass through th' Suðureyjarsund to lay Þridrangar to south. Then it's to—'

'Thank you, Captain. Helm orders will be understood, however.'

All on deck gazed out at the near-vertical dark cliffs in wonderment.

'Here it was, you Irish monk come. Before even Flóki Vilgerðarson.'

'Are they still here?'

'All gone. Not strong enough t' stand wi' us.' Kydd tried not to think of the fate of the Irish hermits at the hands of the Vikings flocking in.

The coast passed by, dark rust-coloured knotted crags, and on some islets a dusting of green promising summer grass. A flat peninsula stretched out, and when they rounded it, the bay that opened up was pointed out as the final approach to the capital, Reykjavík.

'An anchorage, if you please,' Kydd demanded of Groos, 'where your ships will remain until we have knowledge of the situation ashore.'

He hadn't intended to be so formal to one within hours of relieving his countrymen from their distress, but Groos looked at him steadily and nodded. 'Hafnarfjörður, then – under our lee five mile.'

After passing instructions to the merchant ships Groos returned to *Tyger*. 'Reykjavík, not far.'

With *Wasp* following in their wake, they closed with the distant town, dramatically set within low island sentinels below the distant ramparts of snow-streaked mountains.

Chapter 83

*T*yger anchored and, in accordance with Kydd's orders, *Wasp* made a sweeping pass before the town in case the French had forestalled them. If there was hostile fire she was to note the positions and withdraw immediately.

The day was chilly and grey, the north-westerly had a boreal menace that was in keeping with the sinister pitch-dark shore-line, and Kydd tensed as *Wasp* reached one end of the water-front at a breakwater and traversed the mile or so of shoreline before another. There was no firing.

Langton returned and brought up alongside. 'Sir, all seems orderly and usual, no hostile movement directed at me.'

'Captain Groos, will you accompany me ashore?'

Prepared for anything, *Tyger*'s boat made for the little harbour, a white flag prominent but, in accordance with the rules of war, no armed men to accompany them.

Two small merchant ships were anchored inside. Groos directed them to a jetty, and as they neared it, the town took shape. It was not an imposing sight. Fewer than fifty houses, mostly sawn pine and painted in red or white, warehouses to one side, with a better class of dwelling nearby – a small church and one or two stone buildings.

Along the foreshore were turf huts, near half buried. Smoke curled from a single vent in each, and nearby racks were festooned with drying fish. Their boats drawn up before them, fisher-folk were busy at their work of gutting, splitting and laying out.

As they prepared to land Dillon pointed to a fort not far from the landing place, the muzzles of guns stark against the timber stockade. A single flag floated above it.

'Is new for me,' muttered Groos, trying to make it out. 'The colour – I do not know it.'

Neither did Kydd – a blue flag with a triplet of white objects that looked uncannily like fish. As a national ensign it was like nothing he'd seen and he had no idea what honours were due.

By the time they'd stepped ashore a small crowd had gathered to gape at the strangers. Most were in coarse woollen cloth and skins, bearded, with long and shaggy hair, wild-looking in their wide-brimmed hats and leggings. Fishermen, labourers.

Kydd looked about for a receiving party but saw none. Better-dressed men watched them from a distance but no one approached.

It was disturbing and unaccountable.

They headed off towards the fort, stepping out on a road that was rough and dusty with black sand.

A figure looked down from the parapet and disappeared. Minutes later a gate opened and two soldiers emerged, in untidy bright-green garb.

Kydd, in full-dress uniform with sash and star, glowered at them. 'Tell 'em I'm captain of the frigate that lies yonder and that I wish to make parlay with their senior officer.'

'*Við eftirspurn til að sjá liðsforingi þinn*,' snapped Groos, importantly.

The soldiers gaped at him. Then one said to the other in English, 'No idea what the bastard's saying, but that there's the navy. What'll we do, Mick?'

Before Kydd could reply, the other said, 'Bad cess t' go athwart 'em, I'd say. Take 'em to the King?'

They entered the only stone building of consequence and were ushered into a palatial room on the upper floor.

A strong-faced, handsome man of Kydd's age rose to greet them, wearing something approximating a naval officer's frock coat and breeches. 'Good morning, gentlemen. You may know me as His Excellency the Protector of Iceland, Commander-in-Chief by Sea and Land. Is there anything I can do for you?'

'Your name, sir?' Kydd rapped.

'Jørgen Jørgensen. And yours, sir?' The reply was courteous and bore no trace of resentment at Kydd's sharpness.

'Captain Sir Thomas Kydd of His Majesty's Ship *Tyger*. I will know why I'm to be greeted by one not apparently in the authority granted by the Danish government.'

'Quite simply, sir, because the Danish government rules here no more. The rights of the people of Iceland have been restored and the flag of my protectorate is token of that fact.'

'There's been an insurrection.'

Jørgensen looked hurt. 'No one has been harmed or inconvenienced, sir. I have merely taken measures to ameliorate an intolerable situation.'

'You claim to be in power in this island.'

'Sir, I do not claim to be – I am the ruler.'

There was a knock on the door and Maynard poked his head in. 'Sorry to disturb, sir, but this was handed to me for your eyes with every urgency.'

It was a letter and Kydd excused himself while he read. He confronted Jørgensen, 'This is from the Danish governor of Iceland – whom you hold prisoner? He complains bitterly of your actions, sir, and demands redress and reinstatement.'

'Count Trampe? Sir, he no longer holds authority and is—'

There was another interruption, this time by a gentleman in respectable dress in a state of indignation, bursting in to confront Kydd.

'*Herra* Magnús Stephensen, chief justice, and I demand you hear me! This – this contemptible and vile person is—'

Jørgensen stirred irritably. 'Throw the fellow out, please. The wretch continues to annoy me with his ranting, not recognising—'

Maynard came back. 'Sir, there's a merchant cove below says you're not to talk to any without you speak to him first.'

'I'll have some order,' Kydd barked. 'Everyone to the large room below and I'll hear you all out in a proper manner.'

Soon they were seated around a big table, Kydd at the head.

'Now, you, sir!' He pointed to the merchant, fair-haired and stout, with a book of accounts he'd slapped on the table.

'Phelps, and this business can be settled very quickly. I have here a one-time licence from the British government permitting trade with the enemy, namely Iceland. My ship lies in harbour with goods as are not contraband, in trade for tallow and eider. This is what the Icelanders want and here I am to give it to them. All very respectable, don't you agree?'

'A pirate's actions!' snarled Stephensen.

'Silence!' Kydd blared.

Phelps went on smoothly, 'The Danes don't want any but Danish ships and cargoes to ply with Iceland, but how can they now? So Trampe, the sly beggar, as governor he cracks down on the rules and won't allow me to trade. An' that's because he's got his own little line in goods as he wants to part with at top prices and –'

'An outrageous slur!'

'– so the people are aggrieved he won't let my goods ashore because they're in sore need, believe me, and petition us to take action, like.'

'Us?'

'Me and, um, His Excellency, as we're business partners.'

'Is this true?' Kydd asked Jørgensen, in disbelief. 'You took action against a sovereign nation for commercial reasons?'

'Certainly,' he said silkily. 'As was not only my right but my duty.'

'What?'

'I hold a letter of marque that entitles me to take reprisal on the enemies of King George. Is there any difference between taking prize a ship or a territory?'

'Only a naval officer can take a surrender.' Kydd was on shaky ground here but the situation had to be damn well sorted one way or another.

'But I am a British naval officer,' Jørgensen said easily. 'Service all over the world – even New Holland, would you credit it?'

'Australia?'

'In *Lady Nelson*, on a voyage of discovery to Van Diemen's Land.'

Kydd raised an eyebrow. He himself had done that very thing and enquired casually, 'Then you're able to tell me something of the hazards around the River Tamar mouth?'

'Why, nothing to concern the cautious mariner. Save perhaps the fearsome Yellow Rock hard by Low Head.'

Astonishingly, it seemed the man had seen genuine service in that far place.

'He lies!' spat Stephensen. 'He's nothing better than a privateer captain.'

'I know that, sir. I have his letter of marque.'

'A *Danish* privateersman.'

The man had a Danish name, but what was this?

'Is this true?' Kydd demanded.

'In a manner of speaking,' Jørgensen said with a sigh. 'I was in Copenhagen with my family when the British bombarded. I was pressed to take out a privateer, *Admiral Juul*, against our enemies. A mistake, of course. I was taken by *Sappho* brig-sloop as it happened.'

'So you're a Dane. And therefore a prisoner-of-war of the British. Then how . . .?'

'By your own government's act and approval, I was released to come to Iceland to trade under the flag of England.'

'With a privateer's papers.'

Stephensen slapped his hand on the table. 'By his own admission, he's a traitor to Denmark,' he snarled. 'Give him to us and we'll hang him!'

The whole position had passed from confusion into madness. Kydd had to take action – and now. 'As of this hour the rule and government of Iceland is in my hands. Until such time that this is resolved.'

The table stared at him.

'Well, you're all free to go for the moment,' he said testily. 'If I need to consult individuals, you'll be sent for.'

Looking up, he saw with relief the open but bewildered features of Maynard at the door and beckoned him in. 'I'll

369

have a file of marines ashore to march up and down, and we'll hoist proper colours in place of that rag.'

'Which, sir?'

Kydd paused. If British, he was in effect claiming Iceland for King George. If Danish, he was admitting that this was still enemy territory within the jurisdiction of the Danish Crown. And if any other it could only be said to be outside his competence to hoist them. 'Leave it for now. Tell Mr Bray to act as he sees fit in command until this raffle gets sorted out.'

'We could put Captain Groos to work,' Dillon suggested.

'Ah, yes. Tell him to walk around a bit, find out what's been going on, while I get my bearings.'

Kydd realised that in effect he had committed acts that amounted to the capture of a Danish colony without orders or authorisation. On the other hand, if Jørgensen was to be believed, the people had risen against their lawful rulers and had succeeded – in which case he was dealing with an independent country whose new-won power and authority he had just overthrown.

Groos came back and brought with him a sheaf of weathered papers. 'See!' he demanded, handing over various proclamations printed in formal lettering.

'. . . the situation we now are in requires that we should not suffer the least disrespect to our person . . .'

'. . . we therefore solemnly declare, that the first who shall attempt to disturb the prosperity or common tranquillity of the country shall instantly suffer death, without the benefit of civil law . . .'

'. . . all acts must be signed by us . . .'

This was the act of a conqueror, a potentate!

'The people, for his airs, they call him *Jörundur hundadaga-konungur* – Jørgen the Dog Days King.'

There was more: he'd made progress around his 'realm' and been free with reforms and boons issued in his name to a bemused and ignorant people who had no idea what a revolution was, having for centuries been dependent on the Danish for their very existence.

'His soldiers?'

'His own seamen, dressed up in what he find in the warehouse.'

So, a crude revolt, and all for crass commercial gain.

Then another story began to come out, one that brought it all into question. One in which a stranger came to Iceland to trade and found it grindingly poor and in want, yet was barred from trade and connections with the outside world by a hidebound governor enforcing the strict law against commerce with any other than Denmark. The country had slid ever deeper into penury and famine, backwardness and hopelessness. With a few armed sailors he had enabled them to throw off the yoke, take their independence and future into their own hands. And among the proclamations there were far-seeing acts of improvement and enlightenment, together with commitments to revive the Althingi, the ancient parliament of the common folk.

Kydd knew that if he intervened it would be to bring it all to a standstill — a movement of the people just as much as the American Revolution had been. Did he have the right to interfere with history unfolding?

He could sail away and leave them to it, but there was then the accusation, not denied, that the man was in fact a Danish privateersman, a prisoner-of-war of the English on the run. But then again he had a perfectly genuine Admiralty Board letter of marque. Did it cover territory as a prize? If so, under prize rules, Iceland was going to find itself under the British flag, probably much to the surprise and displeasure of the Portland government, who would have to find the means to defend it.

It was no use — he was going in circles. He had a brief vision of Brooks's club, the members in their armchairs with an evening rummer lordly discussing the elements of the case — but that was a world away now.

'Mr Dillon. I've decided on my course.'

'I'd be gratified to know it, Sir Thomas.'

'Very well. It is this: that I sail for England forthwith. I bear the person of Jørgensen to justify his actions before their lordships at the Admiralty, and they shall judge the matter. I convey also Count Trampe, who shall then be enabled to argue the case why Iceland should not be made prize. How does that sound?'

'Umm. If the count will not consent?'

'Ha! He cannot refuse, for if he claims Iceland as Danish he's the enemy and is now my prisoner-of-war.'

'Who will rule Iceland while we're absent?'

'Why, your chief justice cove. What's his name – Stephensen? Then do inform them both that I shall sail in forty-eight hours – in writing. Damn, but this has been a rare to-do!'

Chapter 84

Finishing the letters, Dillon assembled them to take to Kydd for signature. He went up the stairs but stopped when he heard voices in the office. It was Kydd, in stiff conversation with Stephensen, no doubt concerning the handing over of power and authority. He'd come back later.

Groos was waiting for him.

'Hr Dillon,' he said respectfully. 'I wish t' see Sir Kydd an' thank him for what he has done for our people.'

'I'm sorry, he's engaged for the moment. I'll tell him you called.'

'Thenk you, sir. I am, too, sorry that you mix up in our quarrel. It is too much.'

'Never worry, Captain, it seems resolved now.'

'And you will be sailing?'

'Within a short time, I believe.'

'I wish longer, we Iceland people may show our feeling for you.'

'Kind in you to say so, sir.'

'Then I will take a leave of you. Oh – if you sail soon,

you might be interest. I heard there's an English at Skarðsheimjökull, along the coast. You will tell them you're here, give passage back to England?'

'Just the one?'

'Yes. Stays with fisherman to recover.'

'I'll let Sir Thomas know.'

Kydd was in no doubt. 'A castaway, poor fellow. We'll have to get word to him. Think how he'd rue it if he finds he's missed his only chance to get back home. Find a guide, we'll send someone.'

Knowing Dillon's insatiable appetite for foreign shores, Kydd grinned. 'Interested in going yourself?'

'Perhaps I will,' Dillon answered equably, but inwardly exulted as it was a great regret that probably his only journey to this extraordinary country looked to being so cruelly brief.

'Then take a trusty with you. Wouldn't want any misunderstandings with the natives.'

Stirk agreed to be his companion. 'Off the barky, stretch out a bit, like. An' Pinto wants t' see how they dry stockfish different to Portugal, the loon.'

Groos shook his head slowly. 'No, no, Hr Dillon. The way, he's not easy. I will guide.'

The four set off, heading out north along the coast mounted on small but sure-footed Icelandic ponies with two pack beasts.

There would be no forgetting this ride, Dillon reflected. So completely different from anywhere else he'd encountered: the black-sand beaches, the distant mountains twisted and dour. Even their colours were alien, iron-black and bare in a barren wilderness that he knew was twice as broad as all Ireland.

Leaving Reykjavík, the track passed fishing villages, the boats pulled up on the foreshore near medieval in their ornamenting, much like a flat-bottomed Scots scaffie. Racks of drying fish spread their odour on the wind, and curious folk came out of their turf huts to watch them pass.

The trail was more a bridle path if anything. There were no wheeled vehicles in Iceland and therefore no cart tracks; there were ruts but they were the result of centuries of ponies and pack-horses following the same way.

It led inland towards a coastal range for they were traversing a small cape. As it did so, they met tussocked plains and meandering streams, then by degrees went up into the higher levels and another, wilder realm of dark, tortured rocks that lay at random where the violent earth had spewed them.

In an apprehensive silence they followed a path marked with cairns, occasionally finding mysterious tarns that smoked sulphurous exhalations from somewhere nearby and caught in the throat. Still higher, and white patches of compacted snow began to appear at the same time as a northerly flurry of wind set Dillon to shuddering.

Once they passed a gully that so captivated him he had to stop and take it in. The focus of three waterfalls of green-white purity, the naked rocks were bedaubed with lichen – orange, yellow, green, red – as if from a mad artist's palette.

The track grew steeper until Groos warned that it would be tough going for a spell. They dismounted and led the ponies, feeling the grey-green moss soft underfoot. Once among the tumbled scree slopes, Dillon caught sight of a snatch of colour on some of the dismal rocks, flowers blossoming in the clefts where none else dared.

They crested a ridge and there before them was a fjord with a fishing village nestled below. On the opposite side, dominating all, was the broad white tongue of a glacier and, beyond it, the endless march of dark, craggy mountains; further still, in the interior, the unearthly white glow of an endless ice-field. The scene had a majestic beauty and grandeur that took the breath away.

In a blustery northerly they began the descent, heads down as the wind brought with it a spiteful sleet to swirl around them.

And then, suddenly, they were at the village.

Chapter 85

A little more light from above, just to bring out the contrast in the old hut, cunningly placed above a raging river scene. The brush reached out and delicately tipped the underside of the cloud with a streak of ivory.

With the artist's sigh of contentment, the brushes were returned to their case and the painting admired. It was really rather good and a flush of pride touched her. Persephone Lockwood knew then she was mending, healing.

It had been an act of misery, of desperation to escape the pain, but it had indeed turned the tide. To withdraw from friends and family completely, not to have to explain, to be on her own, here to find herself again. Would she return soon? Kydd had betrayed her unforgivably but it was out of his power to hurt her again. She was even able to reflect charitably that it was some derangement of the mind that had led him, even against his will, to act as he had. In any case it was all over now.

The light was getting bad and she should be packing up. The kind couple she was staying with would want her to join them at the evening meal when the men returned home and she had every intention of being there.

It had been necessary to flee to somewhere she would not be known, away from the feverish wartime clamour of the south.

The road to Scotland had been long and wearisome but there she had hoped to find among the wild and romantic Highlands the solitude she craved until she was ready to return.

It had not answered: for some reason she needed to put a physical gulf between herself and the land of her forebears. Quite by chance she'd brought along Niels Horrebow in translation and had been seized with longing for what she read. A true romantic pilgrimage and perfectly remote, somewhere she would be truly secure from any chance discovery. It would be where she saw out her pain.

It had been remarkably easy to journey to Iceland. Scottish fishermen regularly made the haul out to the cod banks south of there, and knew the waters well, together with their Icelandic brethren of the seas. A fair sum forthcoming overcame their astonishment that a lady – for entirely her own reasons, of course – desired to make passage to that heathen land.

Off some unpronounceable island, within sight of a wondrous great ice river, she'd been transferred to an Icelandic cod boat. The Scottish skipper, his bearded face comically concerned for her, had nevertheless told them in guttural Danish that all she wished for was a kind soul to take her in while she recovered from an ordeal and in the meantime painted the wonders of their land.

They'd agreed doubtfully. Then she'd endured the chill whipping of wind and sleet until it had cleared as they approached a harbour set in the terrible beauty of a great fjord. Gripped by a fierce longing for what was around her, she was landed with her modest baggage at a tiny wooden jetty and, in a short time, a gnarled old fisherman, his wife clutching at him from behind, had come to look her over.

She could not answer their questions in what, after Horrebow, she guessed was Old Norse, but something passed between them, the man's fierce grey eyes relenting, and, by means of signs, she was taken to one of the turf huts.

She followed inside. A low passage led into a quite sizeable room with a central fireplace venting through the roof and well-worn articles of furniture in favoured positions. The reek of fish oil and smoke caught her unawares and she coughed a little as she looked around.

It was a remarkably snug abode, the roof held with drift-wood beams and soaring whalebones. There were cunning places for oddments and trinkets, and at one end a single cherished picture of a younger man, looking stern and martial; at the other stood a three-legged stool and spinning wheel.

Light came from both sides, a muted illumination, for the windows were nothing but a wooden frame on which was stretched a thin membrane of sorts.

Further on, turf walls separated out other rooms and, after a brief consultation between the husband and wife, Persephone was shown a chamber with its own window. It had a bed and quaint dresser encumbered with skins, which the man was at pains to mime would be taken out. Just the space she needed for her easel. Perfect! She signalled her pleasure and there was visible relief and smiles.

That evening, over a bowl of *kjötsúpa*, a hearty lamb soup, they had shyly tried to communicate, the rolling syllables oddly familiar in their lilt but quite beyond her comprehension. She picked up, however, that he was Baldur and his

379

wife Gudrun – or was that Gudthrun? And she must be content with 'Persa'.

The following days were all she had dared hope for.

Baldur still followed the sea, and a full rack of split cod was his pride, but in the daytime she went with his son Sigardur and his straw-haired girl, who took her proudly around the sights. And what an experience to thrill the bleakest soul! Cascading waterfalls of ice, gloomy canyons lit with livid colours, the mighty and irresistible spectacle of a glacier close to. On the shore she spotted walrus and seals and in the bay the rhythmic progress of killer whales. There were geysers, steaming pools warm to the touch, and always the grand and limitless prospect of the snow-clad mysterious interior.

Persephone spent days at her easel trying to capture it, at times despairing that any would believe the wild grandeur she had seen, and all the time feeling the desolation within her retreat.

Sometimes at night there would be visitors, and out would come the *mjöður*, mead, and the old men would give forth with what she assumed were the terrible tales of long ago – the sagas she'd seen mentioned in Horrebow. Afterwards the girls would break into some haunting chant accompanied on a bone flute and small drum. And she herself would come in with a wistful 'Sweet Lass of Richmond Hill' or other trifle that would set the whole hut to the stillness of rapture at its exotic, unknown cadences.

She would then retire for the night to her bed of furze and eider, with its bear-skin throw-over, and dream of what she'd seen.

And today she was completing her third picture: *Troll Maidens at the Gorge*. It had everything – the terrifying precipice, the mysterious allure of subterranean forces at work, the—

Suddenly intruding, voices floated to her from outside, probably supplicating hands for a herring haul.

She went back to her work as Gudrun bustled off to see what the fuss was all about.

And she almost missed it. After weeks of hearing nothing but rough Icelandic, she was shocked rigid. English was being spoken!

Dropping her brush, Persephone hurried into the communal room in time to see a bedraggled traveller inch his way in. As usual she was in her Icelandic country smock, coarse but well suited to weather that could change in an instant, her hair wild and free, in no way fit to receive a visitor. Flustered, she faced him.

'Ah, we have been told that an Englishman, a castaway, is within—' The man broke off, staring at her as if at a phantom.

'There is no castaway here, sir,' she said cuttingly, incensed at this intrusion into her eyrie.

He was peering at her in puzzlement and confusion. 'Madam. I believe I'm addressing Miss Persephone Lockwood,' he said carefully. 'Can this be so?'

Frozen with shock, she gathered her wits. 'Who enquires, pray?'

'Why, Miss Lockwood, do you not remember me?'

'Should I, sir?'

'Lisbon, the passage back to England that never was,' he answered softly.

'The secretary to Captain Kydd,' she said, in a brittle voice. 'And what are you doing here, might I ask?'

'We've been told there's an English castaway here, recovering. I was sent to offer passage back home for same.'

'In Captain Kydd's ship.'

'Just so.'

With a dawning horror she understood. By some super-natural means she'd been tracked down to her sanctuary fastness to begin her time of torment all over again.

Never! A wave of panic washed over her. 'No! I will not, do you hear? Leave me alone! I'm happy here. Go!'

'Miss Lockwood, the ship sails in hours.'

'Get out!' she shouted. 'Go back to your master, but leave me alone!'

'But—'

'Go!' she screamed, only just in control. 'Leave this place, go away!' She turned and fled to her room.

Dillon faltered, then went outside where Stirk waited. 'She won't come away,' he blurted. 'Wants to be left here alone.'

'She?' Stirk demanded.

'Miss Lockwood. She fled here to be on her own after . . . after . . .'

'Well, if she's here, an' I won't ask how, she has t' go. Ain't natural for a lady.'

'Stirk, you don't know what happened.'

'Don't know? The whole barky knows, Mr Dillon. No use in tryin' to keep a secret aboard any hooker as keeps the seas for more'n a dog-watch. I'm right happy she's safe 'n' all but I reckons she's on to a wrong steer wi' the captain. Doesn't know the whole griff. I'll set her right on it.'

'She won't hear you.'

'Oh? We'll see how a mite o' straight talkin' serves.'

He bent to enter the low passage, then stopped and looked back. 'Not you, Mr Dillon,' he said.

She was in one of the small rooms, bent over and sobbing.

'Ah, Miss Lockwood. I'm here to put you square wi' the captain.'

'Get out,' she croaked feebly, then, more forcefully, 'You've no right to—'

'Ah, but I have, miss. Has you got any clue how many folks you've mightily distressed? Let's start with your own ma and pa. They think you've done away wi' yourself and are payin' good money to have the canal dragged.'

'I'll send them a letter, now get out of here!'

'Worst is the captain. Do y' know he—'

In a fury she lashed out at him but Stirk caught her wrists. 'Now, miss, I ain't never hit a lady but I won't take this from any biddy.'

'How dare you?'

'I'm not goin' t' let up until you've heard me out, s' listen.'

She glared at him in impotence.

'Cap'n Kydd I know much better'n you, m' lady. If there's one thing y' need to hoist in, it's this: the man's true north. A real, double-barrelled, copper-bottomed, bevel-edged gent, who cares more f'r his morals than a miser does his gold.

'Anythin' you may've heard other is tommy-rot. Now he cares f'r you like nothin' else on this sainted earth and you treat him like this? I'll have you know he's run back to sea, swearin' he'll never marry anyone else.'

'I saw him with my own eyes go to a common doxy in Southwark. You can't tell me—'

'Listen to me good,' Stirk grated, her wrists clamped harder in his big horny hands. 'He's too square-sailin' a cove. Caught up by a tomrig cuttin' a wheedle and he's easy meat. She pitches the gammon about a child an' he falls for it. No truth in it a-tall but he wants t' do right by her and visits t' see what he can do. Would ye rather he's the kind o' man who turns his back on a sad case? He didn't an' he couldn't.'

'No truth in it?'

'I've got a lord as'll stand by m' words.'

He released her wrists slowly.

Tears pricked as the import of what he was saying flooded in.

'I'm only a simple ol' shellback, but it seems t' me there's somethin' at work in your stars, m' lady. Here we is, the furthest bit o' land afore we run up agin the North Pole, and we've both of ye, brung together the same day for some reason. Can't think what it is.'

The tears came.

'Not my place t' say it, but he's had a rare hard time an' needs you t' hang out a signal to come alongside.' His voice softened. 'Y' cared for him once, why not now?'

It was too much.

The hard sailor's simple words laying out the truth of it all, that she'd been betrayed by her own deep love of the man into a foolish misreading of his actions, that he in turn had been struck down and hurt by her – and to hear he cared for nobody else! She had to go to him, go now – to make them both whole again.

She fell on Stirk's shoulders, all the bitterness and rage crumbling and washing away in a flood of tears.

He awkwardly held her while the storm surged and spent itself, then led her out.

Thankfully, with Groos there to translate, the white-faced Gudrun was reassured but bluntly refused to take payment for her stay, bashfully asking for one of the paintings to keep.

'We'll be off then, Miss Lockwood,' Dillon said respectfully.

'On the way I'd crave pause while I make good use of the hot pools,' she said shakily, 'And perhaps find something fresh to wear – your captain will have enough of a shock to see me without I appear like this!'

Chapter 86

'Damn it all, Mr Dillon, you know the ship's sailing directly. Does it take so long to fetch in a wretched castaway?'

Kydd had felt his secretary's absence in this ridiculous situation and wanted to hand over the whole madness to the new administrator, Stephensen, and be away from Iceland just as soon as he could manage it.

'I do apologise, Sir Thomas. The country does not lend itself to celerity, I find. We did meet with success, however, and your wretch is below in a back room having expressed a desire to speak with you.'

'No! I'm out of my mind with this tomfoolery. He'll have to wait until I've got more of a steer on all these papers.'

'Sir, I rather think—'

Kydd sighed heavily. 'Yes, yes. Poor devil probably wants to thank us for deliverance. I suppose I can spare him two minutes.'

He followed Dillon down and out to a small outbuilding.

Stirk was there by the door and offered, 'I'll see if y' castaway is in shape t' see ye, sir.'

He slipped in and was back shortly. 'Waitin' for ye.'

Followed by Dillon and Stirk, Kydd entered, his eyes unaccustomed to the gloom within. A figure stood motionless opposite him and the room fell to a strange stillness as his eyes adapted to the dimness. Not quite believing it, he took in the colourful Icelandic garb and saw that this was a woman.

He looked closer – and was shocked rigid. She was exactly like . . . It was Persephone!

Dazed, he swung round on Dillon. His secretary's expression was politely noncommittal, Stirk's blank and patient, both apparently noticing nothing unusual.

The woman regarded him for a long moment, a soft smile playing.

It couldn't be! It was not possible! It had to be that the events of the past days had unhinged him and his mind had substituted his lost Persephone for the pitiful sight of a shipwrecked seaman . . . or was this a ghost?

'I – I have to get out!' he said hoarsely, and turned to go.

'Oh, Thomas – you're not pleased to see me?'

It was too much. He froze in a panic of unreality as she moved across the room.

Then she kissed him.

Broken by a tide of emotion, Kydd fell to his knees. She knelt down beside him and stroked his face gently, as his senses whirled insanely.

'P-Persephone, it's y-you.'

'Yes, my sweet darling, it is.' She raised him up.

'W-what are you doing here?' he stammered at last.

'Never mind explanations, my love, that can come later – know only that we're together once more. You and I.' She kissed him again.

He responded, long and hard, then pulled away, breathless,

incredulous, stunned by the inconceivable turn of events. He blinked back tears. 'Persephone – my love. If you've heard ill of me I pray don't think it—'

She put a finger on his lips. 'I know everything, dearest. Rest your mind. For now . . .'

'Does this mean . . .' he dared.

'That we're engaged to be married when we return to England?' she answered – but it was with a slight frown. 'I have to tell you, Thomas, that things have changed between us and therefore my views have altered.'

His heart lurched. Struck dumb with anguish, he saw her frown dissolve into a teasing smile. 'We will not be wed when we're returned, this I will not have. Instead I desire that . . . that we shall be married here and now. In Iceland, the most romantic of places, as we shall remember all our lives!'

Kydd crushed her to him, then, too late, looked about guiltily, but they were quite alone. 'B-but married, here? We're not—'

'I spoke with Captain Groos. He's of the strong opinion that your humanity in allowing through the convoy will count with the bishop – they have one, you know – who will grant us special licence to be wed here.'

Kydd beamed. 'And I as ruler of Iceland – *pro tem*, of course – do order it so!'

Chapter 87

Dillon was put in charge.
In quick succession he secured the necessary licence from an effusive bishop, whose incomprehensible protestations of delight and willingness Groos translated and relayed on. The quaint wooden cathedral was put at their disposal for three days hence and it was settled that while the good woman Gudrun would perform the office of attendant to the bride she would be given away by a much gratified Groos. A proud Dillon would act as Kydd's best man.

As for the ceremony there would apparently be no lack of bridesmaids among the awe-struck maidens of Reykjavík, led by Sigardur's intended, but it seemed there was serious disagreement brewing among the two organists as to who would secure the honour of playing on the day.

A wedding feast of the very best that springtime in Iceland could provide was promised, but for the more important matters it took a little thought.

The Lutheran sacrament required the exchanging of rings to signify the sealing of the bond, and in the absence of a convenient jeweller, *Tyger*'s armourer stepped forward and saved the day by producing two highly polished rings fashioned from brass cringle eyes, hardly to be distinguished from gold.

Persephone was adamant: she did not pine for an elaborate gown and train and would be delighted to make her appearance in traditional Icelandic garments. Taken in by a merchant couple, she was prepared for her nuptials by Gudrun who fussed about her as if Persephone were her daughter.

And then the day dawned.

Kydd took particular care with his attire: full dress uniform and sword, the star and sash of his knighthood immaculately adjusted, and his tall best cocked hat with its gold lace gleaming, the very picture of a famed frigate captain.

At the due hour his barge, manned by his officers and warrant officers, made its way inshore to the little pier where he stepped off the boat before a silent crowd of hundreds who had come from all parts of the island to be present at the occasion.

Kydd gave a polite bow and was rewarded by a ripple of applause and respectful greetings.

As he moved off with Dillon, there was movement – and, to his embarrassment, he saw that flowers were being strewn in their path on the way to the cathedral, the cries of joy and well-wishing leaving no doubt about the feelings of the Icelanders.

He arrived in a haze of happiness, still not quite believing it was happening, into the packed cathedral – for all its timbered appointments a darkly handsome House of God in the Nordic tradition with few churchly embellishments.

Overhead a pair of bells burst into life, summoning the bride to her appointment with God and her betrothed.

Kydd stood in thrall of the moment: in a very short while he would be joined to the woman he'd come to adore and who most truly loved him, a thing of miracle and wonder.

As the organ played on, an intricate descant he couldn't recognise, he stole a glance about him.

With Dillon next to him in clerkly black they were by some margin the most richly dressed present, most being garbed in homespun, with the bishop himself in a plain robe edged with Arctic fox and—

The music stopped.

He turned to see two figures standing at the entrance, limned by the bright sunlight. The doors closed and, as the organ began a quite different, grander air, on the arm of Captain Groos Persephone Lockwood processed up the aisle towards the altar.

She was wearing a stunning Icelandic wedding gown in vibrant blue, richly embroidered with gold and red, and a tall white and gold headdress. Her eyes fixed steadily on Kydd's as she moved towards him to take her place by his side.

Coolly she turned and attended the bishop as he took up his book and made proclamation, his words ringing out in the hush. Prompted by a whispering Groos, the ceremony proceeded – and then abruptly it was over.

Arm in arm, they made their way in procession to the church door, Kydd's heart overflowing with pride and happiness until they stood blinking in the sunshine.

It was a wildly improbable scene, as unlike a wedding day in England as it was possible to be, the only familiarity the pealing of the bells in the wooden tower. In front of them a frigid sea with stark black rocks and a beach of raven-sable sand, to the right a coast that ended in a tortuous up-flinging of crags, and from the mysterious interior the eerie glow of glaciers a hundred miles wide.

The wheeling keen of sea-birds and the distant cries of seals brought them back to earth, and Kydd turned to Persephone to meet her ecstatic eyes and gently, longingly, kissed her.

It brought on a storm of applause from the waiting crowd, whence Stirk emerged in his best shore-going rig, his hair unnaturally plastered back, Doud and Pinto his awkward supporters.

Stepping up, he touched his forehead to them both and said gruffly, 'An' it's me who's goin' to have the last say, which is to mean as the Tygers want me t' let ye know that they welcomes Mrs Kydd to the barky and . . . begob, an' I'm adrift in m' bearings! That is t' say, we welcomes right heartily Lady Kydd, as who is now, to our crew.'

'Why, thank you, Mr Stirk,' Persephone said softly. 'I'll look after your captain for you most willingly as is within my power, but then it must be you who takes care of him for me.'

Stirk blushed, shuffling his feet. 'Ah, we'll see t' that, never fear. An' as we say an' mean, it's right dimber to see ye both spliced – and let it be a long one!'

He wheeled about and faced the rest of the Tygers who had magically appeared and roared, 'An' it's three times three for the captain an' his lady as they's now outward bound on th' seas o' life.'

The cheers rose deafeningly, one after another, ringing and echoing in the bay, on and on as if the very mountains had joined in the paean.

Author's Note

I pen each Author's Note last of all, somewhat wistfully because another Kydd tale has been finished and I must move on to the next. As a writer you get quite attached to a book, especially if there is a strong emotional content, as in this one.

As always, this story is firmly based on the historical record. The flight of the royal family and the entire government of the nation of Portugal was an unprecedented event. Behind it lay the secret treaty of Fontainebleau, enacted between Bonaparte and the treacherous Spanish minister Godoy. In it, the corpse of Portugal was to be shared between them, and Britain's last and oldest ally would disappear from the pages of history. That Godoy was comprehensively fooled by Napoleon is quite another story but certainly the Portuguese navy of fourteen battleships and eleven frigates added to the forces arrayed against England would have been a catastrophic reversal. As it was they sailed with the Regent of Portugal to Brazil where the world was treated to the sight for all of thirteen years of a mother country ruled by its colony.

The village of Ivybridge slumbers on. The London Inn is there still, under another name, its stables and cobbled courtyards now housing craft workshops. The modest mansion Corinthia remains and is in fact where your author has the good fortune to dwell now. It nestles in the beautiful Erme valley, which winds on up to the moors, a place so idyllic it lured Turner, Rowlandson and many others from London to capture its loveliness in paintings.

Quite at another extreme is the Pentland Firth. This is truly a fearful place when out of temper and is strewn with wrecks beyond number. The concentration of currents and races is probably the worst in the world, certainly for a navigable seaway. Twelve-to-fifteen-knot sustained tidal streams are common, which, to put it into perspective, is about five times walking speed. In the only passage I've ever come across in this vein, *The Admiralty Pilot* breaks out of its normally weighty and restrained prose to declare, 'With smooth water and a commanding breeze, the firth is divested of its dangers, but when a swell is opposed to the tidal stream, a sea is raised which can scarcely be imagined by those who have never experienced it.' This is by no means an overstatement: even as recently as 2006 the 73,000-ton supertanker FR8 *Venture* lost two seamen killed on her decks while in transit.

Iceland is one of those places that are truly unique in the world and is quite unforgettable for the adventurous visitor, the stark black offshore skerries possibly the most frightful sea sight I've experienced.

One of the most fascinating characters from real life in this book is the Dane Jørgen Jørgensen, the King of Iceland. As an able seaman convicted of mutiny at the Cape of Good Hope, he joined the crew of the tiny *Lady Nelson*, making her way to Port Jackson to figure later in a voyage of exploration to Van Diemen's Land. Today, a splendid replica under full sail can be seen where once she sailed.

A mariner under the British flag, Jørgensen then plied the seas until caught up in the bombardment of Copenhagen after which he was made a (Danish) privateer captain, having the misfortune to be caught by a frigate and taken in chains to England. Improbably, even as an enemy alien, he talked his way into the command of a pioneering trading voyage to Iceland under licence.

The outcome for the King of Iceland of his removal to England by the sorely vexed captain of the frigate *Talbot* was to be imprisoned on the dubious charge of having broken his parole as a prisoner-of-war. For Iceland it was a better result. Touched by stories of hardship and isolation, Sir Joseph Banks led a movement to annex Iceland to the Crown but the British government compromised: the country, while still enemy territory, was granted extraordinary trading privileges, which greatly relieved the situation.

For Jørgensen, his release saw him just as implausibly move on to become a paid British spy on the continent in the desperate years before Bonaparte's downfall, but after the war he took to drink and gambling. Taken in petty theft, he was transported to Van Diemen's Land, which he'd last seen as an explorer. After his sentence, he elected to stay, entertaining tavern visitors to enthralling stories. He died in a hospital on the site of the very one in which, a century and a half later, my wife Kathy drew her first breath.

My research trips as always have been greatly assisted by those on the spot, and in Lisbon I was particularly helped by two eminent maritime historians: former commander of the Portuguese Navy's magnificent square-rigger *Sagres*,

Malhão Pereira, who pointed me in the right direction with various primary and secondary sources, and Professor Adolfo Silveira Martins, who opened my eyes in the splendid Museu da Marinha to the extraordinary seafaring heritage of Portugal. And in the pretty town of Oporto, long-time Kydd reader Paolo Meireles and his wife Carla so delightfully furthered my education in things Portuguese.

I must also mention retired merchant service captain Gudjon Jonsson, who in Iceland went out of his way to drive Kathy and myself to secret haunts and sights of his remarkable country, including the reconstruction at Eyrarbakki of the turf homes of Persephone's time there.

As usual, my sincere appreciation of their efforts goes to my editor at Hodder & Stoughton Oliver Johnson and his team – and my wife and literary partner Kathy.

It is of great sadness to me that my agent of over fifteen years Carole Blake will not see this book in print as she passed away in October 2016. She is sorely missed.

Glossary

amity	friendship
a try	in a gale, show sail enough to keep bows to sea
biddy	woman
Biscayman	coastal merchant ship plying between Spain and France
Blue Peter	since 1777, blue flag pierced with white, flown at fore masthead to indicate ship is about to sail
bower	the largest type of anchor on the ship's bows
braw	Scots, meaning fine or splendid
brimmer	an offering of wine in generosity where the wine brims over
brow	planking, generally with supports placed to enable communication from a wharf to a ship
buffer's nab	a false seal used to authenticate a financial document
capstan pawl	the part of a ratchet that prevents cable running out again
catblash	nonsense, nothing in it, as with a cat vomiting a fur ball
claw	in the nautical sense, a vessel hauled as close to the wind as is possible to get to avoid peril
Code Duello	set of rules governing single combat between gentlemen; the 1777 Irish Code Duello the most common
conn	the responsibility for directing the ship on a given course
contumely	contempt or rudeness intended to mortify
Corinthian	well-built sporting cove in dress cut to accentuate his physique
cully	cullion, amiable fool
dandy	extravagantly and immaculately dressed, known for his wit
dead reckoning	to find a current position by extrapolating from a previous known position
dimber	fine, outstanding

397

drabble-tail	sad-looking, inadequate
drogher	small coastwise vessel for carrying bulk goods
favour	mark of allegiance, generally ribbons or a rosette in the favoured colour
fop	he who is vain about his clothes and manners to a ridiculous degree
fribble	an effeminate fop
furbelow	a piece of showy ornamentation, frill
hooker	ship big enough to cast an anchor
jarvey	driver of a hackney coach
kedge	anchor normally used to haul off from
lie-to	a-try; keeping bows to sea, going nowhere
moil	confusion, upheaval
offing	to put a safe distance between ship and shore
pantaloons	men's breeches that extend from waist to ankle
partido francés	at court, the informal party in support of the French
pig's ear	arrangement of bunt of sail in a harbour furl to curl back over gear for a smart showing
pink	a man at the height of fashion
post-chaise	fast and light enclosed carriage for travelling far
pot-walloper	frequenter of taverns
pousada	inn, lodging house of the better sort
ragamuffin	small and scruffy child
ratchet	mechanism seen as a pawl that engages the sloping teeth of a wheel or bar, permitting motion in one direction only
rhino	wealth
rummer	large drinking glass with a stem intended for toasts and the like
scot and lot	householder paying taxes and therefore entitled to vote
scud	to run before a gale with sail enough to keep the ship ahead of following seas
scran	a sailor's meal
shab	shabbaroon, an ill-kempt and disreputable person
shellback	an old seaman marked by the sea, as with a barnacled sea-turtle
surety	formal promise to pledge security on an act
the *ton*	those people who are at the forefront of fashionable society
toiler	those who labour for their bread
tomrig	rude, wanton girl
touch-hole	hole communicating from the exterior of a cannon to the interior firing chamber
transports	vessels hired by the Navy Board for the express purpose of conveying stores or passengers
two-wheeler	small urban horse-drawn conveyance
wheedle	criminal trick